BOOKS BY ROBERT HARDAWAY

Novels (Western Reflections Publishing)
Murder at Mont St. Michel
Alienation of Affection
Lily Queen
The Papyrus
Six Queens Naked
Dreamlet

Academic Books on Law and Public Policy
Colorado Evidence (Lexis-Nexis, co-authored, 14 editions)
The Great American Housing Bubble (Praeger)
Marijuana Law and Politics (Praeger)
Saving the Electoral College (ABC-CLIO)
Airport Law and Regulation (Greenwood Press)
Crisis at the Polls (Greenwood Press)
America Goes to School (Praeger)
Population, Law, and the Environment (Praeger)
The Electoral College and the Constitution (Praeger)
No Price Too High: Victimless Crimes (Praeger)
Preventive Law Casebook (Anderson)
Aviation Law and Regulation Treatise (co-authored) (Butterworths)
Preventive Law in corporate Practice Treatise (Mathew Bender)
Colorado civil Rules Annotated (West Publishing, co-authored)
Aviation Law and Regulation—student Edition
      (Butterworths, co-authored)

Critical Praise For Books
By Robert Hardaway

MURDER AT MONT ST. MICHEL

"A Colorado John Grisham! Truly an engaging book from first to last. I loved it!"

—Richard Lamm, former Governor of Colorado

ALIENATION OF AFFECTION

"...An Extraordinary novel...superbly crafted novel of obsession, sex, scandal, betrayal and prejudice which raged through the high society of Chicago, Paris, Denver, and even the doomed voyage of the Titanic. Attention Hollywood! Alienation of Affection is the very stuff of which block-buster movies are made...."

—*Midwest Book Review*

"University of Denver School of Law Professor Robert Hardaway has seamlessly incorporated reports from Denver's daily newspapers and transcript of the trial proceedings into his own creative work to produce a spell-binding book...more than just a riveting take.... (Awarded an 'A' rating)"

—*Rocky Mountain News*

"...a fascinating look at a bygone era...."

—Bob Ewegen, *Denver Post*

LILY QUEEN

"...(A) compelling story set in the context of a great American tragedy, which educates, entertains, and enlightens...."

—Richard Lamm, former Governor of Colorado

SIX QUEENS NAKED

"...A wild heart stopping ride...."

—Richard Lamm, former Governor of Colorado

CRISIS AT THE POLLS

"Enhanced with a chronology, glossary, and an extensively annotated bibliography of print and electronic materials for further study, *Crisis at the Polls* is a seminal work of meticulous scholarship and an invaluable acquisition for academic and community library political scene and American history reference collection."

—Midwest Book Review

NO PRICE TOO HIGH: VICTIMLESS CRIMES AND THE NINTH AMENDMENT

"Professor Robert Hardaway provides an interesting assessment of the so-called victimless crimes and our societal battle to restrict them... *No Price Too High* is interesting reading with a powerfully presented and strongly argued theses. It is likely to provoke useful discussion about important issues."

—Law and Politics Book Review

"We are indebted to Professor Hardaway for bringing together the common effects of the so-called victimless crimes of drugs, prostitution, and gambling and demonstrating quite persuasively that such laws produce unintended consequences far more damaging to our society than the defined crimes themselves....Professor Hardaway gives us that much needed comprehension in his book. *No Price Too High* provides a sense of the heft and purpose of the Ninth Amendment, a source of wisdom in this age of folly."

—John L. Kane, Federal Court Judge

"I found this book to be both interesting and enlightening. Hardaway shows us the historical mistakes we made from the criminalization of such personal problems such as prostitution and gambling. By making these acts illegal, prostitutes and gamblers received no solution to their problems; in fact, their problems worsened...."

—Gary E. Johnson, Former Governor of New Mexico and former presidential candidate

SAVING THE ELECTORAL COLLEGE: WHY THE NATIONAL POPULAR VOTE WOULD UNERMINE DEMOCRACY

"A readable account of an immensely important Constitutional provision that few truly understand. An important history lesson!"

—Richard D. Lamm, former Governor of Colorado

"Robert M. Hardaway has long been a thoughtful ad effective advocate for the Electoral College. His critique of the national popular vote legislation is much needed at this critical moment in our nation's history. *Saving the Electoral College* is a welcome resource for any student of the American political system."

—Tara Ross, author of the *Indispensable Electoral College and Enlightened Democracy*

A Judy Alexander Mystery

Murder On the Concorde

Robert Hardaway

WESTERN REFLECTIONS PUBLISHING COMPANY®

ISBN: 978-1-937851-56-9

Printed in the United States

Text design by Steve Smith, FluiDesigns
Cover design by Hans Hollenbeck

Western Reflections Publishing Company
P.O. Box 1149
951 N. Highway 149
Lake City, CO 81235
www.westernreflectionspublishing.com
(970) 944-0110

Dedicated to
Judy Trejos

Chapter One
Present Day

Judy Alexander sat on the rim of the circular fountain in the village square of St. Jeanette. In quiet contemplation she surveyed in the distance the azure waters of the Mediterranean and felt the soft ocean breezes caress her face.

She and her late partner of three years, Robin Hammond, had come to this place every summer during the time they had worked and lived together in New York City after her graduation from the Oliver Wendell Holmes School of Law. Robin had been her law professor and faculty advisor in the Exoneration Clinic. With his untimely death the previous year, she had dealt with her loss by returning to the solitude of this little French outpost on the Cote d'Azur, reliving in her mind the blissful years she had spent with him—years which now seemed all the more precious. She had intended to take a full year off from the law firm where, after her graduation from law school, she and Robin had been partners in a boutique law firm specializing in criminal defense. Now, after eight months on the Cote d'Azur she finally felt she could move on—even if she still had not decided how she would do so. If time had not healed her wounds, it had mercifully lessened the sharpness of the pain they inflicted.

In her self-imposed sabbatical from the firm, she had not insisted upon remaining completely incommunicado with her law partners. Although she had asked them to refrain from calling her except in matters of dire urgency, she had remained open to receiving short texts inquiring as to routine matters occasioned by her having passed all her clients to them during her absence. She had also retained iPhone and FaceTime contact with her closest friends, including Amber in Houston, and

"Uncle Timothy," who was still living in Avalon on Catalina Island across from Long Beach in California.

Over the past seven years she had been dutiful in maintaining at least weekly FaceTime contact with Timothy Hoxley who had taken her under his wing during her first year of law school as a student in the Exoneration Clinic and given her the commission of a lifetime to find his long-lost daughter. Bonnie had mysteriously disappeared many years before from the island of Mont St. Michel off the coast of Normandy in France. The generous remuneration he had insisted on awarding her for her most satisfactory completion of this commission had enabled her to pay the tuition for her remaining two and a half years of law school. He had offered her much more, but she had declined, protesting that the payment of her tuition was more than sufficient for the services she had provided. After Robin's death, knowing that Judy would decline any further remuneration, Timothy had given the Holmes School of Law a five million dollar grant in honor of Robin to fund its Exoneration Clinic.

It had been during her performance of Timothy's commission that she had also become close to Timothy's goddaughter, Amber, who was now a senior partner in the prestigious Houston law firm of Crocker and Rutherford.

Timothy had been eighty-five at the time he gave Judy her commission eight years ago, at which time he claimed he was suffering from a progressive illness which doctors had advised him was terminal. Although Timothy had never confided to Judy the nature of his illness, the fact that he was still alive and kicking at the age of ninety-three belied his gloomy prognosis. He was also in full possession of his faculties, though he was physically disabled, confined to a wheelchair, and attended by a team of nurses.

Judy knew that he could pass away at any time, and made sure to FaceTime him at least once a week to monitor his well-being. Amber told Judy that her regular FaceTime calls always raised his spirits, and she even attributed to Judy much of the credit for extending his life beyond expectations.

Since escaping to St. Jeanette the previous October, Judy had made weekly visits to her old friend, retired French Police Detective Jacques Montagne, and his wife Clara. The now elderly couple was still living in a cottage outside St. Jeanette, though Clara was suffering from the early stages of Alzheimer's. Judy had stayed in regular contact with them since she had met the couple seven years before while working with them on solving the murder at St. Michel.

Judy stood and walked away from the fountain toward the shade of a nearby tree to make a call to Jacques and ask if she could drop by later that afternoon for a visit. Just as she started to dial the cell rang.

"Hello?

"Judy?"

"Yes. Amber? Is that you? My connection isn't that great. Hold on while I walk down to the corner where I get better reception."

"Sure," said Amber in a muffled but anxious voice.

"Okay. I hear you fine now."

"Judy, it's about Timothy."

"Oh my God, is he okay?"

"No, he's not. That's why I'm calling. I think it's really bad this time."

"What happened? I just called him last Friday and he seemed fine."

"He had an episode last night. The night nurse called about three this morning. You knew he was in hospice, right?"

"Yes, of course, but I also know he's never accepted or even believed that he is in hospice. When I asked him about that a couple of weeks ago, he accepted that designation only to the extent that he thinks that hospice gives him more benefits—though considering that he's a billionaire I can't believe that's really a consideration for him. I guess he thinks he'll live forever—contrary to when I first met him when he thought he was at death's door—and maybe that's a good thing. Optimism is supposed to be good for your immune system. And I must say that when I FaceTimed him last Friday he was alert and looked fine. I know he has good days and bad ones. And we had a nice conversation. He asked me when I was planning to come back to the states."

"And what did you tell him?"

"I told him I wasn't sure, but that I probably wouldn't be staying in St. Jeannette for more than a few more weeks. I told him that when I got home I'd be sure to come see him. I feel badly now, Amber. If I had known he had taken a turn for the worse, I would have come back right away."

"I know, I thought he was okay too. According to the nurses he really did take a turn for the worse last night. I think you'd better come now. The nurse let me talk to him later this morning. He had recovered somewhat from his episode and was able to talk. The nurse seems to think we're talking now about hours, not days."

"Oh nooooo, Amber! I can't believe it! I'm so sorry. What did Timothy say?"

"Not much. But he wants us both to come as soon as we can."

"So you're going out today?"

"He wants us both to come, Judy."

"Well of course I'll come as soon as I...."

"Together, Judy. He wants us both to come together."

"But you're in Houston and I'm out here in St. Jeanette. Why don't you go now, Amber? You're the goddaughter, so you'll need to get there right away, and I'll come out to Avalon as soon as I can. As soon as we hang up I'll make reservations for the next flight to Paris, and then to LA. Then I'll rent a car and drive down to...."

"No, Judy. Listen. We need to go together. He was adamant about that. Together. He's told me many times that you're his goddaughter too. We've never actually said this to each other, but now is as good a time as any: that makes us, you know... godsisters. So we need to go together. That's what he wants."

"But he may not have much time, so shouldn't I...."

"Judy, stop. Chandler has already sent the G-500 down from Paris to pick you up at the Cote d'Azur Airport. How long will it take for you to drive there?"

"Whew, all right. I guess now is not the time to argue. I can pack in fifteen minutes and get to Cote d'Azur in two hours."

"Okay, that's good. The G-5500 should be there by then and fly you direct to Sugar Land. I'll meet you about…I'm thinking about…let's see…you'll gain about six hours—thank goodness—so probably I'll meet you around, let's say…well, anyway, I'll meet you when you arrive, join you on the G-500, Chandler will gas us up and fly us to Long Beach, where we'll board the…."

"Oh, yes, the *Bonnie*. I remember it well. Who wouldn't? But slow down, Amber. I'm coming, I promise. I'm leaving now."

"Sorry. Of course. If all goes well we should both be in Avalon by, maybe, before noon tomorrow…."

"You know if it was for any other reason…."

"Yes, I know, you don't feel comfortable jet-setting around in Timothy's toys like some decadent potentate, but…."

"It's not that…."

"Shut up, Judy. Timothy loves you, and so do I. The three of us are family, and we're the only family he's got. He wants us to come together—not really sure why, but that's what he wants. We both owe it to him…." Amber stifled tears. "I only hope we get there…before…before…."

Judy was trying to reconcile the vision she had always had of her god-sister as the ferocious and fearless courtroom advocate, with the now distraught, distressed, and even scared woman she was hearing on the phone. "Now it's your turn to stop, you little squirt. I love you too! It will be okay. We'll get there, we'll get there together, and we'll get there in time. I promise. Maybe things aren't as bad as you think. Please don't worry, and hang in there until I see you tonight. I'm hanging up right now, and I'll see you in Houston tonight when I get there."

"And I'll be waiting for you! Kisses! Go sister! Go!"

Chapter Two

Chandler was standing at the Cappuccino machine in the business terminal of the Cote d'Azur airport when Judy appeared at the glass doors to the lounge and pressed the buzzer.

Chandler turned and waved to her, then motioned to the lounge receptionist to let her in.

Judy put down her small bag, ran to Chandler, and uncharacteristically—for she had never before felt comfortable hugging Timothy's somewhat stuffy executive secretary—quickly withdrew her formal offer of a handshake and instead wrapped her arms around him.

"How is he, Chandler?" she asked breathlessly, for she had broken every speed limit in getting to the airport.

"Come, let us sit down," he said, taken aback by her emotional embrace, but awkwardly managing to return the hug. "It will be another half hour before the refueling is completed."

"Of course."

"Can I get you some coffee or something?" said he as he ushered her to a lounge chair in front to the big picture window through which she could see the G-500 being refueled.

"I'm afraid coffee is the last thing I need. Perhaps some wine?"

"Of course." Chandler stood to go to the bar and pour a glass. Returning, he handed it to her. "It's been a long time, Judy."

"I know, I know. But Robin and I did visit last year. You remember, don't you? And since then I've FaceTimed Timothy at least once a week, often more times than that."

"Yes, and I can tell you that he looked forward to it every time you and Robin called, especially when Amber also joined you on the calls. It was always the high point of his day. Amber thinks your calls have inspired him to hang on and fight this terrible...."

"Amber did tell me that, and I'm glad. But now I wish I had visited him more often in the flesh. I don't know if Timothy told you, but Robin passed away last October when...."

"Yes, Timothy did tell me of that, and I was so sorry to hear that. Timothy was most saddened by the news. He and Robin had gotten to be very close friends ever since you completed that commission for Timothy. And of course, he always thought that you and Robin were perfect for each other. I think you know that our success in finding his daughter gave him new life. He thought that finding Bonnie would give him acceptance of his impending death and the peace of knowing what happened to his daughter before he died... and perhaps it did, but you and Amber have given him a new will to live. After the tragic deaths of his wife and only two children, you and Amber are his only family now. But the disease which afflicts him, though slow moving, is inexorable, and cannot be put off forever."

Judy had never asked for the details of his affliction, but always assumed it was some kind of cancer—perhaps prostate, or pancreas. But since Timothy had never told her, she had never felt compelled to ask. In fact the only time he had ever mentioned to her that he even had an affliction was on that day seven years before when he had summoned her to Avalon and mentioned his affliction as the reason why he needed her to find his daughter's killer before he died. From that day on, she was happy to believe that whatever the nature of his affliction, perhaps he had or hoped to beat it; perhaps he could then look forward to the ignorant bliss enjoyed by the more fortunate human beings of not knowing in advance of their expiration date—at least not too precisely.

"The nurse told Amber that it was a matter of hours not days. I hope that is not true, for I would be devastated if I did not see him in time." Judy paused to see if Chandler might not offer better hope than what the nurse had offered to Amber.

"I could not say," Chandler finally responded. "His doctor, in talking to me, did not use those same words—hours, not days—but I think he agreed that his time is very short."

"But what I don't understand is that, if his affliction is truly slow moving and gradual, why all of a sudden is he literally at death's door?"

Chandler shook his head. "Judy I'm going to tell you something that I'm not sure Timothy would approve of me telling you."

"Yes?" Judy leaned forward.

"For the past two years Timothy has confided in me, and me alone, that he had no intention of ever allowing himself to pass away in extremis—chained down in a hospital bed with tubes emanating from every orifice, a ventilator or some other hideous medical contraption shoved down his lungs while he gasps for breath like a victim being buried alive, or screaming in pain like a victim being pierced by the spikes of an 'Iron Maiden' or the diabolical instruments of the Spanish Inquisition—all because of society's obsession with insuring that no expense be spared by the medical profession in insuring that the hapless patient live a few extra days of pain and agony. Doctors, he was convinced, were too frightened of being prosecuted to ever permit him any dignity in dying."

"He really thought that?" said Judy taken aback by this description of Timothy's disturbing vision of what he believed awaited him on his deathbed. "Didn't he understand that hospitals can provide painkillers, opiates...?"

"He feared those almost as much as the pain and asphyxiation itself—that he would be so sedated that he would lose all power to control the manner of his death."

"Is that why he's not in a hospital?"

"Yes, absolutely. At his home in Avalon, he felt more in control."

"But surely the doctors and nurses who attend him there would be under the same legal restrictions as doctors and nurses in a hospital...."

"That is precisely why he never intended to die in Avalon, even at home. He had already made advance plans to travel to Switzerland where he would be allowed to die on his own terms.

It is the only country in the world where one can visit a thanatorium and be asked only two simple questions: are you competent, and do you understand what you are requesting? If the administrator and medical board of a thanatorium is satisfied that the applicant is of sound and rational mind, his death can be arranged on the applicant's terms with humane medical assistance provided as requested."

Judy was about to ask if the American states of Washington and Oregon did not offer similar assistance to those wishing to die with dignity. But then she remembered a similar intense discussion she had had with Robin on their first 'date'—at the Hilton in New York City—when the subject of assisted suicide had come up in the context of a case she was later to work on with Amber. In that case, her client had offered to plead guilty to murder in return for receiving a death penalty by lethal injection. Robin had told her that the law in those two states had far more restrictions, and fell far short of the right to die in dignity that was provided by Swiss law.

"So why didn't he go?"

"Timothy? He waited too long, I'm afraid. As revealed in last night's episode, he physically could not endure it. In wanting to live his life to the fullest until his time had come, he waited too long—his greatest fear. As you assumed when you last talked to him a few days ago during your FaceTime together, he too believed that his disease would continue to only afflict him gradually—that he would have plenty of time to make his plans to go to Switzerland. It was not until his episode last night that, gradual as his decline had been before, and bearable as his pain had been, he and his nurses realized that he would not be going anywhere. I regret to say that, while he was successful in preserving his mind—saving it from the ravages of opiates, particularly the OxyContin the doctors were always trying to foist on him—he never anticipated that his physical parameters could decline so precipitously in a single episode. Last night's episode was so severe that, as you learned from Amber, the nurses were amazed that he actually survived until this morning."

"Did the doctors never correct Timothy's assumption that his decline would continue to be gradual, and that a single episode might make it impossible for him to ever leave Avalon?"

"I don't know that he ever asked his doctors that particular question, and even if he had, I doubt if they would have disabused him of that possibility since they did not know of his plans to go to Switzerland. In any case, they would certainly not have approved of his plans—which, of course, he knew and which was why he never told them."

Judy could only shake her head in sadness.

Chandler looked out the window and saw that the fuel truck for the G-500 was disconnecting.

"Judy, it looks like the refueling is complete. Are you ready to board?"

Judy nodded. "Yes, absolutely. Perhaps one more glass of wine?"

"There are plenty of spirits to choose from on the plane. I think we should go right now. I'll call the pilot and stewardess to let them know we're walking over now."

"Of course." Judy picked up her bag and waited for Chandler to finish his call.

"Okay! Let's go" he said as he finished his call to the pilot and snapped his cell phone shut. "Next stop Sugar Land. It's a long flight, even though the G-500 can travel at mach.90—at least six and a half hours. I've prepared the back bedroom for you, and you may wish to take a shower before you take a nap—if you feel you can nap that is. Timothy insisted that I make you as comfortable as possible."

"You're joking. He actually called you to tell you that?"

"He's still talking, Judy, at least he was when he called me this morning. In fact he called me right after he called Amber. He would have called you too, but the nurses couldn't find your cell number. As physically diminished he is after last night's episode, his mind is still sharp as a tack, and his voice, though subdued and hesitant, still booms."

Judy shook her head. "I know it well. I'll follow you!"

Chapter Three

It was dusk when the G-500 made its final approach to Sugarland. The cabin attendant, who had been sleeping on one couch while Chandler slept on the other, knocked on the back bedroom door.

"Judy, this is Sophia. We're landing now, Judy. Are you up?"

"Yes," came the answer, "out in a minute."

Minutes later the Gulfstream came to stop on the tarmac. Judy looked out the window and saw Amber waving to her. As Chandler pushed out the stairs, Amber clambered up, shook hands with Chandler at the door and then embraced Judy at the door.

"You've come! Thank goodness!" said Amber as she turned to Chandler. "When can we leave? Have you had word from the nurses?"

"Yes," he replied. "Just prior to our landing I called and talked to Jan, the head nurse on duty. He's resting comfortably now, though breathing heavily, but was awake earlier and taking liquids. That was about an hour ago, and he was asking when you both would arrive. As usual, he's declining sedatives. I told Jan not to wake him, but that if he did wake up to tell him that we were just landing in Sugarland, and should be in Avalon before midnight. I've already alerted Captain Smith on the *Bonnie*, and he assured me that it would be waiting for us at the pier in Long Beach when we arrive."

Amber took Judy's hand and squeezed it as she asked Chandler: "Can we leave right away?"

"I just checked with Captain Heath. He's still in the cockpit arranging for the refueling. We previously arranged for priority, and the truck is on the way as we speak. We also have two mechanics on their way from the terminal who will be inspecting all the aircraft equipment and preparing the pre-flight check list for Captain Heath."

"So a half hour, maybe?"

"We'd better give it an hour, but perhaps less."

"Thank you so much Chandler. I don't know how Timothy would ever have gotten along without you all these years."

Chandler nodded. "It has always been my pleasure, Ms. Hartman. Your godfather was"—Chandler corrected himself—"is a very fine man. Now, would you and Ms. Alexander like to wait in the lounge, or would you prefer to wait in the plane while we refuel?"

Amber turned to Judy. "I think we'd like to remain on board if that's all right."

Judy nodded.

"But Judy and I have some catching up to do. Perhaps we could retire to the bedroom so both you and Sophia could stay in the main cabin if you wish. Or you could go to the lounge if you prefer."

I think I'd better stay on board to help the captain in case he needs me during the refueling. And Sophia can bring you something to drink and a snack if you wish."

"I don't have much appetite," said Judy. "Just some Voss with lemon would be fine for me."

"Well, I'll take a strong martini," said Amber. "As you can see I have been very worried all day about Timothy."

"Of course," said Sophia. "I'll have them to you in just a minute."

"Come," Amber said to Judy as she took her hand. "Let's go back to the bedroom where we can talk."

Amber shut the bedroom door behind them, sat on the bed, and patted the bed beside her. Judy smiled and sat.

"I'm so sorry about this morning," Amber said sadly. I was just so upset when I got that call this morning from the nurses. I'm sure I was barely intelligible."

"It's okay. I'm a bit of a basket case too, and I'm sorry if I was short with you. I know he's been ailing, but it was a shock to hear—you know—that it's hours not days. But Chandler says that he was awake this afternoon, and we'll be there tonight. We'll be on time."

There was a long silence before Amber said," you know, we've both been very good goddaughters. I know we've both FaceTimed him regularly, and you and Robin went to visit him last year, didn't you? But I'm afraid we haven't been as good staying in touch with each other, have we?"

At the mention of Robin, Amber saw Judy's expression change to one of distress. "Oh, Judy, I was so sorry to hear about Robin. That commuter plane crash up in Maine. Have they ever determined the cause?"

"No, a report is due out anytime, and of course there will be litigation. I'd rather not think about that right now."

"Of course. Sorry."

"No, it's okay."

"Well, if you ever want to talk about it...."

"Sure, thanks."

There was a knock on the door and Sophia arrived with the Voss and martini. Amber took the tray and handed it to Judy.

"Thank you, Sophia."

"Of course, let me know if you need anything else."

"Now, where were we?" said Amber as she passed the Voss to Judy.

"You were saying that we should have stayed in better touch with each other over the past few years.""

"You know I really wanted to join you in St. Jeanette. I really meant to, but you wouldn't believe my case load at the firm. And you had said you really wanted to be alone for a while."

"You're right. We definitely should have stayed in touch better. We were planning to come down, you know, visit you in Houston, until...until...."

"I told you my firm is now Crocker, Rutherford, and Hartman, didn't I?" asked Amber, changing the subject away from any reference to Robin's tragic death.

"Yes, Timothy told me that! He was so proud of you. Senior partner—look at you!"

"Well, one of three."

"Are you handling death cases anymore?"

"Actually, no, and very few criminal cases either. I'm afraid it was one of the conditions for making me a senior partner. I wasn't bringing in enough income for the firm doing the criminal cases—so I now do mostly civil, personal injury, wrongful death, that sort of thing. Not that I mind. I'm afraid the Gardner case really took it out of me. Of course without you it would never have been solved. I'll never forget that, and neither will Timothy. Did you ever write your law review article about the ethics of plea bargains in which the defendant offers to plead guilty to murder in exchange for being given the death penalty?'

"Actually I did! It was actually published by the Oliver Holmes law review."

"I'd love to read it. You must send it or give me the citation. But I remember you were about to drop out of law school at that time. Why didn't you?"

"Robin, of course. I know I was really bored after the first semester, but Robin finally convinced me that it could be an exciting career. And as you know, he resigned his professorship and returned to his law firm right after we found Timothy's daughter...."

"You mean you found Timothy's daughter on Mont St. Michel—it was all you, Judy, and you did it as a first year law student...."

"You are kind, Amber, but let me continue. After Robin left the law school we were able to date right away, and moved in together soon after. I clerked at his firm during law school, and after my graduation he brought me on to the firm as an associate. Last year I was made the senior partner along with Robin."

"So it's Hammond and Alexander now?"

Judy smiled. Not quite, but Hammond, Alexander, James, and Henderson.

"Well now look at you!"

"It's just a small firm, hardly in your league. I have two junior partners, both women, former public defenders, and six associates, two of them Holmes alumni and former students in the Exoneration Clinic. Two of the former partners in the firm have moved on. We specialize in criminal defense, and liaison with the Exoneration Clinic at Holmes. Thanks to Timothy the clinic is now well funded. We don't make a lot of money, and that wasn't really our goal. But I'm afraid I kind of left my junior partners in the lurch, taking a year off. But Susan James and Megan Henderson are both doing quite well in my absence from what I can glean."

"I remember your 'honeymoon' in St, Jeanette. But you didn't marry. I always thought you would."

"It was a mutual decision. We didn't think it was necessary, really. My son Yee had gone back to Hong Kong to go to university there, Robin had no children from his previous marriage and…well, long story—I'll tell you about it sometime, but in the end we just decided to stay perpetually engaged as it were. Of course we were very happy and loved each other quite madly."

"And so here we are. I'm sorry it takes a tragedy for us to be together."

"By the way, I wanted to ask you. How is Dr. Gardner these days?"

Amber's face dropped. "Judy you saved his life, and because of you, he and his sister have led full and happy lives ever since we got him released from prison. But I am sad to tell you that after a brave fight with pancreatic cancer he finally did succumb. Last June I think it was."

"Oh, Amber, I'm so sorry to hear that. He was a fine man, though I can never forget how he was manipulated by that…."

Just then there was a sound of clanking hoses. Judy stood and opened the bedroom window curtain. "I think they've finished the refueling. Amber, why don't you stay and rest here in the bedroom for the flight to Long Beach? I'll go and join

Chandler and Sophia in the main cabin. I got a good rest on the way over from Cote d'Azur."

Amber gulped down her martini, handed it over to Judy, and plopped over to the side.

"Thanks, Judy, I'll take you up on...."

She was out. Judy covered her with a blanket and tip-toed out to the main cabin.

Chapter Four

It was near midnight when the *Princess Bonnie*, a Cecelia 165 sporting five cabins and a crew of eleven, tied up at the Hoxsey pier in Avalon. A black Hoxsey Industries Range Rover was waiting to take Chandler and the girls up the road to the Hoxsey Manor overlooking Avalon Bay.

Betty, the head housekeeper, was at the door to greet them with open arms. Tears and hugs followed between the three women as Chandler, roller bags in tow, stood back at a respectful distance from the emotional reunion.

As Judy entered the circular atrium, lined with nautical art and aquaria of exotic tropical ocean denizens and jellyfish, she looked out through the twenty-foot windows at the lights of the glittering boats in the bay below. Visions of her first visit to this Hoxsey paradise some seven years before raced through her head.

Back then, as a wary, timid, but curious first year law student she had come in response to a mystifying summons she had received from the reclusive tycoon—none other than Amber's godfather. The mysterious commission for which he had summoned her had seemed incredible to her at the time, even preposterous. It was nothing less than to find the killer of Timothy's beloved daughter, who had disappeared without a trace some twenty years before from the iconic island of Mont St. Michel off the coast of Normandy in France.

Her skepticism at being summoned for such an undertaking had been understandable. After all, as she was soon to learn, the grieving father had devoted his entire life since Bonnie's disappearance to finding both her remains and her killer. He had spent millions of dollars hiring the most experienced and able detectives, the most accomplished researchers and investigators, technical experts, and communication specialists.

He had called in chits from every politician with whom he had contacts, and even sent moles to ferret out information form the French constabulary and Police Nationale.

Her first question to Timothy had been why he thought that she of all people would be able to solve a mystery which a small army of detectives and investigators had failed to do.

Judy still remembered how Timothy had responded with an odd non sequitur by asking her a puzzling question of his own: "Judy, have you read the writings of the Greek philosopher Aristotle? Any of his sayings?"

Sensing that she was being tested—though for what reason she had no idea—she had recited a few of the eminent philosopher's aphorisms she vaguely remembered from her college philosophy class: "'the whole is greater than the sum of its parts," and "the roots of education are bitter but the fruit is sweet."

"Very good." He had said. "But now I have one which you may have overlooked: 'Beauty is a greater recommendation than any letter of introduction.'"

"Aristotle really said that?"
"Indeed he did. You can google it up if you doubt it."

"And what would that have to do with why you have brought me here?" she had queried.

It was then that Judy learned for the first time that it had been Amber who had mentioned to Timothy during one of her FaceTime conversations with him that Judy, whom she described as extraordinarily beautiful, had accomplished the impossible by convincing a womanizing Assistant District Attorney to let Judy gain access to Roger Gardner, the man who had theretofore rejected Amber's appointment as counsel to represent him in a murder case that had gained national headlines.

Timothy had gleaned from Amber's description of Judy a last opportunity to find his daughter's killer—something all his detectives and investigators had failed to do. His investigators' primary shortcomings, he was sure, had always come down to their failure to gain access to those in the French Police Nationale who knew more than they had reported in the available official documents of their investigation.

Alarmed that Timothy had planned to use her as a honeypot, Timothy had assured her that he had nothing of the kind in mind: "If all I wanted was to use you as a honey trap," he had protested, "there are legions of young woman I could retain for the purpose—and they all would have been seen for what they were, and thus useless. That's not what I want."

"Then what are we talking about...." Judy had asked.

"It is precisely because you would not have to do any of the things that odious term implies that I believe you could gain access where others could not."

Judy had remained skeptical, but in the end, even with Robin's disapproval, she had undertaken Timothy's commission— but only because it had connections to the Gardner murder case with which she was already involved.

In the end, Judy had confirmed Aristotle's reflections on the power of beauty, and had not only saved the life of Roger Gardner, but found Bonnie's killer and Bonnie's remains as well. Timothy's gratitude had been profuse, and though Judy had refused any remuneration other than her law school tuition, he had expressed his regard for Judy by referring to her thereafter as his second god daughter, along with Amber.

Judy now quickly recovered from her reverie of the past, and before either Judy or Amber could ask, Betty said:

"Mr. Hoxsey is okay for now. He's resting. He woke up a few hours ago, and asked about you both. Dr. Haggerty just looked in on him, and took his signs. Jan and the nurses are with him and monitoring all the equipment. He's breathing very heavily. But...."

"Can we see him?" Amber asked.

"Come up. I'm sure it's okay. Come on up. Oh, Mr. Lauridson, Timothy's lawyer is in the south bedroom, and two of the nurses are in the third floor bedrooms upstairs. But both of you have the west second floor bedrooms. Chandler, can you bring up the bags?"

"Of course, "said Chandler." Why don't you all go up and I'll bring the bags up shortly."

"Why is the lawyer here?" Judy asked as they followed Betty up the grand staircase.

Betty turned around on the landing. "Oh, they don't tell me," she said in a low voice, "but he's been here all day. Two of his associates from the law firm were here all day as well, setting up video equipment in the library, but they've gone down for the night to one of the hotels down in the village. I guess Mr. Lauridson will tell you what that's all about. He asked me to wake him when you got in, but first I know you want to see Timothy."

"Yes, please, thank you," said Amber.

Judy and Amber followed Betty down the hall to Timothy's bedroom.

"Wait here a moment and let me check with Jan to see if it's okay for you to come in," Betty whispered as she opened the bedroom door.

Betty returned, put her finger to her lips and led them in. The light was dim, lit only by a single lamp by the bed and the flashing diodes of the medical devices. The silence was broken only by the soft whirring sounds of an infusion pump and the beeping of the monitors.

Jan was replacing a saline bag when she turned around and waved them forward.

Timothy was breathing heavily through an oxygen mask, but otherwise was sleeping peacefully.

Jan approached and said in a low whisper. "I'm so glad you have come. Mr. Hoxsey has been asking about you this afternoon, and asked me to wake him when you came in."

"Is that a good idea? Shouldn't we let him sleep?" Judy asked.

"It probably would be better, but he made me promise. I think it will be all right."

"Okay," said Amber. "Be as soft as you can."

"Of course." Jan leaned over, turned up the light on the lamp, and lightly touched his free right arm which had no IV attached. "Mr. Hoxsey," she whispered in his ear. "Judy and Amber are here to see you. Can you hear me?"

For a brief moment it looked like there would be no response, but then his eyes opened. For a moment he seemed to be just focusing, but as he recognized his goddaughters in the dim light he smiled and attempted to say something.

Jan said, "I'm going to remove your mask for a moment so you can talk with your goddaughters. Is that all right, Mr Hoxsey?"

Timothy nodded and brightened as he raised his free arm. "You have come!" he said in a low hoarse voice. He motioned for Jan to come closer and then whispered something in her ear.

Jan nodded and turned to Amber. "He asks me to leave so he can talk to both of you privately. I'll be right outside. Call me if you think he needs anything?"

"Of course." Amber approached, took his free hand and squeezed. Judy went to the other side of his bed and gently touched his shoulder.

"I guess I didn't quite make it to Switzerland," he said with a soft chuckle. "But that's okay. Well, sit down, my two beautiful girls! I'm not done for yet!"

"The nurses say you're doing better. We were so sorry to hear you had a bit of a setback last night, but happy to see you looking good this evening. Judy came all the way from St. Jeanette in France to see you."

Timothy raised his other arm with the IV inserted, and held it out for Judy. She placed one hand palm down under his, and the other on his upper arm, careful not to touch the IV on his wrist.

Timothy smiled knowingly. He knew there really was no point in denying that his time was now to be measured in hours. He and his girls knew that he would never have summoned them if it were otherwise.

"Tonight was supposed to be our FaceTime night, Dad." said Judy. "But this is better, right?"

Timothy squeezed Judy's wrist. She knew he loved it when she called him "Dad." For the past several years he had insisted that she call him that.

"I was so sorry to hear about Robin," he said. "He was a very fine man, and I was so happy when you and he finally got together. I like to think I had something to do with that."

"You did, Dad. You practically put us in each other's arms. And I'm grateful for that and for the years he and I had together."

Timothy could see the tears well in Judy's eyes. "Judy, what you did for me—finding Bonnie and bringing her killer to justice—what all my investigators were unable to do…gave me the extra years of life I'm sure I did not deserve. Without you…."

"And she helped me save another fine man who would have been executed without her help," Amber added.

Timothy now turned and squeezed Amber's hand. "Sweet daughter" he said with emotional affection, "it was you who came into my life, when Bonnie…when Bonnie…."

"I know, Dad. But it was you who came into my life when both my parents died and left me as an orphan. Without you…."

"Daughters, I cannot tell you how happy it makes me to see you two together…."

Judy began to hold back tears. "We should have come to see you more often…."

"Yes, we should have," Amber agreed.

"We enjoyed that miracle of communication with this FaceTime. I see and hear you better on the screen than I see you now. And I wouldn't have dreamed having you come all the way out here when…Judy, you and Robin were saving the world from injustice…and Amber, you were working yourself like a dog fighting for your clients…though it would have been nice to hear that you had found a good husband to take care of you. How is that coming by the way?"

Amber forced a smile. "Oh, Dad. I've had some interesting…still working on that…but nothing yet. If it happens, it happens, otherwise I'm perfectly happy, I promise you. I have a good life because of you."

"That's all that counts."

Timothy suddenly took a labored breath and wheezed.

"Get Jan, quickly, Judy." Amber cried.

Judy went to the door to fetch Jan. "He's having a problem. Please come!"

Jan came in, checked the monitors, and replaced the oxygen mask. In moments he was breathing regularly again. "Perhaps you should go now," she said.

"Thank goodness, said Judy. "We'll go now. Please call us if anything else happens. We'll just be down the hall."

Timothy began shaking his head and trying to say something. Amber and Judy stopped and waited.

"Are you okay, Mr. Hoxsey?" Jan asked.

Timothy tried to pull off the mask.

"We can take the mask off for a moment, Mr. Hoxsey," said Jan. "But breathe with it on for a few more minutes, and then if you're okay we'll take it off for a few minutes and you can talk. Okay? The girls can wait."

Timothy nodded in assent that he understood.

"Are you ready to take it off, Mr. Hoxsey? Just for a minute, though, okay?"

Timothy nodded and took a deep breath. Jan gently removed the mask. "Now you can talk for just a minute, okay?"

"I'm going to leave the door open," Jan said to the girls, who returned to the bedside.

Timothy held both girls' hands. "I have just one last request before you go to bed," he said.

"Of course," both said in union.

Just at that moment, Mr. Lauridson, still wearing his suit pants, white shirt, and tie, appeared at the door. "Is everything all right?"

"Yes," said Jan. "Mr. Hoxsey wants to say something to the girls before they retire for the night."

"Ah," said Timothy, now seemingly recovered from his wheezing attack. "Just the man I wanted to see. "Jan, can you leave us for a few minutes?"

Jan nodded. "I'll be right outside the door if you need me, sir."

"Girls," said Timothy, "this is Mr. Lauridson, of the eminent law firm of…of…."

"Lauridson and Meyers, Mr. Hoxsey."

"Of course. Mr. Lauridson has been my personal lawyer for…how many years?"

"About thirty-two years, Mr. Hoxsey."

"Yes, quite right. I know Jan is going to be back very soon to put this obnoxious mask on me again, so I'll make this quick. Last year…it was last year wasn't it?"

"Yes, Mr. Hoxsey, last July." Lauridson turned to the girls, and said, "Last July I advised Mr Hoxsey to update his will which he had not updated for some years. Although Mr Hoxsey has no close relatives—his wife and two natural children have passed away, he does have some…."

Timothy wheezed again, prompting Jan to return. Before she had a chance to put the oxygen mask back on, Timothy, barely audible now, managed to say, "Okay girls, go with Mr. Lauridson. He knows what I wanted to ask you to do for me. I'll see you all in the morning."

With that, Jan replaced the mask. "All, I'll ask you to leave for now. I'll call you if there's any change. I'll be with him all night, but come back at eight in the morning. My shift isn't over until ten, when Cindy will be here. The support nurses are resting on the third floor, and will be back on duty at that time, as will Dr. Haggerty. Good night."

Lauridson, Amber and Judy left the room and entered the hallway, and Jan shut the door. Lauridson said, "I know it's late, but Mr. Hoxsey was quite clear that he wanted to ask you to do something for him. I think he was about to ask you when the nurse thought it was best that we leave for a while. Do you have a moment so that I can be sure to convey his request to both of you?"

"Of course," said Amber. "Shall we go down to the atrium?"

"That's fine. I know you both must be tired, but I do think it's important that we talk this evening."

Left unsaid was that Timothy would probably not make it through the night.

Chapter Five

"Mr. Lauridson, I don't feel comfortable leaving Timothy tonight, "said Amber as she and Judy followed the lawyer down the spiral staircase to the atrium. I feel we should be with him tonight."

"I agree," said Judy. "Can't this wait until tomorrow?"

"It will only take a moment, and then you can both return to stay with him tonight. Please, have a seat."

"For just a minute, then" said Amber as she took a seat and motioned Judy and Lauridson to do the same.
Lauridson sat, opened his briefcase and took out several sheets of paper.

"Amber Hartman and Judy Alexander, I have here Timothy Hoxsey's Last Will and Testament. I am not at liberty to show it to you as long as Mr. Hoxsey is living. However, I will tell you that it is an exceedingly simple Will, only three pages in length."

Amber and Judy looked at each other as if to ask "then why are you telling us about it now?"

Reading their minds, Lauridson continued:" The reason it is so simple and brief is that it contains no provisions for complicated trusts; there are no provisions for individual bequests or other restrictions. It is as simple a Will as the ones I used to churn out on the word processor for thousands of young sailors for whom I wrote Wills while I was a Navy JAG officer many years ago. It is essentially no different than a standard form Will that can be obtained from any mail order legal assistance clinic. Nevertheless, upon my urgent counsel, he permitted me to draft it in consultation with him to insure that it was legally enforceable in all respects in accordance with California law. It replaced his former Will, which was several hundred pages long and contained many provisions and conditions, tax efficient structured trusts, and bequests to multiple beneficiaries and charities. To be honest with you, I counselled him against writing so simple a Will, proposing that he at least retain a number of stratagems to minimize federal and California estate tax, but he was insistent he wanted none of that. Of course I complied with his instructions."

"Do you know why he insisted on replacing his former Will with such a short and simple one?" Amber asked.

"I'm coming to that, but I can tell you that one of his reasons was to avoid what he feared most might occur after his death—namely a contentious, expensive, and disputed probate proceeding that would surely consume a disproportionate portion of his estate in legal costs, expenses, and estate tax appeals, and thus almost certainly drag on for many years after his death....."

And probably greatly diminish your legal fees as well, Amber was thinking, but did not say it.

"...and in that respect he was almost certainly correct. However, because of his current Will's simplicity, and lack of such estate tax avoidance contrivances as remainder trusts and generation skipping bequests, it is very likely that the bulk of his estate will be subject to the top 40% federal rate."

Judy looked at her watch. "This is all very interesting, but frankly I don't think either of us knows much about tax law, and we'd really like to get back to Timothy now. Surely we can discuss all these matters tomorrow morning and....."

"Just another five minutes, please. As I said, Timothy wanted to ask you both a favor himself. But this morning he realized he would probably not be in any condition to ask himself by this evening, and if so, he made be promise I would ask it for him. In fact, I was surprised he was able to speak at all to you this evening. He was in very bad shape this morning when I spoke to him, and....."

"Please, sir, ask it now," said Amber with some impatience.

Lauridson took a breath." He wishes you to both watch a video tape which he made on the same day that he had me draft the current Will to which I just referred. He further expressed the wish that, if possible, you watch it before his death, or failing that, as soon after his death as possible."

"You mean, we should watch this tape now?" Amber asked.

"Yes, that is precisely the request that he wished to make to both of you—together. Since he was unable to make it, I am asking it now on his behalf. My associates have already set up the video equipment in the library for your immediate viewing. I know you are both very tired, but if at all possible I think you should watch it now before you retire for the evening."

Amber and Judy again looked at each other in puzzlement.

"How long does this tape run?" Judy asked.

"There are actually three tapes. The first tape is about a half hour. That tape you need not view before his death, and you can watch it at your leisure any time after his death. It was made at my insistence at the time he signed the Will. Present at the signing were myself, two of my associates, Timothy's personal physician, Dr. Haggerty, and two independent board certified psychiatrists. After extensive questioning by all present, and in particular after questioning by the independent board certified psychiatrists, Timothy signed the Will in the presence of everyone present. This morning, he also signed a number of inter vivos transfers of property—again with Dr. Haggerty, myself, and my two associates as witnesses, which property will pass immediately to the grantee without going through probate. These inter vivos transfers were also video-taped—a third tape, which again, you may view at a later time. But to be clear, it is only the second tape which Timothy has asked that you view before his death if possible."

"Why were all these tapes necessary?" asked Amber. "He's never suffered from dementia, to which both Judy and I can attest. For many years, including up to the present, we have both FaceTimed him at least twice a week, and in that time he has never exhibited any indications of mental incapacity or lack of situational awareness."

"But you will permit me to say that neither of you are mental health professionals. Were his Will and the recent transfers ever to be challenged, your opinions would be quite irrelevant in any probate hearing. But it is precisely such contentious hearings that Timothy wanted his heirs to avoid after his death."

"Are there any potential challengers to his Will?" Amber asked.

"Not really—at least none of any real consequence—but you'd be surprised at who can come out of the woodwork when substantial assets are at stake in a probate hearing. While Timothy has no living spouse or natural children, we've located some more distant relatives, second cousins and the like. When an estate is substantial, such relatives have been known to file challenges based on a claim that the testator lacked testamentary capacity—not with any real chance of prevailing in a trial, but with the purpose of filing countless petitions and interrogatories to leverage their power to delay as a means of extorting a payout. That's why I recommended making this first tape documenting Timothy's competency beyond any doubt."

Just at that moment, the front door chimes knelled.

"I'll get that," said Lauridson as he rose.

It was Dr. Haggerty.

"Hello all. Don't get up. I'm just here to check on our patient."

Lauridson introduced Amber and Judy. "Doctor, these two beautiful young ladies are Timothy's two goddaughters."

"Two?" said the Doctor, extending his hand to both. "I know Amber of course, but I've never had the pleasure of meeting you, Judy."

"We saw Dad about an hour ago," said Amber. "He was talking, but I'm afraid the nurse thought we should leave when he faded back to unconsciousness."

"I will go up now and check his vital signs."

"Doctor, we plan to stay up for the night. Will you let us know if there is any change? We'll be in the library for another forty-five minutes or so, but would like to come back up to be with him after that if you will permit us."

"Of course. I suppose you know...."

"Yes, we know. We plan to stay with him until...or until he recovers."

"I'm afraid you should not count on that."

"We understand. But you'll let us know?

"Of course."

Doctor Haggerty turned and ascended the stairs.

"Now, ladies," said Lauridson, "if you will join me in the library."

Chapter Six

Lauridson led Judy and Amber down the hall to the library and ushered them in. A large screen had been set up on a stand in the middle of the room, flanked by stacks of various digital and communication equipment. A couch had also been set up about twelve feet from the screen.

"Please take a seat," said Lauridson. "I have set the tape to begin playing in five minutes. It is about fifty minutes in playing time. Please stay here until I return in one hour. It is now 1:25 A.M., so I will return at precisely 2:30 A.M., at which time I am sure you—and myself as well—will be ready to retire for the night."

"You're not staying?' Judy asked.

"No. I have specific instructions that no one is to ever view this tape except for you two ladies. In fact, my instructions include destroying the tape you are about to see immediately after you view it. You will find on the coffee table a notepad and pencil if you wish to take notes. But even those you must take care to destroy as soon as you are confident you can remember the highlights of his message."

"But why...."

"I'm sure the tape will speak for itself. Timothy videotaped this message with no one else present. He taped it shortly after we taped the first tape showing him answering questions from his doctors and signing his Last Will and Testament in the presence of myself, my associates, and the doctors."

"And both tapes were made on the same day...."

Lauridson flipped through his note pad. "Both the tape showing him answering questions from his doctors and signing the Will, as well as this second tape, were made beginning at 11:34 A.M. on the morning of May 17 of last year. That first tape will be preserved and presented as evidence if for any reason his

Will is ever challenged on grounds of his mental incapacity—an event we do not anticipate, as we believe that first tape speaks for itself in terms of establishing his mental competency at the time he signed the Will."

"And the Will itself...?" asked Amber

"I have that Will in my possession, but I alone know the contents of it, and have strict instructions that it is to be released, made known to others, and submitted for probate only after his death. Even my associates are not aware of its contents."

"So you are the only one who knows the contents of the Will itself, but you have no knowledge of the nature of Timothy's message in this second tape we are now to view?" asked Amber with a look of puzzlement.

"I thought I was clear on that. That is correct. And now I must leave before the tape begins. I will be in the hallway to insure that you are not disturbed while the tape runs.

"But what if there is a change in Timothy's condition during the time that the tape is running? The doctor said he would let us know immediately so we can come be with him. We both need to be there if...."

"In that case I believe I have the discretion to stop the tape—which I can do remotely—and restart it later. Hopefully that will not be necessary."

Lauridson looked at his watch. "And now I must go." He walked out and shut the door firmly.

For the third time that evening, Judy and Amber looked at each other in bewilderment.

"I don't understand...." said Judy.

"Shhhh, girl... It's starting...."

The video showed Timothy sitting on his favorite chair in the library, looking rested, calm, smiling, and alert. Timothy spoke:

"Welcome, my precious goddaughters. It is my hope that you are both together with each other listening to this recording. If you are, it means I have delayed for too long my plan to go to Switzerland to pass away with dignity, and I am now either dead, or am still alive but at death's door and physically incapable of making that journey. My hope now is that if it is the latter, that there will still be time for both of you to come to me before I exhale my final breath and assure me with a simple nod, that you have viewed this tape, and assent to the simple provisions of the Will which I have this day signed.

"The time and date of the making of this recording should be well documented by my long-suffering attorney, Mr. John Lauridson, and I am recording in the library of my Avalon home with no one else present. I have also left strict instructions that this recording is to be destroyed immediately after you have viewed it, although one or both of you may take brief notes if you wish. However, I would ask that you destroy any such notes as soon as you are confident you can recall all the important highlights of what I am about to say.

"First, let me explain why I believe it was necessary to make this recording. Earlier today I signed my Last Will and Testament in the presence of Mr. Lauridson, his associates, and a group of doctors who asked me a lot of silly questions supposedly designed to test my mental competency and acuity. Although I did not believe any such signing ceremony was necessary, John convinced me that, in light of what my accountants advised me was the true value of my estate—an amount which I must confess astonished me— prudence dictated that it should be conducted as insurance against any future attempts to challenge the Will.

"My previous Will was a most ponderous document, consisting as I recall, of several hundred pages of legalese gobbledygook, in which I made various bequests to institutions and individuals, including, of course, to both of you. It also contained a number of very complex provisions designed—or so John and his people advised me—to minimize the amount of estate tax which the government would extract. I did not pretend, nor do I pretend now, to understand any of those provisions except to find them exceedingly complex, problematic, and, frankly, boring. John even advised me that some of those provisions, though meticulously concocted by my army of accountants to pass legal muster, might, or even probably would, invite litigation and challenges, both from the government and beneficiaries named in the Will—all of which could tie up my estate for years, benefitting no one, at least for a long time.

"And so it was, one evening after an exhilarating FaceTime chat with one of you—I forget whether it was with Amber or Judy—that I had found myself with some extra time before finding myself ready to retire. I'm not sure what masochistic impulse induced me to use that precious free downtime to review my Will, but I did—pulling a copy of it out of my file cabinet and endeavoring to plow through it. By the time I had gotten to page 150 or so, I put it down and resolved to write a new Will—a simple one which, combined with the video tape which John had advised me to make in any case, would make it both unchallengeable and amenable to virtually immediate distribution of the assets in my estate after my death. I have left instructions that my new Will, the contents of which only John is aware, must not be divulged until I have breathed my last.

"Nevertheless, I wish to tell you now the contents of that Will—though I will leave it to John to later advise you of the current value of my estate inasmuch as that value may have changed significantly from today until the time of my death."

"Before I advise you of the contents, I want to tell you why I am doing all this."

"Amber, after both your parents passed away and left you an orphan at the age of fourteen, the close ties of friendship between our two families resulted in my becoming your "Uncle Timothy." As both my parents and siblings had died—my elder brother in an air race accident in Long Beach—you became the closest living members of my family. When Bonnie was murdered, it was you who gave me consolation and the will to go on. Since then you have become the light of my life, and nothing has given me more pleasure than seeing you succeed as a lawyer in your chosen vocation. It has been my privilege to be your godfather ever since. Of all the reasons for being grateful that you have been in my life, not least of these was bringing Judy into my life. Had you not done so, I would be facing my maker without knowing what ever happened to Bonnie, and bringing her killer to justice."

"Judy, you were a disillusioned first year law student when you first came to me. But I recognized in you my last remaining hope for finding my daughter, and you did not disappoint me. Despite the danger you risked in accepting my commission to find Bonnie, you undertook it with determination and unbelievable courage and resourcefulness. For that I have always been grateful beyond words that I can express. Along with Amber, I feel privileged to be your godfather."

"Since the death of my only daughter, you have both given me a new life worth living. Accordingly, I have decided to leave my entire estate to both of you— jointly."

Amber and Judy both turned to look at each other in disbelief, less now in puzzlement than with astonishment, and with mouths open. Timothy paused his narrative for several moments to let the import of this bequest sink in.

"I think I have already explained why I wanted to simplify my Will, but now I wish to explain why I have simplified it in this particular way.

"It is still my wish that full accommodation be made for all my domestic staff who have served me so loyally over the years. Furthermore, having been blessed with a considerable fortune passed down to me from my father—for which I did nothing to deserve—I also wish a significant part of my estate to be passed to worthy charitable causes. For the reasons I have given you, however, I do not wish to make such bequests in my Will. Rather I leave it to both of you—not because you are legally required to do so, which I underscore you are not—but because I have every confidence that you will both fulfill my wishes out of respect for me as your godfather.

"With regard to authorizing distributions to my domestic staff, I suggest that you consult with Lauridson as well as my accountants with regard to suitable amounts to be given to staff in like circumstances, taking into account both their contributions to my household and the length of their service—then double it.

"Regarding charitable contributions, I have no reason to believe that my opinion as to which charities are the most deserving is any better than your own thoughts in this regard. Therefore I leave it up to the two of you to agree on what contributions to make. You might also want to instead consider forming your own charitable trust, with both of you as joint founding settlors. I would suggest that you allocate 25% of the estate—after all taxes, fees, and legal expenses are paid—to such endeavors.

"That said, however, I believe there will be more than enough for both of you to enjoy the fruits of my legacy to improve your own lives and live your own dreams. I know that both of you are unlikely to live with undue extravagance just because you have the wherewithal to do so—though that will certainly be an option for both of you if you believe that will make you happy."

"I know that Judy has never been completely comfortable jet-setting around in any of my own toys or extravagances—yachts, airplanes, mansions, and the like—or she would never have eschewed the generous remunerations I offered her to express my gratitude for the invaluable service she rendered me in finding my daughter. Nor would she have chosen a law professor as her mate—though I believe they gave each other greater happiness than either would have had with anyone else—when, given her extraordinary beauty, she could not only have had her pick of any millionaire or celebrity she wanted, but had them melting into warm puddles at her feet."

"Nevertheless, I do have several rather selfish requests in hope that one or both of you would be willing to accommodate them."

"First I would like to express my hope that you will jointly take title to my Avalon home, use it as a holiday home for you, your friends and relatives whenever your schedules permit, and continue to retain all the domestic help currently now serving to maintain the property."

"Second, I ask that you jointly take title to the *Princess Bonnie*, avail yourselves of it as your primary mode of transportation to Avalon, use it for whatever other recreational purposes that might give you enjoyment, and retain the current captain of the vessel, and all others who serve aboard and service it.

"Finally, it is my wish that you retain title to three of my current homes—one in Knightsbridge in London, another in the 16th Arrondissement of Paris, and a third in Switzerland—again insuring retention of the staff and maintenance personnel. If you can agree, you might decide to put one or more of those homes in one of your individual names, or lease any or all of them to render income.

"As John will no doubt soon apprise you, the bulk of my holdings are in the form of shares of Hoxsey Industries. It is currently privately held and I own all the shares. On the assumption that neither of you would be interested in running the company, I have, during the past year, worked with John and other retained counsel and bankers to take the company public within thirty days of my death. This will provide sufficient liquidity to pay all estate taxes, fees, and legal expenses, and leave more than adequate liquid assets for you to invest or spend as you wish. I have no doubt you will both wisely do so.

"I would only have re-written my Will and expressed my wishes in this manner if I had complete confidence that the two of you would work together in harmony as joint grantees of my estate. I reiterate that all the wishes I have expressed in this video are advisory only, and in no way bind you legally to honor them.

"And so I close with this final request—that if I am still alive and conscious when you finish this viewing that you come to me if I am near to you, and give me a nod that you accept my requests, and pledge to honor them. With that I leave this life with love in my heart for both of you."

As the screen turned blue, Judy and Amber continued to stare at it in stunned silence. Both were speechless as they waited for Lauridson's knock at the door.

It came seven minutes later, and Lauridson entered.

"You saw it all?" he asked.

Both girls nodded.

"Very well. Now as I promised my client, I will go, and as you watch, destroy the video disc."

As he did so, breaking the disc into a thousand pieces, Judy asked, "Is there any word from the doctor?"

Lauridson turned and said, "I just talked to Dr. Haggerty. There has been no change in the last hour. He says you may go up now. If you wish to sleep in his room with him, there is a comfortable couch. I have also had another bed brought in, so there are beds for both of you."

"Thank you," the girls said in union and followed the good lawyer to Timothy's bedroom.

Chapter Seven

"I can't believe he's gone," said Amber somberly as she looked out at the ocean panorama in the distance.

It was 7 A.M. on the third day since the passing of Timothy Hoxsey. On the veranda of Hoxsey Manor overlooking Avalon Bay, Betty was serving a breakfast of coffee, egg whites, wheat toast, and yogurt to Lauridson, Amber, and Judy.

Lauridson handed each of the girls a copy of the day's schedule he had prepared. "After the memorial service at Avalon Community Church this morning, you two, Chandler and I will lead a procession from the Church back here to the Manor for the reception. If you would prefer, Chandler can arrange for the Range Rover to bring you."

"Not at all, said Judy. It would be our privilege to lead the procession. Do you know how many people will be at the service?"

"The service will be open to all permanent residents of the island, so we'll see. He has a number of friends here, of course. I have also invited several of Timothy's closest business associates, plus Betty and Mary. We have arranged for a complete catering service so all of them will be free to attend the service—also Timothy's old friend Sophie Dorleac...."

"It will be nice to see Sophie again," said Judy. "She gave me my crash course in French when I was preparing for my mission to France...."

"That was, what seven years ago...?" asked Lauridson.

"Judy nodded. "Yes, and she worked me hard night and day. I could never have done what I did in France without her help."

"I have also invited my two senior associates," Lauridson continued, "Shawn Pierson and Ed Mason, as well as Hector Shane, the lead attorney for Madison and Shane Investment

Bankers. I don't know if they'll come to the service, but they will be here for a meeting with me at 4 P.M. down in the library."

"That's the investment Banking Firm that's handing the Initial Public Offering for Hoxsey Industries?" Amber asked.

"Yes, and just to confirm, will both of you approve of moving forward with taking Hoxsey Industries public?"

"Yes," said Amber and Judy in unison. "That's what he wanted."

"Good. Over the past year, Timothy has taken all the preliminary steps to do so. Madison and Shane filed the Form S-1 seven months ago with the Securities and Exchange Commission, comments have been exchanged, and the Preliminary Prospectus was filed....."

Amber held up her hands." It's all fine, John. Judy and I are in complete agreement that it should go forward."

"But it's important that you both understand that as the sole beneficiaries of Timothy's Will you would have complete authority to withdraw the SEC application if you wish since the process for going public is not yet complete."

"We understand," said Judy, "but we are in complete agreement...."

"Nevertheless, it is important that your decision to go forward is communicated to Madison and Shane directly, rather than indirectly from me...."

Amber's face showed surprise. "You mean the investment bankers don't yet know the contents of the Will?"

"As named executor, I will be submitting the Will for probate first thing tomorrow morning, but to answer your question, at this moment only you two and I know the contents of the Will. You will remember, as I told you on the evening before Timothy's death, that he had given me strict instructions not to divulge the contents of the Will until he had passed away—instructions which I have followed to the letter. You will recall that I only showed the Will to you after Doctor Haggerty had signed the death certificate."

Amber and Judy looked at each other, as if to ask each other if they should divulge to Lauridson that they did indeed have advance knowledge of the contents of the Will because they had watched the second tape.

Lauridson immediately gleaned the meaning of that look between the godsisters and said, "Of course I could only assume that in the second tape Timothy not only told you of the contents of the Will, but also asked that you never divulge that contents of that tape to anyone."

Amber was about to say something, but then did not, unsure of what she could say and still respect Timothy's expressed wish that they never divulge the contents of the tape. Finally she changed the subject slightly. "You did destroy that second tape, didn't you?"

"Yes, I did destroy the second tape, as you know, and as Timothy instructed me. I will therefore not presume to speculate as to its contents, but can only assume that he expressed therein his advice, or wishes—not legally binding, of course, as it could not have been since the Will itself is clear, simple and unambiguous—as to how you might dispense certain assets in his estate, make charitable contributions, or make accommodation for his staff and members of his domestic service."

Both Amber and Judy momentarily froze. Judy finally said, "We thank you for not speculating, John."

Lauridson held up his hands. "Just as I, in the confidence of the attorney-client relationship, had to respect his wishes not to reveal the contents of his Will until after his death, I respect fully any request he may—or may not have made to you. I will only say that if—and I underscore if—he did ask you not to divulge his wishes therein expressed, it would have made sense for him to do so. He doubtless had greater confidence that you two together would carry out his wishes than he had confidence in a legal system that would have given scope to opportunistic lawyers and potential claimants to tie up the probate of a more complicated will and expose it to delays, unnecessary fees and legal expenses, and even extortion in return for abstaining from even frivolous challenges, petitions, and interrogatories, and appeals. I do know he wanted none of that."

Both girls put on their best poker faces.

"But," Lauridson continued, "I must point out that the soundness of his plan to leave his estate unmolested rests upon a basic premise."

"Yes, John?" asked Amber with just a hint of irritation.

"That the two of you would always agree on how his wishes would be carried out, and that—God forbid—you would never turn on each other, either in a court of law, or otherwise."

Judy now spoke up firmly. "That would never happen, John. After you showed us the Will, Amber and I discussed the possibility that you might raise that concern. And we can assure you that every decision we make will be a joint decision. Under no circumstances will we ever allow any disagreement between us to jeopardize how Timothy would have wanted his legacy to be carried out."

Lauridson nodded, smiled warmly, and after a pause said, "Well, I'm glad to hear that, and from everything Timothy has told me about both of you, I have every expectation that it will be so."

At that moment, Betty returned to refresh everyone's coffee. "Can I bring you anything?"

"We're fine," said all.

"Betty," said Amber, "would you like to ride with us down to the church? "We'll be leaving in about an hour."

"Oh, thank you Amber, but no, I need my morning walk. You all go ahead."

"All right. There will be spaces reserved for you, Mary, and all the staff. Chandler will be available if any of you need a ride."

"Thank you, Ma'am." After a short silence, Amber again took the lead. "John, do you have a pen and paper?"

"Of course," said he, picking up his brief case.

"We have an hour and a half before we leave for the service. Perhaps now would be a good time for Judy and me to tell you our wishes with regard to certain matters relating to the estate."

"Your wishes—yours and Judy's?"

"Yes, John," said Judy indulgently. "We have already discussed them between ourselves. We want to tell you our wishes now so that you can work out the details and give us a final plan to carry them out."

"Of course," said Lauridson as he opened up a small notebook. He had no doubt that what he was about to hear in fact reflected Timothy's wishes, but that was understood if not stated. "Fire away."

Amber now turned to Judy, who pulled out from her purse a small notebook.

"First," said Judy reviewing her notes, we are fine with the initial public offering of Hoxsey Industries to go ahead. We trust you will keep us apprised of all developments."

"Of course."

"Second, we wish to make full accommodation for all current personal staff and domestic help, with generous options provided to them, including the choice to continue working at their current jobs at Hoxsey Manor, as well as at Timothy's estates in Paris, London, and Switzerland...."

Amber added: "And also options for taking a pension, or appropriate lump sums, based on time of service."

"Does that include staff and boatmen on the *Princess Bonnie*?"

"Yes," said Judy.

"And the pilot and staff for the G-500?"

Judy looked at Amber who said, "Yes, if they are employees of Hoxsey Industries—not contract workers, of course."

"Got it. I will talk to Timothy's accountants and prepare a proposal of generous options to be offered to all current employees."

"And then, double it," said Judy.

Lauridson nodded. Sounds like words Timothy would use, he thought.

Judy continued: "Once the proceeds from the initial public offering are received, we would like you to set aside twenty-five percent of the total value of the estate, after all estate and other taxes are paid, to set up a charitable foundation, with Amber and I as trustees. If you will give us a list of the charitable bequests Timothy made in his previous Will, we will see that those charities are given first priority in any future grants made by the foundation."

"I have a law firm in mind which specializes in setting up charitable foundations."

"Great," said Judy. She turned to look at Amber.

"The houses," Amber reminded Judy.

"Oh yes, Hoxsey Manor here in Avalon, and the homes in Paris, London, and Switzerland are to be retained in our joint names."

Lauridson finished writing a long note. "Are they to be retained for your exclusive private use, or may they be rented out and leased?"

Judy again turned to Amber. They had obviously not discussed that.

"Are they being leased out now?" Amber asked.

"I will have to check that, but I believe so, yes—with the possible exception of the Knightsbridge property in London. The Swiss property on Lake Geneva I know is rented out to celebrities—$30,000.00 a week."

"Whew!" said Judy. "But you know "I'm perfectly happy with Madame Durand's little B&B in St. Jeanette. As far as I'm concerned, I doubt if I'll ever use those houses for personal use. Amber?"

"Well, for now, let's rent them out. If either of us did want to—maybe for a wedding someday—well, we could talk about that. We'll let you know."

"All I need to know now is whether you wish to retain title in your joint names. You can decide about rentals or leases at a later time."

"Yes, we'll retain joint ownership," said Judy.

"Okay, anything else?"

"I think that's it. Judy?" Amber asked.

"No, I think that's all we have."

"How long would it take to draw up a detailed plan for these distributions?" Amber asked.

"Well, the accountants can probably draw up a plan for the offering of options to the staff and household help within the next couple of weeks. Everson and Klaxton make all the payrolls and also have the means to survey comparable accommodations to staff in similar situations."

"And double it," said Judy firmly.

"Got it. In the meantime, all staff and help will continue to be paid, of course."

"How long before the IPO is consummated?"

"Actually, it could be done in just a few weeks. It's been in the hopper for over seven months now, and your investment bankers just needed your okay to set a date and proceed."

"I guess that's all we have, then," said Amber.

"Great. Let me set myself a personal goal of presenting to you, one month from today, a final proposal for your approval, including a disbursement plan for staff, a timeframe and projected legal costs for setting up your charitable foundation, and a preliminary estimate of federal and state probate taxes. If by that time the IPO is concluded—or even if it is not, a projection of anticipated proceeds—I will also provide to you an estimate of the remainder value of the estate after payment of all disbursements, taxes, probate fees and expenses, including attorney and accounting fees, and the funding of the establishment of the charitable foundation and trust."

"Thank you, John."

"All right. It looks like we still have an hour before the service. If you refer to the schedule, you'll see that the reception is planned for 12-3. Then at 4 P.M., the bankers and attorneys will meet us in the library for the reading of the Will."

"It's only three pages long, so that shouldn't take long, should it?" Judy asked.

"No, but the main reason for having the meeting is for you to directly give your consent to the Investment bankers to proceed with the IPO."

"So I guess Amber and I need to be there," said Judy, though immediately biting her tongue for having asked what might seem to be a silly question.

Lauridson gave an indulgent smile. "Since you are the sole beneficiaries, I would say so. Legally speaking, of course, it's not necessary to be there, nor even that there be a formal "reading" of the Will of the kind you see on all the Agatha Christie-type mystery dramas. But don't you want to be there?"

"To be honest not really," replied Judy. "We already know the contents of the Will and…I mean all those high-powered corporate types looking at us and wondering what on earth Timothy was doing…."

"Nonsense. None of them are potential beneficiaries, though we did find some very distant cousins, second and third removed, whom we notified of the probate proceedings in accordance with California law—but none of them would have any claim on Timothy's estate. The last thing Timothy wanted was to have what we lawyers call 'laughing heirs'—that is distant heirs whom he's never heard of, trying to horn in on his estate. No, Timothy's Will is airtight, and no legitimate lawyer would try to challenge it, especially after the elaborate pains we took to establish Timothy's competence in that first tape."

"John, could I ask you just one question before we go?" Amber asked.

"Of course."

"Timothy must have confided in you his wish to re-write his Will to favor Judy and me, right?"

"Of course. I'm the one who wrote the Will for him."

"Yes, I know. Silly question. But what I really wanted to ask is if you ever expressed to him any disagreement as to what he wanted to do?"

"Not at all. He has no close living relatives who are being disinherited. I was a little concerned about his deletion of charitable bequests he had made in his previous Will, and did question him as to whether he was sure he wanted to do that. But, of course, he must have known that you two would make sure his charitable wishes would be respected."

Lauridson paused for a moment, as he had not meant to imply that he actually knew the content of the second tape. He didn't, of course, at least not for sure, but was now satisfied that he correctly surmised it.

"Anything else, as to the form of the Will, or its simplicity?"

"To be honest, I did say to him that, even if he did intend to make other arrangements for his charities outside the confines of the Will itself, it would be better from an estate tax standpoint if he included the charitable bequests in the Will itself, as such bequest, if qualified, could reduce the amount of estate tax the estate would be liable for."

"And what did he say to that?"

'He said he was prepared to pay the full estate tax—that he had spent his entire lifetime hiring the best tax lawyers in the country to minimize his taxes, and that he was fine with now paying the full freight on the estate, especially if it meant he could leave a simple, airtight Will for his two goddaughters. That's one reason he initiated the IPO process shortly after he wrote the will and made the second tape. He wanted his estate to be able to pay the estate taxes up front in cash, and not be subject to delay as the government's appraisers battled in court with the estate's appraisers over the true value of the company. The IPO will establish an incontrovertible value to the company. The government would be crazy to do anything other than take their forty percent of the estate in cash and close the case as soon as possible."

"Wow," said Judy.

"Yep, wow is the right word. I've never had a client like him, and never will." Lauridson looked at his watch. "Well, we'd better get going. Shall I call Chandler to bring up the Rover?"

Judy turned to Amber. "Let's walk."

"Yes, we'll walk," Amber agreed. John, we'll see you and Chandler at the church."

Chapter Eight

Chandler sipped his martini and checked his iPad. "It looks like we'll arrive in Houston by around 4 P.M. this afternoon."

Judy and Amber, facing each other, were each seated in a window seat of the G-500 looking down at the Rocky Mountains below.

"Thank you, Chandler," said Amber. "It's been a difficult week for all of us. I think we're all exhausted." Seeing that Chandler was absorbed with his iPad, she turned to Judy, pressed her index finger to her lips and then pointed it towards the bedroom door.

Judy nodded.

"Chandler," said Amber. "I'm going to go back and take a shower, if that's all right."

Chandler looked up. "Of course, it's your plane now."

"I think I'll go back too to freshen up," Judy said.

"Of course. It's your plane too. Let me know if you need anything. He put down his iPad. "I'll be here if you need me," he added

Judy and Amber entered the bedroom and shut the door.

"Finally, some privacy," said Amber as she plopped down with arms outstretched on the bed. "We really didn't have much chance to talk in Avalon. It seems like there were always bankers or accountants all around us. It's been so overwhelming. I wanted to ask you something."

Judy faced the basin mirror and checked her face and hair. Her beauty was unabated, but her exhaustion showed, and she turned away. "Anything, Amber. You know there will never be secrets between us. There can't be if we're going to make this all work."

"You know the night that Timothy passed away."

"How could I forget it? It was horrible."

"Remember how he asked us, at the very end of the tape, to let him know before he passed away—you know, to give him a nod I think was how he put it—that we will carry out his requests?"

"Of course. I do. We both wanted to tell him that we promised—together we promised—to carry out all his requests to the letter. How could we not? He has done so much for us, and he loved us both so much."

"As we loved him."

"I know. We do and always will."

"It's a bit of a blur now, of course… we were both so tired, neither of us had slept for almost twenty four…and we were both overwhelmed by what Timothy was telling us…but as soon as the tape was finished…Lauridson came in we watched him destroy the tape…then we both elbowed right past him and ran upstairs to Timothy's bedroom."

"Neither of us wanted to even be downstairs watching anything while Timothy might be breathing his last…we wanted to be with him… we wanted to be there when he…." Judy's eyes started to water.

Amber got up from the bed and threw her arms around her. "Timothy wanted us to hear the tape. He left instructions that we were to see it before he died…we couldn't know that he would die that night…."

"I know, I know," said Judy, wiping her eyes. "I guess it's everything. It's just too much. First I lose Robin, then…."

"I'm so sorry about Robin, you know that, but we both lost Timothy, and I really need to ask you something. I wanted to ask you before, but there never seemed to be the right time."

"Sorry. Please ask."

"When we got upstairs we tried to convince the nurse— Jan, I think—to try to wake him…that it was very important."

"At first she wouldn't listen…told us to come back in the morning…."

"But we finally convinced her to try to wake him."

"Yes, and she did try…."

"But he never woke up, he never...."

"He never woke up, but...."

"But do you remember...he did open his eyes, didn't he... didn't he...just for a moment?"

"He did! And you whispered to him 'we both promise to carry out your wishes....'"

"Do you think he heard us? He knew, didn't he, before he died... even if he couldn't talk...he knew we promised him...he heard us, right?"

"I think so, Amber. I think so."

"So we are going to, right?

"Yes we are. Absolutely. Let's sit down."

"Lauridson is putting it all together for us, right? I mean, he's liquidating the company, paying the estate taxes, using twenty-five percent of the remaining estate to fund this charitable foundation, taking care of all his staff and domestic help...."

"I know. And of course he didn't limit us if we wanted to make additional charitable contributions—which we could, maybe should do, right?"

"Of course, we should do that. We'll have plenty of time to decide such things."

"And I understand why he wants us to keep up Hoxsey Manor—it was his family home, after all. I think he likes that we would continue to use it, at least for holidays"

"You said your son is going to school in Hong Kong. Perhaps he could join us there sometime. Have you told him about any of this?"

"I will soon, just need some time to absorb everything first. But it will be a nice place to hang out together for holidays, though, like you said, I still want to spend some holiday time in St. Jeanette. But I wonder why it was so important to him that we keep those houses in Paris, London, and...."

"Switzerland. I wonder what that house is like. It must be something if it gets 30k a week in rent, so I assume all the houses are good investments."

"Well, he didn't say we needed to live in any of those houses. I assume they're all paid for."

"You don't think any of them are mortgaged do you?"

"He couldn't expect us to keep them if they were, could he?"

"I'm sure not. But that does bring up another question. We still don't know the value of the estate."

"We never even asked Lauridson for an estimate of the estate's value. After paying all those estate taxes, funding the Charitable Foundation...."

"Well, until the IPO is completed, he probably can't give us an accurate estimate. To be honest, I didn't feel comfortable asking him for one. Maybe, after everything, it won't be as much as we think."

"And what if it isn't?"

"Fine with me, Amber. I can't say I don't care, but honestly, even if it does turn out to be a lot, I don't know that I would want to change my life very much. I'm more than content to maintain Robins' legacy at the law firm he founded, taking cases that we think are just, working with the Exoneration Clinic at Holmes...."

"And not making much money...."

Judy shrugged. "I'm content. Honestly I am. Aren't you as well, Ms. Senior Law Partner in the distinguished law firm of Crocker, Rutherford, and...."

Amber smiled. "Hartman, but as to satisfaction, I'd have to answer both yes and no. I'm making decent money, and the work is in many ways rewarding, but also...very stressful. At my last medical checkup, my doctor told me, for the first time, that my blood pressure is...well, elevated... I'll leave it at that."

"Do you have any interesting cases right now?"

"A few, actually. I've had to change my mindset from that of a defense counsel to plaintiff's counsel in almost all my cases now—civil cases that is—but I'd love to get you involved in some of them if you were game."

"Sure, I'd like to hear about them. But I think I'd better check first with my own firm back in New York as soon as we get to Houston. I kind of left them in the lurch somewhat after I absconded to St. Jeanette after Robin...."

"Judy, why don't you stay with me for a while in Houston before going back to New York? Lauridson will be coming to Houston within the month to show us his distribution plan and give us the results of the IPO, so you'd want to come back to Houston then anyway."

Judy thought for a moment. "Hmmm. I might like that. The last week has left me rather numb, and I guess we do have a lot to talk about...."

"We have an empty office right now, and you could work there until you have go back to New York."

"Let me talk to my partners. I'll see if they can do without me for another month. When I told them I was taking my sabbatical they didn't expect me for another couple of months anyway."

"That would be so great! I guess we should go back and keep Chandler company." Amber looked at her watch and wound an extra two hours. "We'll be landing in about a half hour."

Chapter Nine

Having slept in the day before, Amber rose early the next morning. She walked down the hallway of her Houston townhome to her second bedroom where Judy was still sleeping and nudged open the door.

"Judy, are you awake?"

Judy turned over lazily, opened her blurry eyes and looked up. "I think so. What time is it?"

"It's nine. I'm going to make some breakfast if you're interested. Also, would you like to come with me to the office today?"

Judy sat up. "Sure, yes to both. Just coffee and juice for me. I'll be down in a few minutes. Do I need to dress up for the office? I'm not sure I have anything suitable."

"No its Saturday, so anything you have is fine. We can go shopping later or I can lend you some of my wardrobe."

"Listen, I wanted to call my office in New York. I'm not sure my associates are in today, but I'd like to check in with them."

"Sure, take your time."

Judy picked up her cell and dialed.

"Annie Brockhurst, Hammond and Alexander. Can I help you?"

"Annie! Good morning, this is Judy."

"You're back then! Are you coming in?"

"No, I'm still in Houston, and may stay here for several more weeks. How are things going?"

"We got a new case yesterday. Judge Leonard appointed us—manslaughter. Couldn't really decline it if we want to keep getting referrals, but we're going to be scrambling to pay the office bills if we don't start getting some more real paying clients. The hourly rate the court pays us isn't cutting it."

Or paying you and Linda a decent salary, Judy thought to herself.

"Judy," Annie continued, "I guess you know. Since we lost Robin we haven't gotten the best criminal clients. He had such a reputation, and always got the best clients. And now with you gone this past year...."

It didn't need to be said that Judy had not had the time to independently develop her own reputation as a trial lawyer. During her three years with Robin she had always acted as second chair in his big cases, though Robin had given her some small cases to defend on her own.

"Have we gotten any interesting cases from the Exoneration Clinic?"

"Not really. As you know we don't get any revenue working on those cases. Of course Robin...."

If Judy heard her mention Robin again, she would start crying. Instead she changed the subject. "Didn't you text me last month that you hired a summer clerk from the clinic?"

"Yeah, a guy. Too many women here now. The firm lost our two experienced men after Robin...."

Judy cut her off quickly. "Annie, I know things are tough now, but there's been a recent development. I can't tell you about it yet, but I may be able to address our financial problems soon— and we can get back to taking cases because their cause is just and not just because they represent a big fee, and we can accept more pro bono cases, working more closely with the Exoneration Clinic to overturn wrongful convictions...."

"Whoa Judy! What, did you win the lottery or something...?"

"No, but listen I can't talk about it now." It occurred to Judy that she still didn't know what her share of Timothy's estate would really amount to, and until she did she was reluctant to mention it. "Hang on, and I'll be in touch soon. Gotta go now. Give my best to the gang, and I'll be in touch soon."

"K, bye."

Judy had dressed while she spoke on the cell speaker, and now walked briskly downstairs to join Amber.

"Coffee's ready," said Amber as she poured Judy a cup. "You almost ready to go? The Rover will be here in a minute."

"Really? We're being chauffeured to work?"

"Well, we're paying Tyrone. Might as well give him something to do."

Judy shook her head. "Amber, I guess we could get used to all this, but do we really want to?"

"Not really. But let's go with the flow for now." Amber went to the window. "Tyrone's in front."

Judy took a last sip and grabbed her purse. "Let's go!"

There being no receptionist at Rutherford and Crocker on a Saturday, Amber opened the glass entry door after fumbling through her purse for the keys.

"Your office is down the hall to your right, second door on the left. Go ahead, and I'll be right down."

Judy entered the vacant office, went to the window to look at the view of downtown Houston, and then took her seat behind the large mahogany desk—definitely nicer trappings than at her well-worn office on the third floor of a modest building two blocks east of Washington Square.

Moments later Amber entered with a stack of files. "Look through some of these and see if any of them interest you. I've got a lot of calls to make, but I'll check back with you before noon and we can go get some lunch. You'll be okay?"

"Of course. Take your time." Judy picked up the top file and waved. "Bye."

When Amber returned several hours later she found Judy engrossed in a file.

"You found an interesting case?

"You're really suing the guy in this case for five million dollars?" She held up the file, which Amber recognized even from a distance of six feet.

"The Walker case. You betcha. The driver was dead drunk—BA of .17—a wealthy businessman coming back from a party at 2 A.M., turned on to a one way street, hit our client's car head on...young woman, beautiful young woman, twenty-four years old, Senta Walker, a former model, now a registered a nurse coming back from her shift at the hospital where she worked... wearing a seatbelt, but the crash still threw her through the windshield and the glass slashed her face to ribbons. She's already endured six painful operations, and still can't go out in public without being stared at in horror. She overheard one man on the street say to his girlfriend 'elephant woman! Did you see that?' People are just awful. Her husband—what a bastard, a doctor too, admitted he couldn't possibly ever make love to her again, said he tried, but with her face so disfigured, he just couldn't. Re-married already. Creep...now he's dumped her, she's alone, in agonizing pain every day, can't even leave her apartment for fear of being stared at and ridiculed, lost her job—too scary for the patients the hospital said. Of course the doctor got a high priced lawyer, and you know what the judge gave him? A seventy-five dollar fine, since there was no death involved. The lawyer and his client had a little celebration in the hallway after the fine was imposed—a lot of high fiving. The doctor only has a million dollar liability policy, but plenty of assets, so yeah! I hope he does go to trial, because I'd love to get him before a jury!"

"Oh my God, Amber, that's so terrible. That poor girl!"

"You said it. Anyway, sorry to get so riled up about that case, but...."

"Amber, it's just so horrible. When I think...."

"I know."

"We should help her, you know if...."

"I agree, we should. The five million dollars, even if we get it, will barely pay for her operations, and her health insurance refuses to pay for 'cosmetic' work...."

"You should wave your fee, Amber."

"I will. And you're right, Judy."

"It's just that, you know, wouldn't it be wonderful if we could just practice law—the only profession we know—that way, without having to worry about our fee, but just about...."

Amber nodded.

"I mean," Judy continued, "don't you think it would give us far greater fulfillment than spending our life gallivanting with a bunch of rich people idling away their lives on their yachts...."

"Yes, I do. I do. And I think Timothy would approve."

"And so would....well, you know who."

"Yes, I know who."

Judy stopped in mid-thought, paused for several moments, and then picked up a second file. "Brenda Masterson—pending. A murder case? I thought you weren't taking on murder or death penalty cases anymore."

"I said I wasn't defending murder cases anymore."

"But you're not a prosecutor either."

"Actually, in a way, I am—just not prosecuting in a criminal case."

"What do you mean?"

"Brenda Masterson is my client. Last summer, her mother, Angela Sterling, died by poisoning. The coroner originally attributed her death to natural causes, but Brenda was convinced that her father-in-law, Ronald Sterling, had something to do with her death. She came to me with her suspicions, which I relayed to the Harris County District Attorney. I convinced him to get a temporary injunction enjoining Ronald from having Angela cremated until additional medical tests were conducted on Angela's body."

"Sterling wanted to have her cremated right away?"

"Yes, he did everything he could to get her cremated quickly.

"So how was it determined that she died from poison?"

"During the pendency of the injunction, Brenda hired several medical experts to conduct a number of additional tests for poison. Brenda was sure that that's how Ronald killed here. The doctors Brenda hired used a number of advanced techniques for detecting poison. They finally found a very exotic but deadly poison that theretofore was thought to be undetectable. These tests later convinced the coroner to change his cause of death to poisoning by means and person or persons unknown."

"So did the D.A. then bring murder charges against the husband?"

"No, at least not yet."

"Why not?"

"The D.A. thought the death was suspicious but at that point couldn't rule out the possibility of suicide. In any case he did not think he had sufficient evidence to prove that the husband was responsible for the poisoning."

"Why not?"

"For one thing, Ronald was out of the state on a business trip when Angela died. She was found dead the next morning by the maid. Since the amount of poison in Angela's system was sufficient to kill her within hours of ingesting the poison, the D.A. didn't believe he had enough proof against the husband to prove opportunity."

"But before he left on his business trip, couldn't he have left poison in a place and in a vessel which he knew she might or probably would, consume in his absence?"

"The D.A. acknowledged that possibility, but he had no proof that the husband had purchased or even had access to the poison. Moreover, there was evidence that many people had had access to the house in the weeks before her death, including a man who, the D.A. discovered, may have been having an affair with his wife."

"But wouldn't that have given the husband a motive to kill his wife?"

"Yes, but still, without more, not enough evidence for conviction. Of course the husband claimed that he was not aware that his wife was carrying on a relationship with another man while he was on his business trips. Without proof that he knew, of course, the D.A. could not even show motive. Without evidence of motive, Hannigan felt he was short of what he needed for conviction."

"So what is the status of the case now?"

"Nothing is happening as far as the criminal case is concerned, at least for now. But Brenda wants me to bring a civil case against Ronald for murdering her mother since the standard of proof in a civil case is only by a preponderance of the evidence rather than the higher criminal standard of proof beyond a reasonable doubt. Of course you know that."

"So do you think she has enough to bring a civil case?"

Amber shook her head. "I told her I don't think we have sufficient evidence for a civil case either—at least not yet. But I'm working on it."

"What might tip the scales for your client, do you think?"

"Well, if a previous wife of his had been murdered by poisoning, that might tip the scales—perhaps like the 'Brides in the Bath' case?"

"Oh you remember that case—from your Evidence class."

"Of course. It established the precedent for Federal Rule of Evidence 404(b): 'Evidence of other crimes is not admissible to prove the character of a person in order to show that the he acted in conformity therewith. It may, however, be admissible for other purposes, such as proof of motive…intent, preparation…identity…or absence of mistake.'"

"Yes. In that case, the defendant left his wife in the hotel room on his honeymoon night to go buy some champagne, and when he came back he found his wife dead, drowned in the bathtub. When there was no evidence of any mark on her body, the coroner had no choice but to conclude that there was no evidence of foul play, that she must have just had a heart attack while bathing. No charges were brought against the husband."

"Until, as you recall from the case, further investigation showed that his previous three wives had all died under very similar circumstances—that is, on their honeymoon night with the defendant, each of the previous wives had been found dead in the bathtub while the husband had gone to get champagne. But with no evidence of foul play on the part of the husband, natural causes couldn't be ruled out, and the husband was never charged in the previous cases...."

"And the evidence of the circumstances in which the previous wives had died was held admissible by the High Court for the specific purpose of rebutting the husband's defense that in the case charged, the death of his wife was a tragic coincidence."

"So he finally got convicted."

"Yes, but I'm afraid there's nothing like that in the Sterling case. I checked. Ronald did have a previous wife who died some twenty years ago, though."

"So there you are!"

Amber shook her head. "Nope. Nothing like in the 'Brides in the Bath' case. Ronald's first wife died in a tragic airplane crash."

"Oh, no. Which one?"

"She died in the crash of the supersonic Concorde in Paris on July 25, 2000. So no help there in showing motive, intent, or the like. After many investigations and lawsuits, it was conclusively established that on takeoff the Concorde hit a piece of metal left on the runway after falling off another plane. This caused a tire to burst, which in turn ruptured a fuel tank and caused the plane to catch fire. With flight controls disabled, the pilots were unable to gain control of the aircraft. It crashed within minutes, and everyone on board was burned alive."

Chapter Ten

Amber stopped by Judy's temporary office and knocked on the half-open door. Before Judy could answer, she walked in and sat down in front of her desk.

"Girl, you've been looking through those files for weeks now. Are you ready to pick one to help me on?"

Judy sat back, patted the top of a pile of five files on the right side of her desk and said, "Here are five cases I picked out which I thought were of interest. If I did pick out one or two to help you with, how would that work? I'm only licensed to practice law in New York."

"I would get you certified by the appropriate court as associate counsel. I'd still be the responsible counsel, of course, but you'd be able to appear in court without me on the case. If we went to trial, we'd appear together. You'd act as second chair, but you could conduct your own cross examinations."

"I thought as much. I think that's the way they do it in New York, though I've never liaised with out of state counsel. I'm still not sure if I should get back to my firm in New York. My junior partners say they're doing okay without me—I've been calling them every day since we arrived in Houston—but they're not making much money and I may lose them if we don't start getting some better paying clients. In any case, I told everyone that I need to stay here until...until...."

"We know what we're dealing with in regard to the estate."

"Well, to be honest, yes."

"Then I guess you'd be interested to know that I just got off the phone with John Lauridson"

"So he's finished writing up the probate plan? The IPO is done? Did he tell you anything? I've been trying not to think about all that."

"I didn't ask. I told him I'd rather we both hear about what's in the estate at the same time. Until then, I guess mum's the word."

"So when is he coming?"

Amber paused for dramatic effect. "He'll be here by six tonight."

"Tonight!"

"I sent the G-500 to pick him up. He should be here by 6 P.M.!"

"Really! I can't believe it."

"Rather than go out for dinner, I thought we'd have more privacy if I rustled something up for dinner at home."

Judy looked at her godsister with skepticism.

"Yeah, I know I'm not the greatest cook, but I can't say you are either—though you've been a great help with the cooking. Anyway, I'm tired of eating out and I'd really like complete privacy when we talk over the plan with John."

"You've sold me," said Judy. "Why don't I pick up some fish this afternoon, and I'll have things going by the time you get home. I'll have Tyrone pick me up in the Rover."

"Good. Just make sure you release Tyrone in time to pick up John at Sugarland. And maybe you'd better pick up some beef steaks too. I'm not sure John eats fish."

"Oh, right. I'll do that. But I wish you'd let me just rent a car. I really feel funny being chauffeured around everywhere like some celebrity...."

"Judy, we've talked about this...."

"I know, I know. Tyrone's on the payroll and so we need to...."

Amber quickly changed the subject. "So, until we know where we stand with the estate, any particular case that catches your eye?"

"I'd love to help you get the five million for Senta Walker."

"She will really need it. I've been trying to negotiate with her health insurance company, but they're still refusing to cover her plastic surgery operations. They're standing behind the exclusion in her coverage for 'cosmetic' work if you can believe it."

"Disfigured for life, and they won't cover it! She can't even get her job back from the hospital where she works because of her disfigurement."

"I suppose we could try to sue the hospital for unlawful termination. They say they'll re-hire her for a job that doesn't require contact with patients—treating her like a leper basically."

"That pretty much leaves mopping the floors, I imagine."

"Certainly it would be a job that doesn't use her skills as a certified nurse and keeps her isolated. I'm doing everything I can. Any other cases that interest you?"

Judy picked up the next file on her stack. "I'm intrigued by this one—the suit you're considering bringing against Ronald Sterling. I imagine that one really did require you to readjust your mindset. Before you moved on to civil cases, you defended murder cases. Now, in effect, you want to prosecute one."

"Not exactly. But you're right. It's true I'm trying to build a homicide case against Sterling, but only by gathering as much evidence against him as I can and presenting it to D.A. Harvey. If he could bring a successful murder case against Sterling it would make Brenda Masterson's subsequent civil case against him a slam dunk. But right now, I really have nothing to give Harvey. And until I do, I have to tell Brenda that we'd have very little chance of getting a wrongful death verdict against her father-in-law."

"So, I guess I should take that case off this pile...."

"Before you do, I should tell you that I did get the final report from the coroner's office today. Apparently the drug that killed Angela Sterling was fentanyl—or a derivative of that drug. I've been asking for that report for weeks."

"Fentanyl? But isn't that a legal drug?"

"Yes and no. It can still be legally prescribed in the U.S. as a pain medication, subject to very strict FDA guidelines, including precertification and quantity limits. Unfortunately, however, at least twelve different illegally trafficked analogues of fentanyl have been identified to date by the U.S. Drug Enforcement Administration—all of them determined to have no medically valid use, and extremely dangerous if ingested. In effect they are poisons. In 2018 fentanyl and its analogues were identified as the most common opioid in drug overdose deaths—even more than heroine."

"I'm surprised fentanyl can still even be legally prescribed."

"It's not the legally prescribed fentanyl administered under strict medical supervision that is the real problem. According to the CDC, only four percent of fentanyl deaths were traced to a prescription. The rest originated from illegally manufactured fentanyl. And apparently it's not that hard to find if you're looking for it. Just last year, the U.S. customs in Nogales found 245 pounds of illegally manufactured fentanyl buried under a pile of cucumbers."

"I take it that's a lot."

"To give you a perspective, just two milligrams—a few grains—is sufficient to kill a person."

"Does the D.A. think that Angela could have taken it herself?"

"Suicide? No, he doesn't think so now. She had no history of any kind of drug use, and no indications that she was in any way depressed."

"Then why doesn't the D.A. think he has a case?"

"Apparently the coroner thinks it likely that the drug was administered through a skin patch, rather than through injection, nasal spray, or by mouth. One of the items found in the bedsheets at the scene was a patch, which presumably came off her skin during her last death agonies. They're testing that patch now for residue of fentanyl. If it's found that it does contain fentanyl residue that would confirm the coroner's opinion."

"Even if that opinion is confirmed, how does that hurt the D.A.'s case?"

Amber took a deep breath. "Apparently, unlike ingestion by injection or by mouth, a patch releases the fentanyl very slowly and produces something called 'delayed respiratory depression.'"

"And the significance of that is...?"

"It means that the patch could have been applied to Angela's skin as much as twenty-four hours before she even had symptoms, though she would have died quite soon after showing symptoms."

"Do you think the patch was self-administered then?"

"Probably, yes."

"What can I do to help?"

"We need to get a lot more information before we make any decision about filing a suit. Could you find out two things for me?"

"Of course."

"First, see if you can find out from the D.A. if the skin patch found in Angela's bed had the appearance of a nicotine patch."

"So you're thinking that she may have applied the patch thinking it was a nicotine patch."

"If we can confirm that the fentanyl patch had been tampered with to look like a nicotine patch—then yes, I do. I was hoping that maybe you could find that out."

"Okay. I can do that. Can you get me an appointment with the D.A.?"

"I'll try by phone, but Harvey usually won't give out that kind of information on the phone, so mostly you'll be on your own trying to get an interview with him."

"Anything else?"

"See if you can find out if Angela had a smoking problem."

"Which would explain why she was using nicotine patches."

"Precisely. See you at the house tonight. By the way, I like salmon. And try getting beef tenderloin for John."

"On my way!"

Chapter Eleven

Amber entered the kitchen with cell phone in hand to find Judy preparing the salad for dinner.

"Tyrone just called, and he's on the way from Sugarland with John. Should be here in about a half hour."

"We'll be ready. I think." said Judy. "You're fixing the drinks, right?"

"I'll have everything ready. What are you having?"

"Just ice tea for me. I'll have some white wine with the salmon, though, and we have some red for John to have with the tenderloin."

"I thought we'd sit on the back patio when he gets here. Not too long, of course. I think we'll be ready to come back in to the air conditioning after a short time."

The two were still scurrying about in the kitchen making last minute preparations when Amber heard the Rover drive up. "That's them," she said. "Can you go out and greet John while I finish up with the rolls?"

Judy put down the salad bowl. "Sure."

Outside, Judy greeted John Lauridson with a hug. "Come on in. So glad to see you again."

"Thank you. You're looking well, Judy."

"The flight was agreeable?"

"Very much so. Had a good shower and nap in the little back bedroom. I appreciate your making the plane available to me. It saved me a lot of time."

"Or course, and thank you for coming. Yes, the G-500 is quite something."

Tyrone was busy extracting a roller bag, a cloth sack, and a large brief case. "Thank you so much, Tyrone," Judy called out to him. "You can just leave the bags here. We'll get them in."

"Yes ma'am," said Tyrone, putting down the bags. "When should I return to pick up Mr. Lauridson?"

"Can you come back about...?" Judy looked at John.

"Let's see," said John as he looked at his watch and turned to Tyrone. "It's 6:45 now. I think we should be able to wrap things up no later than 10 P.M. Can you pick me up then to take me to the Four Seasons?"

"Yes, Mr. Lauridson. You have my cell number if you need anything before then."

"Of course." John picked up his brief case. Judy grabbed the roller bag.

"This way, John."

Amber was at the door to greet him. "Welcome John. Please come in. You can leave the bags here. I thought we'd go out to the patio for drinks."

Lauridson left the briefcase and roller bag in the hallway, but picked up the cloth sack as he followed his hosts to the patio.

As all were seated, Lauridson withdrew from the cloth sack a mahogany box.

"I thought it would be best if you two had this," he said as he handed it to Amber.

There was silence as Amber reverently held the box, and then gave it to Judy to hold.

"Thank you so much, John. Judy, would it be all right if we put it on my mantelpiece for now? We could decide on a different place later."

"Of course." Judy withdrew to place Timothy's ashes on the mantelpiece and returned with mint julips for Amber and John, and an ice tea for herself.

After a short silence as each of the three took sips, Lauridson said, "Well, first of all I'd like to thank both of you for not calling me every day to ask for updates. I have clients who do, and it definitely slows me down."

"We wanted to give you time and space to prepare your probate plan," said Amber. "We both decided we would rather have you provide us with a complete and finalized plan rather than giving it to us in bits and pieces."

"I do have the plan to give you, and it is substantially complete. The IPO took place two weeks ago, and I have the figures for the sale of Hoxsey Industries. I can tell you the public offering went well, with demand for its shares above the original asking price, which in turn gave you higher proceeds. Timothy left you a well-managed company, with hardly any debt, a skilled and efficient work force, and factories manufacturing a variety of industrial products all across the United States, several in Canada, and one in Australia."

Lauridson retrieved his briefcase from the hallway and returned to open it. He took out a portfolio of documents from the briefcase and laid it on the patio table. "These are the IPO instruments which include a complete accounting of the number of shares sold, the prices paid, commissions, investment banker fees, and all legal expenses."

Lauridson waited for one of the girls to ask what the IPO proceeds amounted to, but realized that both preferred not to interrupt him and were content to wait until he presented a final summary and accounting. He extracted another portfolio which had been prepared and provided to him by the accountants.

"This is a final accounting of Timothy's payroll for all household staff presently employed in all four of his houses, including Hoxsey Manor in Avalon, as well as the houses in London, Paris, and on Lake Geneva. It also includes payroll for the G-500 pilots, and crew for the *Princess Bonnie*. Included are the offers to be made to all such employees, including options to accept a lump sum, to remain employed, or to retire based on length of service...."

"At double the market levels for comparable terminations in other...." Judy interjected.

"I was about to say—yes absolutely. Subject to your final approval, of course."

Lauridson next withdrew a heavy notebook, with dividers separating documents in each of several areas of taxes, including income tax and estate tax.

"In compliance with Timothy's request that all taxes, and in particular estates taxes, be settled quickly, we promptly filed income, estate and gift tax returns. In return for prompt settlement we negotiated with the I.R.S. and have paid all such taxes in advance."

Next Lauridson placed on the table a fourth portfolio labeled "net assets." It was organized into different sections, including appraisals of all real estate, personal property, including the value of the G-500 and the *Princess Bonnie*, and liquid assets consisting of stocks, bonds, and bank accounts.

The last folder consisted of documents pertaining to the establishment of the Amber Hartman and Judy Alexander Trust. "So that's it, then?" asked Amber.

"That's it, "said Lauridson. "Debt is almost negligible. During the last twenty years of his life Timothy became determined to pay of virtually all of his outstanding debt. Quite a change from his younger years when as an early pioneer in the aircraft industry he borrowed huge sums from the most gullible investors and friends he could persuade. Fortunately for him, those early investments paid off for him as well as for his investors, which is why his estate is what it is today."

"I suppose it will take some time for us to go through all these documents," Amber said.

"Except I did anticipate that, though neither of you has as yet asked, you might be interested now in what the estate's bottom line is—that is what remains in the estate after taxes, disbursements, and funding for the charitable trust?"

He withdrew two single typed pages from a thin leather notebook. "Accordingly, I have taken the liberty of preparing a one page summary of everything contained in these portfolios. I have one for each of you. The figure at the top is the total value of assets in the estate, including the proceeds of the IPO. The lines below subtract the amounts set aside for payment of all taxes, pension disbursements to all employees, and the funding of the charitable trust. The final line on the bottom of the page is the net value of everything that remains, to which you two are the sole beneficiaries."

Lauridson held out copies of the summary to both Amber and Judy.

Amber looked over at Judy. "Whew! I'll tell you what. Let's have dinner now, and then afterwards we can sit down for coffee and take a look at your summary."

"That was a fine dinner," said Lauridson. "To which of you should I address my compliments?"

Each gave effusively credit to the other. "But now," said Amber, the coffee is ready. "Why don't you and Judy retire to the living room, I will fetch the coffee, and then we can take a look at that one page summary together?"

"Actually," said Judy, "Could we change the order from coffee to a generous glass of your best Chardonnay?"

"I'll second that," said John.

"Okay, a flask of Chardonnay coming up."

As everyone took ample sips, Lauridson again took out the summary copies and handed them upside down to each of the girls. "Now," he said, in the manner of a grade school teacher administering a test, "don't turn the page over until I tell you to do so."

After a dramatic pause, he said "now!"

All eyes immediately skipped over the top entries and immediately went to the bottom line.

As the mouths of both dropped simultaneously, Judy shook her head in disbelief and in a soft voice managed only an "Oh Dad, I can't believe it."

Amber on the other hand was more effusive. "Holy shit!"

Chapter Twelve
July 24, 2000

Audrey Turner Sterling sat at the "American Bar" of the Savoy Hotel on the Strand in Westminster, London. After consulting her copy of the famous Savoy Cocktail book, she ordered the "Leap Year" a classic Savoy cocktail reputed to have been "responsible for more proposals than any other cocktail that has ever been mixed."

The cocktail recipe consisted of two ounces of gin, one half ounce of Grand Marnier, one half ounce of sweet vermouth, and a dash of fresh lemon juice. The Savoy archives meticulously documented that the Savoy Bar Master Henry Craddock created the concoction for the leap year celebrations conducted at the hotel on February 28, 1928. Among his other famous concoctions were the "Hanky Panky," and the "White Lady."

Subsequent Savoy Bar Masters such as Eddie Clark had created the "New Contemptible" during World War II to attract high ranking military officers, especially Americans. Reginald "Johnny" Joe Gilmore had invented "Wedding Bells" to honor of the wedding of Princess Elizabeth and Prince Phillip. In 1969, Jon Gilmore had concocted the "Moonwalk" to honor Neil Armstrong's walk on the moon, and in 1976 Harry Vicars had created the "Speedbird," one of the three drinks commissioned for the inaugural flight of the first commercial flight of the Concorde.

Decorated in Art Deco style with ochre walls, and featuring electric blue and gold chairs, the bar was on many a visitor's list of "must see" places, along with Westminster Abbey and Big Ben.

Ordinarily, Savoy guests had to wait at a table for as long as an hour before being called to sit at the iconic "actual bar"—a special privilege that tourists from all over the world wanted to experience.

Audrey Sterling, however, had been ushered to the "actual bar" by the Bar master almost immediately upon entering, bypassing the dozens of other patrons who assumed she was some kind of film celebrity or royal.

Though she was none of those, as a stunning beauty she could have passed for one. With luxuriant dark hair and dressed in skinny jeans, silk blouse, and black Gucci patent leather flats, she was a young woman used to getting preferential treatment.

"An excellent choice," said the high toned and smartly turned-out young bartender, dressed in white coat and black tie. "I haven't been asked for a "Leap Year" for quite a while. You might want to sip it slowly, though, if you know what I mean."

"Jolly good advice I'm sure!" replied Audrey saucily mimicking a British accent.

"Oh, you can do better than that," the bartender rejoined flirtatiously. "I'll bet you're American."

"Guilty as charged. What gave me away?"

"I've never known an American who can do a proper British accent," he said as he started mixing the drink.

"Maybe you can teach me sometime."

"Maybe I can. Waiting for someone?"

"Well, yes, actually. But not here. I'm meeting an old friend, well long lost relative, I should say—for dinner at the… the…."

"Well, if you're dining here at the Savoy, it would be either the Savoy Grille, on the north side of the hotel, or Kaspars on the south side, overlooking the Thames."

Audrey opened her purse, took out a pack Virginia Slims Menthol cigarettes and lit up. "Which one is better?"

"They're both excellent, love, but Kaspars is probably the best in London."

"Kaspars? Funny name for a restaurant."

"If that's where you'll be meeting your…relative…you'll see the sculpted three-foot-high art-deco cat sitting by one of the tables. He has a place setting and has a napkin tied around his neck. You can't miss it."

"I certainly won't. So that's Kaspar the cat?"

"The story is that back in 1898 there was a dinner party planned by Wolf Joel, the South African diamond tycoon, for a party of fourteen. When one of the guests failed to appear, that left a table for only thirteen, whereupon another diner predicted that whoever first left the table would die. Joel was the first to leave, and was shot dead a few weeks later in Johannesburg. After hearing that, the Savoy commissioned a sculpture of Kaspar, the cat who had been hanging around the front entrance who became the hotel mascot. The sculpture is now seated by staff at any table consisting of only thirteen guests to ward off any bad luck—a fourteenth guest, as it were."

"Too bad my relative friend and I will only be at a table for two." By now, Audrey had taken a number of "sips" and was beginning to feel a little woozy.

"Lucky him. You must not have a husband."

"Oh contraire, I have one. Unfortunately. Back home in Houston. Very nasty character, though. He's probably looking for me now."

At any of the other less prestigious bars in London, the bartender would have been tempted to follow up as therapist with his beautiful customer. But just then the head bartender drew close to him. He turned to see his boss giving him a look of disapproval.

"Well, love, looks like I gotta attend some other blokes. I'll be back in a few to see if there's anything else you want. How long will you be here?"

Audrey looked at her watch. "Actually I think I'd better be going. I'm supposed to meet my friend at seven, but he didn't say which restaurant."

"I'm betting it's Kaspars. Have a great dinner with your friend."

Audrey smiled and rose from her bar stool. "Thank you!" Just as she left the American Bar to look for Kaspars, her cell phone rang. "Hello?"

"Audrey, this is Jeremy. Sorry, I got held up. Long story, but I should be there by 7:30, maybe 7:45, but no later, I promise."

"No problem, Jeremy, but I can't stay up very late tonight. I've got to be at the St. Pancras station by 5:30 tomorrow morning to catch the Eurostar to Paris in time to board the 2:00 Concorde flight to New York. By the way, for which of the Savoy restaurants do you have the reservation?"

"Kaspars. I meant to tell you."

"I'll just wait in the lobby until you get here."

"Okay, see you then."

Audrey found a plush chair in the lobby and pulled out her itinerary and guide book. She hadn't counted on this delay in meeting Jeremy for dinner, and now began to worry.

It had been a week since she had left Houston. She still remembered Ronald's last words to her before she left: "If you go out that door, don't bother coming back!"

And yet Audrey had been preparing to go out that door for several months before she worked up the courage to actually do so. It had taken only two years of marriage for her to realize that her friends had been right. Ronald had married her to be a trophy wife. She hadn't listened. She had been seduced by Ronald's power, his wealth, and his status. As her friends had warned her, she had paid the inevitable price. Now she wanted out. Having given him the irretrievable years she could have had with a more suitable, nurturing and supportive mate—she would not settle for walking away with nothing. Instead would take him for all he was worth to compensate her for two years of abuse she had sustained.

It would take time for any divorce to play out, but this had been her first step in asserting her independence. She was going on a trip, she told herself, to give herself space to decide whether her marriage could be saved. But that was a lie. What she really needed was time to think about how best to go about freeing herself from this man. She had already sold her jewelry—the only real assets she possessed within her control and which over the course of several months she had secreted in a safety deposit box. In the early days he had showered her with such baubles in his quest to buy a woman whose beauty would make her worthy of being his consort. All of the assets she had brought into the marriage as a result of her former modeling career had somehow been subsumed by Ronald into his hedge fund business.

With the funds she had raised from the hocking of her jewelry she had planned a trip of a lifetime. The trip was to include not only a summer sojourn to Tuscany and Venice, but also a week's stay in London at the iconic Savoy, a trip to Paris on the Chunnel, and finally a flight back to the states on the Concorde.

In preparation for her trip, she had retrieved from her mother's archives a list of relatives who lived abroad. Many of them now lived in the UK since her mother had married a British citizen many years before. From that list she had found a second cousin by the mouth-filling name of Jeremy Heathcote-Fox-McKenzie, and had begun an email correspondence with him. He actually had the title of Viscount, but like many of England's aristocrats had fallen on hard times, and was now working as a warehouseman in Southwark. He had generously agreed to take her under his wings while she was in England, and for the past week had squired her to the places she had wanted to see.

In her previous email correspondence with Jeremy she had asked the name of the best Hotel in London. In his opinion, the Savoy was not only the most luxurious hotels in London, but also the most interesting because of its fascinating history.

The origins of the hotel could be traced back to the year 1032 and the House of Savoy which was descended from Humbert I, the Count of Maurienne. What Jeremy had told her of that history had whetted her desire to stay there. Now as she put her head back and closed her eyes, she reviewed that history in her mind as she took in the lavish lobby surroundings.

Many years after the Humbert line had come to an end, King Henry III gave the Earl of Richmond the land between the Strand and the Thames, on which the Earl built the Savoy Palace. In 1505 Henry VII built a hospital for the "poure, nedie" people, which lasted several hundred years before being burned to the ground. In 1880, Richard D'oyly Carte bought the premises and built the Savoy Theater specifically for the production of Gilbert and Sullivan operas, of which he was the producer.

Carte later built the Savoy Hotel on the land adjacent to the theater. He hired Cezar Ritz to manage the hotel, but later dismissed Ritz on grounds that he had embezzled funds. (Perhaps Ritz used those embezzled funds to later build his own hotel, the 'Ritz'.)

As the Savoy became renowned for its luxury—not to mention for introducing for the first time electric lights and elevators—it began attracting millionaires and celebrities from around the world. It reached its zenith in 1905, when the American millionaire George Kessler hosted a spectacular "gondola" party in which the Savoy re-created Venice by flooding the courtyard with over four feet of water. Over two dozen invited guests dined on a giant gilded gondola as it plied this Venetian "canal." The great tenor Enrico Caruso entertained the guests, and a baby elephant brought in a five-foot birthday cake.

In 1923 a notorious murder took place in the lobby of the Savoy, when the French wife of an Egyptian Prince shot her husband dead. (She was later acquitted by a British jury on grounds that the husband had treated her with extreme cruelty during their six month marriage.)

During its early decades the hotel became associated with the arts when it appointed the French artist Monet as its artist in residence, and in 1925 George Gershwin premiered Rhapsody in Blue, which was simultaneously broadcast on the BBC.

Future King Edward VII often frequented Kaspars with his mistresses, including the renowned beauty Lily Langtry, and the Savoy's guest list included such notables as George Bernard Shaw, Charlie Chaplin, Errol Flynn, President Harry Truman,

Audrey Hepburn, Fred Astaire, Judy Garland, Marlene Dietrich, Cary Grant, and even Babe Ruth.

Laurence Olivier and Vivien Leigh met at the hotel. Also visiting the hotel during this time were such celebrities as Frank Sinatra, Marilyn Monroe, John Wayne, Humphrey Bogart, Elizabeth Taylor, Sophia Loren, Julie Andrews, Marlon Brando, Barbra Streisand, and not least, the Beatles.

The Savoy suffered greatly during the Fascist Blitz during World War II, though its famous glass cupola was protected by a sturdy covering. Winston Churchill regularly conducted lunchtime cabinet meetings in Kaspars, and the hotel's air raid shelters were acclaimed as the 'smartest in London'. Churchill, a great cat-lover, even insisted that the Kaspar sculpture join his dinner table on such occasions.

In 1953, a Coronation Ball was held at the Savoy for Queen Elizabeth II, attended by over 1,400 movie stars, royalty, and notables from around the world.

A number of movies have also been filmed at the Savoy, including The French Lieutenant's Woman, and the romantic finale to Notting Hill with Julia Roberts and Hugh Grant.

"There you are cousin! So sorry I'm late!"

Audrey awoke from her reverie with a start. "Oh Jeremy, you've finally come. I was worried."

"I'll figure out a way to make it up to you. I called Kaspars and rescheduled our reservation for eight. We've still got five minutes." He held out his hand and pulled her gently from her chair.

"Jeremy, I know this restaurant must be frightfully expensive," said Audrey after they were seated by a table with a magnificent picture-window view of the Thames. "You must let me take care of the check this evening."

"I wouldn't think of it, cousin. I am a Viscount you know. And what would people think if they knew I had invited such a beauty as you to dinner only to ask her to pay the check."

"You are kind, Jeremy. I'll tell you what, let's do what we Americas call going 'Dutch', and we'll split the check.

"Very well, if it will make you feel better."

"Good, then that's settled. Now, what do you recommend?"

"I've heard that the Cornish Crab Salad is superb, as is the Lobster Bisque. For the main course I am told that the Hereford beef sirloin is excellent, as is the beef Wellington and Creedy Carver Duck."

"Jeremy, a girl like me needs to watch her figure. I think I'll be happy with the Cornish Crab salad and Crab bisque."

"How about the Monkfish tail? I'll even split it with you."

"Maybe a few bites, and you have the rest. Now tell me more about the Savoy."

"I think I've told you all I know. But tell me, why are you going to Paris to take the Concorde? You could take it from here, you know."

"Well, I've always wanted to see Paris...."

"But you'll only be there a few hours before you head back to the states in the Air France Concorde. Fess up now, cousin. You must have another reason."

Audrey smiled sheepishly. "Okay, you got me. There is another reason. I'm meeting someone there."

"Aha, the truth comes out! Very mysterious. I think I'm jealous. Who might that person be? Someone very special, I assume."

Audrey shrugged. "I'm afraid I'll have to do what we Americans often do and 'plead the fifth.'"

"Fair enough. Sorry, I didn't mean to pry."

After the main course dishes were taken away, Jeremy asked "do you care for desert? The Dawson millefeuile is supposed to be good."

Audrey shook her head. "Thank you. Jeremy. Sounds delightful, but, well, like I said, I have to watch my figure. I'd love coffee, decaf if they have it. As I told you, I have to get up in just a few hours to get to St. Pancras by 4:30. The Eurostar leaves at 5:30 and I have to check in forty-five minutes ahead of departure."

"I understand. Well, I'll just join you with the coffee, then."

While they waited for the coffee, Audrey took out her package of Virginia Slims. "Do you have a light?"

"Oh, I'm sorry. I don't. But here...." Jeremy held the table candle and bent it toward Audrey to take the light.

"I'm so embarrassed to still be smoking," said Audrey. "But I'm really trying to quit." Holding her cigarette with her right hand she extracted with her left another small package. "See?"

"Ah, Nicobans. I've heard of them. Do those patches really work?"

"I don't know. I think they do help somewhat. But not enough I'm afraid. Listen, would you excuse me for a moment while I powder my nose? I'll be right back."

"Of course. You can leave your purse and things here if you like."

"Okay, thanks. I'll be right back. I just need to...."
Jeremy just held out his palms. "No need to...I'll be here. Take your time."

"Thanks, back in a jiffy."

Chapter Thirteen

"I guess I'm still in a state of shock," said Amber as she and Judy sipped ice tea on the patio.

"Yes, it does put a different perspective on things," Judy agreed. "I mean we didn't really do anything to deserve it, which makes it all the more difficult to comprehend."

"I guess we have to remember that Timothy spent his whole life building up Hoxsey Industries. It was his whole life. It was only after he lost Bonnie that he realized he would give it all up—every penny—just to have her back. And Judy, you couldn't bring Bonnie back for him, but you did the next best thing by finding out what happened to her, bringing her killer to justice, and giving Timothy closure."

"I don't know. It still just doesn't seem right, somehow. I mean 2.6 billion dollars? It's just hard to even comprehend. I had no idea the company was worth so much."

"Actually, a lot more. That's just what was left over after taking forty percent off the top for estate taxes, giving continued employment or pensions to his personal staff, and funding the charitable trust. I'm perfectly amenable to putting a lot more of what we have into the trust. We just have to decide who is most deserving to share in the bounty. I'm sure you have some ideas."

"I do actually...."

"I mean, you could give your share away if it would make you feel better. But I think we could do a lot of good with it."

"Yesterday I called my two hard working partners at Hammond and Alexander. I think they were both about to call it quits because we haven't been getting enough good paying criminal clients, and the cost of living in New York is high. So you know what I told them?"

"That you were going to make them all millionaires?"

"No, silly. But I did tell them I'd double their partner's share and that I would fund the partners' pool with my own personal funds. I also suggested that they go out and look for the best criminal law attorneys in town and get them to join the firm."

"I imagine they were somewhat surprised."

"Yes, but not as surprised as when I then told them that we would start taking only cases in which the cause was just, regardless of the client's ability to pay."

"And...."

"Then I told them that I wanted to change the name of the firm from 'Hammond and Alexander' to 'The Justice Institute.'"

"Wow."

"I also called the dean at Holmes and told him I wanted to make a contribution of $10 million dollars to fund a Chair in Criminal Law in honor of Robin Hammond: The Robin Hammond Chair in Criminal Law."

"Double wow."

"And what about you, sister? Are you going to let all this change the way you live your life?"

"Well, I am going to buy a new car. And I did cruise the internet to look for fancy big houses for sale in the Houston area. But you know, then I thought what would be the point of that? I have no husband or children to share it with, so why do I need some huge mansion just so I can walk alone at night through its long corridors from one room to another. It would be like living in some museum."

"Now it's my turn to say wow—I mean that you look at it that way."

"I've had some time to think about it, and I've come to the same conclusion that I think you've already come to. For the first time I realize I have a very good life the way it is, and I really don't need to change it. And if I do ever feel the need to change it, I wouldn't do so by using money."

"It's true. You read about all these people whose life was ruined after they won the lottery. Half of them were in their grave within two years, most of them having squandered their windfall, gone into debt, gotten divorced, taken to drugs, or worse."

"And look at Warren Buffet. One of the richest men in the world—worth what, fifty or sixty billion—and he still lives quite happily in a split-level in Omaha that he bought for 30k in the 1950s. I read that every morning his wife puts out $2.18 for him to go to McDonalds and buy an Egg McMuffin and a coke. And then once a week, as a special treat, she gives him an extra dollar to buy the deluxe Egg McMuffin with extra cheese for $3.18. He's almost ninety but goes to work every day, happy as a clam, looking for the next great financial investment. He says he'll leave his kids a little something, but doesn't want to ruin them with a huge inheritance, so his charities will be the real beneficiaries of his will."

"And then there's Jeff Bezos' wife, who's getting forty billion or so in the divorce. I'm sure she gave great support to her husband in his early years of struggling to create Amazon, but does she really deserve...."

"Exactly! So what's our little 2.6 billion compared with her...."

"Now we're both being silly. The fact is, if nothing else, Timothy's legacy is making both of us realize that we are just fine doing what we were doing before—only better. So you'll still keep working at your firm?"

Amber thought for a moment. "Absolutely. I really want justice for Senta. An irresponsible man disfigures her for life, laughs it off after spending thousands on a high-priced lawyer, and now she's the one who's lost her job, in deep debt, and scrambling to get her health insurance to pay for her "cosmetic 'surgeries"—while he gets a $75.00 fine."

"I'll be happy to help you with that case, and also with the Sterling case. I've been studying the file."

"Speaking of that, have you gotten an appointment with D.A. Harvey to see what evidence he has now?"

"Yes, after several tries, I finally got his secretary to give me a fifteen minute appointment for next Thursday at 10:15.

But since he knows you, I still don't understand why you couldn't make the appointment and get the file from him. You know he's not going to just give us the file. I think our best hope is that he might be willing to cough up some information—like whether the fentanyl patch found in his wife's bed was of the type that Angela could have mistaken for a nicotine patch."

"You mean ask if it's possible that Sterling could have taken one of the nicotine patches from his wife's box of patches, scraped off the nicotine substance, substituted fentanyl, and then put the patch back in her pack of nicotine patches."

"Yes, but if you know Harvey personally, wouldn't it be better if you went...."

Amber shook her head and put on one of her sheepish smiles.

"OMG, Amber, What are you not telling me?"

"Well...."

"You've had a run-in with him, haven't you?"

"Actually, just the opposite. A few months ago...."

"Don't tell me you were dating him...."

"It was just for a few weeks. I had known him for years, always gotten along well with him on a professional basis despite the fact that we were always on the opposite sides of a case... but then after I had given up my criminal practice, neither of us thought we'd have any further professional contacts that might create some kind of conflict, but then, you know...."

"Let me guess. It ended badly."

Amber shrugged. "Well, yes, you could say that. I realized within a few weeks that we were not right for each other, or rather he was not right for me...his divorce seemed to be dragging on forever, he was basically living in a flophouse, his ex was making him jump through hoops to see his kids so he was always preoccupied...."

"So you dumped him?"

"As nicely as I could, but he didn't, you know...."

"Take it well."

Amber nodded. "But at least he did take no for an answer, which was a relief.

"And now you think that if you approached him for information in the Sterling matter that it might be awkward."

"I'm afraid so. He might resent that I'm trying to ask him for a favor even after I...."

"Dumped him."

"Uh-huh.

"Also, he might expect that in return for doing me a favor I should let him...."

'But if I .meet with him, I'll have to tell him I'm asking for this evidence on your behalf, so I don't see how...."

Amber now put on her inescapable guilty smile.

"OMG, Amber, don't tell me you want me to do a reprise of that interview you had me do with that sleaze ball...."

"Assistant D.A. Brett Hillman of Appaloosa County? Well it worked for you didn't it? You had him eating out of your hand in no time, and you got him to get you that critical interview with our good doctor Gardner, which turned out to be the first step in finding Bonnie's killer for Timothy."

Judy shook her head.

"Judy, just remember the quote from Aristotle that Timothy always cited to you as the reason why he chose you to find out what happened to Bonnie, a task which his army of investigators had failed to accomplish: "Beauty is a better recommendation than any letter of introduction"

"Amber, I'm in my mid-thirties now...."

"And still a stunning beauty. You know it. I know it."

"And you really think I can get information from Harvey that you couldn't get? Is this guy really as big a sleaze as Hillman?"

"Not at all. He actually a very fine man, an excellent and, I might add, very ethical District Attorney—which is why I really don't want to put him in an uncomfortable position. If you go, I believe he will give you as much evidence as he feels ethically proper, but without having to worry if I'm offering to rekindle a relationship in return for a favor."

"He could still think that I'm just your proxy...."

"I'm willing to risk it. It's our best chance of getting the evidence we need to bring our civil case of wrongful death against Sterling—and maybe even enough to enable Harvey to get a criminal conviction as well."

"All right, I'll try, but please don't be disappointed if I don't get the evidence we need. And if this guy is still on the rebound...."

"Oh, he's an attractive man of forty-two, and I don't doubt that he might be smitten and even summon the courage to ask you out for coffee or something to 'further discuss the case', but he's no Brett Hillman, and he will take no for an answer—which hopefully you will give him."

"Absolutely. But Amber, this is the last time I...."

"Understood. Now go girl, and get the evidence we need."

Chapter Fourteen

"Mr. Harvey will see you momentarily" said the District Attorney's Office receptionist. She ushered Judy into the D.A.'s office. "Please have a seat. He'll be right with you."

Judy, wearing black slacks and silk top, her hair pulled back in a ponytail, sat and waited.

Twenty minutes later Harvey appeared at the open door to his office. "Good morning. Martin Harvey. Ms. Alexander is it?"

Judy rose and held out her hand. "Yes, sir, Judy Alexander. I'm a New York criminal defense attorney, and this week I've been visiting with an old friend here in Houston, Amber Hartman. I think you know Amber."

"Yes, I know Amber," Harvey said curtly. His rugged but youthful face—which reminded Judy of the film actor Matthew McConaughey—already showed signs of discomfort. "Please have a seat."

There was an awkward moment of silence as Harvey took his place behind his huge mahogany desk, looked up, and took in the measure of the alluring woman who sat before him—and whose appearance did not square at all with his preconception of what a New York criminal defense attorney should look like.

"So, will Ms. Hartman be joining us, then?"

Quite a hunk, thought Judy, wondering what deficiencies in this man's character might have caused Amber to dismiss him despite his youthful good looks and position as the district Attorney of Harris County.

"No, Mr. Harvey. She did want to come, but is fully booked with depositions today."

Harvey looked at his watch. "I see," he said skeptically. I assume you are here concerning the death of Angela Sterling, which this office is currently investigating."

"Yes. As you may now, Amber was hired by Angela Sterling's daughter, Brenda Masterson, to pursue a wrongful death action against her step father, Ronald Sterling, whom she believes was responsible for her death."

"Yes, I did hear of that, but I think a civil suit would be premature at this point. We are still developing the evidence in the matter of Angela Sterling's death, and as yet we do not believe we have sufficient evidence to sustain a murder indictment against Ronald Sterling. And before I discuss this matter further, I think I need to ask what your involvement is."

"At the moment, none. But Ms. Hartman has asked me to liaison with her as counsel should her client decide to proceed with her civil suit. I have told her I would consider co-counseling with her if the judge in the court where suit is brought would permit it. If not, I've told her I would assist in any way that I could."

"I see. So tell me, Ms Alexander...."

"Please call me Judy...."

"As you wish. Judy. So, what is your real interest in this case? It's not often that we get New York lawyers down here, let alone criminal defense lawyers. I've known Amber for some years, and it's only recently that she has 'switched sides' as it were. Just a few years ago she defended a sensational murder case brought in this county—I was only an ADA at that time and wasn't involved—and she made quite a reputation for herself as a criminal defense lawyer. I was surprised she gave up criminal defense in favor of personal injury litigation."

"I guess I was too. I've known Amber for quite a few years as well."

"Well, here's the problem, Judy. I'm sure Amber knows that I'm not really at liberty to share evidence that our office collects in these serious cases. If any of our evidence were to leak out prematurely, it could compromise our investigation."

"You'll have to divulge that information eventually though, would you not? The defense has a right to it, including exculpatory evidence."

"Yes, but that's only after we file an indictment."

"But we're on the same side, aren't we? Amber and I are seeking the same evidence of guilt on the civil side, just as you are on the criminal side. The evidence we both seek is the same."

"Not exactly. It's true that evidence we discover would probably also be very helpful in your civil case. But there are important differences as well. Your client is seeking money damages from a particular person. She's already decided who is responsible for the death of her mother, and would have no particular interest in eliminating others who could have committed the crime. On the prosecution side, however, we have no monetary interest, or any preconceived notion of who committed the crime—just an interest in justice, which means that we first have to eliminate all those who had opportunity, motive, and means to commit the crime before we decide to make a case against a particular individual. That takes time, and we first have to check the alibis of all those who had opportunity and means to commit the crime."

Judy realized that these were all good points, and she now wished she had taken more time to anticipate them before agreeing to pursue this interview. However, she didn't want to go back to Amber empty handed. She decided to be content if she could extract from Harvey the one piece of evidence which Amber had been sure would be critical. She had also noticed that Harvey had stopped impatiently looking at his watch, allowing the interview to go over the time scheduled. She hated to admit it, but just maybe she was, as Amber had hoped, softening him up—Aristotle style.

"Perhaps," she suggested sweetly, "if I could just tell you what I know, and you could confirm or deny it?"

Harvey finally smiled. "Sure, shoot. I wouldn't mind hearing what you and Amber think you know."

"Well, first of all, we know that Angela died from an overdose of fentanyl. The autopsy and coroner's report confirms that, and Amber already has copies of those reports."

"Not sure how Amber got access to those reports, but go on."

"The coroner's report also states that the fentanyl was likely ingested by means of a patch, rather than orally or by injection."

"Yes, that was his opinion, but as a criminal defense lawyer, I'm sure you know that effective defense counsel might be able to challenge that conclusion."

"But why would they? Your own report documents that what appeared to be a nicotine patch was found in Angela's bed by the CSI investigators."

Judy waited and then continued. "I would be most grateful if you could just confirm one fact for me—that your lab results show that the patch found, despite appearing to be a nicotine patch, had been tampered with and in fact contained fentanyl."

"How did you know that?"

I didn't until…just now, Judy thought to herself. "Amber just deduced it from everything else she knew from the reports your office has already released."

Harvey sat silent for several moments.

"I'm not asking you to give me a copy of the lab report. I know you'll release it, if not now, during the discovery process—such as the discovery process is these days in criminal cases."

"You know…." he said.

"Yes?"

"I will confirm that fact, just for you, Judy—you're a very persuasive young woman—if you will promise absolutely that you and Amber will keep that information absolutely confidential until we release the lab report at the proper time. I think you must realize the import of that information."

Finally. "I do, and we will promise to keep that report confidential until you let us know otherwise. Thank you, Martin."

"Sure. Does that mean you'll be staying on in Houston for a while? If so, maybe you and I could…."

Judy sensed that he probably wished he hadn't been so obvious, but his tone said it all.

Chapter Fifteen

"So how did it go yesterday?" Amber asked. "Sorry I got in so late last night from our partners' meeting, and you'd already gone to bed. I didn't want to wake you."

Judy had risen early and was now in the kitchen making the morning coffee. "I didn't get a copy of the Sterling file, of course, but I think I did get some useful information. How was the partners' meeting?"

"Dreadful, actually. Being a senior partner isn't what it's cracked up to be. I spend most of my time refereeing disagreements between the other partners—percentage distributions and all that. I'm afraid the firm is still pretty much a boy's club, and some of the other partners still resent that I was ever made a senior partner. And then, of course, they all wanted to stay up 'til all hours drinking."

"Oh no, you didn't...."

"Drinking? I guess I did have a few too many, but I didn't drive home. I learned my lesson that night you had to drive me home from the restaurant. So I called Tyrone to come get me, and left my car in the garage."

"I'm sure Tyrone was thrilled to get your call at 2 A.M."

"I know, I felt bad about that, but he's getting a full salary, and he doesn't have to drive much these days, except to take you back and forth from the office."

"I really would rather have my own rental car...."

"You're cute, but isn't it interesting that we both seem to want to just go about what we were doing before."

"I know. I'm hoping that won't change actually."

"Me too, but I did tell you I'm getting a new car. I'm thinking of a Lexus. Anyway, we'll see. Now, about your meeting with Harvey."

"Well…it was a little awkward at first, of course. I'm not sure if he knew that I knew about your prior relationship with him. He was a little defensive at first, gave me a little lecture about not compromising their investigation by leaking evidence prematurely."

"It wouldn't be leaking. It would be sharing evidence with each other which would be mutually beneficial to us in our civil case and to him in pursuing a criminal case."

"I'm not sure he sees it that way, at least not yet. I mean what evidence do we have that we could share with him?

"Well, we have our client, Brenda Masterson, for one thing. While you were at the D.A.'s office, Brenda stopped in to see me. She really opened up to me about the relationship between her mother and Ronald. It was not good. The wedding cake was barely cut before the abuse began."

"How old is Brenda?"

"Eighteen or nineteen, a sophomore at UT. Very sweet girl, and devastated about her mother's murder."

"And how old was Angela when she died?"

I think about thirty-five or thirty-six. You'll have to check the file. She married her first husband when she was only seventeen or so. They eloped, and she got pregnant with Brenda shortly after, but the marriage didn't work out. He was a car mechanic, but often out of work, and neither of them had much money to speak of. He wanted her to get rid of the baby, but she insisted on keeping it. Partly because of that he left her and the baby shortly thereafter. He later died in a car accident, drag racing or some such."

"Sounds like a charming fellow. So how did Angela manage to make it on her own with the baby?"

"Well, she hadn't even graduated from high school at that point, and had no money to get an education. No family to speak of able to offer her support. She ended up getting a job at a fast food outlet, but didn't even earn enough to cover her child care. She was in desperate straits at that point, living in a flophouse outside Sunnyside which, by the way, had the distinction of being the second most dangerous neighborhood in the United States. When she finally started getting welfare checks, she was about to quit her job at the fast food place and stay home to raise Brenda. And then something of a miracle happened."

"Really!"

It turned out that an exec from a New York modeling agency was on his way to an agency in Houston when he took a wrong exit and ended up in Sunnyside. Being hungry, he decided to make a quick stop at the fast food place where Angela was working her last day on the job."

"Don't tell me. She was 'discovered.'"

"Sounds so terribly unlikely, doesn't' it, but that's exactly what happened—like out of a story book. Angela was young, naïve, and desperate enough to believe the exec's offer to come to New York for a modeling audition, and even to pay for her child's trip and accommodations in New York. Except in her case, the offer was absolutely legitimate."

"Amazing."

"Within a couple of years she became one of the top models in the county, flitting between New York, Paris and Milan and earning millions."

"And how did Ronald come into that picture?"

"It was some years later, shortly after Angela retired from modeling. He was a very successful hedge fund manager, and met her at a gala benefit for the Metropolitan Opera in New York. Thereafter he pursued her relentlessly on his business trips to New York. Although he showered her with gifts, Brenda insists that she never married him for his money. She had plenty of money of her own by that time. Rather, she just wanted to settle down to a life with an attractive, suitable and successful man outside the modeling world—a fantasy world with which she had become disillusioned."

"When were she and Ronald married?"

"About four years ago. He was a widower, his first wife having died some years before in that Concorde crash back in 2000. Although Ronald had been regarded as somewhat of a womanizing 'player' in the world of Houston high society, apparently he had decided that he needed some permanent eye candy on his arm."

"Did she bring any assets to the marriage?"

"Brenda thinks so, but not sure how much. It was probably at least a couple of million or so based on her very successful modeling career."

"So there's a motive for murder right there."

"Not really. Ronald is worth hundreds of millions—supposedly."

"Still...."

"Brenda doesn't think so. She thinks his motive was threefold—first, jealousy because he believed she was seeing another man; second, fear that if she divorced him he would lose a large percentage of his net assets; and third, the humiliation that he would suffer by divorce in his high society world."

"I'm not sure about the third motive. Divorces are not that uncommon in high society. The second motive seems more likely. How much would he lose given that they were only married for four years?"

"Enough. Brenda tells me that she signed a prenuptial agreement that guaranteed her—not a specific dollar amount—but a percentage of his net assets if the marriage lasted at least three years."

"What percentage?"

"Brenda tells me it was twenty percent, and that his net worth had risen substantially since the pre-nup was signed. So if he really is worth, say, 200 million, that would be 40 million."

"Forty million sounds like a motive to me."

"Agreed. But the real reason Harvey still can't make a case yet is this thing about the fentanyl patches. A fentanyl patch, disguised as a nicotine patch, could have been placed in her packet of patches at any time—weeks or even months before. And even if we could prove when she attached the fentanyl-laced patch to her arm, there could still be a delay of as much as twenty-four hours before the patch had its deadly effect—depending on the dosage and the speed with which her body absorbed the poison."

"But how could the killer be sure that Angela would actually attach the fentanyl patch to her arm at all? What if she discarded the packet of patches before she had used them all, or innocently offered it to a friend who was also trying to break the smoking habit?"

"I think the killer was willing to take that chance in return for what he considered to be an absolutely safe method of committing murder without getting caught. By using this method, the killer created opportunity for anyone who ever interfaced with Angela over the course of weeks or months to kill her by slipping the single fentanyl-laced patch into her packet of nicotine patches. It's a prosecutor's nightmare because it requires him to eliminate a huge number of potential suspects in order to isolate the true killer as the perpetrator. Alibis become meaningless in such a scenario."

"But surely only Ronald had a motive."

"We don't know that. Defense counsel is very skilled at finding motives among other suspects who had opportunity—jilted lovers, potential blackmailers, disgruntled employees. I know because I used to be a defense counsel."

"As I still am, though, in the interests of justice I'm willing to help you in your role as de facto prosecutor in this particular case. I've always admired the British system in this regard. Barristers practice in a group at the Inns of Court, and can either accept commissions from defendants to defend them, but equally free to accept commissions from the Crown—through the CPS—to prosecute. So a barrister could be prosecuting an armed robbery case in the morning, and defending a separate armed robbery case in the afternoon—all in the same courtroom. Much better system in my view. You don't see the 'siege' mentality developing in prosecutor and defender offices like you do under the American system—you know 'us against them.'"

"I'm embarrassed that I didn't know that. What's the 'CPS'?"

"Crown Prosecution Service. That's the government department that retains private barristers in the Inns of Court to prosecute the crown's cases in court. Robin and I took a sabbatical together from our firm a couple of years ago, spent some time at the Inns of Court learning about their system. He later wrote a law article in the Holmes Law Review about the differences between the American and British systems of justice. I think we both think the British system is better."

"Hmmm. Interesting. Shoot me the citation to his article sometime. Anyway, I think you see our problem now. Basically, we've got to do Harvey's work for him. Now, tell me what evidence you got him to cough up for us."

"He confirmed that the patch found in Angela's bed appeared to be a nicotine patch, but that in fact, based on the lab report, the killer had substituted fentanyl for nicotine."

"That is an important piece of evidence. How did you manage to get him to confirm that?"

"Well, I inferred that you already knew, so that there was no reason why he shouldn't confirm it."

"So now, he thinks I got someone from his office to leak that report to me? Judy, he could...."

"No, I told him that you had just deduced it, not that you knew it or had seen the report itself."

"So you think he bought that?"

Judy smiled. "I think so. But you did want me to get some evidence, right?"

"Hmmm. So tell me truthfully. Did he come on to you?"

Judy shrugged noncommittally.

"Judy...."

"Not really," she hedged defensively. "He just asked me how long I was going to be in Houston, and if maybe I might...."

"Say no more, but he's not aggressive in that way. Probably just a feeler, but it would be well to watch him. I won't send you back there unless it really becomes necessary. In the meantime, let's get down to brass tacks. What do we have now, that we didn't have before?"

"Not much more, I have to admit. We know that Angela was murdered. We know that the means of committing the murder was by inserting in Angela's packet of nicotine patches what appeared to be a nicotine patch, but which had in fact been tampered with to substitute the fentanyl for the nicotine. Is there anything more we can do at this point?"

"For starters, we could find out when and where Angela bought the packet of nicotine patches. That would give us a starting point, before which the murder could not have been committed. Then we would need to trace Angela's whereabouts from that time up until the day she died."

"And also track Ronald's whereabouts during all that time."

"Which means tracking down everywhere he travelled during that time, and the precise dates he travelled. The goal would be to find a time and place where Angela and Ronald could have interfaced, and when Ronald, or someone he hired, would have had the opportunity to substitute the fentanyl patch for the nicotine one."

"But even if we did that, wouldn't we also have to prove that Ronald had access to fentanyl? How would we even begin to go about that?"

"Yes, that would be difficult. In most of the successful poisoning prosecutions I've looked at, the prosecution was able to prove where the defendant obtained the poison—whether from a hospital pharmacy, a drugstore, doctor's prescription, or hardware store. It would be more difficult to prove the source in his case because it is highly unlikely that the killer got the fentanyl from a legitimate source. It is far more likely that he got it from a black market, probably in Mexico."

"So it could be the perfect crime, then?"

"I would hate to even think so."

"So what are you saying, that even if we got all the information you described—the travel dates and times of both

Angela and Ronald over the period since Angela bought the nicotine pack and the time of her death—and even if we could somehow track the source of the fentanyl, we still wouldn't have a case?"

"I think we'd have the beginning of one, but then there's the bigger problem."

"Which is...."

"It's the cost of getting all that evidence. I haven't been able yet to get a copy of Angela's Will, if she even had one, but it's likely Ronald is the beneficiary. In most cases spouses leave their assets to the other spouse—at common law the spouse was entitled to at least a life estate in half the estate, regardless of what was in the Will—trusting that the spouse would leave the assets to children. But be that as it may, we're talking about the cost of tracking down the whereabouts of perhaps dozens of people who may have interfaced with Angela over what could be a very long period of time. The cost would be enormous, with very little chance of a payoff in the end even if we got the evidence that we were seeking, it still wouldn't be enough, and therefore almost certainly not worth the cost of getting it."

Judy thought for a moment. "But Amber, don't you see how things really are different now than before we received Timothy's legacy? Cases that before we might have had to give up on because of the client's inability to pay, we can now pursue just because the cause is just. I'll gladly pay for the costs of conducting this investigation out of my share of the estate if Brenda cannot pay."

Amber smiled. "If we do it, we'll each pay half. But Judy, even if we're successful, it still won't be enough."

"Amber, for the last couple of weeks I've been going through the Sterling file. I've also boned up on the Texas rules of Evidence, which in most respects are identical to the Federal Rules of Evidence with which I'm more familiar. Texas Rule of Evidence 404(b) is similar to the Federal Rule and provides that...."

Judy consulted her notes, and continued, "TRE 404(b) provides that while 'evidence of a prior crime is not admissible to show that on a particular occasion the person acted in a similar way, a prior crime may be admissible for another purpose, such as proving motive, plan, identity, absence of mistake, or lack of accident.'"

"Yes, I'm aware. We talked about that. It's based on the old English 'Brides in the Bath' case. But as I also told you, that principle can't be applied to the Sterling case because Ronald's former wife, Audrey, died in a plane crash, not by fentanyl poisoning."

"I wonder."

"What do you mean?"

"What if she was poisoned before she got on the plane, and had either died, or was afflicted with the symptoms of poisoning before the plane actually crashed?"

"OMG, Judy. That would have to be the mother of all coincidences, would it not? And how incredibly convenient for the killer who poisoned Audrey with fentanyl. I mean, really! So you're saying that Angela could have attached the poisoned patch to her arm within the twenty-four hours prior to boarding the Concorde, but that the symptoms only began to take effect as the plane was taking off or shortly before."

"It's not impossible, is it? Maybe the symptoms were slight at first, but she didn't want to cancel the trip because she just wasn't feeling well, or thought a cold was coming on. But she still would have been a dead woman from the moment she boarded that plane— regardless of what happened thereafter."

"Judy, come on...."

"Did you know that smoking was banned on the Concorde in 1997? I've been reading up on this. Even though it's only a three and a half hour flight—flying at 1,500 miles an hour, faster than a bullet—that can be a long time for a person addicted to smoking. Wouldn't that be the very time that Audrey Sterling would want to apply the patch? Why ruin a trip of a lifetime by suffering from nicotine withdrawal?"

Amber shook her head. Even if that were true—a remarkable coincidence in itself—it would be impossible to prove now."

"I wonder."

"Now what are you wondering?"

"As I said, I've been reading everything I can get my hands with regard to that terrible crash—there's no doubt about the cause of the crash—a piece of metal fell off a previous plane, which caused the Concorde's tire to burst and get sucked into the undercarriage causing a catastrophic fire. In the aftermath most of the bodies were burned beyond recognition, but most were still able to be identified by means of DNA, and returned to their families in France, Germany, and the United States."

"But surely fentanyl could not still be detected in those bodies after all these years."

"I've looked into that, too, Amber, and depending on the condition of Audrey's body, it might still be possible using the very latest developed methods of poison detection in corpses—assuming only that there has been no complete cremation of the body. Poisons have been detected even in bodies that were exhumed many years after burial and despite being significantly decomposed."

Amber continued to look skeptical. "Judy, it's one of the bedrock principles of common law jurisprudence that criminal defendants should not be judged by their prior behavior, but only by the evidence against them in the case charged."

"I know, but as you know too, 404(b) provides exceptions where evidence of prior crimes can be introduced to show motive, identity, plan, and lack of accident or coincidence."

"I know that, Judy. But…well, just go on."

"Okay," said Judy as she withdrew some cases from her file. "Here's another interesting American case applying the "Brides in the Bath" principle. In the 1973 case of U.S. v. Woods, the 4th Circuit Court of Appeals held that evidence of seven previous unexplained deaths of children in the defendant's care were admissible to prove that she was responsible for the death of an eighth child. All the children who died were foster children and unrelated to the defendant, who claimed that all eight of the deaths, being unexplained, could only have been caused by 'infant death syndrome'—a tragic but extremely rare cause of death. The evidence of the prior deaths was held admissible under 404(b) to rebut the defendant's claim of accident or coincidence."

"I'm impressed. Any more cases you've found?"

"In the Bill Cosby sexual assault case, testimony of prior instances of the defendant giving women sedatives and then sexually assaulting them was held admissible. Similar testimony by witnesses of prior sexual predation was also found admissible in the Harvey Weinstein case. In the 1983 case of Wayne Williams, the defendant was charged with the murder of an African American boy. The court permitted evidence that the unusual carpet, car, and dog fibers found on the victim were identical or similar to those found on eight prior African American murdered children. It did so by applying the 404(b) 'identity' exception."

"Judy, this is such a longshot you're talking about, and the costs of litigating exhumation procedures—not to mention the costs of lab tests and fees of experts employing the latest scientific techniques for identifying poisons of corpses—would be staggering to say the least. I doubt seriously if Harvey would be willing for his office to undertake that cost given the low likelihood of it bearing admissible evidence."

"I'll pay it, Amber."

"Anything you pay, I will too, of course, because as you said, we can now. But first things first. First, you have to find out where Audrey is buried. Second, you have to find out what the condition of Audrey's body was at the time of her burial. Next, you have to find Audrey's next of kin and get him or her to sign the petition to initiate the exhumation process—not a slam dunk, given the number of years that have passed since burial, and with no indorsement by the state or the D.A. Finally, give me all the information you can find on the latest advancements in the science of poison identification in corpses."

"I'm ahead of you sister. Tyrone's picking me up at 6 A.M. in the morning, and Chandler will be standing by in the G-500 to take me to Las Vegas to meet with Madeleine Turner, Audrey's sister."

Chapter Sixteen

As the G-500 Gulfstream began its descent into Las Vegas McCarran International airport, Judy reviewed from her file what she knew of Madeleine Turner. It wasn't much. Just two days before she had assigned to Timothy's old detective firm the task of tracking down the whereabouts of all known relatives of Audrey Sterling, who had died in the 2000 crash of the Concorde in Paris. With only short notice, the agency had found only one living relative, a younger sister of Audrey, and its preliminary report revealed little information about her background other than her present occupation and location in Las Vegas. A follow-up report, which Judy had received by text only minutes before landing at McCarran provided additional helpful information.

Madeleine had apparently been blessed with many of the same attributes that had attracted a twenty-seven year old Ronald Sterling to her sister whom he married back in 1997—not least of which was that her father was CEO of one of the largest hedge funds headquartered in New York City. A graduate of Wharton Business School, Ronald had already rapidly climbed the corporate ladders of several major banks and brokerage firms, and was well on his way to compiling a fortune when he met Audrey at a debutante ball and married her shortly thereafter. It look less than a year for that marriage to crumble, and only two more years for it to degenerate to the point that Audrey had felt compelled to consult a divorce lawyer.

What struck Judy most from these reports was the similarity of the nature of the relationships Ronald had had with each of his two wives. Aside from the fact that Audrey and Angela had risen from dramatically different backgrounds before meeting and marrying Ronald— Audrey from a life of privilege, societal status, and wealth, and Angela from the depths of poverty—both had died during a period of marital alienation and at times that were remarkably convenient for Ronald, particularly from a financial standpoint. In both cases, the bride had been sought as a trophy wife, though in the case of Audrey more for her societal status than her beauty.

Having not had time before leaving Houston to order a car, Judy waited in line for a cab to take her to the Lucky Diamond Casino where Madeleine was a senior manager of operations. Having arrived more than an hour before her 3 P.M. appointment with Madeleine, she sat at the Casino's bar and nursed a watered down Bloody Mary. Dressed only in black slacks, while blouse, and heels, she had not anticipated being approached by raunchy male tourists and gamblers apparently drawn to any attractive female sitting alone at the bar, but especially to a woman of Judy's fresh cover-girl looks. After several failed attempts to sip her drink in peace, Judy retreated to a roped off area of high stakes slot machines and waited until shortly before 3 P.M. She then left the machines and took the elevator to the third floor offices where Madeleine said she would meet her.

"Hello, I have an appointment with Ms. Turner," Judy announced to the office receptionist.

"Just a moment," came the response. Several minutes later a smartly dressed and attractive woman of about forty-five appeared in the reception area and extended her hand to Judy.

"Ms. Alexander? I'm Madeleine Turner. I'm sorry I'm running a little late today. Won't you come in?"

Judy entered a corner office with a floor to ceiling picture window view of the Strip.

"Please have a seat," said Madeleine as she took her seat behind a large glass desk. "I understand you wanted to talk to me about my late sister, Audrey. I must confess I am curious about what interest you might have in her. I'm sure you know she was killed in the crash of the Concorde in France in 2000."

"Yes I know that, and that is one of the reasons I wanted to talk to you."

"Then I'm sure you also know that all the investigations and litigation concerning the crash were resolved many years ago.

I don't know what Audrey's husband received in compensation for her wrongful death—I think the total was $100 million in total compensation for all 109 victims—but I know he didn't deserve whatever he got!"

Judy had obviously pushed one of her buttons. "Forgive me, Ms. Turner. I'm not here to ask about any of that actually. But I am interested in why you think your sister's husband didn't deserve any compensation."

"Because he was a fucking bastard, that's why! She hated his guts. He knew she was about to divorce him and get what she was entitled to in the courts for enduring his years of abuse. That horrible crash not only took away my only sister, but saved his rear end. He not only avoided the cost of a divorce, but he got a million dollars or more in compensation."

"And you received no compensation yourself?"

"No, of course only the spouse was entitled to compensation as next of kin. But I didn't care about that. All I wanted was my sister back, and no amount of compensation would bring her back."

Both women sat silently for several minutes as Judy thought best how to approach the real reason she was there.

Finally, Madeleine said, "So why are you here then?"

"I am working with an attorney in Houston who is representing Brenda Masterson, the daughter of Angela Sterling."

"Ronald Sterling's second wife? If Ronald treated her in the same way as he treated my dear Audrey, I hope she's finally going to bring that…bring that horrible man to account."

"I'm sorry to tell you that Angela Sterling died several months ago. The Harris County coroner recently determined that her death was the result of fentanyl poisoning."

"Oh my God. So this time he actually had to get rid of his wife himself! Couldn't wait around for fate to intervene and do it for him."

"I'm sorry Ms. Turner. I didn't mean to upset you."

Madeleine took a deep breath. "It's all right. I was very close to my sister. It's been so many years since I lost her, but there's not a day I don't think of her."

"I understand. I lost my partner this past year."

"Then you know. So why has Ronald's daughter-in-law retained the services of this Houston lawyer? What's the lawyer's name?

"Amber Hartman. She's very good. Her client, Angela's daughter Brenda, is convinced that Ronald murdered Brenda's mother by substituting a fentanyl-laced patch for one of her nicotine patches. Because a patch releases the fentanyl very gradually, and because fentanyl has been known to produce unexpected delayed respiratory depression, she could have applied the patch as long as twenty-four hours before suffering either symptoms or rapidly relapsing into either unconsciousness or death."

"Fentanyl, you say?"

"Yes, have you heard of it?"

"It's some kind of pain killer, isn't it?'

"Although it can be prescribed under certain very controlled restrictions, we believe that the killer obtained a more deadly analog of the drug on the black market. Brenda believes that Ronald is the one who planted the fentanyl-laced patch in Angela's packet of nicotine patches."

"Wow. I can certainly believe it. He is certainly capable of it, and knowing him, I'm sure he had a motive. I have no doubt he would have murdered my sister if he thought he could get away with it."

Judy paused, and then said, "I will tell you I think it's quite possible that Ronald did exactly that."

Madeleine's jaw dropped in amazement. "What? I mean, how could he have…I mean she definitely died in the Concorde crash…not that he wouldn't have…."

"We do not doubt that your sister could have died in the crash. But that does not exclude the possibility that she could have died after she boarded the aircraft, but before it crashed.

We think it is at least possible that she was administered poison before boarding the Concorde."

Madeleine shook her head. "But how is that possible? If Audrey died on the aircraft before takeoff, or even showed symptoms of illness, surely they would have aborted the takeoff, and called for medical assistance to have her taken off the plane and to a hospital."

"There was a delay of some forty-five minutes after the passengers boarded the aircraft and the time of takeoff. If fentanyl did enter Audrey's body very gradually—in the same way that we believe it entered Angela's body—she could have expired during that time. But even if she was still alive at the time of the crash, or had not yet even showed symptoms, the person who substituted the fentanyl-laced patches would still have been guilty of attempted murder—the crash having intervened to kill her before the fentanyl did."

"But how could you possibly prove that now? What evidence do you have?"

"As of now, absolutely none."

"Then why...why are you here...."

"Because we believe that you may have the means to provide at least some of the evidence we would need to prove that."

"Me? But how could I possibly...."

"That's why I'm here. We want your permission to exhume your sister's body and test if for fentanyl."

"Oh my God. You're serious! How could her body ever be tested for that after all this time?"

"We're not sure it can be. However, in the past twenty years there have been quite a few advancements in the science of poison identification in bodies—depending on the condition of the body."

"So now you're asking me about what the condition of my sister's body was after the crash?"

Judy nodded.

Madeleine's face now showed her distress. "I can't believe you're even asking me that! I mean how you can come down here like this and expect me...."

"I know we're asking a lot. And I have to tell you that the chances of finding anything are very slim even if you give us permission to petition for the exhumation of your sister's body. And even if you do give us permission, there's no guarantee a court would grant your petition."

Madeleine shook her head. "I don't know...I mean you're really asking a lot."

"I know it. And both Amber and I will understand if it's something you feel you cannot do."

"What do you need to know?"

"In reviewing accounts of the condition of the remains after the crash, we know that most of the bodies were badly burned, most beyond recognition, and that many of the body parts were in pieces."

"Please stop it! Judy is it? I think it's best you go now!"

"Of course. I'm so sorry. I'll go now." Judy rose from her chair."

Before Judy reached the door, Madeleine said, "Wait."

Judy turned. "Yes?"

Madeleine got up and went to a large filing cabinet and pulled out a file. "I've kept this for all these years. It will have the details you need." She handed it to Judy.

"Are you sure you want to give me this?"

"Audrey's body, or at least her torso, was identified by DNA...God it's so hard to talk about this... I provided the sample they needed for comparison. At my request her remains were shipped to me in Houston where Audrey had lived with her husband. I held a memorial service for her in the church she attended, and she was buried at Olivewood Cemetery. It's all in the file."

"I'll take good care of it. And...."

"I'll also sign the petition."

"Thank you. I will send you the petition by express mail within the week for your signature. Also be assured that we will take care of all expenses involved in litigating the petition, all the costs of exhumation if the petition is granted, and all the costs of conducting the laboratory tests should any experts we retain find that any available tests for fentanyl would be viable given the condition of the remains. And I have to reiterate that the chances of finding anything are...."

"Very slim. I understand. But if there is any chance at all that my sister was murdered, and that her killer might be apprehended or at least identified, then I want to go forward."

"Thank you. I will keep you informed."

"Before you go. Judy? May I call you Judy?"

"Of course."

"I'm sorry I was short with you before. I realize you're just trying to find some justice for your client and want to bring a killer to justice. If you don't have to rush back to Houston, perhaps you'd like to join me for a light early dinner, or just coffee, in our Diamond Café downstairs. We have a pretty good menu, if I say so. On the house, of course."

Judy smiled. "I'd be delighted. I just have to make a quick call."

"Great. I'll meet you at the elevator in just a minute."

Judy called Chandler to let him know she wouldn't get back to the G-500 for the flight back to Houston for at least an hour or so.

Minutes later Madeleine ushered Judy into the executive dining room of the Diamond Café.

"What would you like?" Madeleine asked.

"Perhaps I'll try your Chef Salad. And just iced tea would be fine."

Madeleine motioned for a waiter, who promptly took their orders and served the orders most promptly.

Judy then asked her final question. "Ms. Turner...."

"Madeleine, please."

"Madeleine, this may sound like a silly question, but your answer could be important. Did your sister ever have a smoking problem, and if so, did she ever try to quit?"

"Funny that you should ask, but yes…she got hooked on cigarettes in high school. By the time she got married, she was determined to kick the habit."

"Do you happen to know if she used nicotine patches to quit?"

"Sorry, I'm not sure,but I think so. But Judy, I do have one last question before you go."

"Of course."

"I know you're working for your client to get evidence to support her wrongful death action against Ronald Sterling. And I'm most appreciative that you're willing to investigate the possible murder of my sister. But given the very long odds against your finding anything in my sister's case, why are you willing to go to all this trouble and expense to look into my sister's death?"

"Two reasons actually. First, for the first time in my life as a lawyer, I have the means and opportunity to pursue a case purely for the cause of justice, and not in anticipation of a fee. And second, have you ever heard of the 'Brides in the Bath' case which arose out of the High Court of Justice in jolly old England?"

Chapter Seventeen
July 25, 2000

Like a gleaming white bird of prey, its sharp beak pointed downward, Concorde waited on the tarmac at Charles de Gaulle Airport in Paris for the arrival of the privileged passengers who would board her that day.

Audrey Turner Sterling looked out her Eurostar window into the Chunnel's darkness, anticipating that at any moment the high speed train would be emerging in to the bright dawn of Coquilles at the Pas-de-Calais. Once she arrived in Paris, she would complete the second phase of her journey that had taken her far away—even if temporarily—from Houston, and her cold-hearted husband Ronald Sterling. Now she looked forward to the final leg of her planned dream trifecta which had included: first the stay at the historical and sumptuous Savoy; second the fifty kilometer trip under the Chunnel, an engineering project second only to man's trip to the moon; and now Concorde, mankind's leap into the future, inaugurated in the same year as man's first voyage to the moon.

It was the prospect of experiencing this third leg that most excited her. It was not just the speed with which she would cross the Atlantic that excited her—though the thought that she would be traveling at the speed of a bullet was thrilling. At a speed of over twice the speed of sound, it was faster than the rotation of the earth, meaning that it could arrive in New York an hour before it left London. For music star Robbie Williams it meant that he could leave London to give a concert in Philadelphia and return the same day to accept two Brit awards back in London. For tycoons and businessmen whose "valuable" time was measured in precious minutes during which millions in profits might be gained, it meant saving a few precious hours in flight time. Indeed, the Speedbird flew from New York to Seattle in fifty-five minutes, a record in commercial air travel never to be equaled in the modern era.

But for the vast majority of passengers, it was not the saving of a couple of hours of flight time over the Atlantic that was worth paying the average ticket price of $12,000.00 for a single roundtrip ticket. This meant that a couple flying roundtrip in 1976 would pay $24,000.00 for the privilege—or $116,000.00 in 2021 dollars. This at a time when a budget ticket on a typical airliner could be had for a couple of hundred dollars.

Nor was it the luxury of the seating or the legroom on the Concorde which was the inducement to fly the great Speedbird. There were but two seats on either side of the aisle, and the width of each seat was barely greater than that on a coach seat on the typical airliner. Even the legroom, though a bit longer than the average coach seat, was far short of first class seats on a 747.

While the typical fare on Concorde was indeed gourmet—a brunch of Lock Fyne salmon with crème fraiche and beluga caviar from the Caspian Sea—such fare could be gotten for considerably less than $116,000.00 land side.

In fact, it was none of these things that attracted either the rich, powerful, and famous, or the less affluent middle class to cough up a chunk of their retirement savings, to buy a ticket.

It was the experience itself.

Audrey had voraciously read the accounts of those who had flown it before, including the account of one of its first flight attendants who famously gushed, "It was a brief glimpse into a life I had not known, polite, considerate, and beautifully decorated. It was impossible not to feel privileged, spoiled, and valued;" or the journalist passenger who had effused, "the flight attendants loved being on it, the passengers loved being on it. You were aware of being part of a very small group of people that were privileged enough to be on Concorde."

Certainly neither Princess Diana, a regular on the Concorde, nor Queen Elizabeth, chose to travel on Concorde because of the extra two inches of legroom on the first row of seats which passed for "First class." For those who sat in the Concorde version of steerage, it was not surprising to be seated next to such veteran Concorde passengers as Robert Redford, Elizabeth Taylor, James Bond (Sean Connery), novelist Joan Collins, Elton John, Mick Jagger, or even a Beatle or two. Across the aisle one might find regular passengers Hugh Grant and Liz Hurley holding hands as Liz looked out her small window to see a lumbering 747, a mere speck flying some 25,000 feet below them and appearing to be dead stopped in the air as the Speedbird flew over and past it at Mach 2.2.

The visionaries who built the Concorde had never conceived that it would be limited to an elite and privileged few. Rather they had envisioned it as the next inevitable step in the evolution of air transport for the masses. Much as the jet engine had made swift air travel accessible and affordable to all those who had theretofore endured long distance travel over many days by slow boat, rail or, most grueling, by bus, the visionaries saw supersonic air travel as the next logical step, particularly in international travel. Once supersonic air travel became the norm, travelers would no more be satisfied with long distance flights on lumbering subsonic aircraft than the rail travelers of the 1900s would have been satisfied with travel to California by covered wagon.

It was on this basis that the "Concorde Project" was conceived as a joint enterprise between England and France in accordance with negotiations to form the European Economic Community (EEC). The French word "concorde," meaning harmony, or agreement, was first chosen as the name for the joint project. However, the use of the French spelling, rather than the English spelling "concord" without an "e" caused considerable consternation in England. In the end, this threshold obstacle to joint cooperation was defused when it was pointed out by the Minister of Technology, Tony Benn that the "e" could stand for both "England" and "excellence." Henceforth the plane would be known simply as "Concorde"—but without the article "the," as in the naming of a person.

The resolving of the political issues, however, was a prelude to the more substantial engineering and technical obstacles. First to raise its technological head was that of heat. As with the space shuttle, an airplane at very high speed also generates heat—about 270 degrees Fahrenheit flying at Mach 2.

In the case of Concorde such heat causes the fuselage to expand by more than a foot. Although consideration was given to developing an alloy that would enable Concorde to fly at even faster speeds, it was decided not to delay the project by developing new alloys and to therefore limit its speed to just over Mach 2. Even so, a flight attendant flying on Concorde would notice that if she left her purse in the space between the workstation and the bulkhead during flight, it would be completely squashed by the time the plane landed.

Another technological challenge was the wings. In order for the plane to reduce drag at speeds of over Mach 2, it was necessary that the wings be small and delta shaped like those found on missiles and fight aircraft—in order to reduce drag. The problem was that such tight and small wings achieved insufficient lift for taking off. This problem was resolved by taking advantage of a little known natural phenomenon first noted by Chuck Yeager, the first man to break the sound barrier in a Convair XF-92: if a plane took off or landed at a very high angle, the vortex that formed over the top of the wings created added lift that enabled it to take off and land at acceptable speeds. As a result Concorde was built with very high and skinny stilt-like stork legs which let it take off nose up without scraping its tail on the runway. The feature led flight attendants to warn passengers of the extreme vertical angle and enormous burst of speed that would push them back in their seats during takeoff. Passengers nevertheless found the experience exhilarating, producing a rush for which many would pay thousands to repeat the experience on future flights.

Then there were the economic and financial issues, never satisfactorily resolved. With Europe chaffing at the aviation predominance of the United States in the postwar years, fear was the primary impetus for England and France to form a consortium to compete with the U.S. in the development of supersonic air travel. France and England were afraid that if they didn't get a head start in taking the next big step in the evolution of commercial air travel they would be forever left behind by the United States.

The fear was justified. As early as 1963, a youthful and energetic President John F. Kennedy had tasked the Federal Aviation Administration with looking into the future of civil aviation. While U.S. aviation had made considerable strides since World War II, the sound barrier had posed a seemingly impenetrable barrier to any further progress. The FAA responded by investigating the possibility of building a supersonic airliner, and launched the quest to build an SST—Supersonic Transport—by asking for proposals from the U.S. aviation industry.

Boeing, the leader in aircraft design, was one of the first to respond and soon presented the FAA with a design that beat out all other American competitors—the remarkable Model 2707-390. By 1969, however, the U.S. had landed a man on the moon, and the push for another expensive project quickly evaporated. Confident that no project in Europe would ever be able to create its own Supersonic Transport, Congress in 1971 decided to cancel all funding for Boeing's SST. This action immediately devastated Boeing, forcing it to shut down its production lines, cancel more than 120 advance airline orders for its SST, and fire tens of thousands of its workers.

As a result, the Anglo-French Concorde Project found that it was no longer in a race to take the next big step in aviation. The United States, awed by what it considered to be daunting technological and economic obstacles, inexplicably and precipitously abandoned the race entirely. The only other competitor, the inferior Russian model Tupolev TU-144 had crashed at the Paris Le Bourget air show, effectively eliminating it too from the race.

The British-French Concorde project was now the only one left in the race. Unwilling to desert the tens of thousands of workers and investors who had put their hearts and souls into the project, it found it was too deep into the project to abandon it. It therefore forged ahead to solve the very technological obstacles that had caused the Americans to simply give up. Claims by sour-grape American politicians that supersonic travel could never be an economical mode of transport proved to be a self-fulfilling prophecy. Boeing's cancellation of its SST orders caused other airlines who had ordered Concordes to cancel their orders as well, leaving British Airways and Air France as the only customers. With so few orders, Aerospatial/BAC, despite having solved all the daunting technological challenges to supersonic air travel, was able to build only fourteen Concordes. Deprived of the opportunity to lower costs by mass production, the opportunity to solve the economic challenges quickly evaporated.

The builders of Concorde had solved the technological challenges, but the costs of doing so had exceeded their expectations. This meant that Concorde would probably never be able to recoup its design and building costs. However, naysayer's claims that Concorde could never make a profit sufficient to sustain its operational costs turned out to be false. Once research revealed that many passengers thought the fare was actually higher than it was, British Airways found that by raising ticket prices to meet their expectations it could operate at a profit. While even wealthy travelers could not justify the high ticket prices just to save a couple of hours of flight time, there were still those willing to pay the price for an experience of a lifetime and a glimpse into what the future could be. Even so, when carrying a full load, Concorde whisked passengers at Mach 2 at 15.8 miles per gallon, comparable to a family car.

The environmental issue turned out to be even more formidable than the technological and economic challenges. When Concorde sought landing rights to American cities, politicians in those cities became discomfited by the thought that the gleaming, streamlined, and futuristic Concorde might upstage the lumbering and unprepossessing American airliners landing at their airports. It was an affront to the very image of American superiority. When predictions of economic doom failed to happen, the politicians resorted to predictions of environmental catastrophe wrought by the sonic boom to justify denial of landing rights in the U.S. Even when Concorde assured the city functionaries that the speed of all its transatlantic flights would be reduced to the subsonic as it approached land, and pointed to noise studies which showed that Concorde's noise was less than many American subsonic airliners, such as the Boeing VC-137 which served as Air Force One, city administrators continued to use noise as the pretext for denying landing rights.

If Americans couldn't have an SST, nobody else would either.

But it was neither economics nor environmental issues which was to bring down the Concorde. Nor was it even the catastrophic decline in air travel after the 9/11 attacks on the World Trade Center in New York.

Rather, it was an event which Audrey Turner Sterling, for all of what she had ever read about the Concorde, could ever have anticipated would be marked as occurring on the very day she arrived in Paris on the morning of July 25, 2000.

As the Eurostar came to rest on track 17 at the Gare du Nord in Paris, Audrey pulled out her mobile and called the man who had promised to meet her.

"Alastair, I'm here. I'll be right out. You're just outside, right?"

"Hi Audrey. Yes, I'm here. Look, it's only 8:30 and you said you don't have to be at the airport until 2 P.M., so we've got some time. Since its Sunday a cab should get you to de Gaulle in about forty-five minutes. Meet me in the Paris Nord Café, just across the street from the front entrance on the Rue de Maubeuge."

"Be right there."

Chapter Eighteen
July 25, 2000

Alistair Devon, MP, sat in a dark corner of the Paris Nord Café while he sipped a cappuccino, nursed a croissant, and slowly puffed on a Lambert and Butler cigarette. He waved as inconspicuously as he could when he saw Audrey enter and look about.

Audrey smiled broadly when she saw him. To her, Alistair was the image of the quintessential English gentleman, in his mid-50s with marvelous silver hair of which he sometimes seemed most conscious, finely featured, and who always spoke in the crisp King's English of a distinguished Member of Parliament.

He stood as Audrey approached. "Please have a seat, my dear. How radiant you look! Now tell me, how was your trip through the Chunnel?"

She looked distracted as she put aside her bag and sat. "Not quite as exciting as I hoped I'm afraid, Alistair."

"Well, my dear, it's really just a very long tunnel with nothing to see while you're travelling through it. Still, since the days when Napoleon dreamed of creating a tunnel conduit for invasion that bypassed the British Navy, it's surely a marvel— just to think that you're whizzing right under the very Channel that's protected our country from invasion ever since William the Conqueror last did it in 1066."

Audrey nodded. She was always impressed with Alistair's knowledge of history.

"Now," he said. "What can I get you? I'm sorry we have so little time."

"I'm fine. I had something on the Eurostar. I know how busy you are Alistair, what with the economic conference you are attending here in Paris. I was afraid I wouldn't get to see you again at all before I had to get back to Houston. Did you get my letter?"

"Ah yes, my dear. I did get your letter, which is why I thought it important that we should meet in person to discuss it. Having you come here to Paris was the only way I could arrange to see you at all as I will be tied up here for at least another week before I can return to London."

Audrey shrugged. "It's okay. I really wanted to go on Concorde, and it doesn't much matter whether I take it from London or Paris. Besides, it gave me the chance to go on the Chunnel, too."

"So, about the letter...."

"You're happy about it, aren't you? Now we can...."

Alistair did his best not to show his incredulity at her naïveté. How could this young woman possibly believe, even for a moment, that he would be happy with the news contained in her letter? Thirty years ago he had married into one of the oldest aristocratic families in Britain. With the fortune and estates that marriage had brought him, he had leveraged himself into a position of some influence in Parliament, as well as a subcabinet post. He had met Audrey at a charity ball dinner two years before in London which she and her husband had attended. Charmed by Audrey's beauty, he had invited both of them for lunch the following day—an invitation which only Audrey had been able to accept since her husband was off to a hedge fund luncheon at that time with his British partners. For the week thereafter, Ronald's business meetings had been such that he had no time for his wife, and left her to her own devices for diversion and entertainment. Alistair had taken advantage of this and he and Audrey had begun a fervid affair. For Alistair the affair had been a diversion from his tiresome and unaffectionate wife, and for Audrey an outright escape from her abusive husband.

After Audrey had returned to Houston, they had kept up the affair by email, and Audrey had managed a return trip alone to London for a charitable function the following year. Six months after that, Alistair had arranged for a plausible excuse to be in Houston, and they had met at a resort outside Padre Island. Her most recent sojourn to London six weeks before had begun with an assignation lasting four days at one of Alistair's ancestral estates in Scotland. All the servants had been given time off.

Since receiving Audrey's letter, Alistair had become distracted by the threat her pregnancy now posed. There had been a reason why he insisted on never being seen together with Audrey in public. Didn't she understand why that had been necessary?

Alistair nervously mashed out his cigarette and quickly lit another.

"Can I try one of those too?" Audrey asked.

"I'm sorry. I know you're trying to quit, and it was thoughtless of me to light up. I'm trying to quit as well, you know...."

Audrey took out her pack of Nicobans and extracted a patch. "Here, try one of my patches."

"No, I tried one of your patches when we were up in Scotland last month. It didn't help."

Audrey shrugged. "Okay, but at least I'm trying. I read in the *Mirror* that your government is trying to pass legislation banning smoking in public places. I can't imagine. But Alistair, we don't have much time. We really have to talk about our situation...."

Alistair held back a wince as he took in Audrey's reference to "our" situation. "Maybe I will try one of those patches, after all...."

"Here, take the pack," said she.

"No, keep the pack. I'll just take a couple of patches." He mashed his second cigarette and took out several patches.

For the three days since he had received Audrey's letter he had thought about what he would say when he next saw her, but hoped that there would not be a next time. He assumed that Audrey would have gone back to Houston by now and that once back home she would be content to handle the situation. But when he had texted back that he was in Paris for a conference, and wouldn't be able to see her before she returned to the states, it was she who had insisted meeting face-to-face before she left, offering to come to Paris and change her July 25 Concorde reservation from British Airways to Air France. What could he say? That he couldn't spare an hour to meet with her even when she was willing to come to Paris to meet him?

He had lost a fair amount of sleep over the last three nights as well. Did she really nurse pretensions of being an English Lady? Had he ever made promises to her?

The night before he had woken in a cold sweat as he remembered the throes of passion on the third night of his assignation with her at his Scottish estate. He rationalized: in response to her entreaties to express his devotion to her, he might…just might…have said something along the lines of perhaps… perhaps, mind you… finding himself at some vague time in the future being in a position in which he could divorce his wife. Had Audrey taken that literally? Surely nothing said in the throes of passion could be taken literally. Surely Audrey understood that divorcing his wife would not only mean that he would be cast out of the aristocratic society which he had heretofore enjoyed, but, perhaps worse be evicted from the family estates.

He shuddered when he thought of the political scandal which had originated some years before from the sexual relationship between married British cabinet member John Profumo and Christine Keeler, a nineteen-year-old model. When the affair was discovered by the tabloids, Profumo was forced to resign from government. Prime Minister McMillan in whose cabinet he served, retired shortly thereafter on "health grounds." The conservative government went down to dramatic defeat in the next election. A later report on the "Profumo Affair" concluded that the national scandal had brought about the gradual ending of traditional notions of deference: "authority, however disinterested, well-qualified and experienced, was increasingly greeted with suspicion rather than trust."

As for the disgraced Profumo, whose affair had managed to bring down the entire British government, he began his penance and search for redemption by working as a volunteer at a homeless shelter in the East End of London mopping floors and cleaning toilets. He died at the age of ninety-one in 2006, still working in the homeless shelter.

As Alistair took one of the patches and applied it to his arm, the vision of himself being disgraced in the same manner as Profumo and ending his days mopping floors in a homeless shelter, caused his normally firm hand to tremble. Still, he nursed the hope that Audrey would see reason.

"So Audrey, are you sure about the pregnancy?" he asked hopefully. "I mean it's only been, what six weeks, and we did use protection, didn't we?"

"I think you did for the first two nights, but then...I think...I've missed my period. I got one of those drugstore tests...."

"Those are not that reliable...."

"No, Alistair, I also saw a doctor. I am pregnant."

There was a long pause before Alistair said, "So what are our plans now?"

"No Alistair," she replied sharply, "what are your plans?"

"I don't know. It's up to you, isn't it?"

"Whether to keep the baby? Yes, I plan to keep the baby."

"Of course that's entirely your decision, Audrey. But I wonder if it's wise given that you are about to initiate divorce proceedings with your husband."

"If you mean that the timing sucks, yes. Is that what you mean?"

"Well, yes. If you keep the child, I take it your husband would know it isn't his."

"Given that we haven't had relations for the past year, I would venture to guess that he could figure that out, yes."

"I'm not versant in American divorce law...."

"Texas divorce law, actually...."

"Well, whatever law applies, I'm just wondering how having this baby in the middle of the divorce proceedings might affect your case."

"'Adultery' you mean. Just say it, Alistair."

"Well, yes...."

"I don't know. I'm not a lawyer. But yes, it probably will. He'll have the best lawyers in the state. We have a pre-nup, but I think there's some kind of 'morals' clause in there that could affect...."

"But you still want to have the baby...."

"Yes, I do. And that means I need to know where you and I stand. Perhaps you don't remember now. Up in Scotland when you were fucking my brains out you told me that you loved me...."

Now Alistair could not control the wince. "I do...."

"And that you would divorce you wife and...."

"I never said that...."

"You said that...."

"I never promised you anything!"

"So that's the way it is, then. The baby and I will be on our own, and...."

"I didn't say that. But, love, please understand...."

"Don't ever call me that!"

"Sorry. But please, Audrey, understand my position. If I were to divorce now, I'd be wiped out. Literally. And then I'd have nothing to offer you and the baby, would I?"

"So you're saying that if you remain married, and hush all this up, you might deign to support me and...."

"Yes, absolutely. I would support you most generously."

"And how would that work, Alistair? And how would I enforce that, Alistair? Bring a paternity action against you in the British courts? I know, you don't know. You'd rather support us in the states, where I'm out of sight and out of mind. But maybe I'd rather live here. I'm a bit tired of the U.S., and I'm sure as hell tired of Houston. Once I do get the divorce I'll want to be as far away from that man as I can. I think I'd have some rights if I came back here, though, you being the father and all?"

Beads of sweat now began to slide profusely down Alistair's face. His nightmares of the night before seemed to be coming true.

"Audrey, I still love you. You know I do. And maybe it will be possible in the future to divorce, or maybe...."

"Maybe your wife will predecease you?"

"I didn't say that. But please be reasonable."

Audrey looked at her watch. "I'd better get going. I like to get to airports early. I don't' want to miss my flight. I have an appointment with my divorce lawyer in Houston tomorrow afternoon."

Alistair nodded. "You know I'll do everything I can. All I can say is that I'm sorry. I regret terribly if I led you to believe...I don't want us to part this way."

Audrey sighed and sat back in her chair. "I guess I knew it as just a dream. I should have known."

Yes, Alistair thought, you should have.

Audrey stood up. "Wait a minute. I've got to pee before I go. I'll be right back." She picked up her purse, but left the pack of Nicobans on the table.

Moments later she returned and grabbed her roller bag. "You can keep the patches if you want."

"No, I know I'm hopeless. You'd better keep them for your trip. I don't know if the Concorde lets you smoke."

Audrey picked up the pack of patches and put them in her purse. "Would you mind getting me a cab?"

"Of course. Please call me when you get to Houston." He kissed her awkwardly on the cheek, placed a ten quid note on the table, and went out to flag the cab.

Chapter Nineteen
July 25, 2000

Audrey felt like royalty as she was led by a personal Concorde representative who whisked her to the front of the Air France security line at Charles de Gaulle Airport. Dozens of passengers waiting in line wondered who the person was sailing past the authorities.

"Par ici, Madame," said the rep as he led Audrey through the crowd toward the Concorde Lounge.

Seeing the sign to the First Class Lounge, Audrey pointed to the sign and asked "Is this it here?"

"No, Madame. That is just the First Class lounge. The Concorde Lounge is separate and has many more amenities. It is exclusively for Concorde passengers, but all First Class passengers on other Air France flights can pay a 500 Franc upgrade and be admitted. Just this way."

The Concorde Lounge was indeed spectacular, magnificently decorated with original artwork, handmade Italian fur "Elemis" spa, cabanas, and private showers. A granite fireplace graced the main lounge area, which featured high floor to ceiling windows giving a panoramic view of the airport. A grand piano was available to whoever wanted to play. Apparently there was little danger that anyone other than a world renowned concert pianist would ever venture to touch the keys.

The rep handed Audrey's Concorde ticket to the concierge, who smilingly invited her to enter. "Welcome, Madame. The bar is out to the left, and you may take the elevator to the private dining booths on the level below. Please enjoy your stay with us. If you wish I can keep your bag until your flight is called."

"No, I'll keep it, but thank you."

"Is there anything else I can assist you with before I go, Madame?" the rep asked.

"No, I'm fine, but I think I'm ready to visit the bar. Is there any particular concoction you recommend before the flight?"

"Mais oui, Madame. You will find that the Laurent Perrier Grand Siècle Champagne served in the main lounge area is superb. At the bar you might try the Zephyr Martini."

"Sounds wonderful. I'll certainly try it." Audrey rolled her bag down the hall to the central lounge area, gazed out at the panoramic windows at the Concorde in the distance, and then took a seat at the bar.

"Qu'auras-tu, Madame?" the white shirted barman asked.

"I understand the Zephyr Martini is recommended?" Despite the rep's recommendation she was not sure the barman would know what that was. She had never heard of it.

It took only moments for the martini to appear and for the barman to say, tongue in cheek, "Shaken not stirred."

Audrey nursed her shaken martini, and then paused to extract a Virginia Slim cigarette from her pack. The Concorde was not due to be boarded for another hour and a half, so she took a look at the spa brochure and meal menu. She had not eaten since taking a snack on the Eurostar very early that morning and considered whether she might have time to shower, visit the spa, and have a light lunch before flight 4590 was called.

When the barman came and asked if she wanted another drink, she asked, "I understand there are dining booths on the lower level. Is it possible for you to take my meal order here?"

"Oui, Madame. I can take your order, and it will be ready in about thirty minutes when you go down to your dining booth. I can reserve your booth now if you like."

"I was thinking of visiting the spa first. Would I have time to do that, and still have time to go down to eat before the flight is called?"

"Of course, Madame. If you visit the spa now, your meal will be ready downstairs when you are ready."

Audrey perused the menu. "The Smoked Haddock fish cake looks good. Would you recommend it?"

"An excellent choice. But even better is the Seared Seabass Fillet with fresh herb salsa."

"Well, then! It is that which I will order. Thank you. Now, which way to the spa?"

The barman pointed to the hallway on the other side of the main lounge area. "Just down that hall, Madame, and to the right."

"Great, thank you." Audrey took a final sip of the Zephyr and mashed out her Virginia Slim in the porcelain ashtray. She pointed left inquiringly.

The barman nodded and said, "Oui Madame."

At the spa, Audrey took a quick hot shower, washed her hair, and enjoyed a ten minute massage. After changing into a comfortable red sleeveless shift dress and applying her makeup, she made her way to the glass elevator which took her to the lower level dining booths.

"Your name, please?" asked the maître d'.

"Audrey Sterling?"

"This way, please. Your booth is ready."

She was shown to a window table overlooking the tarmac, and saw that Concorde was already at the gate. She looked at her watch, saw that she would have over an hour to eat before boarding, and relaxed.

"Wine, Madame?" asked the server.

"Please. Your house white will be fine."

While she waited, she withdrew both her Virginia slims and her Nicobans and placed them next to her glass on the table. Thinking that her meal would be served momentarily, she resisted the urge to light up, and returned the cigarettes to her purse. After her meal, she thought, she would apply a patch to get her across the Atlantic.

Sipping the wine, she looked down to read a brochure about Concorde. Then, she felt the presence of someone sitting directly across from her in the booth. Startled, she looked up, and could hardly believe her eyes.

"Oh my God! What are you doing here?!"

Chapter Twenty

Amber knocked lightly on Judy's office door.

Judy looked up from her desk. "Morning, girl. Come on in. Sorry I slept in this morning and didn't make breakfast. Just got in actually. What's up?"

"I saw you in the living room last night, but you seemed so engrossed in a file—the Brenda Masterson file I assumed—that I didn't want to disturb you. What time did you finally get to bed?"

Judy sighed. "Not until after 3 A.M. I'm afraid. I think I'm ready to talk about what we've really got at this point in the Masterson case."

"Great. But before you begin firing away on that, I was wondering if we could talk about something else first."

"Of course. Sit!"

"You know, Judy, you've been working here in my office suite for two weeks now, and...."

"Oh, if you need this office I can...."

"Not at all. As a matter of fact, just the opposite, and that's what I wanted to talk to you about. I think you should take this office permanently."

"What do you mean?"

"I think you should join the firm here. I can make you a partner. I think I could even convince my partners to make you a named partner.

Judy shook her head. "You mean 'Crocker, Rutherford, Hartman...and Alexander.' You're sweet, but I really wouldn't care about that. I'd rather not have my name on the marquee. Anyway, what would your partners think? You and they have far more experience than I. Besides, I've got my own firm in New York, and I think they need me now."

"Well, you wouldn't have to have your name on the 'marquee', but, well…hear me out. We could merge our two firms. Lots of firms have branches in different states."

"I'm not taking another bar exam. The one I took in New York was brutal enough."

"You might not have to. The Texas bar is considering a proposal to waive in out-of-state lawyers without taking the Texas bar exam if they scored a 270 on the Uniform Bar Exam in the state where they originally took the bar."

"I took the bar in New York the year before they implemented the UBE. So that wouldn't help me. And I've only practiced for three years."

"Okay, but you wouldn't need to be licensed in Texas if we merged. You could still take cases under your own name in New York, keep your office here with me, and assist me…."

"We'll see. I'll think about it. As you know, I've asked my New York partners to see about getting our firm qualified as a non-profit and naming it the Justice Institute. We would only take cases based on the merits of the case and the interests of justice—and not one who pays the highest fee. I think Timothy would approve—using his legacy to seek justice for others just as I got justice for Bonnie and Timothy. Both our firms could do that now, Amber. It was just a dream before, but now with Timothy's legacy, we could really do it."

"All right, it's something to think about. I do like the idea. But now, what have we got in the Masterson case?"

"I did get one important piece of information out of Madeleine Turner last week, though not much more: just like Angela, Audrey was addicted to smoking. And she used Nicoban patches to kick the habit."

"Yeah, I've read that addictions can run in families. You know, genes. But so what?"

"So, just like Angela Sterling, Audrey Sterling was using nicotine patches to kick the habit."

"And…?"

"Don't you see, Amber? What if they both used patches? That would have given Ronald Sterling the opportunity to kill both of them in the same way. Brides in the Bath."

"Judy...."

"You see it, don't you?"

Amber paused to find the right words. "Judy, you know I appreciate your helping me with the Masterson case, but that's my point here. It's the Masterson case, not the Audrey Sterling case. We can't afford to spend a disproportionate amount of our resources on what happened to Audrey Sterling. Yes, it would be helpful evidence in our civil suit against Ronald Sterling if we could establish that he poisoned his previous wife. But we both know he couldn't have killed her. The cause of the Concorde crash had nothing to do with Ronald Sterling."

"I know that. And Audrey was probably still alive when the Concorde crashed, though I still think it's possible she died from the fentanyl before the crash itself. Even if the crash intervened to kill Audrey before she died of fentanyl poisoning, if we can show she was poisoned by fentanyl that would still show plan, intent, identity—which would make her poisoning admissible under FRE 404(b)"

In the face of Judy's obvious passion for this line of thinking, Amber decided to lighten the mood. "You know, you remind me of the examples I used to give the children of some of my friends who wanted me to talk to their kids about whether a law school career would be suitable for them. So I posed these examples, to kind of test these kids' legal IQ aptitude. I would pose this factual scenario to them: 'A' really wants to kill 'B,' so he shoves 'B' off a high cliff. But 'C,' who is half a mile away, also wants to kill 'B,' so when he sees 'B' falling to his death, he fires his rifle and kills 'B' before 'B' hits the ground. Is 'A' guilty of murder?"

"Well, Professor Amber, the answer is no because 'A' didn't actually cause 'B's' death."

"Very good. Now one more: 'A' and 'B' both want to kill 'C.' Both 'A' and 'B' learn that 'C' is about to make a long journey across the desert. 'C' knows he cannot carry enough water to make it all the way across the desert, so in advance, he places a barrel of water at the half way point between his starting point and his destination. 'A' then finds the barrel before 'C' arrives to retrieve his water, and poisons the water. Then 'B,' unaware that 'A' has poisoned the water, finds the barrel and empties it into the sand. When 'C' arrives at the barrel, there is no water and he dies of thirst. Is either 'A' or 'B' guilty of murder?"

Judy decided to play along. "Well, it would appear that at least one of them must be guilty of murder, since 'C' died as a result of 'A' and 'B's' actions. But that would be wrong. Neither 'A' nor 'B' would be guilty of murder. 'A' is not guilty because even though he poisoned the water, he did not actually cause 'C's' death because 'C' never drank the poisoned water. 'B' is not guilty of murder either, since, if anything, he saved 'C's' life—at least temporarily—by spilling the very poisoned water that would have killed 'C' had he drunk it. So neither killed him. Am I right?"

Amber smiled. "Okay, girl, I pronounce you as having sufficient legal aptitude to have a successful career in the law. But as you know, there is not necessarily any one correct answer to any of these hypotheticals I pose to prospective law students. What establishes aptitude is the reasoning one uses to arrive at a conclusion."

"So I passed."

"Sure. Now, seriously, let's talk about Audrey's death in the Concorde crash. First of all, regardless of whether we could prove that Audrey was poisoned by a fatal dose of fentanyl before the crash, it would be almost impossible to prove that she actually died before the crash. That being the case, the most that could be proven in regard to Audrey's death would be attempted murder. That's different than the Brides in Bath case in which all the previous wives actually died under similar circumstances."

"Assuming that no confession was forthcoming, I agree. But wouldn't the fact that Audrey was poisoned by the same means as Angela was poisoned still be admissible under 404(b) as showing intent, design, motive, opportunity...."

"Maybe, maybe not. Depends on the judge. But that's the least of our problems with admissibility. First and foremost we would have to prove that Audrey was in fact poisoned with fentanyl...."

"I know that. But we now have Madeleine Turner's permission to exhume Audrey...."

"I'm skeptical that even if we can get a court to grant permission to exhume, that any lab today would be capable of finding fentanyl after so long given the condition of Audrey's body."

"That remains to be seen. Madeleine told me that her body was in better condition than most of the others because...."

"Regardless, I'm still skeptical that we can find a lab that can perform such a procedure. And even if we can find such a lab, any such procedure would have to be on the cutting edge of what is possible now in forensic science. The cost would be exorbitant in proportion to its value in the Masterson case."

"But Amber, we've talked about this. If anyone can afford to commission such a task, it's us. When Timothy commissioned me to find out what happened to Bonnie, he knew it was a longshot. But he was willing to pay anything to find the truth. You gave me this case to look at, and now that I have looked at it, I want to find the truth—regardless of the cost."

"Of course, I'd pay my share because I know Brenda couldn't afford it, but that brings me to my next point. We'd have the same problem in showing that Ronald snuck the fentanyl patches into Audrey's pack of nicotine patches as we have in proving that he snuck them into Angela's pack of patches. How do you propose that we find evidence of either?"

"With regard to Audrey's death, we'd have to hire a detective agency—maybe the one Timothy used—to track all of Ronald's movements in the twenty-four hours prior to Audrey boarding Concorde flight 4590 on September 25, 2000. Ronald was always travelling around that time, taking flights, buying tickets, making reservations at hotels for business meetings, functions...."

"Are you kidding? Tracking his movements twenty years ago? I suppose it could be done by gathering up old plane reservations, hotel receipts and the like, but the cost...."

"Amber, I hate to be a broken record, but I don't care about the cost. Yes, I know I'm a millionaire now—maybe even a billionaire, we both are—but do you see me in line to buy a Lear jet, or yacht, or Lamborghini, or a palace somewhere? I honestly could care less about those things! You gave me this case to look at, and I see the opportunity to bring justice to not just one, but two victims. That's what I want to do. Before I fell in love with Robin, I looked at the law as just something different that I could do with my otherwise purposeless life. It was he who taught me that the law could be something more. I want to find out the truth in both these cases, and for the first time in my life I can do what I want to do."

Amber smiled indulgently. "Okay, I get it. And I'm with you. But now let me ask you something."

"Anything."

"What if you...and I...spend all this money investigating Angela's death, and we not only find evidence that it was not Ronald who killed Angela, but also that he never attempted to kill Audrey either. I mean it's possible isn't it?"

For the first time, Judy did not have a quick answer. She thought for a moment, and then said, "So be it. We'll have still found a murderer and brought him to justice. And if our evidence exonerates Ronald, that's okay, too. We'll have done something that the legal system couldn't do, or didn't have the resources to do. I want to do this for the two most important men in my life— Robin and Timothy. I owe both of them everything."

"Judy, since the first moment you stepped into my office seven years ago, you've never ceased to amaze me. I mean, with your looks, and now your money, you could, literally, have the world lapping at your feet. Instead you seem to want to be something like a legal version of 'Batman', out to do justice in the world for its own sake with no expectation of remuneration other than the satisfaction of doing good. If that's what you want to do, okay. I'll do it with you. I ask only one thing."

"Yes?"

"In this particular matter, remember that we only have one actual client, and that is Brenda Masterson. I would not for a moment want us to divert our attention from what is in her best interests. I certainly wouldn't ever ask her to bankroll an investigation into the possible poisoning of Audrey Sterling when, at least at this point, there seems to be so little chance of finding any real evidence that would be helpful in Brenda's case. We're only talking about one particular item of evidence here that would be relevant in Brenda's civil case—namely evidence of Ronald's prior attempt to poison his first wife—which might or might not be admissible under 404(b). But given that you and I will be paying that cost, and that it could conceivably, though not likely, be helpful in Brenda's civil case, I'm willing to go ahead."

Judy smiled. "Thanks, sister. And when this is all over, let's talk about your idea of a merger. However, let's not put our names on any new firm just yet. The name 'The Justice Institute' for our merged firm would suit me just fine."

Chapter Twenty-One
July 25, 2000

The crisp voice emanating from the Concorde Lounge announced, first in French and then in English, that Air France flight 4590 was now ready for boarding.

Audrey Sterling was still in the lounge washroom when she heard the announcement. It had been a full hour since she had first seen the one person she never expected to see sit down across from her in the dining room. Soon after the unexpected visitor had joined her, she had felt the need to visit the ladies room. When she returned to the table, she nervously applied one of her last remaining nicotine patches and smoked one final Virginia Slim cigarette.

Now she was feeling a little woozy, and wasn't sure why. Perhaps it was the wine—she had gulped down several glasses—but had barely touched her meal. That was it, she decided. She had imbibed too quickly. But she now realized it might be something more. She leaned forward and grabbed the basin for several moments to gather herself. Perhaps it was just the excitement of being about to embark on the trip of a lifetime, travelling faster than a speeding bullet. She tried diverting her mind from how poorly she now felt, and conjured up what she had long imagined in several dreams—that someone at rest adjacent to the plane had fired an actual bullet, and she could look out her window and see the bullet frozen in the air yet travelling at twice the speed of sound.

The announcement was repeated, so she shook her head, then splashed water on her face, dried it, and began to re-apply her makeup. As she looked at herself in the mirror she was not satisfied with the way she looked, despite the makeup she had applied. Her paleness showed through. But she was determined that she would not let what could only be a momentary, if most unwelcome, attack of wooziness jeopardize this trip she had dreamed about for so long.

She grabbed her roller bag and retreated out to the bar where she asked her helpful barman if he happened to have an aspirin. He cheerfully obliged, pulling a two pack from a hidden drawer, and handed it to her.

"Are you all right, Madame?" he asked.

"Oh, yes. I'm fine. Just a bit of a headache. Merci."

Stepping out into the lounge's private concourse, she stood momentarily in front of the panoramic floor to ceiling window to gaze at the great white bird on which she was about to embark. Exhilarated by the sight, she convinced herself that she was experiencing a second wind.

She noticed that the majority of conversations among her ninety-nine fellow passengers were in German. She had heard that many of the passengers were with a group planning to join a Caribbean cruise in New York. Many of the passengers were flying with families. Audrey noticed a family of two grandparents, two parents and three children—all chattering enthusiastically and obviously excited.

Although Audrey did not recognize any celebrities, she was surprised that so few of her fellow travelers fit her preconception of wealthy businessmen. The man who stood in front of her in the boarding line looked distinctly middle class, thirty-ish and even boyish. Perhaps, she thought, he was a business wunderkind who had made a fortune selling an internet company he had created. Though she had heard him speaking German earlier, he must have recognized her as an American as he turned to her and asked her in heavily accented English:

"Exciting, isn't it? Is this your first trip on Concorde?"

Audrey did her best to conceal her increasing physical discomfort and forced a smile. "Yes, it is! And you?"

"Bestimmt! I have saved for over seven years to fly the Concorde. It is my dream."

"Mine too. Are you flying to New York on business?"

"Ich? Nein. I teach school at the USI international school in Frankfurt. It's a high school. I don't make much money, but enjoy teaching my math courses. Ever since Concorde made its first flight, I've wanted to fly on it. Ever since I was hired as a teacher there I've been saving to buy a ticket. I have a window seat, 15A. What's your seat number? My name is Hans by the way."

Audrey delved into her purse and pulled out her ticket. "Let's see. I'm in 15B."

"Then you have the seat next to me. I'm sorry, you don't have a window seat."

"Oh no. I changed my reservation from the B.A. Concorde flight from London at the last minute and didn't even think about that."

"No problem. I'd be happy to switch seats with you during the flight. You don't want to miss the view. The Concorde flies at almost 70,000 feet, twice as high as old-fashioned airliners. The windows are small—they have to be because the air pressure outside the plane is so low at that height—but they say you can see the curvature of the earth at that height. Of course I want to see that for myself."

"Oh, thank you. Yes, I'd love to see that too. But please don't feel you have to. You've waited many years to take this flight and...."

At just that moment, Audrey faltered and grabbed Hans' arm to keep from falling.

Hans grabbed her by her other arm and pulled her up. "Are you all right, Fraulein?"

Audrey recovered. "So sorry. I'm afraid I had a few too many martinis waiting for the flight to be called, and didn't sleep much last night. Too excited, to be honest. Just got a little dizzy. Please forgive me."

"Are you sure? I can call someone...."

"Oh, no. I'll be fine as soon as we're seated. But thank you." Audrey held out her hand. "I'm Audrey by the way."

"All right, if you're sure. I think we're about to board now."

Audrey followed Hans as each gave their tickets to the gate attendant.

"May I help you with your bag? I see you're travelling light," said Hans as they made their way down the jet bridge.

"Yes, I hate checking bags and having to wonder if I'll ever see them again. "You seem to be travelling light as well. Did you check a bag?"

"No, I only have this small bag as well. I will only be staying in New York one night. I return tomorrow on a budget airline."

The smiling steward greeted both at the doorway, checked their tickets at the doorway and directed both to the 15th row. Hans took Audrey's small roller bag and deposited it in the overhead.

"Would you like to sit by the window for takeoff?" Hans asked chivalrously.

"I wouldn't think of it. You've saved for seven years to take this flight. I'm fine. I can still see from here. Please go ahead."

Hans slipped into the window seat while Audrey collapsed into the aisle seat and closed her eyes. Moments later a flight attendant came by offering champagne.

Hans held up his hand. "Not right now, thank you." He looked over at Audrey. "Champaign, Audrey?" Seeing that she now looked distressed, he repeated, "Audrey?"

Audrey opened her eyes. She felt flushed. "Just some water," she said.

Hans called for the steward. "Could you bring us some water? I think this lady is...."

"Of course. Is she all right? I could call...."

Audrey forced a smile and looked up. "I'm fine, really. I just need some water."

The steward hesitated.

"Please, I'm fine. If you could just bring the water."

"Of course. But please let me know...."

"So sorry. I guess I'm a nervous flier."

"If you're sure." She came back in moments with the water. "I'll have to come back for the glass before takeoff."

Audrey nodded, settled back and shut her eyes. Several minutes later the steward came back to retrieve the glass.

"She says she's fine," Hans said. "I think she's just resting now."

"All right. Let me know if she needs anything."

Hans looked out the window. "We're moving!" he said excitedly. He turned to Audrey who seemed to have gone to sleep, but hesitated to wake her until just before takeoff. He wanted to be sure she would be awake to experience the 250 mile an hour takeoff and ultra-steep climb that would push everyone back in their seats for the thrill ride of a lifetime.

Several moments later the captain's voice came on the intercom. "Bien accueillir! We are first in line for takeoff after the DC-10-30 in front of us. Please insure that your seats are in the full upright position, that your seat trays are secured, and your seatbelts are fastened."

Just at that moment, Hans turned to see Audrey's face contorted and in unmistakable distress. "Steward!" he called out. The thunderous roar of the four Rolls Royce Olympus Turbo afterburners drowned out his call as Air France Concorde flight 4590 began its 400 kilometer per hour run down the runway.

Chapter Twenty-Two
July 25, 2000

Captain Christian Marty pushed forward the throttle of Concorde's four Rolls Royce engines, bringing them to life with a rumbling roar and initiating the long trek down the runway.

Captain Marty was a daredevil skier who had once windsurfed across the Atlantic, and was one of the elite group of pilots qualified to fly the Concorde—a group said to be smaller in number than that of astronauts qualified to fly to the moon—and he was now ready to take up his bird for the three-hour journey to New York City without further ado.

He had waited patiently for the DC-10-30 ahead of him take off, and with Controller's permission to take off, the flight crew was now fully engaged in calling off the speed of the aircraft—100 knots, 150 knots 175 knots...."

Before it reached its takeoff speed of 200 knots, Captain Marty felt a slight thump and noted the aircraft veering to the left. Had he allowed it to continue doing so, it might have gone off the runway and hit a Jumbo 747—carrying French President Jacques Chirac and his wife—waiting to cross Concorde's runway. Accordingly, Captain Marty called for "rotation" (lift off) at a speed of 188 knots, which was below the recommended lift off speed.

At that moment, the voice of the Controller came over the intercom. "Concorde zero 4590, you have flames, you have flames behind you!"

Moments later flight engineer Gilles Jardinaud called out "Breakdown, engine, breakdown engine two!"

The fire alarm rang loudly in the cockpit.

The captain cried "Engine fire procedure!"

Flight engineer Jardinaud shouted: "Cut engine two!"

In alarm, First Officer Jan Marcot screamed "Warning, the airspeed indicator, the airspeed indicator, the airspeed indicator!"

The voice of the Controller on the intercom warned: "4590, you have strong flames behind you!"

Marcot yelled "We need to get to Le Bourget! Le Bourget!"

The Captain cried "No time! No time!"

Back in row 15 of the cabin, Hans looked out his window to the rear and saw the shooting flames. Then he turned to Audrey, who fleetingly opened her eyes and then stiffened, thrusting forward, and then backwards into her seat. In terror, he took Audrey's hand and squeezed it. There were screams from all the passengers, and cries from the children.

The stricken plane banked hard to the left. Below through the window could be seen the outline of a small hotel, which loomed larger and larger as the plane twisted on its side and streaked headlong to the ground.

Within seventeen seconds of takeoff, the lives of all 109 terrified and screaming passengers, men, women, children, and crew ended in a ball of fire.

Chapter Twenty-Three

Judy picked up the report from the NXR Detective Agency which she had commissioned soon after her visit to Madeleine Turner in Las Vegas. It was the first report she had received. She was disappointed that it did not report all the information she had requested, but that was to be expected since the tasks assigned to them would not be easy to fulfill. Nevertheless, the report did contain one piece of information she found intriguing.

"Anything useful?" asked Amber as she tapped on the door frame of Judy's office. "You've been holed up here in this office all week since you got back from Vegas."

Judy looked up, sighed, and threw the NXR file down on a pile of documents she had found on her own. "Not really. But I knew that the information I really need might be impossible to uncover."

"Like what?"

"For one thing, I need to be able to trace Ronald Sterling's movements, where he stayed, where he made reservations, in the weeks before Audrey died in the Concorde crash."

"I understand. That was over twenty years ago."

"Still, Ronald was quite the travelling man at that time, as he still is today. He was probably on the road on 'business' more than he was home. We know he went to conferences, symposia, partner meetings, meeting with bankers and investment groups all over the world. All those trips should be documented somewhere. He had to have made plane and hotel reservations, and there must be receipts. It's just a question of tracking them down."

"He didn't ever take Audrey with him on those trips?"

"Actually, he did a few times. I've been in touch with Madeleine a few times since I got back. Madeleine told me that Ronald actually took Audrey with him on a few trips to

London in the years before she went by herself to escape him in 2000. Audrey loved London, always hoping to find some of her mother's relatives. Her mother often told her that she was related to the British aristocracy. Of course he pretty much abandoned her once they arrived, and she was left to her own devices."

"Not surprised. He is by all accounts a despicable human being. But, Judy, you seem to be spending most of your time now investigating Audrey's death—which is fine, but remember our client is Brenda Masterson."

"I've got the NXR looking at Ronald's movements in the weeks before Angela's death too. But like you said, without some proof that Ronald had something to do with Audrey's death, you wouldn't be able to use Texas Evidence Rule 404(b) to admit that evidence to buttress the case against Ronald for Angela's death. Also, as I understand 404(b), you don't have to prove the prior act beyond a reasonable doubt—only that the circumstances likely occurred."

"Well, there's still some legal question regarding the 'corpus delecti' problem."

"How so?"

"Defense counsel have been known to argue that before a prior act can be admitted under 404(b), the prosecutor must not only show that the prior act occurred—in our case showing that Audrey died from fentanyl poisoning but also show by convincing evidence that the defendant—in our case it would be Ronald—is the one who poisoned her."

"Yes, I understand that. But it always goes back to the Brides in the Bath case in which the prosecutors were not required to actually prove that the defendant killed his previous wives, but only to prove that they died under exactly the same circumstances—dead in the bathtub after the defendant went out for champagne. So far, the cases support application of 404(b) along the same lines as the British High court outlined in the Brides in the Bath Case."

"I still have to come back to the threshold problem: how can we show a similar prior act if it's clear that Audrey died in the plane crash and not from fentanyl poisoning?"

At this Judy smiled to hide her exasperation at her friends' failure to understand her premise. "Of course there is no question that Audrey died in the Concorde crash. But if we can show that Audrey was poisoned by fentanyl before she ever boarded the Concorde, I see no reason why a court would not allow us to show that as a similar circumstance. Either Audrey actually died of fentanyl before the plane crashed, or, if she was still alive when the plane crashed, that she would have died from the fentanyl if the plane crash had not intervened as the immediate cause of death. We talked about this before."

Amber smiled indulgently. "I know, I know. I just wanted to make sure you were still up on the law, and I see that you are. But one question: I see you have a stack of documents and reports concerning the cause of the Concorde crash. If there's no question that Audrey was a passenger on the Concorde on the day it crashed, and there is no question about what actually caused the crash, why are you looking into the cause of the crash?"

Judy nodded. "Point taken. The cause of the crash certainly has nothing to do with whether Audrey was poisoned prior to boarding Concorde. But since I spoke with Audrey's sister about the crash itself, I have not been able to stop thinking about that crash itself and what Audrey must have gone through if she was still alive at the time of the crash—and of course what all those other passengers, men, women, and children, must have gone through in the those terrifying seventeen seconds after the takeoff."

"I understand. I take it that all the various government agencies which investigated the accident agree on the cause of the crash?"

"Well, yes and no. All the investigators agree that the series of events which ended up in catastrophe began when Concorde hit a small metal strip on the runway. That strip measured only seventeen inches long and less than half an inch thick, and may or may not have fallen off the Continental DC-10—Continental denies it—which took off just ahead of Concorde. But when Concorde struck it at a speed of 188 knots, it caused the tire to blow—no question about that. Debris from the shredded tire then entered the underside of the left wing at a speed of 310 mph, causing the number five fuel tank to rupture and gush fuel, and which was ignited by an electric spark in the landing gear bay. This caused engines one and two to lose power."

"A freak accident, then."

"Very much so. Prior to that moment, Concorde was the safest airplane in the world, having flown for twenty-seven years without a single fatality—a record that immediately ended when it hit that tiny metal strip."

"Couldn't the plane have aborted the takeoff once it was apparent that an engine was on fire?"

"Another cruel fact: at the very moment that the Controller called the pilot to report the fire, the plane reached V-1 speed."

"V-1?"

"The speed at which it was too late to abort without crashing. So the pilot had to take off, despite the fire. But with insufficient speed and lift to stay in the air, it managed to stay airborne for only seventeen seconds before turning on its side from asymmetrical thrust and crashing upside down into a small family-owned hotel outside the Paris suburb of Gonesse, killing all passengers and crew as well as four hotel residents."

"So why do you say there is still some controversy about the cause of the crash?"

"There is no disagreement that the shredding of the tire by the impact with the metal strip initiated the series of events that resulted in the crash. The French Accident Investigation Bureau concluded that the sole cause of the accident was the shredding of the tire and the consequent rupture of the fuel tank and fire."

"So who disagreed?"

"Some Concorde pilots, for one. While they agreed that it was the shredding of the tire and consequent fire that was the immediate cause of the accident, many of them believed that it was not the whole story. They suggested that an improperly serviced 'spacer' in the undercarriage caused the wheels to be misaligned, which in turn caused the plane to veer to the left as it sped down runway. This in turn led to the Captain having to take off at lower than the recommended speed to avoid veering off the runway. They also noted that the last minute loading of nineteen bags caused the weight of the aircraft to exceed the aircraft's certified maximum weight, and that the wind had shifted from being still to an eight knot tailwind. These factors in turn prevented the plane from taking off before it reached the fateful metal strip. Finally, they noted that the flight engineer's decision to shut down engine two was premature, and that if left in action it would have been quickly extinguished as the fuel from the tank was depleted, and thus been able to provide sufficient thrust to keep the plane in the air."

"No one listened to them?"

"The French Investigation Bureau rejected their conclusions. No one wanted to believe that 'man', not God, caused the crash. But in later years, many of the pilots' conclusions have been quietly accepted by the aviation community. After many years of litigation, manslaughter convictions of Continental for shedding the metal strip on the runway were overturned by a French Appeals Court."

"Interesting, for sure. But have you found anything that might suggest that Audrey's boarding of flight 4590 was anything but ordinary?"

Judy picked up the NXR report. "As I said, the report did find something puzzling."

"Yes?"

"They found that Audrey originally had reservations to fly the Concorde on British Air from London. But then on July 24, 2000, the day before she was scheduled to fly, she changed her reservation to fly from Paris on Air France instead."

"What's so unusual about that?"

"She left London on the Eurostar at 5:30 on the morning of July 25. That gave her just enough time to get to Paris, perhaps catch a quick meal, and then go directly to de Gaulle Airport for the Air France flight."

"So?"

"Why would she do that? It would be understandable if she changed her plans to fly from Paris so that she could have time to take in the sights of Paris, stay a few days, shop on the Champs-Elysees Elyse, maybe visit the Eiffel Tower, or whatever. But what would be the point of going to all the trouble of changing her reservation, getting up at the crack of dawn, just to go directly to Charles de Gaulle? It doesn't make sense. Apparently she even lost her window seat by changing her reservation."

Amber shrugged. "Maybe she hadn't ever seen Paris before, and thought she could get a taste of it on the cab ride to the airport. Unlikely, I agree, but what are you thinking?"

Judy pursed her lips. "I think she went there to meet someone—someone whom she could only meet there and not in London for some reason."

"What, you're thinking she might have wanted to meet some French lover who couldn't be bothered to come over to London and meet her before she returned to the states?"

"I don't know. I just think it's curious."

"Well, I just hope you don't get so focused on Audrey that you lose sight of our client. With Audrey we're just talking about getting a piece of evidence that might—and I underscore might—be useful if we ever bring a wrongful death action against Ronald Sterling. I'm wondering if you're so focused on Audrey now, that you want to pursue that matter in its own right rather than to simply provide evidence in Brenda's case."

"I suppose you could be right. I think I do, and must confess that I find the matter of Audrey's death very compelling. Is that a problem?"

"Not at all. With our legacy we can do what you always wanted. Pursue Justice. It's okay."

"Thanks."

Amber noticed a book beside the piles of reports and documents. "I see it's not all work and no play. What's that book you're reading?"

Judy picked up the book she had bought several days before. "In a way it's related." She handed it to Amber. *The Bridge of San Luis Rey*. I just started reading it."

Amber turned it over and looked at the back cover. "What's it about? How did you happen to pick it up?"

"I had been reading about all those people in the Concorde crash, about the families, the children, how they all happened to be at that particular place at that particular time, and wondering if it really was an act of God. In particular, I read an article about Michele Fricheteau, the owner of the Hotelissimo into which the Concorde crashed, who wrote a book, *Putaine de Crash*, about the two chambermaids and two Polish hotel students who were killed—how they had come to be working at her hotel on that particular day. Madame Fricheteau had bought this crumbling, cheap hotel at the end of the runway and had somehow made a go of it, charging about twenty dollars a night. Her business was wiped out."

"So sad."

"Anyway, the next day I was at Barnes and Noble looking for a good book to read. They didn't have *Putain de Crash* but I did see this book I remembered reading in grade school. After leafing through it much of the story came back to me. It's about five interrelated people, each with their own individual stories and backgrounds, who happened to cross a particular bridge in Peru between Lima and Cuzco at the very same time on July 20, 1714. The rope bridge, woven by the Inca a century earlier, collapsed at the very moment the five people were walking across it, hurling them all to their deaths in the river far below."

"I've heard of it," said Amber as she leafed through the book.

"It was Thornton Wilder's second novel, and it won the Pulitzer Prize in 1928, and was also the bestselling book of that year. In 1998 the book was rated as number thirty-seven by the Board of American Modern Library on the list of 100 best 20th century novels."

"I'll definitely have to read it."

"It traces the lives of each of the five victims and asks the cosmic question of why each of them had to die at that particular time and at that particular place. The book is framed from the perspective of a Franciscan Friar, Brother Juniper, who witnessed the catastrophe, and seeks empirical evidence of God's divine providence by interviewing everyone who knew the victims."

"If it received the Pulitzer Prize, it must have a theme."

"Thornton Wilder said his book poses the question: 'Is there a direction and meaning in lives beyond the individual's own will.'"

"Kind of embarrassed I haven't read it. But didn't they make a movie of it?"

"Yes, I think there have been several movies of it, the last in 2004. There was also an opera based on the book in 1954. The book was quoted by British Prime Minister Tony Blair during the memorial service for the victims of the September 11 attacks in 2001, and was also quoted during the 2007 Minneapolis bridge collapse by Brian Williams of NBC."

"All right, I'd definitely like to read it after you're finished with it," said Amber. "Now back to work."

Chapter Twenty-Four

It was a warm but not too warm Sunday morning, and both Amber and Judy had slept in until almost noon.

It was Amber who first arrived in the kitchen to prepare coffee, fruit, and yogurt for a late breakfast. She had already laid it out on the back patio when Judy, still in robe and slippers came out to join her.

"Nice of you to join me, sister," said Amber amiably. "Catch up on your sleep?"

"I think so," replied Judy as she sat and poured a cup of coffee."

"You've had a hard week working on the Audrey Sterling case. Anything new to report?"

"Not really. So far the only useful info I've gotten from NXR is what I already told you—that for some reason Audrey cancelled her British Airways Concorde and reserved a seat on the Air France Concorde the day before the crash. Not much to go on, I know."

"You're paying a fortune to NXR to get more information. Do they say they're making any progress in tracing either Audrey's or Ronald's whereabouts in the weeks before the accident?"

"They claim that they are, of course. They've dug up documentation showing Ronald's travels in the weeks before July 25—a partners meeting in San Francisco, including his reservations at the Hilton, and hotel reservations in San Diego where he had an appointment with a barker. Tracking Audrey's movements are more difficult, because, at least according to her sister, she stayed with friends or at small bed and breakfasts. However, they did find that she did stay at the Savoy on the nights of July 23 and 24. There were records of that. Amazingly, they even found that she may have had dinner reservations at Kaspars restaurant at the Savoy on July 24."

"Do they know who the other person on the dinner reservation was?"

"Not yet, because the Savoy generally only put the reservation in the name of someone who's also a guest at the hotel and could therefore sign for the dinner. But they're working on it. The problem is the time. After more than twenty years most hotels, even major ones, discard records of reservations, receipts and the like. There's no reason to keep them. So finding this kind of documentation means contacting the various hotels and airlines, and getting access to their deleted computer files. Even if they get access—that isn't easy either, and generally requires paying the hotel or airline a lot just to locate the hard drives—they then have to hire forensic specialists to retrieve the deleted files."

"But if they get the hard drives, they can retrieve them?"

"Theoretically it's possible, yes. As they explained it to me, even deleted files don't go into a black hole. They can be retrieved, but it can take hundreds of hours of labor by experts to do it. My point person at NRX is a guy named Jake Everett. Used to work at the CIA. As he explained it to me, whenever the CIA needed to delete sensitive material or abandon a computer or laptop, they didn't just throw it in the trash. They literally took it out to a vacant field and dropped some kind of belly bomb on it, blowing it to smithereens. That's the only way they can be sure that the data on the memory or hard drive can't ever be retrieved."

"Huh. So unless it's been belly bombed, retrieval even from old computers and hard drives can always be retrieved."

"Yep, apparently so, if you have the right expert to do the job—although there are precious few experts around who are capable of doing that—and you are willing to pay them a fortune to do it."

"Speaking of that, dare I ask how much it's costing you?"

Judy looked down with eyes up.

"Sorry. I meant 'our' money, of course."

"Let's just say that the cost is way beyond what any

financially challenged police department or D.A.'s office would be willing to pay on a cold case with so little chance of retrieving any worthwhile evidence."

"I know. Thanks to Timothy, money is no object for us now in finding the truth. The truth is worth a thousand Lamborghinis to me right now."

"All right, sister, but perhaps we should agree on a division of labor here. How about you continue to work on the Audrey Sterling matter exclusively, since you're so deep into it now, and I'll concentrate on Brenda Masterson's civil case."

"Fair enough, but aren't I working on Audrey's case in order to help you find evidence you can use in Brenda's case?"

"Yes you are. I didn't mean that we can't help each other on each end of this. What other lines are you pursuing?"

"Well, Jake is researching and screening a number of laboratories working on cutting edge DNA and forensic developments in identifying poisons in cadavers, particularly cadavers in burned, deteriorated, or damaged condition. He said that within the next week or so he'd be able to present me with a short list of certified labs that might be doing that."

"And what's the status of the exhumation petition?"

"I filed it. It's set for a hearing on September 13."

"So in the meantime, you have to sit and wait."

"Not entirely. I've also been researching the law."

"Really, in what area?"

"Attempted murder. Most state laws and cases are fairly consistent when it comes to defining murder—the act of intentionally causing the death of another human being with malice aforethought. However, state laws and cases regarding attempted murder differ in a number of respects."

"Wait just a minute," said Amber. "I'm going to go in to get another muffin. Can I bring you something?"

"How about some juice?"

"Oh, of course. Be right back."

When Amber returned she handed Judy a glass of grapefruit juice. "So how is the law of attempted murder relevant in the Audrey Sterling case?"

"Well, it's like you said. Even if we exhume Audrey's body, and even if we find a lethal amount of fentanyl in her body, it would probably be impossible to prove that she died before the impact of the crash."

"Yes, and you answered my little hypothetical about that correctly: When 'A' pushes 'B' off a thousand foot cliff, 'A' is not guilty of murder if from a distance 'C' shoots 'B' in the head before 'B' hits the ground. However, you didn't say whether 'A' might be guilty of attempted murder."

"I'm thinking that yes, he would. In the same way, even though Ronald might not be guilty of causing the death of Audrey if the crash killed her before the fentanyl had a chance to kill her, I'm thinking that Ronald could still be guilty of attempted murder. Am I right?"

"I'm afraid that, depending on the jurisdiction, the law might not be quite that clear cut."

Judy took a final sip of her coffee. "Why not?"

"Maybe the best way to explain the vagaries of the law of attempted murder would be to give you another set of hypotheticals."

"Oh no! Don't tell me you have more hypotheticals of the kind you gave to test the legal IQ of your perspective law school applicants."

"You're not game?"

Judy took a sip of juice. "Sure. Go ahead."

"All right. Here's the first one: 'A' hates 'B' and wants to kill him. One day, 'A' decides to take a hike out in the desert. There is no one around him for tens of miles. Not having properly prepared for his trek through the desert, 'A' soon runs out of water and starts having hallucinations. Soon he thinks he sees 'B,' but what he actually sees is just a mirage. 'A' then takes out his gun and with intent to kill and malice of forethought, he shoots the mirage full of holes. Is 'A' guilty of attempted murder?"

"No one around for tens of miles?'

"Yep."

"So how would anyone even see him shoot the mirage?"

"Don't confuse the issue of proof with the issue of the law for attempted murder. Maybe he later confessed. Just answer the hypothetical on the basis of your legal reasoning."

"Then I would say no. All 'A' did was shoot in the air with no one around him for many miles. That can't be a crime."

"Even though he had malicious intent to kill, but was just mistaken in thinking that 'B' was right in front of him?"

"Hmmm. I'd still say no. Am I right?"

"Remember, it's not a question of whether you're right or wrong. It's your legal reasoning that I'm testing. Now, consider my next hypothetical: An assassin wants to kill James Bond, and learns that Bond is staying in a hotel room. The assassin enters the hotel room, and sees James Bond in the bed. He then shots at Bond, but misses him by inches. Is the assassin guilty of attempted murder?"

"There I would say yes. He wanted to kill Bond, had the malicious intent, and failed to kill him only because he was a bad shot. Right?"

"Wait, first a couple of more: same hypo as the one I just gave you, except that this time Bond has been careful enough to put pillows under the bed covers to make it look like he's in the bed, but in fact Bond is ten miles away. The assassin then riddles the pillows full of holes. Is he guilty of attempted murder?"

Judy thought for a moment. "I think so. He had the intent to kill, and just missed Bond because Bond was very clever."

"Even though the assassin never even came close to killing him?"

"Sure."

"Then how is that different from the first hypo in which you said that 'A' was not guilty of attempted murder because 'B' was tens of miles away?"

Judy hesitated. "So what's the answer?"

"Not finished yet. I've got a couple of more to give you first: An assassin wants to kill Bond. He finds Bond in a back alley, and gets the drop on him. He then fires his gun at Bond, but miraculously the gun jams and Bond gets away. Is the assassin guilty of attempted murder?"

"I think yes. The assassin had malice of forethought, intended to kill, and only failed because his gun jammed. Right?"

"Hold on. Wait. Next hypo: the assassin wants to kill Bond. He sees him, pulls out his gun, aims and pulls the trigger. However, he has forgotten to load the gun, which now has no bullets. Is the assassin guilty of attempted murder?"

"Well, yes. He had the malicious intent, and just failed to kill because he forgot to load the gun, so...."

"Wait. Next hypo: the assassin wants to kill Bond, and picks out one of the guns he keeps in his collection to do the job. However, unbeknownst to the assassin, his son has placed in his collection a fake gun, used for theatrical purposes, which looks exactly like a real gun, but is in fact a gun with a blocked barrel which is incapable of firing a bullet. The assassin takes the gun, finds Bond, aims it at Bond and pulls the trigger. The gun doesn't fire, and in fact can't fire a real bullet. Guilty of attempted murder?"

"I think yes, because, again, the assassin had the intent, and thought the gun was real...."

"Even though he never had the actual means to commit the murder when he attempted to fire the gun?"

"Last one, and then you can give me what you think is a sound legal principle which resolves all the hypotheticals with consistency: a woman from a Caribbean country has a firm religious belief in voodoo. She believes with all her heart that if she creates a doll in the image of a person she wants to kill, and then utters an incantation, that she can kill a person in whose image she created the doll. The woman wants to kill Bond, creates a doll in Bond's image, and then with intent to kill utters the incantation. Assuming that the incantation doesn't work despite her intent and belief that it would, is she guilty of attempted murder?"

"Of course not! There was never any possibility that her incantation would work. So no."

"But how is that different from the previous hypo in which you said the assassin was guilty of attempted murder when he tried to fire an unloaded gun? Just as with the woman who believed in voodoo, it was absolutely impossible that the unloaded gun would succeed in killing anyone."

"It's different because in the case of the woman, the belief was based on a crazy religious belief that...."

"But I thought you were coming to the legal principle that intent to kill rested upon the intent to kill, regardless of whether it was in fact possible that the attempt would be successful?"

"But no rational person believes that voodoo would actually...."

"Half a billion Christians believe that one could rise from the dead. Are they all irrational?"

"That's different because...."

"Because...."

"Amber! You've exhausted me now. Can you just tell me what legal principle if applied would give the correct answer to all your hypotheticals?"

Amber shook her head and broke out in laughter. "Don't you see? There is no one principle that resolves all of those hypotheticals predictably. Every state's law and cases might give you a different answer on each of those hypotheticals. And that's my point. As you research the law of attempted murder you will see that. I have defended both murder and attempted murder cases, so I talk from some experience."

"And you've had a lot more experience than I...."

"When I posed these hypotheticals to those prospective law school applicants, I wasn't looking for a specific legal answer which, in any case, could only be obtained by legal research of the law in different state jurisdictions. They had not yet taken a course in criminal law, so there was no way they could arrive at such an answer. Rather, what I was testing was their ability to reason and arrive at a legal principle on their own."

"Wow. I wish Robin were here to help me on this. So how did I do?'

Amber smiled. "You did just fine."

"Come on give me a grade."

"No...."

"Come on!"

"Okay. How about a C+...."

Both women broke into laughter.

"Hey," said Judy. "How about we get on our bikes and ride to the park!"

Chapter Twenty-Five

On a hectic Monday morning at the law office, Amber knocked at the doorframe of Judy's open door. "Got a minute?"

"Sure. What's up?"

"I was hoping you might do me a favor."

Judy put down the NXR file she was reading. "Of course. Name it."

"I'm afraid it might be the one thing you'd be reluctant to do for me."

"Impossible."

"Well, it involves going back to Harvey's office...."

"Amber, anything but that!".

"I know you hate going there, but I just can't go—for the same reason as before. And I'm sure you're the only one who can get the information I need."

Judy sighed. "You and Timothy, and your exalted notions of my charm. Okay, what information do you need?"

Amber sat. "From my experience, any murder investigation involves immediately obtaining a warrant to search the primary suspect's house. I'm sure Harvey did so, and I'd be surprised if he didn't manage to seize both Ronald's and Angela's computers."

"What were you thinking might be on them?"

"In Ronald's case, I would think there'd be emails to and from hotels and airlines confirming reservations. That would help us track his movements in the weeks before Angela's death. In the case of Angela's computer I'm hoping for the same, but also something more."

"Like what?"

"Like correspondence with...."

"You mean co-respondent..." Both laughed at the Judy's allusion to the term used in British divorce litigation which referred to the person charged with adulterous misconduct with the petitioner's spouse.

"Something like that, yes."

"I don't think he's going to hand over the computers, so I take it that what you want are copies or transcripts of all the retrieved emails."

"Yes, for now, that's probably all we can get. If some emails were permanently deleted by either Angela for Ronald, and therefore need additional forensic work to retrieve them, we can try to get those later—maybe offer to pay for the extra expense that would entail."

"All right, I'll do it. Hopefully this will be the last time I need to do that. I wish we could somehow get access to Audrey's computer and files. It would be a lot easier if we could gain access to her emails at that end rather than NXR trying to access them from the other end after all this time."

"Do we even know that Audrey even used email? I mean, was email even routine back in 2000?"

"Yes, I believe so. As I recall reading somewhere, the first email was sent as early as 1971, but by 2000 over half of Americans were using it. Now, of course, almost everyone does."

"I wonder what the chances are that Audrey's computer still exists. I would imagine that it would have been thrown out by now."

"Maybe, maybe not. I'll have to contact Madeleine Turner again and ask what she did with Audrey's belongings after her death. Maybe they're still sitting in storage somewhere, or maybe Madeleine even kept some of her belongings, including her old computers."

"Unlikely. But feel free to contact her again after you see what you can do with persuading Harvey to cough up Angela's and Ronald's email and computer downloads and tapes."

"All right. Now, do you think I should try to make an appointment with Harvey through his office, or just try a walk-in?"

"I suggest the walk-in. I need to get moving on this case without delay. Brenda is getting a little impatient. Why don't you go right now as a matter of fact? I'll call Tyrone to come get you. He can take you home and you can change."

"Why do I need to change? What's wrong with what I'm wearing?"

"I thought you might like to try a shorter skirt, or...."

Judy shook her head. "No Amber! I'm fine with what I'm wearing."

"Okay, Okay. Let me call Tyrone."

"Good afternoon, Ms. Alexander. Very nice to see you again. I assume this is not a social visit." Harvey held out a chair for Judy in his office.

"Thank you for seeing me, Mr. Harvey. Yes, I'm afraid I'm on another mission for our mutual friend, Amber Hartman. I think she might be of great assistance to you in the Sterling matter."

"I have no doubt. So what does she want now?"

"I think she was wondering if perhaps you might have already served a warrant to retrieve the computers of both Ronald Sterling and Angela Sterling."

Harvey paused, sat back in his chair, and then rose. "Ms. Alexander...."

"Judy, please."

"Well, Judy, I was wondering if you might join me for a cup of coffee."

"I'm fine, sir...."

"Martin. Only fair that we're both on first name basis."

"Actually I'm fine...Martin. I...."

"I wasn't thinking of our coffee here in the office. Dreadful brew if I say so. And I'm due for an afternoon break. There's a

Starbucks just down the block. Perhaps we could discuss any requests over a latte?"

Judy shifted uncomfortably. So sharing an intimate cup of coffee would be the price of getting the transcripts Amber wanted, and no guarantee of that. "Uh, well...."

"It's just a minute's walk. I often do business in the corner table. I know the manager, and he can guarantee our privacy."

Judy nodded. "I'll follow you, then."

"Great. This way. I don't know about you but I need a little caffeine this late in the afternoon."

After leading Judy to the Starbucks, which turned out to be a bit further down the block than he had intimated, he ordered two cappuccino's and led Judy to his corner table.

After taking a few sips he said, "Now, assuming I have seized the computers Amber was referring to, I suppose she wants me to just turn them over to her."

"Oh, not at all...Martin. But if you have transcripts, they might be useful in tracking Ronald's movements in the days and weeks before Angela's death. Amber has a detective agency trying to track his movements by scouring the database of airlines and such, but it would really help if we had his computer."

"I'm sure it would. May I ask what detective agency Amber is using?"

Judy realized that perhaps she should not have mentioned that Amber and she were using a detective agency. Maybe it was all right that she did so, but she should have asked Amber first. "Let me ask Amber...."

"No problem. I was just curious. Now, I'm afraid I can't turn over the actual transcripts...."

"So you do have the computers, then...."

Harvey ignored Judy's question and continued, "...at least not at this time. However, I will give you one piece of information that we gleaned from the transcripts, and which Amber might find useful."

Judy waited.

"Angela did plan to meet with someone just one week before her death here in Houston."

"Oh. Yes that would be useful information. Where was she going to meet this person?"

"London."

Judy was stunned. For the moment, all she could think about was 'Brides in the Bath'.

"London, England? Angela?"

"Yes, and we have learned that she did in fact go. We have her plane reservations and boarding pass. She stayed overnight at the Savoy. And we also know that she returned to Houston the very next day."

"Oh, and do you have a name of the person she planned to meet?"

"Now…Judy…I'm afraid I can't tell you that, at least not now."

Judy stood up. "You can't? Why not?"

Harvey was taken aback. "Please, Judy, sit…."

"No, Mr. Harvey. I won't sit down. You have information that would be most helpful, and you refuse to give it to us." Judy took out a card from her purse. "Here's my card with my cell phone. Let me know when you feel like telling us."

Chapter Twenty-Six

"So the waiting may be over?" Amber asked over a breakfast.

"I hope so. I'm expecting a call at 11 A.M. this morning, which will finally tell me if I'll have anything to go on in Audrey's case."

"It's all right if you don't. We'll just concentrate on getting more evidence in Brenda's case against Ronald Steeling."

"And I haven't just been sitting around waiting for the toxicology tests on Audrey. After all, I did spend two weeks in my New York law office in late October, interviewing perspective criminal law attorneys applying for associate positions, looking over the books, helping my partners find more upscale offices, and getting the paperwork started on becoming a non-profit firm specializing in unjust convictions—the Justice Institute."

"Not to mention replenishing the firm's bank account, I assume."

"Well that too of course."

"We missed you around the office here while you were in New York. And remember you promised to talk about merging our firms."

"And I will—as soon as I find out if I have anything to go on in in the Audrey matter."

Judy pulled a calendar and notebook from her briefcase and began reviewing her calendar entries for the last three months.

"Let's see. As you know, I finally got Madeleine's petition for Audrey's exhumation signed last September 27 after one short continuance. On October 8, I signed the contract with RFL Toxicology Laboratory out of West Virginia to do Audrey's autopsy and poison analysis."

"I know you had a difficult decision to make before settling on RFL."

"Yes, Jake gave me a list of the best certified private forensic toxicology labs in the country that might be willing to do the tests on Audrey's body in its present state of decomposition. We contacted all of them and sent them copies of the DNA report which identified the body as being that of Audrey Sterling back in 2002—Jake had tracked that report down—as well as detailed pictures of the body. Three of them declined the commission stating that the body appeared to be in too great a state of decomposition for any of their existing instruments or tests to be able to identify fentanyl. A fourth lab said that they believed they might have a chance of success, depending on the extent of damage and decomposition, but that they were backed up with official government requests for tests which they could not delay, even for an incentive payment to give us priority, and therefore could not begin testing for up to a year."

"So that left RFL."

"Yes, they were also willing to give us priority, though only for a substantial incentive payment for doing so. We shipped them the body on October 11."

"I hate to ask how much they wanted to bump you to the top of the line."

"Then don't. Let's just say it's enough to buy a late model Ferrari, so thank Timothy. But even that's just for them to attempt to get a result. They wouldn't guarantee any results at all, positive or negative. They knew they couldn't just use any of their off-the-shelf tests, or even use their preferred tests on blood and urine because of the body's state of decomposition. However, they did think that if they tried some of the cutting edge experimental tests just becoming available, like...," Judy consulted her notes, "...experimental mass spectrometry tests in combination with the latest high performance liquid chronographic and gas chromatographic detection tests on bone and hair—which were still preserved on the body even in its state of decomposition—

they might, and they underscored might, be able to get some results."

"And if these tests don't work and they can't get results?"

"Like I said, the payment is non-refundable if they can't get any results at all. We're paying them to try, that's all."

"So how soon did they say they would know something?"

They said that, one way or the other, they'd let us know by November 22. These things take time, even when I pay to get to the top of the pecking order."

"November 22—that's another week."

But I just got a text from Jake who said they got some results early. But because we asked for confidentiality, the lab didn't want to email or fax it. They're sending it by express registered mail, and I should get it tomorrow. But Jake has a hard copy that was hand delivered, and said he would call at 11 A.M. to give me the bottom line—whether their tests were successful and whether they found fentanyl or not."

Amber looked at her watch. "It's 10:50 right now."

Judy got up from the patio table. "Will you watch my cell for a moment? I'm just going to hop into the kitchen to get my Voss fix."

Judy had no longer entered the kitchen when the cell rang. She rushed back frantically and picked up phone.

"Hello? Hello?"

"Judy?"

"Jake Everett from NXR. Good morning. Do you have a minute?"

"Yes! Yes! Of course! Did the lab get some results?"

Jake paused for dramatic effect, which Judy hoped might be a good sign—but then maybe not.

"Are you sitting down?"

"Yes! Yes! Now tell me, please!"

Another pause. "Okay, there's good news and bad news. Which do you want first?"

"Oh my God, Jake! Okay, then give me the bad news first."

Chapter Twenty-Seven

"Nope, I want to give you the good news first," Jake said.

"All right, any order you want!"

"They found fentanyl in Audrey's body."

"Oh my God! I can't believe it!"

"Apparently they used an experimental bone toxicology test they'd never used before—something called a multiplied liquid chronographic sequencing test. It's cutting edge. You can read the full report which you should get tomorrow."

"I can't believe it! But…then what's the bad news?"

"By extrapolation, they also determined that it was a fatal dose…."

"But that's good news, not bad."

"I wasn't finished with the good news."

"Jake, stop playing around. So what's the bad news?"

"Okay. There no question it was a fatal dose, because even a minute quantity can cause death, and the amount found was in excess of that amount. However, the test was not precise enough to determine how long after it was administered that it would have been enough to cause death. The best they can do at this point is to give us a window of forty-eight hours. And, of course, they can't tell you whether the dose, however lethal, actually caused Audrey's death before Concorde crashed. I doubt if any test will ever tell us that."

"But they're sure of their window for when the poison was actually administered."

"Yes, but even that is based on some assumptions…."

"Such as…."

"Such as what Audrey's weight was at the time that the poison was administered, what she had to eat prior to applying the patch to her person, assuming she is the one who applied it, how porous the particular patch was, and how soluble the fentanyl solution was that was applied to the patch."

"We provided the lab with examples of Nicoban patches...."

"Yes, but if the patches were tampered with, there's no way of knowing how concentrated the applied fentanyl solution was. The lab is willing to conduct further tests to tighten the window—if you authorize them."

"I do. Tell them to keep testing and tighten the window using different sets of assumptions."

"Will do. Do you want an estimate of the costs before you authorize these additional tests?"

"No. Just tell them to get started on the additional tests as soon as possible. For now, just knowing that Audrey was poisoned makes a case for at least attempted murder."

"I take it that you have dismissed any idea that Audrey took her own life."

"I find that very unlikely. From everything I know now she was excited to fly home on Concorde, and looking forward to getting back to Houston, to begin divorce proceedings, and to begin a new life away from Ronald Sterling."

"Right. Now...."

"While I've got you on the line. Any more progress on finding out who Audrey had dinner with the night before she took the Eurostar in London?"

"I think we're getting close. We've made some connections, gotten some interviews. We'll let you know as soon as we find something."

"I do have one further task—an even bigger longshot than that one."

"Ugh oh."

"Look, we know that for some reason Audrey cancelled her reservation on the British Airway Concorde the day before she took the Eurostar to Paris. We also know that she took the fatal Air France Concorde from Paris just hours after she arrived in Paris. I've been discussing this with my colleague Amber, and neither of us can think of a reason why she would do that. The only reason we can think of is that she went there to meet someone. She certainly didn't go there to do any sightseeing. And if she did meet someone there, that meeting would fit very neatly into the window timeline you just gave me."

"Hmmm. I see. But you're right, the chances of finding that person after more than twenty years would be impossible—certainly there would be no chance of finding witnesses to any such meeting after all this time. I suppose we could try to see if the Paris Concorde Lounge kept any records of who visited the lounge, but the lounge itself was shut down after Concorde stopped flying, and...."

"I know that's not a viable line of inquiry."

'Can you think of any other?"

"I can only think of one, though one that's almost as likely to lead to a dead end. Audrey Sterling had a sister, Madeleine Turner, who is still living. She's a manager for the Lucky Diamond Casino in Las Vegas. I went to see her a few months ago. As Audrey's next of kin, she signed the petition for Audrey's exhumation, which is why we were able to provide RFL Labs with Audrey's remains. If she has kept any of her sister's possessions—I'm thinking especially of her computer—I was thinking that we might be able to retrieve her emails, and to whom she might have sent them to arrange a meeting."

"Well, I could look into that. But wouldn't it be simpler if I just interviewed Madeleine and asked her if she knew anyone that Audrey might be meeting in Paris?"

Judy smiled. "Yes, I suppose I could have asked her that when I talked with her. I didn't think of it at the time. So maybe you could send one of your investigators down to Las Vegas to ask her?"

"Sure, we could do that. But Judy, would you mind if I asked you a personal question? Of course I will understand if you don't want to...."

"It's all right. What?"

"Look, I'm happy to pursue all these lines of inquiry, no matter how unlikely they are to lead to anything you're looking for. You're paying us by the hour, and we're always grateful for the business. But I've just got to ask why this matter is so important to you. From what you've told me, you think that if we can uncover evidence that Audrey was murdered...."

"Or the victim of attempted murder...."

"Yes, and that she was poisoned by fentanyl, and that it could be used as evidence in a case brought by a client of your colleague."

"Right."

"But I just have to ask if this piece of evidence, if we are ever able to uncover it, could possibly be worth the price you are paying for it. I mean...."

"Jake, don't worry about any of that. Just send me the bills and I will pay them. But yes, I do have some personal reasons for pursing this matter. My late partner was a professor of law, and as my advisor on a law school clinic dedicated to overturning unjust convictions, he inspired me to pursue truth and justice for its own sake. Until recently, I have not had the means to do so, and now I do."

"Okay. I didn't mean to pry. Just wanted to make sure you wouldn't get a heart attack when we send you our next bill."

"I have confidence that you're giving me my money's worth. As long as you keep getting me results, I'll be satisfied. I know the information you got about Audrey meeting someone at the Savoy—well, I was amazed you were able to ferret that out. So keep getting me results, and I'll take care of your bills."

"You're an amazing lady, Judy. It's a privilege to work for you."

Chapter Twenty-Eight

Amber held up her hands. "I gotta hand it to you, girl! I never thought you had any chance of finding fentanyl in Audrey. You are amazing!"

Judy nodded. "I didn't either. I'm kind of amazed myself."

"So where do we go from here?"

"I'm still kind of dazed. Let's sit down and think about it."

Amber and Judy sat for about ten minutes, until Judy said, "So do I now have some admissible 'Brides in the Bath' evidence for you?"

Amber thought for a moment. "Well, yes and no. I think we need more."

"How so?"

"Remember that in the Brides in the Bath case, there was proof that the husband had actually been with the brides on their honeymoon nights. So far it looks like you have evidence that Ronald Sterling's first wife died of the same poison as his second wife, Angela. But under Evidence rule 404(b), I don't think that's enough of a connection."

"But I thought you didn't need the 'corpus delecti' to bring in evidence of a prior act?"

"Yes, that's true, in this sense: if in our civil case against Ronald for poisoning Angela with fentanyl we wanted to present evidence that his previous wife had also died from fentanyl poisoning, we wouldn't have to prove that Ronald actually poisoned Audrey with fentanyl; we'd just have to show that at or about the time that Ronald was with Audrey, that she ingested a fatal dose of fentanyl. But as of now, you have no evidence that Ronald was with Audrey at or near the time that she ingested the fentanyl. Do you understand?"

"I think so, so you're saying I still need to...."

"Remember—in the Brides in Bath case, the prosecution was not required to prove that the husband actually killed his previous wives. But it did have to show that on those prior occasions, the husband was actually with his previous wives—that is, that he had some physical connection with them—at or about the time that they died or had inflicted upon them the means to kill them. You will also recall that in that case, the husband's current wife died from unexplained circumstances. According to the husband, he went out to get some champagne on their honeymoon night, and returned to find his wife drowned in the bathtub. Without forensic evidence to prove that the husband actually held them down in the bath until they drowned, the prosecution couldn't make a case against him—until, of course, they found that his previous wives had died under the very same circumstances."

"So you're saying that I need to find some physical connection between Ronald and Audrey at or near the time that Audrey ingested the fatal dose."

"Right. I think you have to show that at some time prior to Audrey ingesting the fentanyl, Ronald was actually with her and had an opportunity—just an opportunity, mind you—to insert a poisoned nicotine patch into her packet of patches. Then I think you'd have the connection necessary to satisfy Evidence Rule 404(b)."

"I see. Now I understand that NXR has already found evidence that Angela met someone in London shortly before she died in Houston from the fentanyl-laced patch."

"Yes. And they're now trying to find evidence that the person who met with her in London was in fact Ronald. But even if they can establish that Ronald in fact did interface with Angela in London on the day before she died in her bed in Houston, that's simply not enough to convince a jury that he was the one who laced Angela's Nicoban patch. And that's where your evidence would come in under 404(b)—if, that is, you can prove a) that Audrey died from fentanyl, and b) that Ronald interfaced with Audrey in the period before the fentanyl would have taken its deadly effect."

"Yeah. I get it. Well, NRX already has evidence that Audrey met with someone at the Savoy in London the night before she took the early morning Eurostar to Paris to board Concorde. NRX now just has to find who that someone was."

"That might do it, yes."

"I also believe that Audrey may have met with someone in Paris in the hours before she took the cab to the airport. I also think it's possible that she might have met someone at the Concorde lounge."

"Another thought occurs to me. If in fact both Audrey and Angela were slipped the poisoned patches while in London, then the crime of at least attempted murder was committed in England."

"So if both Audrey and Angela were poisoned in England, but didn't die until they were outside England—Audrey in France, Angela in Houston—then the crime scene shifts to the jurisdiction of Great Britain."

"That's an interesting legal question actually. What if someone fatally shoots someone in Wyoming, but the victim manages to make it across the border of Colorado before actually expiring. Is the crime of murder committed in the jurisdiction of Wyoming or Colorado?"

"I would say Wyoming."

"I think you're right, but I'll need to research the law on that—and not just Texas or American law, but both British and international law."

"In the meantime, it looks like the center of gravity of both these cases may be in Great Britain."

"Didn't you tell me that you and Robin took a sabbatical to study the British legal system?"

"Yes, and we learned that prosecutions there are authorized by the CPS."

"Child Protective Services?"

Judy laughed. "No, silly, I told you—it's the Crown Prosecution Service. That's the government organization that authorizes prosecution of all serious offenses. I wonder whether it might be worthwhile to pay them a visit and report to them the evidence I have thus far that at least one murder, and possibly two were committed within their jurisdiction."

"Shouldn't you bone up first on how you would go about reporting a possible murder in England? I mean I've heard it's a complicated system of justice."

"I will do that, but I can bone up on that over there just as well as here."

"So what are you saying, Judy? That you want to go to England now?"

"That's what I'm thinking. Yep. I'm going to call Chandler right now and tell him to have the G-500 ready by tomorrow morning."

"Wow, just out of the blue you're deciding to go to England? So as soon as you get there, are you planning to just waltz into the CPS—or whatever it is—ask for the director, and report these possible murders to him directly?"

"Sure, why not?"

"If you were anyone else, I'd tell you start at the bottom—with the London police—and work your way up the system. I mean you'd be an American who just appears and starts talking about a twenty-year-old murder that may not even have happened in England. But I remember how you started at the top in France by arranging a meeting with the Inspector General of France. I don't know how you managed that. Actually, I take that back. Maybe I do—I still can't forget Timothy's favorite Aristotle quote about beauty being a better recommendation than a letter of introduction."

"Silly."

"Not really, and you've proved it. But all right, if you really think you have to go right away, I should probably tell you something before you go."

"You've got some new information?"

"No, I'd have already told you if I did. But Harvey called me yesterday."

"Really! I thought you two weren't corresponding."

"Well, he did. Correspond that is. He said that you kind of left in a huff when you met with him the other day."

"Why would he call you to tell you that?"

"I guess he thought you were mad at him or something."

"Well, I was frankly. He told me that he had discovered the name of the person who met Angela in London the day before she was to return to Houston shortly before her death. But when I asked him if he could tell me who it was, he started giving me excuses as to why he couldn't tell me."

"Judy, he's the D.A.. for Harris County. He can't just start leaking all the evidence he has in a pending investigation. He'll release it when he feels he can do so without compromising his investigation."

"I understand that. But I really felt he was trying to, you know trade information for...."

"What? A date?"

"To be honest, I got that feeling, yeah. I mean his office was perfectly private, but he told me we'd have more privacy at the Starbucks down the block—but it turned out to be several blocks away, and...."

"Judy, you know how important that name would be to me in Brenda's case. If that person she met happened to be Ronald Sterling, it would enable me to show that Ronald had opportunity, in addition to motive and means to kill Angela."

"I'm sorry. I guess I overreacted. But seeing Harvey come on to me like that...."

"Judy, you've been used to that all your life. He wouldn't be the first guy to have an alternative motive to get you into bed."

"But this was different. I mean, you were dating him. I just wouldn't feel comfortable leading him on in any way, knowing that you and he used to be...."

"Oh Judy, you're sweet! You thought I'd be like the woman who divorces her husband, and doesn't want to see him, but would still be hurt if she saw her best friend dating him. It wouldn't be like that. I wouldn't have minded if you and he actually got together for real. He really is a fine man, amazingly attractive for that matter as well, and I hardly think asking to cloister with you at Starbucks detracts from that. I mean he's on a double rebound—first from his wife, and then from me. I mean he wouldn't be a man if he didn't deal with those losses by...."

"Amber, stop. Do you hear yourself?'

"What?"

Judy gave her that look of skepticism with which Amber was by now familiar—looking down with eyes up.

"You don't think...."

"I think just maybe, yes."

"You think I still have feelings for him? That I regret having left him?"

"Well, he did call you, not me, didn't he? If he was just after me, he could have called me. But he didn't. Do you think he just might have come on to me to make you jealous? Is that so terrible? He must have known that I would tell you about his moves on me."

"Oh, I don't know."

"Of course, if you still want me to have another shot at him to try to get the name of who Angela met in London, I'll do it for you. But you've got to get it out of your head that every man I meet dissolves into warm puddles at my feet and falls desperately in love with me. I'm over thirty, you know. Pretty soon I'm going to have to worry about men coming after me for my money rather than my looks. I'm not the same woman who went to France seven years ago and...."

Amber shook her head. "Actually you are. You just don't' know it. I see things that you don't. But no, I won't ask you to hook up with Harvey again."

"Thank you. You know what I think you should do? I think you should call Harvey back and tell him that you'd like to meet with him about the evidence he has in the Sterling case. It would give you a chance to see if you still have feelings for him.

If not, you can still use your wiles on him—all in the interest of justice, of course."

"Of course."

"So will you come up and help me pack? I want to get an early start tomorrow. And then I want to spend the rest of the evening researching everything I can find about Britain's Crown Prosecution Service."

Chapter Twenty-Nine

Chandler stood at the bottom of the stairs to the G-500.

"Good morning, ladies. Judy, your pilot has arrived, and the mechanics have made their final pre-flight check of your plane. I arrived earlier to start the fueling, and your new flight attendant, Josephine—I just hired her last week—is already aboard. So we're ready to go whenever you are."

"Thank you Chandler. What would we do without you?"

Judy gave her brief case and roller bag to Chandler who carried them up the stairs. She turned to Amber.

"You know, you can still come with me you know."

"I'd love to. But I've got too many things going on at the firm. I have an important pretrial hearing next Tuesday in the Senta Walker matter. The bastard who disfigured her for life is making a motion to suppress the sobriety test, and if it's successful she could end up not getting a dime. I've got to be here to oppose that motion."

"I understand." She hugged Amber. "I'll call you when we refuel in Teterboro."

"I assume Chandler is coming with you."

"Of course. He handles all the plane stuff and arranges for landing permission—all that. I couldn't do without him."

"Now you have to admit, having Timothy's plane is a lot better than flying coach."

"No doubt, but to be honest I'm still not used to it."

"Just remember—Timothy wanted us to have and use the plane."

"I know, I know. So be it. Listen, if I have time in London I'll try to help on your cases, though I'm not sure what I can do from London."

"Don't worry about that. You concentrate on Audrey, and I'll hold the fort here until you get back."

Judy turned to Chandler who was now waiting at the top of the stairs.

"Coming!" she shouted.

Amber took Judy's hand. "Where will you be staying in London?"

"The Savoy, of course. I'm hoping I might pick up some clues following in Audrey's footsteps in the days before she went to Paris. Maybe I'll get lucky and find someone who worked there back in 2000 and still works there."

"I should have guessed. I suppose you have no idea how long you'll be in London."

"Not really. You think I'm going on a wild goose chase, don't you."

"For the first time in our lives we have the means to pursue a challenge to justice that comes our way. Do what you need to do in London, and call me as much as you can."

After a final hug, Judy walked up the stairs and waved.

Each blew the other kisses until Chandler waved and closed the hatch.

Chapter Thirty

Judy looked up from her desk and the pile of google printouts she had downloaded the night before. The refueling at Teterboro had taken longer than anticipated, and it now looked like the Gulfstream would not arrive at Farnborough outside London until early in the morning.

She was anxious to get through most of the printouts and learn as much as she could about the British legal system before she arrived in London.

She looked over at Chandler, who was dozing peacefully. Josephine was busy preparing a light lunch.

"What would you care to drink, Judy?" Josephine asked.

"Iced tea is fine," Judy replied. "But fix something for yourself as well."

Judy stopped to look out her window at the blue waters of the Atlantic below. Then she turned to her printouts and learned that the Crown Prosecution Service was the principal public agency for conducting prosecutions in England and Wales.

The history of the CPS traced back to 1829, the year when Sir Robert Peele, a former Prime Minister, established the Metropolitan Police Force. Prior to that time, criminal prosecutions cases could only be brought by private citizens at their own expense. After the creation of the Metropolitan Police Force, the police gradually took on the burden of bringing criminal prosecutions in the courts—though technically, still only on behalf of private citizens.

In 1880 a Department of Public Prosecutions was established and conducted as a department of the cabinet post of Home Office. However, the jurisdiction of this office was limited to prosecuting only the most serious cases such as treason, murder, and rape. Police forces still continued to bear responsibility for bringing all other criminal cases before the courts.

It wasn't until 1962 that a Royal Commission recommended that the police set up independent prosecution departments in order to avoid the conflicts of interest that had arisen when the investigators were also the prosecutors. When a number of police departments declined to adopt the recommendations of the Royal Commission, and continued to prosecute cases themselves, another Royal Commission recommended that a single and independent Crown Prosecution Service be established to assume responsibility for conducting all serious criminal prosecutions.

Finally, in 1985, Parliament passed the Prosecution of Offences Act which created the Crown Prosecution Service. Under this Act, police forces would still have the authority to undertake prosecutions on their own for less serious offenses, including common assault or property damage. However, police could not prosecute offenses for treason, murder, or rape without authorization from the Crown Prosecution Service. The CPS makes the final decision to prosecute in such cases.

Unlike a District Attorney's Office in the United States, the CPS does not actually try cases. Rather they hire barristers listed on an "advocate's panel" to actually try the cases.

Barristers are courtroom specialists who are independent and self-employed. However, they are permitted to organize into a group, or "set" which shares expenses in "chambers." Unlike a law firm, however, each member of chambers is independent, and does not share profits. However, like roommates, they can and do share expenses, such as rent, secretarial services, and utilities.

Only solicitors can form law firms. These solicitors perform office work, screen and interview clients, and prepare "briefs" and "instructions" from clients. Then they tie up all the paperwork in a neatly tied ribbon—literally—which when provided to the barrister contains all the material that the barrister will need to try the case in court.

Being independent, barristers can and do try cases against each other. The CPS might hire one member of the set to try a serious criminal case against a charged defendant, while a defendant in another case might hire the same barrister to act as his defense counsel in a separate case. Thus, a particular barrister might try a criminal case on behalf of the Crown in the morning, and in the afternoon act as defense counsel in another case.

All Barristers must belong to one of four professional barrister associations called "Inns of Court." There are four of them: Gray's Inn, Lincoln's Inn, Inner Temple, and Middle Temple. These Inns provide libraries, eating facilities, and other professional accommodations. Each Inn also has a "chapel" or "precinct" associated with it, where aspiring barristers can train and practice.

Once a barrister earns a reputation as an outstanding advocate who has made outstanding contributions to the legal profession, the sovereign may appoint that counsel as "Her Majesty's Counsel Learned in the Law," and grant the honorific "Queen's Counsel." "QC's" are entitled to wear special silk gowns to indicate their lofty status, and are entitled to sit in the first row of the court in front of other barristers.

Fewer than ten percent of barristers are ever offered the honor of "taking the silk" and gaining QC status, and not surprisingly they command the highest fees.

Judy recalled much of this information from when she and Robin together had taken their sabbatical some years before at the Inns of Court, but had had little contact with the CPS itself.

Now, as she contemplated what her first course of action would be when she arrived in London, she decided she would first try to make contacts at the CPS rather than in chambers or the Inns of Court. Whether she would later regret that decision she would have to wait and see. For now, however, she would concentrate on familiarizing herself with what the CPS procedures were for deciding whether to authorize prosecutions for murder and attempted murder.

Chandler was still dozing, and Josephine too was sacked out on the couch with eyes closed. Judy didn't want to disturb her. Before retiring to the back bedroom, she read a section of the "Code for Crown Prosecutors" which set forth five conditions that must be met before the CPS will authorize prosecution:

1. There are reasonable grounds to suspect that the person charged has committed the offence.
2. Further evidence can be obtained to provide a realistic prospect of conviction.
3. The seriousness of the case justifies making an immediate charging decision.
4. There are substantial grounds to object to bail.
5. It is in the public interest to charge the suspect.

Now exhausted, Judy let these conditions rattle in her head, as she tiptoed to the bedroom, took a quick shower, and slipped into bed.

Chapter Thirty-One

Upon arriving at Farnborough, Judy released Chandler to fly the G-500 back to Houston, and took a cab to the Savoy. Although she had gotten a decent night's sleep in the G-500 bedroom, she was still jet-lagged. She decided to crash in her Savoy suite and not further her mission until the following day. When she awoke at 3 A.M., and couldn't get back to sleep she decided to check in with Amber who answered after one ring.

"Hey girl, I take it you arrived okay."

"Yep, but I should have held out and not gone to bed until tonight. Now I'm all out of kilter."

"It's only early evening here, but I'm still at the office writing up an offer in the Senta Walker case."

"What are you offering?"

"That we'd take five million flat, not a penny less—take it or leave it. I actually hope they don't accept, because I'd love to get her case before a jury. But she needs the money now for her operations, so if I can get her five million quickly, and not wait for years of litigation and appeals, I feel I should do it."

"Good luck on that, and give Senta my best.""I will. Now what are your plans?"

"I'm going to start by visiting the CPS tomorrow. I'm sure it's not the proper place to get an investigation going into the poisoning of Audrey, but maybe someone there can point me in the right direction."

"Well, if anyone can get something going, it's you. I need to get this offer out, so I'd better let you go. Keep me posted."

"Sure. Talk tomorrow."

After lying in bed for another several hours, Judy rose, showered, and changed into her black suit and heels. After a quick breakfast of coffee, yogurt, and juice at Kaspars, Judy stepped out on to the Savoy Circle and asked the doorman to hail her a cab. Judy nestled into the black cab, first in the line of three.

"Where to, Miss?" the driver asked.

"I don't know the exact street address, but it's the London South Crown Protection Office."

"Of course, Miss. It's on Petty France in Westminster."

"Petty France?"

"Just a street name, Miss. I have no idea why it's called that. It links Buckingham Gate with Broadway and Queen Anne's Gate. It's next to the Ministry of Justice which I happen to know is 102 Petty France. The CPS for London is right in there."

"Thank you. I was hoping to get there when it opens at 9 A.M."

"No problem, Miss. Traffic's not too bad. I'll get you there in about twenty minutes."

"That's fine. Thank you."

The cab arrived in less than fifteen minutes. The CPS building was much as she imagined—a typical modern structure of concrete and glass. There were several people already lined up waiting for the 9 A.M. opening.

Inside, she approached the reception desk.

"Yes, who would you like to see, Ma'am?" asked the white haired receptionist who reminded her of an Agatha Christie matron.

"I was hoping I might be able to see"—Judy consulted her research notebook—"let's see, Chief Crown Prosecutor Adrian Blakely."

The receptionist smiled indulgently. "You have an appointment with her?"

"No, but I wish to report a serious crime. I am a lawyer—American—and have come here to report it."

"Ma'am, crimes are not reported here. But if you are not familiar with our procedures, I can call a deputy prosecutor who may be able to advise you." She called on the phone, and after a brief conversation, turned to Judy and "Your name Ma'am? And do you have any identification, passport?"

Judy showed her passport, and the receptionist read her name to the person on the line. "Very well, sir." She turned to Judy. "Is this an emergency?"

"No. It is not."

"Deputy Prosecutor Williamson will be with you in a few minutes. You can wait for Deputy Williamson in the reception area down the hall.

Judy nodded. "Thank you."

Judy followed the directions to the reception area where she sat and read her notes as she waited.

It was a half hour before a personable young man approached with dark curly brown hair and what appeared to be a pleasant disposition. "You are Judy Alexander?"

Judy rose and held out her hand. "Yes Sir."

"I am DP Henry Williamson. Will you follow me upstairs?"

Judy couldn't help thinking how young he looked—surely not too many years out of school.

Judy followed Williamson up an elevator to a small fourth floor interview room.

"Now Ms. Alexander, what is the purpose of your visit today?"

"Sir, I am in possession of evidence that on July 24, 2000 an American woman by the name of Audrey Sterling was deliberately poisoned by a fatal dose of fentanyl while in this country...."

"Ms. Alexander, I don't mean to interrupt. I was only inquiring in order to ascertain the general purpose of your visit, not the specifics. But since it is a crime you wish to report, I must tell you that this is not the department to which you must report. All such reports, other than those involving national security, must be submitted to the police. It is then up to them to investigate the crimes, and for anything but the most serious crimes, to prosecute as well. If it is a serious crime, such as murder or rape, the police must refer the matter to us for a final decision on prosecution."

"I understand, but I was hoping that someone in this department might be able to advise me as to how to proceed and to which police department I should report the matter."

"Certainly I can give you some advice in that respect—as to who might advise you, that is."

"Thank you. I would appreciate that."

"First, may I get you some coffee?"

Judy doubted that any institutional coffee would be up to her standards, but thought it impolitic to decline. "That would be nice. Thank you."

Williamson left and returned in a few minutes with the coffee.

"I could certainly give you the address of the police district where it would be best to file your report, but given that you seem unfamiliar with our procedures, I'm thinking it might be best to refer you to a solicitor or barrister who might help you navigate."

"That would be wonderful. Thank you."

"I'm giving you the number of a friend and classmate of mine at Oxford. He's actually a barrister, not a solicitor, and I'm sure he could help you. His name is Braxton Thomas. I'll give him a call and let him know you'll be calling. Good guy. He practices now at the Quadrangle Chambers on Bedford Row, which is associated with Inner Temple. Wait until tomorrow and then give him a call. Here's his info and number."

Judy took the information. "I really appreciate this."

"Good luck."

Chapter Thirty-Two

Despite her contact that morning with someone who might be willing to help her move forward, Judy realized there was not much she could do for the rest of the day. She decided to walk back to the Savoy, where she retreated to her room for a nap, and then called Amber.

"Hi girl. How's everything on the home front?"

"Got the Offer of Judgment letter out in the Walker case. I gave them a week to answer, so now just waiting to see if they respond. How is your quest going? Any progress?"

"Not really. I went to the CPS, but as I expected they can't do anything until I first file a report with the police. However, a nice young DP did offer to put me in touch with a barrister who might be willing to help me navigate their system, so maybe something will come of that."

"Nice young DP, huh? Well, hopefully that will get you going. But hey, your friend Jake called early this morning but couldn't reach you. They found who Audrey's dinner mate was on July 24, 2004."

"Oh my God! Really! Tell me!"

"I don't know how they did it, but they're 99% sure that on the evening of July 24, 2000, at Kaspars restaurant, Audrey Sterling dined with a down and out British Viscount by the name of Jeremy Heathcote-Fox-McKenzie."

"Say again?"

Amber repeated the mouthful title and name.

"And did they get an address?"

"Yes, that too. Check your email. They said they're sending you all the info they have."

Judy quickly rolled to her email. "Got it! How did Jake ever find this?"

"He said don't ask. I assume they checked everything they could get their hands on—deleted emails, computer records, cameras—God knows what he checked. Whatever he did, it cost a bundle to do it. He sent us a huge bill...."

"Never mind. Pay it. I'll call you back after I read the report!"

Chapter Thirty-Three

After a long day at CPS and a sojourn to the local pub, Henry Williamson lay back on the couch of his Bloomsbury flat and called his old Oxford classmate Braxton Thomas.

"Ay mate, how's everything down there at the Quadrangle?"

"Hey Henry, long time no hear. Madhouse. Clerk Baldy is running us ragged. He gave me two instructions from Sharkey Lewis today—armed robberies. No choice, really. Had to take them."

"That mangy old solicitor? I thought Baldy was trying to transform Quadrangle into a prosecution set."

"That's the key word, Henry, trying. In the meantime we still gotta pay the bills. Baldy talks a good game, but I've yet to see him come through for us—at least not in any kind of volume. We get prosecution referrals from CPS now and then, but it's not enough to go exclusive. We took Baldy on as clerk when Scofield retired—I thought it was a mistake at the time—and he claimed to have contacts with you guys at CPS. Speaking of...."

"Brax, you know I'm just a desk jockey here. If I tried to help out buddies like you—as if I had any influence at all here...."

"I know, I know. But we are on the list you know. So if you do see an opening to put in a word for us...."

"Of course. Just don't hold your breath. There's a lot of sets who want to go exclusively prosecution, but hey, someone's gotta defend, right?"

"Yeah, sure. So, how's everything at the workhouse?"

"Okay. I'm mainly just screening now—at my desk all day—just trying to work up the ladder."

"Well, you wanted a steady salary, so you got it. Here in Chambers, we junior barristers really have to scramble to get decent cases, and we're at the mercy of Baldy who doles out the cases and instructions."

"You've been out of pupillage for three years, Brax. You should be making it by now. Doesn't your old master still help you?"

"Hodges? Oh he does, when he's got time and isn't distracted, but he's got another pupil now—a pretty cute bird too—but I'm not complaining. He got me into the set, and that was huge. He got silk, you know, so just up to me now."

"Right. I didn't know Hodges got the silk."

"Just last year. So we've got three now, and they always get the good prosecution cases. Anyway, haven't heard from you for months now. You just ring to talk over old times?'

"Pretty much, but also wanted to give you a lead on a bird if you're in the market. Last I heard, you and Sharon had broken up."

Braxton groaned. "Yeah, it was rough. Just baching it these days. In a way it's good, though. Gives me time to concentrate on my career—such as it is—here at the Quadrangle. So why do you ask."

"Just wondering, because I had a very interesting visitor today at the office."

"Really, I didn't know you got visitors."

"I usually don't, of course, but when Sally, the CPS receptionist, doesn't know what to do with someone who comes in, she calls one of us to talk him...or in this case her."

"So what was interesting about her?"

"She's an American, says she's a lawyer, though you'd never guess it by looking at her."

"And...."

"Well...she was quite a...."

"Bit of alright?"

"You could say that, yes...."

"Fit, then?"

"Quite."

"Well, Henry, aren't you the sly dog. Sounds like she made quite an impression on you. So what did she want?"

"She began to tell me about a murder she wanted to report—something about a woman who had been poisoned with fentanyl...."

"fentanyl? Here in England? In London? What did you tell her?"

"What we're supposed to tell people who come to the CPS thinking we're some kind of police station—that she needed to go a police station, or the Yard, and report it. But she obviously wasn't familiar with how best to make such a report...so I thought of you."

"Me? Why me? I can't make a report for her."

"No, but I couldn't really see her just wandering around like a forlorn tourist and just dropping into one of the local police stations and trying to make a report. She looked a little out of her depth, so I thought you could help her navigate, hold her hand, maybe accompany her down to the South Side station. You know the officers there...."

"And of course you just wanted to help her. Out of the goodness of your heart, of course."

"You got me, Brax. I shouldn't have. If you don't want to help her, I can call her and tell her to figure it out herself. She left her cell number with me."

"Well, you've got me curious now. She must be quite a bird. So what, am I supposed to call her now?"

"No. I gave her your number at Quadrangle, and told her to call you tomorrow. Maybe she won't even call you."

"Okay. I owe you a favor anyway. What's her name?'

"Judy Alexander."

Chapter Thirty-Four

Judy woke early, but had time to kill before her meeting with Braxton Thomas at 4:30 P.M. that afternoon. She had called the young barrister at 9 A.M., who had kindly consented to meet with her after his court hearings. He told her that he was short of time, however, and would only be able to meet with her for at most fifteen minutes.

After showering and changing into her black suit, white blouse, and tie, she sat down on the couch in front of the picture window of the Thames, and began looking through her book of London maps. She saw that Quadrangle Chambers were on Bedford Row—only a twenty-minute walk from the Savoy. That would give her time to walk to the British Museum and see its exhibits before doubling back to Bedford Row.

At 4:30 P.M. she presented herself to the doorman at 241 Bedford Row.

"Who are you here to see?" he asked.

Judy consulted her notebook. "Braxton Thomas. He's a barrister."

"That would be in Quadrangle, Ms. Down the hall to the lift, second floor, and then turn to your right."

Following the directions, Judy stood at the door and was reading the names on the door when two harried barristers carrying bags and instructions emerged. Rushing past her she asked "Are these the chambers of Braxton Thomas?"

Without turning around, one said "see clerk Harold inside."

Judy opened the door to a scene which reeked of bedlam. Sitting around a large table were a dozen or so men and women busily attending to paperwork and answering phones. At its head was a bald headed man calling out instructions to several assistants who gathered around him.

Judy decided to take a seat on the only vacant chair along the perimeter of the room and wait until the throng of people surrounding the bald man—whom she deduced was the clerk of chambers— had dissipated.

As she sat, a distinguished looking man in full battle array of silk and wig walked by and did a double take.

"Good afternoon, Madame. You appear to be waiting for someone. May I be of assistance?"

Judy rose. "Yes, sir. I have an appointment with Braxton Thomas. Am I in the right place?"

"Indeed you are. Braxton is a former pupil of mine. I regret that I do not know where he is at the moment. I am Michael Hodges." He extended his hand.

Judy took the hand offered, apparently unaware that by long tradition, barristers rarely shook hands. The tradition could be traced back to sword-bearing times, when a handshake was considered a way to show that you were not armed. Since barristers were gentlemen, there was no need to shake hands to show your trust. Had Judy known this, she would have realized that for whatever reason, Michael Hodges was breaking the tradition for her.

Judy paused for a moment to size up the man in silk. He looked to be a man in his late fifties, with an air of the aristocrat. With his forensic wig, which consisted of a frizzed crown with four rows of seven curls in the back, he reminded her of Agatha Christie's classic barrister, played by the inimitable Charles Laughton, in the 1957 Billy Wilder film *Witness for the Prosecution*.

"I am Judy Alexander, sir. I am visiting here from the states."

"I am pleased to welcome an American cousin. If you like, Ms. Alexander, you may wait in my office."

"Thank you, but I was told to check in with the clerk."

"I can do that for you if you wish. Now if you would care to follow me."

Judy followed Hodges down the hall into a large and well-appointed office that was almost the size of the entire central chambers. He motioned for her to sit on the leather couch in front of his monumental mahogany desk, took off his wig and placed it in a wooden box.

"If you wouldn't mind waiting here, Ms. Alexander, I will see if I can find Mr. Thomas for you." He returned moments later and took a seat behind his desk.

"I have checked with our clerk, and he advises me that Mr. Thomas is expected back from court momentarily. While we wait, might I ask what brings you here to see Mr. Thomas? Have you been referred by one of our solicitors?"

Judy shifted uncomfortably, unsure what to make of the attention being paid to her.

"No, not at all sir. I am lawyer, licensed to practice in New York. It has recently come to my attention, through a client, that a murder, or attempted murder, may have been committed here in London some years ago. On behalf of a client, I have come here to England to look into that matter. We have evidence that a young American woman, named Audrey Sterling, was poisoned by an overdose of fentanyl, administered by means of a doctored Nicoban patch, on or about July 25, 2000. I am trying to discover who in London may have had contact with her during that time...."

"Audrey Sterling, did you say?"

"Yes, sir."

"A daunting task, especially given that any such contact would have occurred twenty years ago."

"Over twenty years, actually, yes sir."

"That's a very long time. It's true, as you must know, British law, unlike American law, does not provide for statutes of limitation in criminal cases except for minor cases brought in the magistrate's courts. Nevertheless, compiling proof in any case that old inevitably involves great difficulty."

"Yes sir, I am aware of that. But actually, my client's case does not necessitate me finding such proof of each and every element of the crime which we suspect, with an eye to prosecution here, but only that a particular person may have had an opportunity to commit a crime. If I can find such evidence here, it would enable me to present evidence in a civil wrongful death action my associate in Houston is contemplating bringing in the courts of Harris County, Texas. We have a rule of evidence in that state, 404(b), which is based on one of your old cases—the Brides in the Bath Case."

"The Brides in the Bath case! My dear, I'm afraid you have lost me now."

"If further evidence of motive, and means were also discovered, I understand that prosecution of that crime would be entirely to the discretion of your justice system here."

"I must say, that sounds intriguing, but...."

"Perhaps I should wait for Mr. Thomas to explain."

At that moment there was a knock at the door.

"Come in," said Hodges.

Appearing at the door was a young man with a shock of light brown hair, an infectious smile, and a face that reminded Judy of a young Hughes Grant, or of Charles Laughton's protagonist Tyrone Power in *Witness for the Prosecution*.

"Sorry to bother you, Sir Michael. I understand I have a visitor...."

Judy rose and turned around. "Hello, sir. I am Judy Alexander. I called you this morning and you said I could come in this afternoon and meet with you."

"Of course, Ms. Alexander," Braxton replied. Sorry I am late." He turned toward his old mentor. "Thank you, Michael. I can take our visitor off your hands now."

"Of course. Your delightful guest has quite a story to tell."

"I'm looking forward to it. Now, Ms. Alexander, if you will follow me?"

Judy smiled, thanked the silk-clad barrister who had taken such in interest in her, and with some relief excused herself to follow the attractive man whom she hoped might now take her under his wing.

Chapter Thirty-Five

"Now Madame, what can I do for you?"

In the chair of a much less imposing office, Judy said, "Thank you for seeing me. May I ask who I was just talking to?" Braxton cold have given a long answer.

Michael Hodges was his old mentor and the senior member of Quadrangle Chambers. Years ago he had achieved a national reputation as one of the great advocates of the British bar. In his heyday, he was so effective in court that he had rarely lost a case, no matter how much the evidence and facts were against him and his client. In court, his opponents trembled to go up against him, and often pled out to avoid confronting him in court. He commanded the highest fees representing the highest profile criminal defendants, and soon became the Crown's first choice of counsel in prosecutions. Before he reached the age of thirty he became the youngest barrister to win the coveted silk. To be taken into his pupilage was considered the highest honor for aspiring barristers, as it had been for Braxton. But his life had changed when cancer took his wife to whom he had always been faithful. Since her death, however, he had played up his celebrity and sought out the movers and shakers in the power structure, including both MP's and peers—and not least starlets and models—whose wealth gave them not only power but access to those in the power structure itself. Although he had never allowed these proclivities to jeopardize his reputation or allow himself to be the subject of any sexual harassment suit, it was well known that he could rarely resist any beauty who came his way, particularly one as stunning as Judy who just happened to waltz into chambers and take a seat outside his door.

Instead, Braxton just answered Judy's question briefly. "That was our senior barrister, and one of three silks we have here at Quadrangle."

"Does he still practice, and take cases?"

"Yes, though very few. Mostly he consults and mentors our younger pupils and junior barristers. He was one of the founding members of our chambers, and we are very proud to have a silk of such reputation in our chambers."

"He sounds very impressive."

"Now, I understand my friend Henry referred you to me, but I'm not sure I know why or what I can do for you."

Judy had no doubt that Braxton was a busy man, but despite his formality and air of patient indulgence, she felt that he was softening in her presence. Such guilt as she often felt in such situations she could easily rationalize as being justified in the cause of justice. She would soon discover if his interest went beyond simply doing a favor for a friend. He had, after all, only offered her fifteen minutes over the phone."

"I know you only have a few minutes...." she said apologetically.

"Plenty of time, Ms. Alexander."

It was a good sign.

"It might take an hour or so."

"I'm all ears. I have time. Please tell me."

Judy spent the next hour and a half telling him the reasons for coming to London—starting with Amber's client, Brenda Masterson, who had hired Amber to file a civil wrongful death suit against her stepfather Ronald Sterling, the death of Audrey Sterling in the Concorde crash, the death of Angela Sterling by fentanyl contaminated Nicobans, the RFL lab report documenting the fentanyl found in Audrey's body; and finally the NXR report of a British Viscount who had met with Audrey at the Savoy on the evening before the Concorde crash.

Braxton listened attentively, taking notes. "Explain to me again how evidence of the poisoning of Audrey Sterling in this country would be admissible evidence in a civil action for wrongful death against Ronald Sterling in Harris County in your country."

"Its admissibility would be based on the same premise as in your High Court's decision in the Brides in the Bath Case."

"I'm familiar with what you call the Brides in the Bath case—Rex v. Smith, 1915, as I recall." Braxton looked at his watch. Judy assumed the interview was over, until Braxton said:

"Listen, Judy—may I call you Judy?—it's almost six. A lot of us unwind from our days in court down at the Brass Monkey—a pub just a short walk from here. Would you like to continue our conversation down there? I'd like to hear more about how our Brides in the Bath case fits into your rules of evidence."

"Of course. I'd love to. Lead the way."

It was a delightfully warm August evening as Braxton took Judy the long way along the Embankment to the Brass Monkey.

"I assume you've already seen all the tourist attractions," he said as he pointed out Big Ben, the Parliament buildings, and the Tower of London in the distance."

"Actually I haven't as yet. But once I finish my little mission here, I would like to."

The Brass Monkey was alive with a different kind of bedlam than in chambers. The two squeezed past the throng of lively barristers, solicitors, court officials, and judges enjoying their pints amid an atmosphere of frivolity and spirited—and very loud—conversation. Braxton spied Hodges, seated next to two other barristers, holding a pint in the air and waving for them to come join him.

"Join us, you two!" Hodges shouted over the bedlam. Two other young barristers, a man and a woman, stood up from the table and excused themselves, leaving their seats for Braxton and Judy.

"We're just leaving," said the woman. "We're going to see *Hamilton* at Victorian Palace, so ta-ta you two. Braxton, I don't know your friend."

"Cynthia, this is Judy, who is visiting from the states."
Judy smiled. "Hello, Cynthia. Enjoy the show. I've always wanted to see it."

Braxton seated Judy next to Hodges and then followed.

"What can I get you two?" asked Hodges, who appeared to have already imbibed several pints.

"Let me get us all something, Michael," said Braxton. "Judy, they have the best fish and chips in London here. Are you hungry at all?"

"Actually, I am. I guess in Rome do as the Romans do, so fish and chips sounds good…and a pint sounds good as well."

"Done," said Braxton. "Michael, anything for you?"

"Another pint will do me fine."

Braxton left to wind his way through the throng to the bar to order. As in most, if not all pubs in London, a trip to the bar to order was required in lieu of waiter or waitress service.

Hodges, now alone with Judy, turned to her and said, "I was intrigued by what little you were able to tell me before Michael came to take you away. Did I understand you to say that the young woman to whom you referred—the one who was allegedly poisoned—had certain contacts around the date of July 25, 2000?"

"Yes, I did say that, sir. Does that date have any special significance for you?"

There was a crescendo of laughter in the pub and Hodges could not hear the question."

"Say again?" he shouted above the din.

"I said, does that date, July 25, 2000, have any significance for you?"

"As a matter of fact, I'm afraid it does…and Judy is it?"

"Yes, sir."

"Then, my dear, could I possibly prevail upon you to call me Michael?"

"Of course, if you like…Michael."

"It is quite possible that I may be able to help you with regard to possible contracts that this Audrey Sterling may have had on or about the date that you mention. You wouldn't happen to have a picture of this woman, would you?"

Judy could hardly believe what he was saying. Was it even possible that this icon of the British bar would actually have information regarding Audrey Sterling? What were the chances of that? She tried to calculate in her head the extremely long odds that he of all people working in London could possess any such information. Or was this simply a ploy to engage her—a male tactic with which she was only too familiar?

Flustered, Judy reached for her briefcase, which contained her files, toxicology reports, and NXL dossier. "As a matter of fact I think I do."

"Oh, not here, dear. We can take a look later. Anyway, here comes Braxton with your fish and chips, and our pints."

Braxton squeezed through a tight group of evening revelers, ducking his head as he did so. "Sorry it took so long, but it's more crowded than usual tonight."

The evening passed pleasantly, as both Braxton and Hodges vied to regale Judy with war stories of their courtroom exploits.

It was shortly before midnight, and the pub crowd had thinned considerably, when Hodges stood. "I'm afraid I must call it a night. But permit me to invite both of you to my humble manor outside Newbury in Berkshire this coming weekend. Can you come Friday night, say about 6 P.M. for dinner, and stay for the weekend? We can discuss Judy's investigation, and perhaps provide some assistance to her. What say you?"

"I would be most pleased to come," said Judy. "You will provide me with directions?"

"Of course. And Braxton, you have been to my humble abode on several occasions, and presumably know the way. Can you bring Judy, or do you have other plans?"

Braxton hesitated. In fact he did have some plans—a dinner date he had made with a woman he had met at a wedding the previous week. But the prospect of interfacing with the loveliest woman he had ever seen was not an opportunity he wished to let pass. He would break the date.

"Of course, Michael. It would be a pleasure. And Judy, I'd be happy to pick you up on Friday—say about 4 P.M.? Where are you staying?'

"At the Savoy. I'll look forward to seeing you then."

Chapter Thirty-Six

Braxton's vintage 1980 Triumph Spitfire, top down, careened around the Savoy Circle, stopped near the front entrance of the Savoy, and beeped.

Judy was not expecting Braxton to arrive in such fashion, and at first did not recognize him.

He beeped again, and Judy finally waved.

"Get in!" he called.

Somewhat flustered, Judy opened the passenger door, flung her small bag into the space behind the front seat, and despite her petite five-foot-four frame found that entering the Spitfire passenger seat required a certain amount of bodily contortion. "Wow" she said.

"You okay? Ready to go?" he asked.

"Sure. I'm afraid I wasn't quite expecting...."

Braxton accelerated the Spitfire around the Circle with a screech. "My little Spitfire? It was my granddads. He flew Spitfires during the war. He was shot down over the channel, but was picked up and lived to fly again. Great little car...when it runs, that is. Is it okay to leave the top down? I can put it back up...."

"No, it's fine. It's just that...." She withdrew a scarf from her purse and tied it tightly around her head.

"You'll be fine," he reassured her.

"Well at least I'm dressed for it. The weather report said we were in the middle of a heat wave, so I hope these shorts and T-shirt will be okay, at least for the drive."

"I love 'em. You look great, by the way."

"Thank you. I did bring a summer dress for dinner. Now where are we going exactly?"

"Newbury. It's about fifty miles west of London in Berkshire. Newbury has become sort of the Silicon Valley of England, but there are a number of country estates outside its immediate surroundings. The manor where they film *Downton Abbey* is just a few miles down the road from his house."

"Really! And that's where Mr. Hodges lives?"

"He has a flat near the Quadrangle, but usually retreats to his country house on the weekends. Since his wife died I suppose it can be lonely with just the housekeeper, gardener—and, he may have a chef too—although I have heard stories that he also entertains quite a lot."

"Dinner parties for neighbors, friends you mean?"

"I suppose, but actually more along the lines of...of...."

"What?"

"Well, let's just say that as an eligible and wealthy widower—attractive I suppose, for his age and something of a celebrity himself—he has opportunities to...."

"Entertain younger woman?"

"Have you heard of the movie actress—more of a TV actress actually—Evelyn Montaigne?"

"No, I can't say that I have."

"No reason you should have. Don't think she's broken into the Hollywood scene as yet. She's been in several successful sitcoms, quite a beauty of course. She and Hodges were something of an item a while back...."

"Are they still?"

"Oh, I don't know, but I doubt it. Like I said, he doesn't really confide in me about his private life, and we haven't been particularly close since my pupillage with him. That's why I was a little surprised when he invited us to his house this weekend—out of the blue."

"Not to mention me. I was really surprised."

"I still consider him my mentor, though, and I often go to him for advice on a case or to consult with him."

"Can I be honest about something?"

"Of course. What?"

"I am very hopeful that you might be able to help me with my...."

"You're referring to your Brides in the Bath case back in Houston?"

"Well, yes, but specifically I need help in filing a police report with the proper people, and I would be most grateful...."

"But....?"

Judy wanted to make clear that she had only agreed to this country weekend in order to get help on her case, and nothing else. "But I wouldn't have agreed to come to Hodge's house if it hadn't been something he said to me just before he invited us to visit"

"I'm all ears."

"Well, he said that he might be able to help me track down possible contacts that Audrey Sterling may have had shortly before she took Concorde."

"He said that?"

"Yes, and he implied that he may even have known Audrey Sterling."

"That's hard to believe. Perhaps you misunderstood. I mean what are the chances?"

"That's what I thought, but at this point I feel like I need to follow up every lead regardless of the odds of it panning out. Does Hodges hang out with those who are similarly situated—like MP's, peers, who have enough power and influence to... I don't know...."

"Seduce young and attractive women?"

"I didn't mean to put that fine a point on it, but yes. It's been my experience that once men like that get some wealth and power, they often delude themselves into thinking that they are also physically attractive to women, and try to take advantage of it."

"Hmmm. Have you had personal experience along those lines?"

"Let's just say I've seen it and been wary. Should I be worried?"

"No, I'll be there for you. Won't let you out of my sight. But now that you mention it, Hodges does seem to belong to an

Old Boy's Club of sorts. Don't know how many of his old cronies still stay in touch, but I wouldn't be surprised if they meet—or at least have met often in the past—in the billiard room of his manor over Brandy and cigars to discuss their latest conquests."

"So maybe it's not so impossible that he would have known someone with enough power, status and wealth to turn the head of a young American beauty making the rounds of the Savoy set."

"Well, I wouldn't worry about visiting him. After all, he did invite me too."

"As my chaperone? Maybe figuring that I might get wind of his reputation and not come unless I had someone like you as my chaperone."

Braxton laughed. "I suppose anything's possible, but I wouldn't read too much into it. He's got too much of a good reputation in legal circles to jeopardize it beyond a few indiscretions that might at most lead to a few whispers and rumors that could never be proved."

"And I suppose such titillating rumors, at least if not confirmed or showing up on the front page of the *Daily Mirror*, might actually enhance his...his...."

"Mystique?"

"Something like that."

"I'm sure...wait, hold on...don't want to miss this exit on to the A-4."

The Spitfire accelerated to pass a lumbering truck on to the freeway and made a sharp right turn.

"Oh!" Judy grabbed her scarf just I time to keep it from flying away in the wind. The spitfire had not gone more than a mile down the freeway at highway speed when the engine began sputtering.

"Is everything okay?"

"What? I can't hear you!"

Braxton and Judy had had no problem hearing each other in the slow traffic, but at the higher speed and noise on the A-4, both now had to shout in order to be heard.

"Hold on!" Braxton shouted. "There's a petrol station just up a few miles! We'll stop and I'll check the carburetor. It sometime acts up like this at high speed!"

With cars now passing them at high speed, Judy grabbed the side of her seat and held on. "Now you tell me!"

She began to breathe more easily as the Spitfire coasted into the station. Braxton got out and opened the hood.

"Carburetor just needs some adjustment," he said calmly. "It'll just be a few minutes."

Judy got out. "Anything I can do to help?"

Braxton turned and smiled indulgently. "Know anything about carburetors?"

"Of course! That's me, the expert auto mechanic."

"Actually, you can do something. I think I gave you Hodge's cell number. Why don't you call him and tell him we'll be a little late."

Judy took out her cell. "Okay. What shall I tell him? How far are we from his house?"

"It's about an hour's drive from here. I should have this thing adjusted in about ten minutes. Tell him we should be there by 6:30."

"Right. And can I ask a favor? Maybe we could put the top up now?"

"You got it, Princess."

Chapter Thirty-Seven

"So you don't think I'm going into the lion's den, then?" Judy asked plaintively as she looked out the spitfire's tiny window at the imposing façade of Hodge's country home.

Braxton stood on his driver' seat, leaped over the door, and hurried around to open Judy's car door to take her by the hand. He then pulled Judy's bag from the back of her seat, and extracted his own bag from the boot. "Well, even if it is, M' Lady I shall be right at hand to protect you."

The two stood for a moment to take in the house and surrounding gardens.

"Well," Braxton said, "it may not be Downton Abbey, but it could be its baby brother. Looks pretty much like it was when I visited a couple of years ago, but the garden seems much more elaborate, and I think I see a new addition in the back."

"Very impressive. Does he still live here alone?"

"I guess we shall see," he said as he led her to the front door and pointed to the large bronze knocker in the shape of a gargoyle. "Shall you do the honors?"

"Sure." Judy took a breath and then tentatively gave a light tap with the gargoyle.

"You'll have to do better than that, I'm afraid."

Judy looked at Braxton with her face down, eyes up expression. "Yes sir!" This time she gave the door a vigorous knock three times."

It was a minute before the door was opened by a ruddy-complexioned middle-aged man wearing a light blazer and scarf.

"Good evening. Braxton Thomas and Judy Alexander to see Mr. Hodges."

"Of course," came the good natured reply. I am Jeffery. Mr. Hodges is expecting you and waiting in the sunroom. You can put your bags down here for the time being. Dinner will be served shortly. Please follow me."

Braxton and Judy looked at each other with raised eyebrows and then followed Jeffery in to the sunroom.

The sunroom was bathed in the summer evening light beneath a glass dome. Amid deep foliage, water from a stone waterfall trickled down into a small pool of Koi. Hodges was seated on a divan, and rose as they entered. He was wearing jeans and a light suede jacket.

"Welcome you two! Please come and sit!"

As they sat, Braxton looked up and around the sunroom. "Michael, I don't remember this sunroom when I last visited. Is must be a new addition."

"Indeed, it is. It was just completed last summer. How do you like it?"

"It's magnificent. I'm most impressed."

"Thank you. I've been enjoying it immensely. Always wanted one, but never got around to it. Hodges turned to Judy. "I'm so pleased you could join us this weekend. I understand you had a problem with Braxton's ridiculous little automobile."

"It was quite exciting, I must say," replied Judy. "I'm sorry we were a bit late."

"No problem at all. I'm just glad you both made it in one piece."

"My carburetor's been acting up lately, but it just took a little adjustment."

"I'm sure." Hodges turned to Jeffery. "I take it dinner is prepared?"

"Yes, sir. All the dishes are prepared, and I've put them all under warmers in the dining room."

"Excellent." Hodges turned to Judy and Braxton. "Jeffrey here is an outstanding chef, the best in Newbury, and is the manager of the Newbury Inn. I have known him for years, as I knew his father. I am most fortunate that he is able to help me with meals when I come here for the weekend."

Turning back to Jeffery, he said, "it sounds like you have worked your usual culinary wonders, Jeffrey, so you may go home for the evening."

"Very good sir. Do you wish me to come tomorrow to clean up?"

"That would be fine. For the rest of the weekend, I think we can make do ourselves with what we have in this kitchen."

"Very good sir," Jeffery repeated as he turned and left.

"Now," said Hodges. "I was hoping that we might spend a little more time here before dinner, but since the dinner is ready and warming, may I suggest we retire to the dining room?"

"Of course. We'll follow you," said Braxton.

"I hope you both like pheasant?"

Though Judy was more of a vegetarian and fish persuasion, she nodded politely. The pheasant certainly looked inviting, and she might be able to partake in a small portion.

The dining room was typical of a nineteenth century manor house, book-lined but darkly conventional for that time period. After everyone served themselves from the warming plates set upon the rustic mango wood hard carved rustic buffet cabinet, Hodges asked his guests to sit while he poured the wine.

"Now," said Hodges as he sat himself at the head of the table. "I've come up with a few activities for this weekend if you would care to participate, although of course please feel free to just veg out and relax in the garden if you prefer."

"Tell me what you've planned, Michael. I'm sure we'd like to join."

"For tomorrow morning, I thought you might like to join a fox hunt my neighbors Justin and Elsa have planned for us."

Hodges noticed Judy's look of concern and quickly reassured her. "We don't chase real foxes, of course. Justin rides ahead dragging a scented rag, and we just follow up after ten minutes or so. And we don't have a whole pack of dogs like they show you in the films—just five hounds—or maybe only four— and half the time they don't catch the scent and just wander off until called. No wooden fences or streams to cross. We call it a 'fox hunt' just for fun, but it's really just an excuse to exercise Justin's horses—and his dogs—a bit."

Braxton looked over at Judy? "Want to try it? I haven't been on a horse for ages, but...."

"Sure, why not? I haven't either. But I really didn't bring any riding clothes—just the shorts I have on and a summer dress. I don't think either would be suitable for riding."

"No problem at all, Judy," said Hodges. "In your bedroom upstairs, you will find in the closet a number of outfits from which I'm sure you can find something suitable."

"I'm afraid I too don't have anything...." said Braxton.

"You'll find something suitable in your closet as well, Michael. So we're all good for tomorrow morning? Bright and early—hope 6:00 A.M. isn't too early."

"Nope, we'll be up. Right, Judy?"

"I'll try," she replied. "I'm still a little jet lagged, so maybe you could wake me at 5:30 if I'm not up yet?"

"Done," said Braxton.

"Excellent," said Hodges. "For lunch tomorrow, I thought we could make sandwiches for our friends before they return home with their dogs and horses. We could relax the rest of the day, and then Justin and Elsa said they could return in the early evening for a game of croquet."

"Sound great," said Braxton.

During dinner, both Braxton and Hodges regaled Judy with more stories of their courtroom exploits. After dessert of a choice of Apple Crumble, Treacle Pie, or Figgy Pudding—all aesthetically laid out on a triple stacked serving dish on the buffet—Hodges invited everyone back to the sunroom for after dinner cordials.

After Hodges served the liquors, he offered a mahogany box of cigars to Braxton. Braxton discreetly shook his head, and out of sight of Judy, pointed to her.

"Of course, what was I thinking!" said Hodges. "None of that tonight."

After an hour of small talk about the garden and the upcoming fox hunt, Braxton noticed that Judy looked a little uncomfortable. The conversation up to that point had been decidedly of the male variety, and Judy looked like she was fading.

"Michael," Braxton said, "we very much appreciate your hospitality, but I'm afraid we may have brought Judy here under somewhat false pretenses. As we discussed on Wednesday, she is looking into a matter for a client of hers back in the states, and she has told me that you had indicated to her that you may have firsthand knowledge of the young woman, Audrey Sterling. I'm afraid that the prospect of obtaining some information about that woman, whose death she is looking into, was the reason I was able to persuade her to join us this weekend—of course, she was also most eager to see a beautiful country home such as yours. But I fear it is a matter of time for her, so we were hoping...."

Thank you Braxton! Judy thought to herself, and grateful that it hadn't been left up to her alone to bring up the real reason why she had agreed to come.

"Of course, of course!" Hodges interrupted. "It is very true that I did intimate that I may have had some knowledge of that young woman—though I believe I underscored the may—and asked Judy to show me any picture that she might have of this Sterling woman. It has been many years since I may have met this woman, and I will need a picture to be sure that I am thinking of the same woman whose death Judy is looking into."

Hodges turned to Judy. "Have you brought the picture of her?"

Judy nodded. "Yes, I have several, as a matter of fact, which I was able to obtain from her sister. They are in my bag, and I can show them to you now, if you like."

"Excellent. But it is getting a bit late now this evening. Might I suggest that we set aside a time tomorrow for me to look at your pictures, and discuss what I might be able to tell you about her—assuming she is the woman I am thinking about."

Judy looked over at Braxton with an expression that

showed her impatience with Hodge's hedges—both as to the likelihood that he really had any information which might be useful to her, and also to the manner in which he seemed to be putting off having any meaningful conversation with her. On the other hand, there were no other leads for her to follow up until she heard more from NXR, and, if nothing else, she seems to have enlisted the help of Braxton in navigating the British justice system. Of course it remained to be seen if either Braxton or Hodges had a hidden agenda, though she was more concerned about Hodges than Braxton, who seems to have taken a genuine interest in helping her.

Judy stood. "Well, boys. If I'm to get up at the crack of dawn in the morning, I think I'd better get to bed."

Hodges put down his liqueur. "Then we shall call it a night. Braxton, could you take Judy upstairs and show Judy her room? It's at the end of the hall on the right, just across from the room you stayed in last time you visited. And you can take the same room you had before. If either of you can make it to the kitchen by 6 A.M., I'll try to have a continental breakfast and coffee ready for you."

Braxton said. "Thank you. Judy, I'll get our bags and you can follow me up."

"Let me know if either of you need anything. My bedroom is at the other end of the hall on the left."

Braxton led Judy up the staircase to her bedroom and opened the door.

"Oh, it's very nice," she said. "I love the canopy bed. She went to the window and looked out over the garden. "Very lovely. I shall be fine here."

Braxton nodded "Then I shall say goodnight. I'm sure you'll have everything you need. You can have the adjacent bathroom, and I'll take the one down the hall."

"I'd invite you in for an evening nightcap, but I'm really tired."

"Of course. You'd like me to wake you about 5:30?"

"Actually, could you wake me up even a little earlier? I wouldn't mind taking advantage of Hodge's offer of coffee in the morning to get me started."

"Of course. Get a good night's sleep, and I'll see you in the morning."

Chapter Thirty-Eight

Justin and Elsa arrived an hour late at Hodge's house amidst great confusion. Both of them arrived on horseback leading three extra horses for Judy, Braxton, and Hodges, while four hounds ran ahead of them barking madly in anticipation of an exciting outing. One disappeared into the neighboring woods and had to be called back.

Hodges apparently knew the horses and took the reins of the one he felt would be least excitable and led it over to Judy.

"Cinnamon here should give you no trouble. Are you ready?"

Although Judy had not ridden a horse in years, she mounted her steed adroitly and took the reins. Hodges and Braxton too were soon mounted.

Justin attached the scented rag to the back of his saddle while Elsa dismounted to attach a leash to the four hounds and held them.

"Go Justin!" she shouted.

"Give me at least five minutes!" shouted Justin as he sped off across the paddock and out the gate. Elsa held the hounds who were straining against the leash.

Several minutes later Hodge's called "Release the hounds!" With some difficulty she unleashed the exuberant hounds, deftly mounted her own steed, and sped after the hounds.

Cinnamon meanwhile, despite Hodge's assurance that he was not excitable began to twirl around in circles as Judy tried to gain control.

"Can I help?" asked Braxton, though he was in no position to do so as his own horse seemed to want to return to his own barn in the opposite direction.

Finally, both Judy and Braxton gained control and trotted off in the general direction of the others. They had not gone far when Cinnamon apparently decided he could take advantage of his inexperienced rider, and headed at a gallop toward a nearby copse of shaded trees, where both rider and horse disappeared from view.

Braxton gamely followed Judy into the copse, where he found her dismounted and sitting against an English Oak. She had tied Cinnamon, seemingly quite contented, to a nearby low hanging branch.

"So," he said as he dismounted, "it seems that your horse has a mind of his own." After tying down his own horse, he came and sat next to Judy.

"I take it you're not really into this fox hunt business," he said cheerily.

"Not really, I'm afraid. But this is nice, sitting her under this big beautiful oak. Very peaceful. You don't think the others will be cross with us for losing our way?"

"Oh, I shouldn't think so. I bet you a quid to a buck that none of the hounds will ever find the rag. They're not really fox hounds, you know."

"I gathered."

"Anyway, I'd rather be here with you under this tree than chasing dogs."

"You don't have to, you know. I'll be fine here for a while. Why don't you go ahead? I can find my way back."

"And leave a damsel in distress? I wouldn't think of it."

"Well, I'm not a damsel, and as you can see I'm not in distress."

"Of course. I'll go if you wish."

"No, I'm sorry." She touched his hand. "It's okay. It's just that...."

"What?" he asked, thrilled by even this slightest innocent touch from Judy. He wondered if she knew it.

"I don't know. I guess I just feel a little guilty. Here I'm supposed to be investigating a murder on behalf of a client, and instead I'm sitting here on the estate of a British aristocrat, feeling this balmy summer breeze, and...."

"But you're here because Hodges told you he may have some information about...."

"Audrey Sterling." She withdrew her hand.

"I know. But do you think he really does? Or did he just say that to...."

"To get you here? Hey, I'm your chaperone, remember?"

"Thank you, but I really can take care of myself."

"I have no doubt of that."

"You can help me, though."

"Name it."

"I mean aside from helping me make a report to the police about the murder."

"Name it."

"Hodges promised that he would set aside time today to discuss what he knows about Audrey Sterling. I don't know when they'll all be coming back from this fox hunt, and then there will be lunch, and then later this afternoon there will be croquet...."

"You're worried that somehow the time will slip away and you won't have your promised private discussion with him."

"Yes, I think I am."

"Well, I'm not sure what I can do...."

"I don't think it will be practical to try to pin him down this afternoon. After the hunt, his friends will probably take their horses and dogs back home, but as I understand it, they will reappear for the croquet game... and if they will be staying for dinner then the day is going to be pretty much shot by the time they leave again."

"So, what are you saying? That we should try to nix dinner?"

"No, everyone will have to eat. But maybe you could suggest that all we want is a very light dinner that we can scavenge from his kitchen. He didn't mention that Jeffery was coming back to fix dinner, did he?"

"No."

"So when we get back, could you maybe mention to him that I do not want a heavy dinner and need to set aside a certain time this evening to meet with him. Can you do that?"

"I'm sure I can, yes."

"And one more thing."

"Name it."

"When I do meet with him this evening I want it to be in private."

"Meaning...."

"I need you to disappear."

"Really? I thought you were concerned about being alone with him."

"I told you I can take care of myself."

"But any information he gives you—if he has any—will be information I will need in order to make as full a report to the police as we can."

"I know that. And any information I can get from him I will relay to you later. But I have gotten the feeling that whatever it is that he has to tell me is not something that he would want you to know."

"That could be true."

"From what you told me about him, he's had some questionable friends and relationships. Perhaps any knowledge he has of Audrey Sterling emanates from one of those contacts. And you say you were his pupil in chambers, so...."

"But wouldn't he know that anything he tells you, you would tell me since he knows I've offered to help you."

"Maybe, maybe not. He would retain some...some...."

"Plausible deniability, as opposed to if I heard him divulge some dark secret to me directly?"

"Something like that."

Braxton looked at his watch. "Perhaps we should be getting back. If the hounds haven't found the rag yet, I'm sure they'll have given up by now."

"Fine by me."

Braxton got up and cupped his hands to help Judy back on her horse.

"I hope your croquet is better than your horsemanship," he said jokingly as they rode back to the manor.

"I just might surprise you."

Chapter Thirty-Nine

It was late on Sunday afternoon when Judy and Braxton took their leave of Hodges' Newbury country house.

"So how did it go last night?" Braxton asked as he navigated the Spitfire through the narrow streets of Newbury. You must have been up late last night with Hodges after you sent me away."

"Yes, and I appreciate your taking off. I guess I had gone to bed before you came back. And of course you and I had no time to converse this morning—Hodges was always around. Where did you go last night? Sorry I had to kick you out."

"I have no doubt Hodges was glad I left. So, last night, I first hung out at the Lock, Stock, and Barrel. I saw some old friends from law school there as a matter of fact. Then we all went to the Old Catherine Wheel, and finally ended up at the Old London Apprentice—all great pubs by the way. So, did the old letch make any moves on you while I was away?"

"No, not really. He did ask me to come back next weekend, though. Of course, he commented on my...."

"I can imagine. Just invited you, sans chaperone for next weekend I assume?"

"Oh yeah."

"You're not going, are you?"

Judy gave Braxton her face down eyes up expression, this time accompanied by a peer over her sunglasses. "What do you think?"

"Just asking. So was it worth it? Did you get anything worthwhile out of him?"

Judy lay her head back on the headrest and shut her eyes. "Actually I did. I think. We'll see. I'll have to check it out, of course, but yes."

"So are you going to tell me?"

"You know, we didn't have much breakfast or lunch—Hodges had us out on that long hike this morning—and when we got back to the house I couldn't find much in his fridge. With no Jeffrey, Hodges wasn't much help in the food department."

"I know. Sorry."

"Don't be silly. I enjoyed the weekend. Your friend did warn us that we'd have to fend for ourselves, so that's alright. But do you think we could stop at a nice quiet place, and I could fill you in? I'd rather do that than shout at you while you're driving, especially if you're going to keep the top down and get back on the A-4."

"I can stop here and put the top up."

"No, I like the top down. Let's just find a quiet little place to talk."

"I know just the place. Afterwards, we can go back by country roads and avoid the A-4."

"I'd like that—see the country. So beautiful."

"Do you like Italian?"

"Sure."

"Then you'll like Mio Fiore, down on Market Street. Just a few blocks from here."

"Sounds great."

Mio Fiore was almost deserted, the Sunday rush having dissipated by the late afternoon hour. They found a quiet corner table near the fireplace. Judy ordered Pasta Al Salmone, and Braxton Bruschetta.

"Look's delicious," said Judy. "Want to try a bite of my salmon pasta?"

"Sure. And try a bite of my Bruschetta."

They fed each other a bite.

After a lull in their conversation about the weekend's highlights—including the fox hunt and the croquet game in which Judy and Braxton as a team beat Justin and Elsa while Hodges watched from his lawn chair—Judy said:

"Okay. Well, we didn't get around to the matter of what he knew about Audrey Sterling—at first. He insisted on giving me a history of the house, so of course I just listened. But I was worried you might come back before we got to what he knew about Audrey. So I just took out the pictures I had of Audrey and just showed them to him."

"And...?"

"He took a while, looking at each picture closely. Finally he told me he recognized her."

"Really! How?"

"It seems that Hodges was a buddy of an MP by the name of Alistair Devon. Alistair and some of his friends used to come to Hodge's house and play billiards. Hodges didn't tell me the details of these...."

"Orgies?"

"As I said, he didn't go into more detail, but I got the impression he was telling me only enough to—you know—maybe justify his invitation to us to visit for the weekend."

"Yes, he would have looked foolish if he had to admit he had made the whole thing up about knowing Audrey. So was Audrey one of the guests that night?"

"Apparently so. There were several others there as well, but they left around eleven, leaving just Alistair and Audrey. The three of them stayed up drinking until the early hours, after which Alistair and Audrey went upstairs to bed."

"Let me guess. Same bedroom?"

"Hodges strongly implied that, but didn't...."

"Obviously he would have known, being the host."

"I didn't press him on that particular point, but I'm sure they did."

"Was that the only time her saw her—Audrey, that is?"

"No, he said he had seen them together on several prior occasions when they came to his house for weekends of sex and play."

"He said that? He really opened up for you, then."

"Yes. Hodges said that Devon was smitten with the girl—you can see from the pictures, even though they're just head shots, that she could turn heads, so I wasn't surprised to hear him say that. Hodges claimed that he tried to tell his friend that he must give up the girl, as well as any delusion that he could avoid scandal and ruin and live happily ever after with Audrey. According to Hodges, Alistair just wouldn't listen."

"So Alistair Devon really did know Audrey. I take it that none of these get-togethers took place shortly before the Concorde crash, so how does that help you?"

"In that respect, it doesn't. But it does establish that Audrey was having an affair with a powerful married man, an MP with a position in the government as well."

"But unless you can establish that Devon actually interfaced with Audrey in the twenty-four or so hours of her alleged poisoning, I still don't see how...."

"But Hodges can...and did establish that."

"How on earth could he?"

"According to Hodges, Devon called him on the morning of July 25, 2000. He was in a panic, and said he needed to consult Hodges about what he should do. Apparently Devon had come to his senses by that time, his passion had cooled, and he had resigned himself to giving up Audrey."

"Let me guess. He was soon to find out it was not going to be that simple."

"He told Hodges that he had just met with Audrey in a Paris bistro. Apparently she was on her way to board the Concorde later that afternoon, but insisted on meeting him in Paris before she returned to the states. Since Devon was in Paris for some economic conference when he got some kind of note, or text, from Audrey demanding that he meet with her, he agreed to meet her at the bistro before she left for the airport."

"What was Devon in such a panic about?"

"He said that at their bistro randezvous, Audrey had told him that she was pregnant, and was insisting that Devon divorce his wife and marry her."

"Oh wow. Or...or what...."

"Or...well she didn't need to say anything, but...."

"If he didn't marry or commit to her, the implied threat was that she could drag him through a paternity action in British courts and...."

"You get the picture. Devon had very little assets of his own. His wife controlled the money, and he had belatedly realized that any scandal would not only jeopardize his position as MP, but almost certainly result in divorce, disgrace, and impoverishment."

"Shades of the Profumo affair."

"Profumo?"

"Never mind. Go on."

"So it all confirms what I suspected—that on the morning of July 25, Audrey had gone to Paris in order to meet someone—in this case, Devon."

"I still don't see how that helps you. First of all, even if he did slip Audrey a fentanyl-tainted Nicoban at that Paris bistro, at most that would show opportunity to attempt murder—but in France, not the UK. And I certainly can't help you navigate the French legal and police system, which is a mystery to me anyway."

Judy shook her head. "You don't understand. Yes, if Devon slipped her the tainted Nicoban in Paris that would be the case. But their meeting in Paris establishes that they began an affair long before. Devon could have inserted the Nicoban in Audrey's purse at any time in the weeks before Audrey even went to Paris to board Concorde. So it could have been weeks before she actually attached the one tainted patch to her arm. And it doesn't just show opportunity, it shows motive. What could be a better motive for murder than avoiding—I'll say it again—scandal, disgrace, and impoverishment—a triple whammy as it were."

Braxton downed another glass of wine and waited for Judy to continue what he was beginning to think was a fantastic story. He wanted to tell her that it was all very thin in terms of showing a case for murder, or even attempted murder, against a respected MP of the realm. But he now found himself so enamored of her that he could not bring himself to tell her so or to discourage her in any way."

"You don't think it's sufficient to go to the police do you?" Judy asked.

"Probably not yet," he hedged. "I think you need more." He wanted to add "a lot more," but refrained.

"I agree. That's why I was thinking...."

"What?"

"Well this morning when you went out to the sunroom to smoke your cigar with Hodges, I googled up Alistair Devon. He's retired now—or at least not an MP. He and his wife live most of the time in London, but on weekends he often goes up to his wife's family estate in Scotland to shoot grouse. It's located a few miles outside the small coast town of Crovie in Aberdeenshire, the district in which he had been elected an MP."

"So...?"

"I think I should go up there and interview him. See what I can find out."

"Judy, you've got to be joking! What could you possibly learn from him now? If you approached him on this now after so many years he'd probably take you for some kind of investigative journalist and throw you out—maybe have you arrested."

"I wouldn't go there in that capacity."

"You don't think he'd see through you?"

"Maybe, maybe not. But I think I could get him to talk to me at some point."

"I'm sure you could, but for all the wrong reasons. All right, then let me go with you."

"No, I don't think that would work."

"You'd just go alone?"

"Yes. But maybe you could help me figure out the best way to get up there. Or are you going to desert me now?"

"Of course not. I'll help you as much as I can. I can help you find the right people to report to."

"Thank you. Now, should we be getting back to London?" Judy noticed that he had by now downed several glasses of wine listening to her tale—almost half a bottle in fact."

"Sure, if you like."

"I noticed you've had about a half bottle of wine, or close to it. I've only had a few sips. I'm thinking you should let me drive."

"Really? You want to drive the Spitfire?"

"You don't think I can? I have my international license."

"I don't doubt you can drive just fine, but...."

"Thank you. But you're right. I wouldn't want to drive it on the A-4, which I've heard is a death trap."

"Well, if you really want to. You're sure you can stay on the left? And what will I do after I drop you off at the Savoy?"

"I could drop you off at your flat, and then take a cab myself to the Savoy."

Braxton took his car keys from his pocket and handed them to Judy. "Well, you shouldn't have to do that. But we'll figure it out when we get there." This should be interesting, he thought.

Chapter Forty

Although Judy had finally gotten the knack of manipulating the Spitfire's temperamental gearshift, she noticed that Braxton was fading—no doubt from all the wine he had imbibed while listening to her long dissertation on Hodges' recollections of Audrey Sterling. She soon realized that that she could never find her way to Braxton's flat in Knightsbridge if he was not awake to give her directions—particularly if she was to navigate back country roads rather than the A-4.

She was also discombobulated by the fact that few of the roads featured street signs—a fact which she later learned traced back to the days of World War II when all the street signs were taken down to thwart any Nazi invasion into the interior.

With Braxton still slumped in his passenger seat, she slid into a petrol station, where she stopped and entered the address Braxton had given her into her map app on her iPhone.

Even as she listened to the crisp voice of the woman's voice on the app, in the darkness she managed to miss several country turn-offs. It was almost midnight when she arrived at the parking garage to Braxton's flat.

She now had no choice but to wake him.

"Are we here?" he said groggily as he wakened with a start.

"So what now?" asked Judy with a scolding tone. "I don't think you're ready to drive yet. Should I get a cab?"

"Look, would you like to come up to my flat? Let me make us some coffee, and then I can drive you back to the Savoy."

Judy hesitated, and then shrugged good-naturedly. "I guess I can come up for some coffee. I'm pretty tired myself since Hodges and company got us up so early this morning."

"Great. I can show you my etchings." He extracted himself from the passenger seat, leaned over to fetch Judy's bag, and then went to the boot to retrieve his own bag. "Follow me, M' Lady. And by the way, great driving. A lot of Americans don't even know how to drive a shift."

"Thank you! My dad taught me, though I drove him crazy teaching me. He told me it might come in useful someday—although you're right. Almost nobody in the states can even drive a stick these days."

"Well it definitely came in handy tonight. Sorry for fading out on you. I shouldn't have had so many...."

It's okay, and I'm sorry. If you hadn't, I wouldn't have had an excuse to drive your...well your little Spitfire is quite a little...."

"Spitfire."

"Right. I think I'd love to have one. Do they still make them?"

"Oh, no. Mine's the last year they made them—1980."

By now the pair were walking the two blocks from the parking garage to an Elizabethan building of flats, up an elevator to the third level, and down a long hallway to the door of his flat.

"Entre."

Judy was not sure what to expect of the flat of an up-and-coming young and hungry barrister, but she was pleasantly surprised. Though unmistakably masculine in décor it was tastefully decorated and furnished. A meticulously detailed model sailing vessel graced a mahogany mantelpiece, and drawings of 19th century courtroom scenes and black robed lawyers lined the walls. In the corner was a cabinet with an old style turntable, and 33 rpm records organized in cubby holes. Law books were stacked in piles on an oak desk, and open briefs littered both desk and chairs.

"Sorry it's such a mess," said Braxton as he set down the bags. "As you can see, I didn't expect any company this evening."

"Don't be. It's got character. I like it. What's this ship?" asked Judy.

"Henry VIII's iconic warship, the *Mary Rose*. It was the greatest warship of her day. One day in July of 1545 she sank in the Solent, off the coast of the Isle of Wight. There she sat until she was discovered in 1971, and finally raised in 1982—the most expensive and complex maritime salvage project in history."

"Where is it now?"

"She's now on display in Portsmouth—though you can only see her through windows. For years she had to be saturated with a water and glycol solution. Then in 2016 a museum was built to house her, and you can now view her dry. It's been visited by over half a million people around the world."

"Amazing."

"Would you like to see it?"

"Actually I would." Judy walked over to a shelf filled with several photographs. "Who's this?" she asked picking up a frame.

"That's my mother."

"She's very pretty," she said, picking up another frame. "And this woman?"

Braxton seemed to hesitate to answer.

"Your girlfriend?"

"No. Just someone I knew. Once, a long time ago." He took the frame and placed it back on the shelf.

"Sorry, didn't mean to...."

It couldn't be too long ago, thought Judy. After all, Braxton looked to be no older than his late twenties—perhaps early thirties.

"It's okay. Now, why don't you sit down and relax and I'll go make the coffee."

"Oh, can't I help?"

"Sure, if you want." He led her into a small kitchen with a small table and two chairs. "Here, please sit." He grabbed a packet of coffee beans and began grinding them.

"Tell me, Mr. Barrister," she said playfully, do you really have some etchings to show me, or was that just to lure me into your lair...."

"Not at all," he replied with an impishly innocent smile. "Wouldn't dream of such a thing. Does my humble flat really look like a lair? I really do collect Daumier sketches and drawings.

Bought my first one at a garage sale back in law school for three quid. I even have some originals. Those are the ones on the wall."

"Daumier? I've heard of him. Yes, I saw them. Interesting. Drawings of barristers in action."

Braxton set a cup of coffee in front of Judy and poured a small amount of milk into the cup. "Something like that."

"How did you know I liked my coffee with no sugar and a little milk?"

"I remembered that's how you took it that night at Hodges."

"Hmmm. I didn't know you were that observant."

"One of the things we barristers have to learn—like observing the demeanor of jurors to understand if we're getting through to them during the course of a trial."

"Perhaps I should be careful then. What can you tell about my demeanor right now?"

"Well. For one thing, you seem much more relaxed than when you were driving. But I was impressed at how you were able to navigate those back country roads without my help. And you didn't drift over to the right side of the road even once."

"That did take some concentration, I admit. I thought you were sleeping off your half bottle of wine the whole time."

"Not really. I managed to look over at you several times when you were preoccupied with making the correct turn."

"You had me fooled. I didn't notice."

After a long silence, Braxton said, "You really are very beautiful, you know."

Ignoring his comment, Judy took a few final sips, and then stood up. "Well, let's take a look at those drawings, and then you can take me back to the Savoy."

Realizing he might have prematurely overstepped, Braxton stood awkwardly. "I'm sorry...I didn't mean. I mean...."

"It's okay. Come on. Let's see these Daumiers of yours." She walked back to the living room, and Braxton followed.

Judy pointed to a drawing of a fatuous, bloated monarch sitting on a throne and spitting out equally fatuous palace sycophants. "Is this a Daumier too?"

"Gargantua. Yes, and it's my favorite as a matter of fact. It's a rather—to say the least— unflattering caricature of the King of France. I'm afraid it landed Daumier in prison for six months back in 1832. Daumier's most common theme was the corruption of the law and the incompetence of government. He had a rather negative feeling toward the legal profession which he may have gotten from his time serving as an employee in a bailiff's office."

"He sounds like he was to art what Charles Dickens was to literature."

"An acute observation. I think you're right. And he was most prolific as well, producing over 500 paintings, several thousand lithographs, and 100 or more sculptures."

Judy moved over to the next drawing. "I take it he drew this during his courtroom and barrister period?"

"Actually, that's not a barrister, but a French advocate in a French court. Same black robes of course, but they were not called barristers. Around the mid-1840s, he began drawing his caricatures of the legal profession which he called 'Les Gens de Justice'—a scathing series of drawings about judges, defendants, and corrupt and greedy lawyers. You can view some of the best ones in the Musee d'Orsay in Paris, the National Gallery in Washington, and the Los Angeles County Museum."

"Fascinating. I'd like to see more of his drawings, but perhaps some other time. It's getting pretty late. I should be getting back."

"Of course. I'll get the car and meet you outside."

"No need. I can go with you to the garage. But before we go, maybe you could show me your record collection over there. You don't see many turntables anymore."

"In our digital age, I'm afraid that's true. I'm a bit of a purist when it comes to musical recordings. A vinyl record is much superior to CD's, because they are analog—and music is analog by definition. A digital recording is just a snapshot of sounds strung together at a certain rate. A digital recording cannot capture the complete sound wave, and is therefore much inferior to records. And of course you get the great artwork on the covers of the records that you never see in the CD versions."

"I'm afraid I couldn't tell the difference in sound, but I'll take your word for it. Would you mind if I looked through your record collection?"

"Of course. Be my guest."

Judy began thumbing through the records. "I see you have a lot from the Big Band period. Also, some of the early Beatle albums. Beach boys? Bob Dylan—*Sad Eyed Lady of the Lowlands*—I like that one."

"Yes, he recorded that on vinyl in just one eight hour recording session at four in the morning. No digital version could ever reproduce the sound of this vinyl version, I guarantee you."

Judy smiled and continued thumbing through his trove of records. She pulled out a vinyl single featuring on the cover a picture of a young woman with dark short cropped hair, looking wistfully to the side. She took out the record and turned it over to the B-side. *Hymne a L'amour.*

"Yes, by Edith Pilaf. Do you know her?"

"I think I've heard of her, but can't remember if I've ever heard any of her songs."

Braxton reached over and gently took the record from Judy's hand, carefully replaced it in the sleeve, placed the sleeve back in the jacket, and returned the album to its cubby hole."

"Oh, I'm sorry," she said. "Is that a special one?"

"Uhhh, I only play it once a year."

"There must be a story behind it. Can you tell me?"

Braxton looked down, and Judy saw in his pained expression a side of him that she had not recognized before. "I'm sure it wouldn't be of interest to you."

"I'm willing to listen, but I understand if it's...."

He hesitated, but finally took the record jacket from the cubby and handed it back to Judy. "I could tell you if you like. Can we sit down?"

Judy sat on the sofa. "Of course, but I didn't mean to pry. Please, if it's personal I don't need...."

"No, I'd like to tell you."

Judy sat with jacket in hand and read the jacket, which was in French. "It says this song was first recorded by Edith Pilaf in 1949."

Braxton did not sit, but went to the window, closed it to block out the street noise, then turned to Judy. "I've never told this story to anyone else. But after being with you these past two days.. I think I would like to tell you."

"Only if you want to."

"Well, first a little about Edith Pilaf."

"Yes?"

"Edith's original name was Edith Gassion. She was abandoned by her mother at birth. When her father enlisted in the French army in 1916 to fight in World War I, he left her with his mother who ran a brothel in Bernay, Normandy. She became blind at age three from Keratitis, but several years later her sight returned—which she later claimed was cured by a pilgrimage she made to St. Therese of Lisieux. Around 1929 or so, when she was fourteen her father took her to join his street performances, playing for centimes, where she first began to sing in public. For some years she made money by singing in the streets. A short liaison with a man from her mother's brothel resulted in a daughter named Marcelle, who died two years later from meningitis."

Judy wondered what the background of Edith Pilaf could possibly have to do with Braxton's story, but she did not interrupt.

"Edith was later discovered by a nightclub owner, who because of her small four-foot-eight-inch frame, nicknamed her "Pilaf, meaning 'sparrow'—and the name stuck. Her performances at the nightclub attracted the attention of numerous celebrities, such as Maurice Chevalier, and she soon became the most popular entertainer in France."

"What a story." Nevertheless, as it was getting very late, and Braxton's story seemed to be taking too long to unfold, Judy was tempted to ask him to save his story for another time so that she could get back to her hotel before falling asleep on his couch. She refrained, but given the very late hour and now felt she was fading, began to regret asking him to tell his story.

"It was not until she was thirty-seven" Braxton continued, "that after many failed and painful romances in her life that she finally met Marcel Cernan, the man with whom she wanted to spend the rest of her life. Although they were passionately in love, and their very busy lives limited the time they could spend together, they never missed a chance to be with each other whenever the opportunity presented itself. In October of 1949, Edith was performing to sell out performances in New York City, when Marcel booked a flight from Paris to New York to be with her."

Judy shifted uncomfortably. She had a feeling that the story might now hit too close to home.

"His flight on a Lockheed Constellation crashed in the Azores, killing everyone on board."

Judy put her hand to mouth and thought how she had so recently lost Robin in just the same way.

"Edith was of course devastated, and dealt with the grief that overwhelmed her by writing the love song on the record you are holding."

Judy turned over the jacket. *Hymne a L'amour.*

"Yes. A hymn to love."

"I'd love to hear it. Can we play it?'

Judy now saw tears welling in Braxton's eyes.

"I'd rather not, if you don't...."

Judy wanted to ask why, but instead sat silent, waiting for him to continue if he chose to do so."

"Judy, when I was in my second year of studies at Oxford, I too met the love of my life. She was working in a photo shop in town when I met her, and it was...."

"Don't tell me. Love at first...."

"No not really. I mean not for me. I mean I was attracted to her, yes. We dated for several months, and we were incredibly compatible. We did everything together. But I was just a law student then and barely able to meet my own expenses, and she earned only a pittance at the photo shop, so when she mentioned marriage, I just wasn't ready for that. I didn't think it would be practical. But Mara thought we could...."

Judy turned to the photo on the shelf which she had asked about earlier. "Is that Mara?"

Braxton nodded. Judy got up and went to look at the photo again.

"She said she would get a second job, any job, waiting tables, anything, whatever, until I graduated and would work a second job to support us. She said she'd be happy living in a hovel if we could be together because she didn't care about any of that. She just wanted to be with me. But I still said no. I told her that I cared for her, but that I just didn't think it would be practical to marry until I could give her the life she deserved, and that maybe we should take some time off from each other to think about it."

"You really said that? So what did she do?"

"I never said in so many words that I loved her. She was devastated, of course, and didn't believe that I loved her. She thought I was just making an excuse not to marry her—and maybe I was. She ended up leaving Oxford and going back to live with her parents in Reading."

"You didn't try to persuade her to stay in Oxford?"

"No. I didn't. I let her go."

"But you did love her?"

"I didn't realize how much, but yes, I did. I tried to return to my studies after she left town, but I couldn't concentrate. My grades suffered. I went to all the pubs on weekends with my friends, to parties, tried to forget her. I dated a few of the most attractive women studying at Trinity—my college at Oxford University—to get my mind off Mara, but nothing worked. Whenever I was with these other women, I found myself thinking of Mara."

Given Braxton's still boyish good looks, Judy did not doubt that Braxton could have had any woman he wanted, and doubtless still could. So that part of this story rang true. But she was still waiting to hear how Edith Pilaf and *Hymne a L'amour* related to his relationship with Mara.

"To be honest, I wasn't willing to—you know, live in hovel—or be distracted from my career path. But the more I thought about Mara, the more I realized that I would never find anyone like her again. Finally, just before graduation of my final year. I gave her a call. She was still living with her parents. I apologized profusely, of course, and really expected her to tell me to bugger off after the way I treated her. You can see from her picture that I had no doubt that she too could have had her pick of suitors in the meantime."

"Yes, she is very pretty."

"So did she tell you to—you know, bugger off?"

"Well, she was of course surprised that I called, and did tell me that she should tell me to bugger off."

"But she didn't"

"I told her, in my winsome way, 'look I'll make a deal with you. If you will promise to never again tell me to bugger off, I'll marry you in six weeks, the day after my graduation.'"

"Really! And what did she say?"

"She said she had a counteroffer."

"A counteroffer?"

"She said she would accept my offer of marriage if we didn't have to wait until graduation, and she could come down the following weekend and get married."

"Wow. And what did you say?"

"I was elated, and I said without any hesitation, 'I accept.' After that, we just talked the rest of the night. I told her how miserable I was after she left Oxford. She confided in me as well, how miserable she had been during our separation as well. Then she said that she had written a letter to me shortly after she had left, but had never sent it. I asked her if she still had it—that I would like to read it—but she said that no, she had burned it the very next day. But then she said a few weeks after that, that a girlfriend of hers had given her a record for her birthday, and that she would send it on to me as a substitute for her letter since the words—though in French—would best express what she had written in her letter."

Hymne a L'amour.

Braxton nodded. There was another prolonged silence before he said:

"The next day, Mara drove from Reading to be with me. I waited all day for her to come, sitting on the step of the church of St. Aladtec's. As soon as she arrived we were going to go to the marriage registry to get our license."

Braxton looked down, and she saw that he could hardly get out his next words:

"I tried to call her on her cell, but there was no answer. Finally, that evening I called her parents. I was afraid Mara had had second thoughts. But she had not. On the way down on the A-4 to meet me, a car from the opposite lane jumped the divider and hit Mara's car head on. She died instantly."

Judy saw his eyes well and she froze. "I'm so sorry, Braxton."

He put up his hands. "So now you understand."

"I do. I do."

"You can't, I'm afraid. I received her *Hymne a L'amour* the next day. And today is the anniversary of the day I received it...."

"Oh my God. I'm so sorry. Do you know the words of the *Hymne*?"

Braxton's voice broke. "I don't speak French, and to this day I've never tried to have someone translate them for me, but I can feel the words from the music, which I listen to on the anniversary of her death."

"You should never have come with me to Newbury this weekend. If I had known how important this day was for you...."

"You had no way to know," he said, struggling to regain his composure.

"Look, on this day...I speak some French, a little anyway. Let's listen to the words together, and I'll translate. And after that, perhaps you would listen to a story I have to tell as well. You are not alone in the grief which you suffer."

Judy handed the record jacket to him.

"Perhaps it is time," he said as he withdrew the record and carefully placed it on the turntable. Judy sat on the couch while Braxton sat on an adjacent chair. The two listened as the *Hymne's* soaring theme of love filled the room as Judy translated, skipping a few words she could not translate:

The sky can fall,
The earth can open up beneath me,
But I wouldn't care,
If you love me.

I would go to the ends of the world,
If you asked me to.

I would steal a fortune,
If you asked me to.

I would renounce my country,
I would renounce my friends,
If you asked me to.

If one day life tears me away from you,
It wouldn't' matter if you love me.

For several minutes neither spoke, the eyes of each wet. When the song was over, the two sat immobile while the record began scratching as it revolved around the turntable.

Finally, Braxton got up to retrieve the record and place it in the jacket.

Judy said, "I can see why you never thought you needed to hear the words. The music, her voice, that haunting theme said it all. It seems to me I've heard what must be a poplar modern version of it, maybe *If You Love Me, Really Love Me*?"

"I know only a few words of French, but enough to know that that's a totally incorrect translation of the words to the main melodic strain—as you have just confirmed with what I can only assume is a far more accurate translation. The modern and English attempts to steal the *Hymn's* most electric melodic strain are all rubbish. I would allow for only one exception—Celine Dion singing the *Hymne* in 2015 at the American Music Awards—she had the entire audience in tears—and of course she sang in French since she understood that French words of love can never be adequately translated into English."

"Maybe I shouldn't have tried."

"You provided the subtitles to Edith Pilaf's words and music. Thank you. Now, I would truly like to hear your story too. Please tell me."

"I don't feel right. Today should be your day—your anniversary—and I shouldn't intrude."

"No, Judy. I want to hear it."

Judy nodded and lay down. With her own voice breaking, she lay down and told it: how the love of her life, Robin, had also died the night before he was to return home to her—from the crash of a commuter plane flying from Maine in the middle of a snowstorm. It seemed to be too sad to be true—that Edith Pilaf, Braxton, and Judy all shared a common bond of grief and loss under similar circumstances in their life—a grief to which the haunting melodic strain of Edith's *Hymn to Love* had united them in a spiritual embrace.

"Judy, I had no idea."

They sat in silence for some time, listening to the sounds of the street outside the windows as both now lay back and closed their eyes. Finally, he rose to look for his car keys, having forgotten where he put them. It took several minutes to find them as he looked in both his bedroom and kitchen. When he came back to the sitting room he saw the Judy had now drifted into a state of soft and steady breathing. He tenderly picked her up in his arms, carried her to his bedroom, and placed her on his bed. He then carefully removed her sandals, and covered her with a light blanket.

"Good night," he said with a soft whisper.

Chapter Forty-One

As the morning sun peeked through the shutters of Braxton's bedroom, Judy's eyes fluttered and she awoke with a start.

Still wearing the shorts and T-shirt she had worn the previous day, she rose in a daze. Barefoot and disheveled, she shuffled out the bedroom to the kitchen.

"Good morning, lazy bones!" said Braxton as he stopped grinding his coffee beans and turned to see Judy standing in the doorway. "Top of the morn'n to yeh, lassie. Now can I rustle up some coffee and scones for yeh?"

Judy, still dazed, shook her head. "What time is it?"

Braxton, looked at his watch and, reverting to his barrister's King's English, said "It is now 7:30—no make that precisely 7:32. How did you sleep?"

"I can't believe I pooped out like that. What time was it when I did that?"

"About 3:30 or so—I think. After putting you to bed, I conked out myself on the sofa."

"So sorry, but thank you."

"Don't be. When grief is triggered it can be exhausting. In this case of last night, for both of us."

Judy nodded.

"Look, sit down. Coffee's almost up. We can talk about something else."

Judy took a deep breath and sat. "I can't believe I didn't wake up when you took me to your bedroom."

"You were out cold. I'm sure that driving the Spitfire through unfamiliar back roads at night must have been tiring. But you did me a great favor in doing the driving. I don't think I would have made it back on my own—at least not in one piece."

"I still can't believe it. I must look a fright."

"To the contrary. You look...."

Judy cut him off. "And I enjoyed the countryside before it got dark. I've really got to get one of those frisky little Spitfires. They're amazing."

"Anytime you want to drive it...."

"I might just take you up on that. Now, you said the coffee's almost up?"

"Yes ma'am. Coming right up." He poured two cups and sat. "So what are your plans today?"

"I've really got to get going up to Scotland to interview... interview...."

"Yes, you said. Alistair Devon."

"You still think I'm crazy don't you?"

"No, but you said that your information was that he generally lives with his wife in London, and only goes up to shoot grouse at his estate in Scotland on the weekends. Today's Monday, so what's the point in going up there now?"

"That's true. In that case I should probably wait until next week and use this week to track down that Viscount I told you about—the one who had dinner with Audrey at the Savoy the night before she left for Paris."

"Do you know where to find... this Viscount?"

"Yes, I have an address. Just a minute." Judy returned to the bedroom where her purse was on a chair. She took out her notebook, and brought it back to the kitchen. "Let's see. According to my information, 'Viscount' Jeremy-Heathcote-Fox-McKenzie lives at 816 Bottlescroft Close in Croydon. Do you know where that is?"

"I know Croydon. It's in South London, about nine miles or so from Charring Cross. Not one of London's better neighborhoods."

"Really? I'm surprised. I mean he is a Viscount."

"That title doesn't carry much weight these days. They're a dime a dozen, and many of them are not very prosperous—though some do try to leverage their title for whatever economic advantage they can get when given the opportunity."

"I guess I can get a cab. I'd better get back to the Savoy first to freshen up and change clothes."

"Let me take you back to the Savoy to do that. Then I can take you out to Croydon to find this Viscount of yours."

"I'll take you up on getting me back to the hotel, but before I try to track down this Viscount I need to review some notes and touch base with my contacts back in the states. That will take a while—most of the rest of the day probably—so I think I'll wait until tomorrow to go on my Viscount-hunt."

"Okay. Why don't I pick you up tomorrow morning then and take you out to Croydon?"

"Don't you have, you know, barrister work tomorrow?"

"Actually, I have my own assistant in pupilage these days—a sweet girl, very ambitious and willing to do everything I ask her. I have no trials set for this week, just a hearing on Thursday, and she could handle that for me if I asked her. She'd be thrilled to do a hearing on her own."

"Really? You're not just saying that?"

Braxton now reproduced one of Judy's face down eyes-up expressions. "No I'm not, Battersea Scouts honor. One nice thing about being a barrister is that we can make our own hours. And I can use the break."

"Battersea? Well, I won't ask. But okay, if you really want to take me, why don't you come to the Savoy tomorrow morning and I'll treat you to breakfast at Kaspars and introduce you to a quite beautiful black cat."

"Yes, I've met him. Shall we say 8 A.M., then?"

"Sure. Now, I just need to find my sandals, and you can take me to the Savoy."

Chapter Forty-Two

Back in her room at the Savoy, Judy sat at her room desk and consulted her notes, compiling a list of the calls she needed to make. The first was to Jake at NXR. Since he was now working for Judy full time, he had given her a number where he could be reached 24/7.

"Hi Judy." he answered after the first ring.

"Hi Jake. Listen, I'm still in London and have some information for you."

"Of course, Judy. What have you found out that I haven't been able to discover hunkered down here in our nerve center?"

"I have confirmation that Audrey did in fact meet with Alistair Devon—a member of parliament at the time and a subcabinet minister in the government—in Paris on the morning of July 25, 2000, in a small bistro."

"How on earth did you get that information?"

"Don't ask. It's the kind of information that's difficult to obtain if you're limited to digital research. As I told you before, we had obtained evidence through our sources that Devon probably had an affair with Audrey, but there was no way to ascertain where they planned to meet, or if in fact that they did actually meet in Paris."

"Well, they did meet. I got that information first hand from a barrister at the Quadrangle Chambers here in Westminster by the name of Michael Hodges. It seems that Alistair called Hodges immediately after meeting with Audrey on the morning of July 25. He was in a state of panic because Audrey had insisted on meeting him that morning—the meeting must have been planned by a phone call, which would have been impossible for you to trace after so many years."

"And...?"

"According to Hodges, Devon said that Audrey had told him she was pregnant, and was pressuring him for a commitment to marry her after her divorce from Ronald Sterling was finalized."

"She was blackmailing him?"

"Not in so many words, but of course she didn't have to. She mentioned that if he couldn't give her a commitment, she might be forced to bring a very public paternity action against him—and that was apparently enough to scare the heebie-jeebies out of Devon."

"I imagine it would. He was probably right to be concerned. If he was in the government that kind of publicity would have been a disaster for him."

"Not just for the scandal it might cause, but also financially, since it was likely that Devon's wife would divorce him—and she had control of all the assets, by inheritance mostly."

"All right, so he had a motive to get Audrey out of the way. But if it was Audrey's pregnancy that constituted the threat to Alistair, he didn't know about that until she actually told him on the morning of July 25."

"According to Hodges, Alistair was anxious to get out of the relationship in one piece even before Angela told him about the pregnancy. So he had plenty of motive to get rid of her even before hearing about the pregnancy and her talk of a paternity action. That just drove him over the edge. If he already had a fentanyl-laced Nicoban in his possession, ready to use if he needed to—but was reluctant to hide them in one of her packs if there was any chance of getting out of the affair in one piece—the pregnancy threat would have been enough to lose all inhibitions to murder. He had too much at stake, and the method he chose must have seemed foolproof."

"Judy, I can't deny that he certainly had a motive, and by meeting her within hours of the time she was poisoned—as you know, we have confirmation of that—he also had opportunity and means. But that still leaves us far short of proving that he, and not someone else, poisoned her. You see that, don't you?"

"Yes, I know we need more. Which brings me to my next assignment for you—which should not be difficult. I plan to go see Devon. You had told me before that he often went on weekends to his family estate in Scotland—somewhere near Aberdeenshire. But I don't want to go on a wild goose chase—go all the way up there and find he's not there."

"Well, we have people who have a very low-tech way to find out when he's going up there."

"Really? How?"

"Simple. We can get his number—that's not a problem—so we just have people who can call his number on some pretext or another. They're quite skilled in getting that kind of information."

"Okay, I won't ask. But if you could give me the information, including directions to Devon's estate, before this coming weekend that would be helpful. I was also planning to make a visit to our Viscount—Heathcote-Fox—whatever his name is. I was going to try to see him tomorrow morning sometime. You already gave me his address. It's not too far from where I am, but I'd just as soon not go all the way out there if he's not going to be there."

"I'll try to get you that info right away—it won't be foolproof, though."

"Whatever you can do. Also, have you had any success in checking the database of the visitors to the Concorde lounge during the late morning of July 25, 2000? If Audrey met with anyone that morning in the lounge, they would also have had the opportunity to poison Audrey."

"Yes, we have been able access the database showing visitors to the lounge on that morning. We've deleted from our list all those who ultimately boarded the Concorde, however, since none of them are alive today. So we are now focusing on the names of those who visited the lounge that morning, but did not board Concorde, and trying to check if any of them had any connection to Audrey. Anything else?"

I'm sure this is a longshot, and I wouldn't want you to spend too much time on it..."

"Shoot. If it can be done, we can do it."

"Well, that's the thing. I don't know if it can be done. Could you call RFL Labs and ask if there's any chance that they could determine if Audrey was pregnant? It's really not critical that I get that info, but if they could it would confirm the story that Hodges told me."

"Oh wow, yeah, I'm sure that would be tough. To be honest, I was amazed that they were able to determine Audrey was poisoned. Pregnancy—that may be a bridge too far."

"Just a shot."

"Expense not an issue?"

"Jake, we've talked about this."

"Yeah, you have. It's just that…well, with the people we service, expense is always an issue…and I guess we're just not used to…I mean…."

Judy did not want to explain that for the first time in her life, money was not an issue. She couldn't even imagine how she could ever spend what Timothy had left her. Nor did she want to explain why she was pursuing a matter which—at best—might only succeed in finding evidence which would be admissible in Brenda Masterson's wrongful death action against Ronald Sterling. But she had now decided what she really wanted to do with Timothy's largess. She wasn't interested in buying a mansion on the Riviera, or retiring to a life of ease and luxury—though she had had no choice in honoring Timothy's request that she maintain Timothy's Catalina home, boat, and plane. She also planned to make even more generous contributions to worthy causes beyond the charitable foundation she had established with Amber, and the Institute of Justice she planned to establish on the foundations of her law firm in New York. What drove her now was the prospect of pursuing justice by solving a mystery. Though she now acknowledged to herself that she was trying to solve the mystery of Audrey's death for its own sake, and not just to find evidence in Amber's case, she didn't feel like trying to explain it to Jake.

"Jake, for the last time, please. Just do what you need to do to get the information I need. I trust you."

"Right. I'll get you the info you need by this evening—just don' hold your breath on the pregnancy thing."

I won't. I don't know that it would be that helpful anyway, even if she wasn't pregnant. The point is that she told Devon that she was, which would have alarmed him whether she was actually pregnant or not."

"Got it, Judy. But could I ask you just one more question?"

"Go on."

"I thought that the thrust of our investigation was to get evidence that Ronald Sterling murdered his wife Angela, and perhaps his former wife Audrey. But now, you seem to be considering the possibility that Ronald didn't murder his wife at all—that maybe it was this Alistair Devon character, or the Viscount."

"As I said, if the evidence shows that Ronald didn't murder either of his two wives, then so be it. I just want to find the truth. I know Amber well enough that she would not want to pursue the case against Ronald if I find proof that he is innocent, in which case she will so advise her client."

"I understand."

"So right now I want to focus on the four people who could have poisoned Audrey: her husband, of course, who had both motive and opportunity; Alistair Devon who also had a motive in spades, as well as opportunity; Viscount Jeremy Heathcote-Fox-McKenzie, who we know met with Audrey the night before she took the train to Paris on the morning of July 25—though I've yet to discover any motive—perhaps I'll find one when I meet with him; and finally our mystery visitor to the Concorde lounge on the day of the crash—though we have yet to discover if he or she even exists."

"It's your money, Judy. I'll get you the info on Devon and the Viscount within the next several hours."

"Thanks, Jake."

Judy next called Amber.

"Hey girl. How's jolly old England?" said Amber after just the first ring.

"Hi sister. Actually I'm starting to enjoy it. I found another suspect, a former MP by the name of Alistair Devon, who had an affair with Audrey, and had motive to get rid of her to avoid a scandal. Tomorrow morning I hope to track down Viscount McKenzie who had dinner with Audrey—supposedly her distant cousin, but that remains to be seen—the night before she went to Paris. Still waiting to see what Jake can find out about a possible visitor to the Concorde lounge and may also have had contact with her."

There was a long pause before Amber said, "Judy, you are keeping your eye on the ball, aren't you? I mean you're supposed to be finding evidence that Ronald Sterling poisoned Audrey, and thus obtain evidence we can use to show that it was therefore more likely that he killed his second wife, Angela. I'm not sure you're helping me by spending a lot of time looking for other possible suspects."

Judy sighed. "I know, Amber. But this Alistair Devon had at least as much motive as Ronald Sterling to get rid of Audrey. It makes sense to eliminate him as a suspect, if nothing else. I'm sure Brenda would much rather that you find the real killer of her mother, whether it's her step-father or not. Anyway, at the moment, I can't do much to find evidence against Ronald until Jake and his crew are able to track his movements in the days before Audrey was poisoned. I hope to hear from him soon on that."

"Of course. I'm sorry. I know you're doing everything you can. Let's change the subject. So it's been all work and no play since you got to London?"

When Judy didn't immediately reply, Amber said, "Judy?"

"Well, yes and no."

"Meaning?"

"I have met someone—a barrister—who's offered to help me navigate the British justice system if I gather enough evidence to report a murder—or at least attempted murder—that took place on British soil."

"Let me guess—he's good looking, and already fallen madly in love with you."

"He is something of a hottie as a matter of fact, and I do think we have found a common bond...."

"Don't tell me—he's just a friend, who within a day or so of meeting you, is going to drop everything to help you navigate...."

"What can I say, big sister? I'm accepting all the help I can get."

"And so you should. You know I'm just teasing."

"I know, but now is my turn to tease. What's happening with you and Martin?"

This time it was Amber who was slow in answering.

"Amber? Tell me."

"Okay, we have gone out a few times. And yeah, I think he is trying to rekindle things with me."

"Enough to make him cough up those transcripts of emails between Angela and Ronald that Martin was able to extract from their computers that he seized?"

"As a matter of fact, he did say he would make them available to me by next week. He says he still needs time to transcribe all of them, and wants to give me a complete set."

"Hmmm. More than he promised me, but that's great. Will you forward them to me as soon as you get them?"

"Of course. Listen, gotta run—client is waiting for me. Keep in touch, girl."

"K, talk soon."

Judy's final call was to Annie Brockhurst at Hammond and Alexander.

"Hi Annie, this is Judy."

"Judy! So glad you called. I was worried. I hadn't heard from you for a while."

"Yes, sorry. I'm working on a case for my friend Amber, and I'm in London now."

"Lucky you! Well, we hired two great criminal law litigators—Howard Wilkinson, and Jamie Pierce. Both have a great reputation for their work on death penalty cases. Howard has already gotten a referral from the governor on an appeal."

"Great. I take it you already believe the conviction was wrongful. Any word yet on changing the name of the firm to Institute of Justice?"

"Well, we tried, but it turns out that name is already taken. I have an idea for several other names."

"Okay, text them to me. You worked out the salaries for everyone, including yourself?"

"Yes, I'll send you those as well for your approval. Of course we couldn't manage those salaries without your contributions to the kitty."

"I'll pay whatever we need to get the best counsel. But I'm counting on you to screen the cases for unjust convictions."

"Yes. Of course I'll send you every case we get for your approval."

"For now, you can do the final approval—at least until I've finished the case I'm working on, which is where all my attention is focused right now."

"Will do, Judy. Any word on a possible merger with Amber's firm?"

"No, but I will get right on that once I'm finished with this case I'm working on now. But send me the new salary schedule. I do need to approve that."

"You'll get it by tomorrow."

"Thanks, and I'll be in touch soon as well."

Judy now closed up her notebook, took a shower, and set her alarm for 7 A.M. the next morning.

Chapter Forty-Three

Early the next morning Judy took her seat at Kaspars and sipped on her freshly squeezed grapefruit juice and freshly brewed cappuccino. Moments later she saw Braxton at the entrance, and waived him over.

"Good morning," he said, beaming as she sat. "Beautiful view, both here at the table and out the window. I haven't been to the Savoy for ages. So have you ordered yet?"

"No," she said, "just ordered my cappuccino and juice. I'm not a big breakfast person, but I hear that they serve freshly baked oatmeal muffins. I might also try Bircher Muesli with berries. But please, order what you like. My treat this morning."

Braxton picked up the menu. "Well, in that case…Ah, they have Cumberland sausages—love those—semi-braised vine tomatoes—love those too—baked beans, and Portobello mushrooms."

"Baked beans?" Judy asked.

"No English breakfast would be without it."

"Interesting. They also have Asian entrees, if you like dim-sum with fry-toasted seaweed and onsen egg."

"Thank you, princess, but I think I'll stick with our traditional English breakfast this morning." He looked around the dining room. "Now, where is that famous cat I always hear about?"

"Kaspar? Oh he's here." Judy pointed to the far corner table next where the famous black ceramic cat was perched on a high chair looking dubiously out at the early morning breakfast guests."

"Yes, I see," he said turning around. Wouldn't be Kaspars without…."

"Kaspar…."

"True enough. People come from all over the world to see the little fella." He turned back to Judy. "Did I mention that you look radiant this morning? You must have gotten your beauty sleep last night."

"Actually, not enough I'm afraid. It was past midnight with calls back to the states, and then I couldn't get to sleep until…probably well after two."

"The jet lag still lingers?" he asked after waiting for Judy to order her muffin and muesli. He then ordered his English breakfast.

"I think I'm over that, or at least I think I am," she replied. "No, it was something else that kept me up."

"Problems back in your law office?"

"No, I think all's well there. I did get some updated information from my investigative agency, some more leads on the suspect in the Audrey matter, but we can talk about that later."

"So…what kept you up?"

"I was thinking about last Sunday night."

"Remarkable. I've been thinking about that too."

"I'm so sorry I conked out like I did. I'm so embarrassed."

"I told you, don't be. I was glad you were there."

"I was thinking about the loss each of us has suffered. No one else can understand the emotional depth of such loss unless they themselves have experienced it."

"True enough. I've only shared mine with you."

"And mine with you, though of course my friends know of my loss."

Braxton nodded.

"I couldn't get that refrain from the *Hymne a L'amour* out of my head last night. I kept thinking of how Edith Pilaf coped with her loss—by writing that beautiful song. But I was wondering—was she able to move on after some time?"

Braxton shook his head. "Not really. She fell into drink, and some say, drugs as well. She died some years later at age forty-seven."

"Oh my. I hope we can cope better than that. Poor thing."

"That wasn't the half of it. She was denied a funeral mass by Cardinal Feltin because of her 'lifestyle', including having been brought up in brothel. But that didn't stop hundreds of thousands of mourners at her funeral procession in Paris, and at the ceremony at the cemetery. It was said that it was the only time since World War II that all traffic in Paris came to a complete stop. It wasn't until fifty years later, in 2013, that the Catholic Church finally relented and gave her a memorial Mass."

"Fifty years too late, it sounds like."

"A Russian astronomer named a small planet, Pilaf 3772, in her honor."

Judy finished her cappuccino, and then said, "I want my legacy in memory of Robin to be the establishment of a law firm, dedicated to uncovering wrongful convictions, a place from which injustices can be righted. Finding who poisoned Audrey will be the first case my new law firm will resolve."

"I wish I had an equally worthy legacy to leave in memory of Mara. Of course, I do want to help you, as I promised.

"Thank you."

"So we're off to interview this Viscount out in Croydon?"

"I just need you to take me there and stay in the vicinity. It could be a very short visit. But I did learn from my investigator last night that he should be home today."

"I can't imagine how your investigator would possibly know that, but he sounds amazing. If I only had an investigative source like yours I don't think I'd ever lose a case—and I've lost my share of them."

Judy started to explain that the exorbitant cost of the investigations she had commissioned from NXR and RFL might be out of proportion to any desired result. But then she realized that if she did so, it might inevitably lead Braxton to ask questions about her financial sources. She did not want her wealth to interfere with whatever might come of her new partnership with Braxton—though romance was the furthest thing from her mind—so she contented herself with changing the subject:

"I hope my interview with the Viscount won't take too long, so after you bring me back to the hotel you'll still be able to return to work at chambers. I've kept you from your job too long already, and I will have plenty to do during this week before making the trek up to Scotland next weekend."

"Not at all, Judy. As I told you, I'm ready for a break. I was hoping you might let me take you to Portsmouth to see the *Mary Rose*."

"I don't know about that, Braxton. I need to call my office in New York and check on some other cases back home. I've got a lot to do."

He shrugged. "Sure. I understand."

Judy looked at her watch. "I'll think about it. Are you almost finished with that amazing breakfast? Would you like anything else?"

"Nope, I've had too much already. But let me take care of the check."

"You treated me to dinner Sunday night. So breakfast is on me."

Braxton sighed. "If you say so. While you take care of the check, I'm going to go over and say hi to Kaspar."

Chapter Forty-Four

The open top Spitfire came to a stop in front of long row houses along Bottlescroft Close.

"My GPS says we're here, but I'm not sure which one is 815. I don't see any street numbers," Judy said as she scanned up and down the road.

"You just have to know where to look," said Braxton as he pointed to a row house two houses down and to the right."

"I see it now."

"Should I pull the car up to it?"

"No, stay here until I check to see if he's home. I don't want to let him see you out in front if he answers the door. If he's not home, just come and pick me up and I'll try another time. If he's home and lets me in, you could just go somewhere and wait until I call you on my mobile, but it could be a while"

"Check. Good luck."

Judy pulled the briefcase from the back of her seat, walked up the sidewalk toward the somewhat rundown row house that Braxton had identified as 815, and cautiously tapped on the door knocker. Getting no response, she tapped again more forcefully. She was about to give up when an elderly woman with broom in hand came to the front door of the adjacent townhouse.

"He's out back, missy," the woman called out, "but I think he heard you. He's coming!"

Judy waved. "Thank you!" Several minutes later, a late middle-aged man with a mustache like that of an Agatha Christie character, opened the door.

"Yes, my dear, may I help you? I'm afraid I'm not in a position to buy anything, but...."

"Hello," Judy interrupted, "Are you Jeremy...." She consulted her iPhone.

"Yes, indeed, Miss. I am Viscount Heathcote-Fox-McKenzie. How might I help you? I would be most pleased to help a pretty young woman such as yourself."

"Thank you, Viscount, sir." Judy gushed. "Then I am at the right place. I'm not here to sell anything, sir. My name is Judy Alexander, and I was a very close friend of Audrey Sterling, who died back in 2000 in the Concorde accident. I understand that...."

"Oh yes my dear! Terrible tragedy it was! She was my American cousin. Such a tragedy it was! Such a long time ago. Such a tragedy!"

"Audrey used to tell me so much about you, and well... it's been so long I know, but this is my first time to visit England, and I thought I might come and visit...."

"Of course, my dear. Come in, come in! Any friend of Audrey...wonderful girl, and such a beauty too...such a tragedy...."

"Thank you." Judy turned before entering so that Braxton could see that see she had been invited in and that he could leave.

Jeremy led her into his sitting room. "Please sit, my dear. And we can talk about dear Audrey. But first, what can I get for you. Tea, or I have some fine Bourbon...Blanton's Gold Edition... or...."

"Thank you, the tea would be wonderful. Thank you."

"Of course, of course. Please make yourself at home. I'll be right back." He retreated to the kitchen.

Judy sat, but when several moments went by and Jeremy had not returned she rose to look at the framed photographs on the wall. She was still looking when Jeremy returned with a pot of tea and a plate of biscuits.

"I'm sure you will like these Milk Chocolate Digestives and Cadbury fingers," he said as he laid the tray down on the cocktail table. "I see you are looking at the photograph of the Chelsea Flower Show. The Queen was there, and there I am with...so many persons of title. Did I mention I am a Viscount? We were all invited, you know...."

"Yes, I see. Very impressive!"

Jeremy proceeded to give Judy a tour of all the photographs displayed around the sitting room, all of which showed a proud Viscount Jeremy in company with one aristocrat or another.

When the tour was completed, both sat while Jeremy poured the tea."

"Now I must ask you—Judy is it?—how were you able to find me? Of course I've lived here all my life, so Audrey must have given you my address."

"Actually, no, I must confess. Though Audrey did often speak of you, it was not she who gave me your address. But since the terrible accident I have had occasion several times to visit Audrey's sister Madeleine who lives now in Las Vegas. She has kept a number of mementoes of her sister, and when I mentioned to her that I would be making a visit to England, she looked through one of Audrey's old address books and found your address—and so here I am."

"How remarkable! And I am so pleased you did so. Are you a relative of Audrey's? I must say that you are quite as beautiful as Audrey, so I'm thinking you must share some genes with her."

"Oh no. As I said we were just close friends. We were classmates at university, UCLA. I understand you and Audrey were second cousins or some such."

"Some such, indeed. I'm afraid Audrey and I may have exaggerated our blood ties a bit, though we did think it quite possible we were related, having a common middle name, and her mother having so many blood relatives here in England."

"So you were actually just friends then?"

"Yes, perhaps a bit more—at least I wanted to think so. She was so very beautiful you understanding. We met at a charitable event down in Chelsea. She had a husband then, of course, but he had left her alone while he attended some business functions. We hit it off, and I offered to show her the sights. I was heartbroken when she had to return to the states, but we kept up an email correspondence for the next couple of years. You never know who might read those missives, so we kind of made up the story that we were… you know…."

"Cousins. I understand."

"So when she came back to London several years later—without her husband this time—I was of course elated. But she soon made it clear that we would have to remain cousins—and not of the kissing variety."

"Did that very much distress you?"

"It did, at first, of course. My wife died when she was very young, and I was lonely. Our email correspondence is what kept me going for those two years before she came back to London back in 2000. But I was just happy to be with her, and it was just as well. I could never have provided for her in the way she deserved—as you can see from my very humble abode here in Croydon."

"But wasn't she about to be divorced from a very wealthy husband?"

"Yes, and there was a time when men of title, divested of their wealth by the crushing taxes of our welfare state, could maintain their status in society by marrying rich American heiresses. But no longer. No, I accepted that I could never hope to marry such a beauty as Audrey was. But I cherished our friendship to the end."

Judy could see the tears well in Jeremy's eyes as he spoke. Were they real, she wondered? Did he really accept his status as a second non-kissing cousin? Or was he capable of alleviating his pain of unrequited love by engaging in an unspeakable act of murder?

Judy sipped her tea. "Do you have a picture of Audrey?"

"Oh, indeed, I have many. Would you like to see them?"

"Perhaps just one."

"Come," he said. He led Judy to his study where an eight by ten photo of Audrey held a center location on his otherwise cluttered desk.

Judy took the picture in her hand. "She definitly was a beauty—kissing cousin or no. You must have been devastated when...."

"You can't imagine. It was many months—no years—before I was able to recover from her death."

"I'm so sorry."

"But she shall always remain in my most precious memories... and in my heart."

Judy looked at Jeremy intently. Were the tears real? She wondered.

They returned to the sitting room, and Judy changed the subject, mentioning that she hoped to visit the *Mary Rose* before returning to the states. After another hour, she rose.

"Well, Viscount. You were very kind to see me. I suppose I must now get back to my hotel."

"Where are you staying?"

"At the Savoy."

"Ah, the Savoy. What a wonderful hotel. You know I have never been there since the night I had dinner with Audrey the night before she went to Paris. It was a night I shall never forget."

"You had dinner with her there the night before she left for Paris?" Judy sat back down.

"Why yes. I did. Why do you ask?"

"Viscount, I wonder if I might ask you what might seem like a silly question. Do you happen to remember whether, on that night, Audrey happened to be smoking cigarettes?'

Jeremy's expression seemed to be one of genuine surprise at the question. "Why I can't say I really remember. I know she was a smoker, just as I was. Back then a lot more people smoked than today. Why do you ask?"

Judy shrugged. "Oh, no reason, I guess. It's just that I knew that Audrey was trying to quit about that time—struggling with it, I think—and I was just curious whether she had managed to break the habit by that time."

"I'm sorry, I'm afraid that's just not something that I have saved in my memory banks. I remember Kaspar the cat, though. Is he still there at the corner table at Kaspars?"

"Oh, indeed he is. I returned his meows just this morning as a matter of fact."

"You are a charming young lady. Well, please give him my regards."

"I certainly shall. And now, I know I've taken up most of your day."

"Not at all. Please call on me anytime you wish. May I call you a cab? I'm afraid I don't have a car or I would be delighted to drive you back to the Savoy."

"Oh no. I have a friend who is picking me up." Judy took out her mobile and texted Braxton. "He should be here in a few minutes."

"Well, how did it go?" asked Braxton as Judy maneuvered herself into the Spitfire.

"I don't know. I really don't know. Can we talk about it? Is there a quiet place we can go before we head back?"

"I don't know Corydon that well. I think I took a pint once at the Dog and Bull—should be close to here if you want to try that."

"I find the pubs a bit loud. Could we find a quiet place?" Judy pulled out her smart phone to google. "Tons of Italian restaurants, but we had Italian the other night. How about this one—the Little Bay Croydon. Modern European, it says. I'm reading the reviews...Here's one that says 'book now for romantic date night'...but later in the evening it says they have live opera...I wonder how they manage that...Here's some more reviews: 'loved the theatrical décor'...loved the Crushed Avocado with Poached Egg...great atmosphere, we were unsure about the opera singer, but she was infrequent enough not to disturb our conversation…guess that answers my question…one more: 'a hidden gem'…so cute and medieval'…'the baked aubergine was fantastic'…What's aubergine? Some kind of British dish?"

"No idea."

"Sounds interesting. Want to try it?"

"Sure, why not?"

"Do you like opera?"

"Not my favorite…I liked *Carmen*, though, and *Phantom of the Opera*."

"So did I. Not sure that's the kind of opera they're talking about, though. Want to try it?"

"Sure, why not?"

"All right. I've got the directions. Turn right here."

After a satisfying dinner—mussels in red wine for Judy and lamb rump for Braxton—Judy was ready to talk about her interview with the Viscount.

"Before I tell you my thoughts, though, promise me one thing," said Judy.

"What?"

"Just one glass of wine for you tonight. We wouldn't want to repeat what happened on Sunday night."

"Why not?"

"Silly. I'm waiting for your promise."

"Okay, I promise," he said sheepishly, as he guzzled the last drops of his one—now rationed—glass of wine. "Now tell me about the interview."

"He definitely had a motive. He was in love with Audrey, but she didn't return the feelings. Just wanted to be his…."

"The friend thing…guys always hate that."

"Yes, but I really can't see him doing anything as evil as poisoning her. I think he really cared for her, and can't imagine him doing anything to harm her."

"Looks can be deceiving. I take it that he did have the opportunity, though."

"Yes, he was very upfront about that. He had dinner with her at the Savoy the night before she went to Paris."

"Was Audrey smoking that night?"

"I actually asked him about that. He seemed surprised by the question."

"I would imagine so. If he's not the one who put the poisoned Nicoban in her packet, the question must have seemed rather bizarre to him."

"Like I said, he seemed genuinely surprised by the question."

"So are you ready to mark him off her list of suspects?"

"I'm not sure. I think I have to keep everyone on the list—at least until I get further feedback from the lab on the dose of fentanyl found in Audrey's body. If they can narrow down the time that the fentanyl would have taken to kill her, that would help eliminate the suspects."

"But, like you said, someone could have put the patch in her packet long before she picked out the poisoned apple."

"But it would limit the extent of the opportunity he might have had to stash the patch in the packet if he didn't meet with her before his meeting with her the night before the crash—and if, say, the lab comes back with a finding that the dose administered would cause death within an hour or so."

"Do you know how often he met with her before the evening of July 24?"

"No. And I agree that's a problem."

"You didn't ask?"

"I guess I should have. But the bottom line is that I don't see him doing something like this. I really don't."

Just then, an announcer took the stage and presented the opera singer who would sing an aria from *La Traviata*.

"I'd love to hear this aria," said Judy. "Can we stay?"

"Of course. Can I get a beer?"

"No."

"Yes, Nurse Ratchet."

Judy shook her head.

Waiter," Braxton called to the waitress, "A Fanta please!"

Chapter Forty-Five

As Judy waited at Savoy Circle for Braxton to pick her up, she was beginning to have second thoughts. Before returning from Croydon the night before she had agreed to let Braxton take her on a road trip to Portsmouth the next day to show her the *Mary Rose* at Portsmouth, but they had not discussed the details. Then, early that morning he had texted her a proposed itinerary which included several stops along the way, including Hampden Court, Codham, Guildford, Chiddingfield, and Liphook before arriving at Portsmouth in the early evening. There they would stay the night at the Queen's Inn for the night, and visit the *Mary Rose* the following morning.

Upon receiving the text, her first instinct had been to call and scold him for being so presumptuous, and tell him that she had only three days to prepare for her trip to Scotland to interview Alistair Devon—that she could not possibly spend more than one day away from the time she had set aside to make those preparations.

Upon further reflection, she decided against such a scolding and that she would go along with his proposed itinerary with the understanding that she be back in London no later than early afternoon the following day—and that any hotel arrangements provide separate accommodations. Accordingly, she had packed a small overnight bag and texted Braxton that she would be ready by 8 A.M.

It was not that she didn't have some positive feelings for him, including gratitude for his help, but they were not of a romantic nature. She was still grieving over her loss—surely he of all people would understand that—and it would be some time before she was ready to embark on any new relationship. Though she was determined to remain focused, she had spent the last hour forming in her own mind how best to make this clear to

Braxton without bruising his feelings—for it was obvious that his inclinations harbored expectations. Even if she could return such inclinations, how could she be sure that his were not just his way of coping with his own grief, and thus not real with respect to any romantic feelings for her?

Long aware of her physical attractions, Judy had all her life endured the unwanted advances of men who reacted ungenerously if not maliciously or even dangerously when she had rejected them or proposed friendship in lieu of romance, however softly and kindly she had done so. What had attracted her to Robin was that he had never pursued her in a way that caused her to interpret his true intentions, but had let her pursue him.

Because of a light rain, the Spitfire top was up when it arrived at the Circle.

"Good morning," Braxton said cheerily as he took Judy's bag, and held the door open for her.

"Morning," Judy replied with just a slight hint of coldness.

They had driven for several blocks in silence before Braxton finally said, "Are you cross with me? You're very quiet."

"Perhaps a little, Braxton. You know we never discussed staying overnight in Portsmouth—your itinerary I got this morning."

"Ah, my texts this morning. Texts can be so impersonal, but I didn't want to wake you if you were sleeping. We got back so late last night, you were tired, so we didn't have time to discuss the details, but you did say you wanted to go to Portsmouth this morning. My text this morning was just a suggestion. I did make reservations for a suite at the Queen's Hotel in Portsmouth—separate bedrooms—but it's only a two hour drive to Portsmouth, and we can return by early evening if you wish. Am I to be forgiven?"

Judy uncrossed her arms, relented, and smiled. "Of course," said Judy as she put her hand on his. "I'm sorry. You've been so kind. I've just been so anxious and focused on this case. I hope you understand. I need to get so much more information before I can draw any conclusions regarding Audrey's death. I feel guilty having a good time when I'm making so little progress."

"But that's not really true, is it? I mean you got Hodges to divulge the name of a prominent politician who had both motive and opportunity to kill Audrey. And you've interviewed that Viscount, who it turns out also had motive and opportunity."

"Yes, but you have to remember that I came here to find evidence that Ronald Sterling killed her, and so far I've found no such evidence beyond what I already knew."

"Motive and opportunity. I wonder if the nature of this case—I mean the diabolical way in which the poisoning of Audrey could have been perpetrated by anyone who had contact with her in the weeks, or even months before she applied the patch—makes it inherently unsolvable. It almost seems a perfect crime in that respect—not to mention that it can never be proved that she died before the Concorde crash. Maybe you will have to accept that it's one of those crimes that can never be solved. I've been honest with you, that neither the police nor the CS will ever bring charges against anyone based on the evidence you have—and certainly not against Ronald Sterling who, on top of everything else, would have to be extradited from the United States. From a jurisdictional standpoint it would be almost impossible to show where the attempted murder occurred. You need forensic evidence."

"I have lab evidence that Audrey was poisoned."

"Not enough."

"I know. I will need something beyond forensic evidence."

"Like what?"

"I don't know. But hey, I'm not going to think about it—at least not for the rest of today and tomorrow. Now tell me about the places we'll visit on the way to Portsmouth."

Braxton turned on to the M-275. "Coming up is Hampden Court—the magnificent house that Cardinal Wolsey built—so magnificent that King Henry VIII thought only a King would be worthy of living in it. He made Wolsey an offer he couldn't refuse, and got the house for himself."

"And the offer?"

"He got to keep his head—for a while at least."

"How long will we visit there?"

"About an hour, if that's okay. We can have lunch there."

"Sounds good. And what's to see in our next stop, Judy opened up her mobile, "in Codham?"

"There's the Brooklands Aeronautical Museum."

"Oh."

"It displays one of the last surviving Concordes."

"Really!"

"Would you like to see it? You can board her."

Judy hesitated. "I'm not sure...."

"We don't have to stop there."

"Yes, I would like to see it. It would be hard, but yes, I would like to see it."

Chapter Forty-Six

After a pleasant day visiting Hampden Court and a more gut-wrenching visit to the Concorde on display at the Brooklands Aeronautical Museum in Codham, the Spitfire made its final turnoff to the port city of Portsmouth on England's south coast.

"How far to the hotel?" Judy asked.

"Just up the road, but I want to show you something first."

Braxton turned left on Wingfield Street, left again on Victoria Street, and finally onto Old Commercial Road which was lined with unremarkable row houses. In front of 393 Old Commercial Road, he stopped and parked.

"Well, this is it," he said as he pointed to the house.

"This is what?" said Judy, bewildered.

"I remembered something you said last Sunday night at my flat about Daumier, and thought you might enjoy seeing this house."

"Really, something I said? I was so tired that night, I'm not sure I can remember what I said."

"After I told you about Daumier's use of caricatures to express his themes against the corruption of law and the incompetence of government, you said something I thought was not only quite perceptive, but also showed your knowledge of literature."

"I can't imagine what I said."

"You said that Daumier seemed to be to art what Charles Dickens was to literature."

"I said that? So—is this house where Daumier lived, or what?"

"Guess again."

"This is the house where Charles Dickens lived?"

"Not only where he lived, but where he was born."

"Really! That is interesting. He was born in Portsmouth? Can we go in?"

"It's a museum now, but it closed at 4 P.M., so we're too late. We could go tomorrow after we see the *Mary Rose* if you like."

"I'll see."

"Great. Now off to the Queen's Hotel. I think you'll like it."

Chapter Forty-Seven

After a quiet dinner at the Queen's Hotel restaurant overlooking the harbor, Judy said:

"Braxton, would you mind if I retired for the night? It's prime time back in the states for connecting with my contacts and associates. I really need to check in with them. Do you mind?"

"Not at all. Let me take you to your room." He led Judy to the elevator up to the fourth floor and the suite which he had reserved, consisting of a living room, two bedrooms and two baths. "I hope this is satisfactory."

"It absolutely is," said she admiring the panoramic view of the harbor. "Very impressive, and I'm sure expensive. I insist on paying half the bill."

"Don't be silly… of course I shall pay the bill."
Judy held up one finger. "No argument. Now I really must say good night."

"Of course. I'll be out here in the sitting room if you need anything. Or I may go out and get something for breakfast. Shall I wake you up in the morning?"

"You needn't. I'll set the alarm on my iPhone, but thank you. I'm sorry to cut our evening short, but I really do have to make a lot of calls. We can go see the *Mary Rose* tomorrow. Shall we plan to meet at in the kitchen at 7 A.M. so we can get a good start?"

"Sure, see you then. Maybe I'll even have breakfast prepared." Braxton approached Judy, but stopped short. He would like to have kissed her goodnight, but realized it was not the right time. "Good night. Until tomorrow morning, then."

Judy retired to her bedroom, took a shower, and then took out her mobile and called Amber.

"Well, it's about time," came the immediate reply. "I was getting worried about you."

"I'm fine—actually having too good a time."

"Really? Are you still in London?"

"I'm in Portsmouth. It's about a two hour drive from London. My new friend, Braxton insisted on taking me here to see the *Mary Rose*, and we're spending the night here."

"Oh, you are, are you...."

"Not what you're thinking—separate bedrooms."

"Sure, sure. You don't have to tell me if you don't want to...now what is this *Mary Rose*?"

"Henry VIII's flagship. It sank four hundred years ago and they just recently pulled it up for display in a museum here in Portsmouth. I'm looking forward to seeing it. But now, tell me about you and Martin."

"Okay, don't be mad, but I guess we're on again."

"I'm glad. Why should I be mad? I'm happy for you."

"We're taking it slow this time. So far, so good. We'll see. And he's promised to cough up the emails we've been asking for."

"That's great. Text me as soon as you get anything that's helpful."

"I will. Anything new from your end?"

"I did go and have a chat with this Viscount character."

"You actually tracked him down? Amazing. What do you think after talking to him?"

"It's hard to say. He definitely had opportunity and a motive. But he just seems so harmless. I have a hard time imagining him as a ruthless killer."

"I'm sure you've read enough Agatha Christie to know that the murderer is always the most unlikely suspect. But I'm glad you've stricken him off your list of suspects if it means that you'll be getting back on track to get evidence against Ronald."

"So far, nothing that you don't already have. But I do have one more person I want to talk to—this Alistair Devon. Now him I can see as being capable of murder."

"Really? A former member of parliament?"

"He just had too much to lose if Audrey really did what she implied she would—file a paternity action against him in a British court. I plan to go up to Scotland on Friday and see what he has to say."

"Be careful, Judy. If he really is the one who poisoned Audrey, he'd have almost as much reason to do something to you as he had to poison Audrey."

"He's not an MP or in the government anymore."

"But still, he has a lot to lose. From what you told me, his wife would probably divorce him in a minute and ruin him financially. And what makes you think that this Devon will even talk to you?"

"Amber...."

"Like Timothy always said about beauty being the best recommendation...."

"Amber, please stop with that...."

"Yeah, yeah. So are you going to have a cover story to get an interview?"

"No, not at all. Just tell him that I had an interest in Audrey, and was looking into...."

"Good luck on that...."

"If I get nothing, then I guess I'll just come back to Houston with my tail between my legs—and just help you with your civil case against Ronald."

"Maybe you'll get a break. I know Jake is working on some leads for you."

"We'll see. I'll let you know if I get anything at all, either from Jeremy, or from here."

"And if not, it's okay. Enjoy yourself. This barrister friend of yours...."

"Braxton. Braxton Thomas"

"Right. Talk soon. Bye."

Judy next called Jake on his private cell.

"Hello, Judy."

"Hi, Jeremy. Anything new?"

"Not yet, but I think I'm closing in on our mystery visitor

to the Concorde lounge. We've checked the backgrounds of nine people who entered during the time that Audrey was in the lounge, but who were not on the Concorde flight. They must have either had lounge privileges or were booked on First Class on another flight. But none of them have any connections to either Audrey or any of your suspects. We still have another six visitors to check out. I'll let you know when we've done that."

"Great, and I'll let you know if anything comes of my interview with Alistair Devon."

"Call anytime, night or day."

"Bye, Jeremy."

Chapter Forty-Eight

Braxton tapped lightly on Judy's door.

Judy was already awake, but had not yet risen from bed. "Come in."

Braxton entered with a breakfast tray of yogurt, plain toast, fruit, and coffee. "Room service," he said. Judy sat up and laid the tray down on her lap.

"Oh wow. Thank you. How did you know what I liked?"

"You do remember that we had breakfast at the Savoy yesterday morning."

"Of course. And you fixed this all by yourself?"

"Indeed I did, and am proud of it. I went out last night after you retired to get a few things at the local grocer. I'm afraid the coffee may not be quite up to snuff."

"It will be fine," she said with a smile as she sipped the coffee and managed to hide a grimace.

"It's the thought that counts, and hopefully the toast, juice and yogurt will pass muster."

"I know they will. Listen, I feel foolish lying here and being waited on. Why don't you go out to the balcony and I will get my robe and come out and join you."

"As you wish. The *Mary Rose* museum opens at nine, and I thought we'd get an early start to get you back to the Savoy by early afternoon."

"I do want to get back by nightfall, but there's no rush, honestly. Go on, I'll be right out."

"What a magnificent view," exclaimed Judy as she joined Braxton on the balcony overlooking the harbor. "What is that old sailing ship in the distance?"

"That, my dear, is the HMS *Victory*, the flagship of Horatio Nelson who won the Battle of Trafalgar in 1805, and set the stage for the British Empire on which the sun never set. Would you like to see it?"

"I would like to see the *Mary Rose*, but after that I was thinking we could just take a walk around the island."

"Then we shall."

There was a long silence as each sipped coffee and took in the sights and sound of the harbor. Finally, Braxton said:

"Are you still planning to go to up to Scotland on Friday?"

"Yes. I need to decide for myself if Alistair Devon is a viable suspect. If I can eliminate him, along with the Viscount, I can concentrate on finding evidence against our primary suspect, Ronald Sterling."

"And you think you can eliminate Devon as a suspect just by talking to him?"

"Actually, I think I can. I consider myself a good judge of character. And to be honest, from what I've learned about Devon, I'd be inclined to consider him a more serious suspect than Ronald Sterling—though I know that's something my associate Amber would not like to hear."

"And if you do decide to strike Devon from your suspect list, does that mean you'll be returning to the states?"

Judy thought for a moment before saying, "I suppose so. Jeremy and Devon were the only leads that brought me to London. If neither of those pan out, then there's really nothing to keep me here. And you've convinced me that I don't have enough evidence to file a report with the police."

"Then perhaps I've managed to hang myself on my own petard."

"Not sure what you mean."

"Never mind. I'd be interested in hearing more about this New York firm you are partnered with. Did I understand you to say that you wanted to convert it into a public interest firm specializing in righting wrongful convictions?"

"Yes, that is what I'm in the process of trying to do. I'm working with my friend Amber Hartman in Houston to merge her firm with mine."

"I wonder if you've ever considered linking a branch of your firm—once your two firms are merged and consolidated—with one of the barrister chambers here in London."

"Really? Would that even be possible?"

"I don't see why not. We have wrongful convictions in Britain too, you know. Or would your new public interest firm only be interested in wrongful convictions perpetrated in the U.S.?"

"Not at all. In fact, I would want our firm—I guess we'd call it a public interest institute—to address wrongful convictions anywhere in the world."

"That would certainly be ambitious. A first step might be to become a barrister in the U.K."

"Huh. How difficult would it be for me as an American with a license to practice law in New York to become barrister in the U.K.?"

"I can't say it would be easy, and the training would frankly be expensive, but there is a barrister at the Quadrangle who did it."

"So what did he or she have to do?"

"First, you'd have to apply to the Bar Standards Board for a transfer to the UK bar. They would look at your legal education and experience in the profession in the U.S., and make a determination as to what additional courses and training you would have to take before taking the Bar Transfer Test. That test would consist of two parts, comprising written papers and oral assessments. You would also have to pass the Bar Course Aptitude Test. Finally, assuming you passed that test, you would have to complete a period of pupillage—that is, engage in work based learning under a licensed barrister in chambers before being granted authorization to practice as a barrister."

"How does the pupilage process work?"

"You would apply to one of the Chambers through a system called the Pupilage Gateway. You can apply to a maximum of twelve chambers each year."

"I'm interested. Tell me more"

"I'll tell you what. I have a hearing scheduled for tomorrow, just a motion, on a burglary case. Why don't you come down and watch me in action, and see if it's the sort of thing you'd like to do. It's a bit different than the court procedures in the U.S. I can get you a copy of the Bar Qualification Manual."

"As I said, I'm interested."

"If your institute was suitably funded, and earning a living was not a prime object, earning a certification would be far less difficult."

"I'll definitely think about it. I'm intrigued."

"Now, getting back to Friday. How do you propose to get up to Aberdeenshire?'

"I was thinking of taking the train. I heard there is an overnight train."

"Yes, the Caledonian Sleeper. It leaves London at 8 P.M. every evening except Saturday, and gets you to Edinburgh the next morning. You can then transfer to a train to Aberdeen, and then either rent a car or take a cab to Devon's estate."

"Actually I don't plan to visit his estate. My investigator told me last night that while Devon shoots grouse on Saturday, he plays golf at the Royal Aberdeen golf club on Sunday mornings. After golf, he hangs out at the club house bar before taking a car to the train station in the evening to board the Caledonian Sleeper back to London."

"Have you decided on your approach?"

"Jake has already arranged for a guest pass for me to play golf with a 7 A.M. tee time. Devon usually has a tee time at about the same time. If I can arrange to meet him, I'm going to be up front with him, just as I was with Jeremy. I'll tell him I was a friend of Audrey, and that she spoke very highly of him before she died on the Concorde…that as long as I happened to be in Scotland on holiday, and had heard that he played at the same golf course, I was hoping to meet the man who meant so much to her—something like that."

"Just use your charm so he overlooks the fact that you are actually grilling him."

Another face down, eyes up look from Judy. "nooooo...."

"Well, color me skeptical, though I will confess that if anyone can pull that off, you can."

"You're right to be so. If I do get incriminating information that we could use in filing a police complaint, then well and good. If not, which is most likely, then so be it— in which case I'll be taking a chartered plane from Aberdeen Dyce Airport to New York."

"You must not be very confident if you've already lined up a charter plane. That must be expensive."

To this Judy made no reply.

"So unless you get incriminating information on Devon...."

Judy finished her yogurt and stood up. "Probably not. But let's go see the *Mary Rose*."

Chapter Forty-Nine

After spending the morning at the *Mary Rose* Museum, Braxton took Judy on the walk he had promised to her earlier. After an hour of walking, they sat on a bench overlooking the harbor.

"I enjoyed the museum," said Judy. "It was most interesting."

"I'm glad you enjoyed it."

For the next ten minutes neither said anything to the other as they took in the panorama of the myriad of ships in the harbor and listened to the sounds of the foghorns, the shouts of seamen, and the waves lapping up against the banks. Braxton seemed lost in thought.

"You're very quiet, Braxton," Judy said to break the silence. "Is everything okay?"

Braxton turned to her and smiled. "Sorry...yes...no...yes...I was just thinking...that I might never see you again...."

She hesitated before breaking him off. "Braxton, I've enjoyed my time with you, and I am most grateful for your kind help and attention...but...you must understand I'm not ready to...."

"I'm sorry...."

"Don't be, please. Perhaps I shouldn't have accepted your help so readily...I didn't mean to...take advantage...I mean it's just that I came here for a particular purpose, and I can't lose my focus now...."

"Say no more. I understand. But perhaps you could answer this one question: was I so very transparent?"

"You mean behind your very charming and confident manner?"

"Truthfully, please."

"I suppose I did...if I had thought about it...it was thoughtless...."

"When?"

"When did you know...how I felt ..?"

"I suppose I should have known the moment I walked into your office...perhaps I did...I can't think about that right now...but my mind was on this case...but then when you followed me into the copse of the woods, and we sat...perhaps I did begin to realize...."

"Last Sunday when we shared the *Hymne a L'Amour*...."

"We both shared our grief...nothing more...."

"Do you believe in love at first sight, Judy?"

Judy shook her head. "I don't think so...well, I do and I don't... I think that ninety-nine times out of a hundred infatuation is mistaken for love...."

"Infatuation masquerading as love...." he mused. "Perhaps you are right. But that still leaves the one in a hundred of which you just spoke...."

"Braxton...."

"Since I must now resign and accept that after you leave for Scotland, I shall never see you again...."

"I didn't say that...."

"If you are so soon to disappear from my life, I entreat you to let me be so bold as to tell you that the moment—the very moment i saw you. I thought you were Lily Langtry come to life. It was all I could do to keep myself from melting into a warm puddle at your feet...."

"Braxton, you are being silly now—such talk as melting into a puddle," said Judy trying to insert a note of levity into the conversation. "And who is this Lily Langtry? Should I know her?"

"You've really never heard of her?"

Judy shrugged. "Perhaps I've heard the name...."

"Ah well, hailing from the colonies, I suppose it is possible that you have not heard of her. She was only England's greatest beauty—of more precisely, the Isle of Jersey's greatest beauty."

"Isle of Jersey?"

"Would you like to hear about her?"

"Sure," she said, relieved to veer the conversation in a different direction. I have a feeling you're going to tell me anyway, and you've got my curiosity up. So tell me about Lily Langtry."

"She was born in 1852 or 1853—anyway, the 1850s—on Jersey, an island off the coast of France, in the bay of Mont. St. Michel."

"Mont St. Michel I'm very familiar with. So she was French?"

"No, Jersey is British, or at least has been since 1259 when the King of France gave up his claim to the Channel Islands in the Treaty of Paris. It was occupied by the Germans during World War II, who shipped hundreds of it residents to concentration camps in mainland Europe."

"How horrible."

"Lily's father was the high deacon of the island, but Lily left the island for London when she was twenty. Her extraordinary beauty soon gave her an entrée into high society. One evening the famous artist Frank Miles saw her at the opera. Stricken by her beauty, he went about to all the clubs in town and asked among friends to discover who she was. When he finally found her, he begged her to let him paint her portrait. She agreed, and when he finished the portrait, he sold it to Prince Leopold for a princely sum. Soon copies of her face appeared on postcards all around the England and Ireland.

"Subsequent artists now sought her out for portraits, including Everett Millais, who christened her the 'Jersey Lily'. Lily was later exhibited at the Royal Academy, and caused such great interest and excitement that it had to be roped off like the Mona Lisa to avoid damage from the teeming throngs that came to admire it.

"Unbelievable."

"Soon thereafter, a friend of Millais, Rupert Potter—the father of Beatrix Potter—took photographs of Lily when she was visiting Millais in Scotland."

"Beatrix Potter? The one who wrote *The Tales of Peter Rabbit*?" asked Judy.

"That's the one....."

"I used to read all her books as a child. But sorry, go on."

"Thereafter, Lily's fame reached the ears of the Prince of Wales, future King Edward VIII, who contrived to sit next to her at a society dinner party. He became instantly taken with her, began courting her with extravagant gifts of jewels, furs, a town house and carriages, and even presented her to his mother Queen Victoria."

"Amazing."

"Unfortunately, the Prince was already married to Princess Alexandra of Denmark. When the Queen made it clear to him that divorce would be impossible, Lily realized that she could never become Queen of England or anything more than a mistress to the Prince. She broke off the affair. Nevertheless, he continued to shower her with gifts—many, but not all of which she refused. After Oscar Wilde encouraged Lily to make a career in the theater, Edward used his influence to launch her career, where she soon became a shining star of the stage. In later years he regularly attended her performances.

"Thereafter, she became involved in a number of affairs, including a notorious one with the Earl of Shrewsbury. Unfortunately, their plans to run off together were cut short when a scandal-mongering journalist unleashed several libel cases in which the Prince was to be named as a co-respondent. The Prince also sued for libel, and the journalist was sent to prison for two years.

"So don't tell me. She must have come to a bad end."

"Not at all. By this time, her fame had spread to the United States, and in—I think it was around 1882—the American impresario Henry Abbey arranged for her to perform in all the great American theaters across the county. She was met by an enthusiastic throng upon her arrival in New York, and was also met by Oscar Wilde who was on a lecture tour at the time. On this and subsequent tours of the U.S. she gave performances to much acclaim coast to coast. She starred in productions ranging from the classical—as Lady Macbeth in Shakespeare's *Macbeth* and Rosalind in *As You Like It*—to the more popular productions. For towns in the American West, the appearance of Lily Langtry was a cause of celebration and pride, and all her performances were sold out months in advance."

"Was she a good actress?"

"Although critics were not as admiring of her as her public, and she endured acrimony along the way from the litany of women who resented the attention paid to her by their husbands, with some of whom Lily had affairs, all her tours of the U.S. were spectacularly successful, and she became a wealthy woman in her own right.

"In 1888, one of her millionaire admirers, Frederick Gerhard, bought her a magnificent mansion on West 23rd Street in Manhattan; another admirer bought her a 4,000 acre ranch in Guenon Valley in Southern California. I understand it survives to this day as the Langtry Farms, and is still in operation as a winery and vineyard in Middletown, California.

"After making her final appearance in the 1913 silent film *His Neighbor's Wife,* she later retired to Monte Carlo, where she passed her final days."

"Amazing. I'll have to read up on her. And you're quite the historian. But doesn't her story just prove my point that love—I mean true love—transcends beauty, and that the whole idea of love at first sight, so enshrined by the romanticists and poets, is rarely a manifestation of anything more than infatuation and lust?"

"I will concede your point, if in return you affirm you concession to me that in one in a hundred cases, it can reflect enduring and selfless love."

Though she was enjoying the history lesson, Judy was determined to bring Braxton back to the present.

"You have to understand," she said, "that too much has happened this past year. I came here to focus on a task, to distract me from losing the one man I ever truly loved…I know the task

I have set for myself must seem like tilting at a windmill, and perhaps it is…and now I feel that perhaps I have used you to hold my hand —though I have not done so consciously—as I go charging into that windmill…."

"Not at all…."

Judy put her hand affectionately on his and said in a sympathetic voice, "I have no doubt that you are physically attracted to me, but I have had so many unpleasant experiences in my life with men who were attracted to me. Those experiences have caused me to always be on guard, to put up walls…I have no doubt that those walls have kept out some with whom I might have found real love. So you must give me time…and I think you must give yourself time as well as I have come to believe that real love is most extraordinarily rare…too often we are deceived, overwhelmed by our senses. You and I have known each other for…what, a week…surely not enough time to…."

"I'm beginning to feel like a character from a Jane Austen novel," said he, disconsolate, but warming to her friendly touch.

"And do you see me as Elizabeth Bennett, then? I'm even more impressed that you read Jane Austen than with your prodigious knowledge of history. I never knew a man who read Jane Austen."

"Then I must keep reading her books—though I hope I'm not a Mr. Darcy."

"Perhaps you are. It took a long time for Elizabeth to warm to him—the whole book as I recall."

"Yes, even after he declared his love for her, it took another hundred pages or so for Elizabeth to return his affections."

"My point entirely."

"Then I'm declaring, Judy, to set the clock for the next hundred pages, which I am prepared to endure if necessary."

She laughed, hoping to lighten his serious tone. "So, you're declaring, are you?"

"Yes, do I have to say it?"

"Please don't, at least not the way Darcy did."

"I certainly won't if it means I have to wait another hundred pages. Do you know what Jane's original title was to *Pride and Prejudice*?" He said.

Judy thought for a moment, taken aback that she didn't know the answer. "I'm afraid you have me."

"First Impressions."

"Really? I should have guessed that."

"And what were your first impressions of me?"

"To be honest, I don't think I had any beyond seeing you as someone who might help me—perhaps a bit of a rake."

"A rake! Ouch. You really took me for a rake?"

"Well, you were the protégé of Mr. Hodges...."

"A pupillage is a bit different than a protégé, but point taken. I can assure you that I'm nothing like him."

"I know that, or I wouldn't be with you now."

With the mood now somewhat lightened, Judy stood up and pulled him up. "Come on, show me the rest of the island."

As they approached HMS *Victory*, Braxton stopped and asked, "So where do we go from here?"

"I'm happy looking at the ship from the outside."

"You know what I mean. Will you come to my hearing tomorrow?"

"To see you in action? Yes, I'd like to, but...."

"But...."

She took his hand sympathetically. "Braxton, I like you. You've been most kind, and I'm grateful. But I think its best that I get up to Scotland as soon as possible, see this Alistair Devon if I can, and mark him off my list of suspects."

"And after that?"

"I hope you understand why I can't make any promises to you. Not now."

"You're not coming back to London with me this afternoon?"

"I'm sorry, no, and I do have a favor to ask. Let me stay here in Portsmouth by myself tonight, and you go on back to London and conduct your hearing tomorrow. Your suite here at the Queen's Hotel is very comfortable. I'll take care of the bill. It will give me time to think, and I need to check in with Amber and Jake. Then Friday I'll make the connection on that Caledonian Sleeper."

Braxton sighed in resignation. "If that's what you want, of course. You'll call me after your interview and let me know how it went?"

"If I can. I'll try. Now, let me walk you back to your car and we'll say goodbye for now."

They walked hand in hand back to the hotel garage. After opening the door to his Spitfire, Braxton turned, took Judy's hand and kissed it. Stammering like a schoolboy, and knowing he might never see Judy again, he declared:

"I love you, Judy. End of story. End of my declaration. Even if it's the end of my life. I love you."

Chapter Fifty

Judy lay back on the bunk of her sleeping compartment on the Caledonian Sleeper, and listened in quiet contemplation to the rhythmic clicks of the locomotive's wheels on the tracks.

She had spent the first hour of the trip enjoying the countryside of southern England, but as darkness had set in and there was nothing to stimulate her visual senses, she turned off her cabin lights and curled up on her bunk in hopes of getting a good night's rest before arriving in Edinburgh the next morning.

After fifteen minutes, she realized there was too much to think about to allow her to sleep, and she reached for her mobile. She didn't know if she could make a connection while travelling on a speeding train through the midlands of England, but thought it was worth a try. Calculating that it was only late afternoon in New York and Texas, she called Jake and got a dial tone. The now familiar voice of Jake came through on the third ring.

'Hello, Judy. Where are you?"

"I'm on a train to Edinburgh, so I'm not sure I can keep this connection. If I lose you, I'll try back later."

"Sure."

"Can you hear me okay?"

"Your voice is distinct, but the volume is very low. Can you turn it up?"

"Not really, but I'll talk louder. I'm just calling for an update. Anything new?"

"Glad you called. I just got a call from the RFL Lab. I don't know how they did it, but they were able to determine that Audrey was pregnant."

"No doubt about it?"

"They don't seem to think so, though they couldn't determine how many months along she was. I'm afraid you can expect a rather hefty bill, though. It was an extensive process."

"I'm sure, but at this point, any evidence at all would help. I have so little to go on now."

"I'm still not sure how this information will help you."

"For one thing, it shows that Audrey wasn't lying when she told Devon she was pregnant."

"But is that really important? Surely he would have demanded proof of her pregnancy before…you know…."

"Poisoning her? True, but if her motive was blackmail she still could have created a scandal for Devon—though without proof of their affair Devon could probably have weathered it with public denials and refutation. In any paternity action, however, DNA doesn't lie. No, I think it's important to know that she was telling the truth about her pregnancy."

"How so?"

"It says something about her character. If Audrey really was carrying his child, she had every reason to feel abused if he was going to abandon her, especially since she was going through a divorce with Ronald and probably had very little expectation of getting anything out of it against Ronald's army of divorce lawyers who would no doubt have found out about her affair with Devon."

"So you don't think blackmail was her motive?"

"I think not, though she may have been naïve in thinking that Devon wouldn't take it that way."

"So you're actually going up to Aberdeen to confront this guy? I gotta say, Judy, I don't see what that's going to accomplish. You can't really expect him to just up and admit that he had an affair with Audrey, got her pregnant, and then poisoned her to get rid of her to avoid scandal."

"Of course not. But I want to take the measure of the man. I've already accepted that I'm never going to find proof—at least not forensic proof—that he, or any particular suspect poisoned her. But I do want to satisfy myself, and I think I can do so by measuring the character of everyone involved."

Judy did not expect Jake to understand. How could he know that this quest to find the truth about Audrey was something she wanted to do for its own sake? Even if she failed in this quest, it would not only be something to occupy her mind as she dealt with her loss, but also be a first step in deciding what she wanted to do with the rest of her life.

"Okay, but as I said...."

"Then don't repeat it, Jake. Instead tell me if you've made any progress on finding our mystery visitor to the Concorde lounge."

"As I told you last time, we have the complete list of visitors on the morning of the crash, and checked the backgrounds of all but four. So far, none of the ones we've checked have any connection to either Audrey, Ronald, Viscount Jeremy McKenzie or Alistair Devon. For all we really know now, our mystery visitor may not even exist."

"All right. Keep checking. I don't know what my mobile reception will be around Aberdeen, but so far I've had no problem receiving emails on my phone."

"I'll send you anything I get as soon as I get it. I've got eight people working exclusively on this."

"I know. Thanks, Jake. Bye."

Judy now considered whether to call Amber, but hesitated. She was sure that she would press her on how things were working out with Braxton, but the truth was that she didn't know herself. Although she couldn't stop thinking about him, she was having trouble dealing with why that was so. After all, ever since Robin's death she had resolved not to get entangled in any romantic relationships for a very long time—perhaps forever. She decided she could preempt any of Amber's questions by asking her about Martin, so she dialed. Getting no answer on her mobile, she called her office and got a soft dial tone.

"Amber Hartman's office. May I help you?"

"This is Judy Alexander. Is she in?"

"Yes, believe so. I'll connect you."

"Judy! Where have you been?"

"Having a very pleasant time actually in the very historical town of Portsmouth."

"Well good for you, sister. I take it that your new beau accompanied you there?"

"Stop. He's just a friend."

"I'm sure."

"But yes, he has been very kind and showed me the sights. I even saw Charles Dickens' house. And how is everything going with our friendly D.A. Martin?"

"Funny you should ask. He's invited me to dinner this evening."

"I don't suppose he's coughed up those emails he subpoenaed."

"Actually, he did. I'm still going through them. But so far, nothing incriminating that I've found. I'll let you know. Where are you now?"

"On a train to Edinburgh."

"To see that Devon character? Well, good luck. But after that, can I expect you back in Houston? I really need you here. I took depositions in Senta's case yesterday. I told the insurance lawyers that if they don't accept our offer of five million to settle the case, our offer is off the table and we go to trial. And we need to get going on merging our firms."

"I've hired two new lawyers for my New York firm and I've funded it while we make the transition to a non-profit. I have John Lauridson working on that."

"Also, Braxton...."

"Oh yes, your friend...."

"Yes, Amber. My friend. He pitched the idea to me of my becoming a barrister here in England. I could fund a chamber here in London, take cases involving wrongful convictions, and liaison with our merged non-profit there in the states."

"Are you serious? I mean you're over thirty, is that really realistic?"

"I would probably have to take another year of courses to qualify, get a pupilage, set up a chamber, maybe try to get dual citizenship in England....'

"Whoa, sister. You really are serious."

"Not really. Just something to think about."

"Well, please stay focused. After you finish with this interview in Scotland—if you even get the interview— please try to come back as soon as you can. The statute of limitations is about to run out in Brenda's case, so I will have to file a claim in her wrongful death action against Ronald very soon, and I'm counting on you to help with the case proper."

"If I can get an interview with Devon on Sunday, I'll try to fly back on Monday. Can you have Chandler fly the G-500 up to Aberdeen? I checked, and there's an airport near it accessible to private jets.

"All right. I used it to fly to a deposition in Dallas last week, but it should be ready to go. Listen, I gotta get home and get ready for dinner tonight."

"Okay, I'll call soon. Good night, and wish me luck."

Chapter Fifty-One

Upon arriving at the Aberdeen train station early on Saturday morning, Judy took a cab to the Jurys Inn which was only a short distance from the Royal Aberdeen Golf Club. With a full day to kill before trying her luck to find Devon at the golf club the next morning, she decided to explore what sights there were to see in the town.

She ran seven miles through woods and dale to see the Craigievar Castle, built in 1626 by the Aberdonian merchant William Forbes, ancestor of the Forbes baronets of Craigievar. From there she took a cab to the Aberdeen Art Gallery to see the 18th century Scottish painting and metal work collections. Before noon she took a cab to the Golf Club to scout out the layout, purchase some golf attire, and also to claim her visitor's pass for the next day and affirm her tee time for the next morning.

"Morning Lassie," said the club house assistant manager the desk in the well-equipped pro shop. "How can I help you?"

"Good morning," said Judy as she handed him the voucher Jake had texted her entitling her to a visitors pass and a tee time reservation for the next morning. "I'm visiting from the states and was told to bring this voucher to you to exchange for a 7 A.M. tee card for tomorrow morning."

The manager examined the voucher closely. "Yeh don't see many of these, mind yeh. Yeh not be related to Prince Charles by any chance," he said in a tone both good naturedly and flirtatiously.

Judy laughed. "Hardly. But it is good, isn't it?"

"Oh yes, Lassie, it seems to be in order. It's just that these passes are very hard to come by. You must have friends in high places. Come all the way from the states have yeh? Well, you'll not find better golf anywhere in the world but right here in Aberdeen."

"I have no doubt."

"I see here you have a tee time for 7 A.M. for tomorrow, a summer Sunday. They may be worth its weight in gold. You are number one on the list for that tee time, missy, but I have to tell yeh that the club policy for single players is to hook up with at least two others on the list. Will that be satisfactory for yeh?"

"Yes, of course."

The assistant manager picked up his clipboard and examined the list. The top two on the list would be—let me see—Sir Robert Logan, and Douglas Callum—he is a councillor for the city here in Aberdeen. Can I ask you about your golfing proficiency Lassie?"

"I'm afraid I'm not very good. Is that a problem? Perhaps these two men wouldn't be too happy to play with an amateur like myself."

"Oh, I wouldn't worry about that, Lassie. One look at you and they'll probably be offering to be your caddy and run down balls for yeh."

"You flatter me, sir," she said sensing his good natured intention. "But I hardly think...."

"We get very few women here—and few who look like you if you don't mind me saying so. It wasn't until 2018 that the male members voted to allow women in at all."

"Then I shall consider myself most privileged to be allowed to play here."

"Don't be. When the vote to allow women was taken back in '18, only three percent voted against it. However, I would advise that if you find yourself getting more than a few strokes behind, that you let them give you a ten. This is a club rule to insure that you don't hold up the people behind you. What be your handicap?"

"Probably the maximum...."

"I'll put you down for a forty, then, and I'll let the other two know."

"Are either of them here today by any chance?"

"You might find Sir Logan in the bar. I'm not sure about the Councillor. You're welcome to see if you like."

"I think I shall, thank you. By the way, do you happen to know an Alistair Devon here at the club? A relative back in the states asked me to look him up if I visited the Royal Golf club here."

"Oh yes," replied Malcom. "He's a regular here on Sunday mornings. His tee time is just behind yours. He's not usually here on Saturdays through—grouse hunting I think."

"Oh, well maybe I'll see him here tomorrow, then."

"Before you go, do you need anything? The club has very strict rules about attire worn on the course." He handed her the rules.

"Oh wow," she said as she scanned the three page sheet. "These rules are very precise…'caps with a peak must be worn with the peak at the front…golf shirts must have collars, turtle, or polo necks…jackets and ties and commensurate non-golfing attire for ladies should be worn in the main lounge and bar on weekends…."

"I think you'd better deck me out, Mr…."

"Just call me Malcolm, Lassie. I can suggest just what you'll need tomorrow. It will only be in the mid-50s tomorrow morning, so better button up. Luckily no rain in the forecast."

"Thank you, Malcolm."

After being fully outfitted with rule-compliant golf vestments, Judy called a cab to take her downtown to find the appropriate ladies attire "commensurate with jackets and ties for the men." She found at the Sirene Boutique Aberdeen a suitable ensemble consisting of a fitted black skirt, silk blouse, tailored jacket, and a pair of three and a half inch Jimmy Choo heels. After returning to the Club House and leaving a suitcase full of her golfing attire with Malcolm, she sat at the bar in the lounge, and ordered a martini.

It was not long before a group of several men seated at a table near the bar struck up a conversation with her. "Are yeh one of our new members, Miss?" one of the slightly inebriated men at the table called out.

Judy turned about and smiled. "Oh, no. I'm just visiting from the states. I'd heard so much about this Club that my friends said I just had to come and have a round. I'm just a visitor."

"Won't you join us?" said another ruddy-faced man at the table. "Can we buy you a drink?"

Judy held up her martini but joined them.

"Are you a professional come from the states to humiliate us on our own turf?" an older man asked playfully.

"Oh, no," she said. "Strictly amateur, I assure you. Could I ask if either of you gentlemen is Sir Robert Logan?"

There were chortles as the men turned to a finely chiseled, middle-aged man sitting at the other end of the table.

Sir Robert raised his glass. "Guilty as charged, My Lady. How might I be of service?"

"It seems that I have a tee time at 7 A.M. tomorrow morning, and that you are on the list to join me. I'm afraid I am not very good, but was hoping you might not mind me joining your group along with a Mr...."she consulted her pass—"

"Not at all, my good lady. I would be delighted."

For the next hour Judy conversed with the men who, with more than their usual abandon in this mostly male environment, competed for her attention.

"By the way," she asked, "do any of you know a Mr. Alistair Devon? A friend of mine, a relative of his in the states asked me to look him up if I ever came this way."

There was a long pause in the conversation before one of the men said, "Indeed, he should be here tomorrow morning. I am in his party. I believe we have a tee time directly after yours."

"Then perhaps I shall see him tomorrow to convey the regards of his relative. Until then, gentleman, I will bid you a good afternoon."

Despite entreaties for her to stay longer, she rose, thanked them all for their good cheer, and returned to the Club entrance to catch a cab back to the Jurys Inn.

Chapter Fifty-Two

It was early Sunday evening when, despite her exhaustion, Judy sat down at the desk in her hotel room to write the report of her interview with Alistair Devon on to her laptop:

> September 5: Everything went as planned at the Royal Aberdeen Golf Club. I arrived early at 6:15A.M., and joined Sir Robert Logan and Councillor Douglas Callum in the lounge before arriving on time for our first tee at 7A.M. Although I had to concede 10's on most of the holes in order not to delay the party behind us, which included Alistair Devon, we finished our eighteen holes before lunch.
>
> After changing and showering, and dressing into our non-golf attire, both Alistair's party and my own all joined together for lunch in the dining room. Apparently, one of the men with whom I had sat the day before in the bar had mentioned to Alastair that I was hoping to meet him to give him the regards of a relative of his in the states. So I was not surprised when I had no sooner sat down for lunch, that Alistair, who had taken a seat next to mine at the table, introduced himself and said that he understood I had been asking about him. I told him that I had asked where I might meet him, and was hoping we might have a private meeting immediately after lunch if he had the time. He readily agreed, and we met in a private sitting room after lunch.
>
> He seemed quite taken with me—which I expected based on what I knew about him—until he asked me about what relative it was who had asked me to look him up when I visited Scotland. At that point I decided that I would have to fess up that there was no such relative. I told him that I had been a dear

friend of Audrey in the years before she died in the Concorde crash, and that Audrey had spoken often of him in glowing terms as the man she hoped to one day marry—and that I was hoping to meet him.

What up to that point had been Devon's charming and pleasant demeanor turned very sour and defensive. He asked if I was a journalist with one of the London tabloids. I said no, and it was only after showing him my New York driver's license that he did agree to continue talking with me. Of course I did not confide in him the true purpose of my visit, as I am sure that would have ended the interview. After we shared a few drinks, he seemed to calm down and talk about Audrey.

He confessed that he had indeed been very much in love with Audrey, and that he had hoped to divorce his wife and marry her. He said that it was only later that his hopes were dashed when his friend Michael Hodges convinced him that such hopes were doomed, and that divorcing his wife would bring only scandal, ostracism, and financial and political ruin. Of course he said nothing of his meeting with Audrey on the morning of the Concorde crash, nor that Audrey had told him she was pregnant or that she threatened to bring a paternity action against him if he did not either divorce and marry her after her own divorce, or generously support her if he could not.

Of course I did not expect he would. In any case, we have only Hodges' third hand account of what Alistair said in his desperate phone call to him on the morning of July 25, 2000, so Alistair must have realized that there would be no way it could be proven, so why would he admit it?

This denial, or failure to confess the cooling of his passion for Audrey, might be taken as evidence of any motive he might have had to poison Audrey. However, I did not take it so. I could never expect him to do so. In the end, I believe that he had loved Audrey, and that he would in fact have married her had not he finally realized that doing so would have caused his own destruction. While his affair with Audrey did show lack of moral character, perhaps no less than so many others in life who follow such a similar path to ruin.

I wanted to interview Devon in order to take a measure of his character. Though by no means exemplary, I cannot believe that he was capable of murder. If I am wrong and he did poison her, he is either one of the most villainous of monsters on a par with the notorious Harvey Crippen who murdered his wife and buried her in his cellar in order to marry his mistress, and whose evil is now enshrined in Madame Tussaud's Chamber of Horrors, or he is just another politician of questionable, but not evil character.

I therefore reluctantly strike him from my list of suspects in the poisoning of Audrey, and will now devote my attention to gathering evidence against Ronald Sterling.

Just as Judy closed the top of her laptop, a text message from Jake appeared on her iPhone" "I have found our mystery visitor to the Concorde lounge, as well as other important evidence. Please call me as soon as you can."

Feverishly, she picked up the phone and called.

Chapter Fifty-Three

Judy listened with dismay to what Jake had discovered.

"Oh my God, Jake! I can't believe it! I just can't believe it! I should have known! I should have seen it! I can't believe I've been so blind. I missed it all, going up blind alleys. Send me everything you have right away! Everything!"

Judy closed the laptop and called Amber.

"Amber, I'm coming back as soon as I can. I think I know who killed Angela and poisoned Audrey. Is the G-500 on the way?"

"Yes, Chandler should be there in the morning at Dyce International Airport there in Aberdeen. He's working on getting clearance as we speak. But Judy, what have you found out! Tell me!"

"I have to pursue one more avenue, and then I can be sure enough to tell you. I'll fill you in when I get there."

Chapter Fifty-Four

The day after returning to London from Portsmouth, Braxton did not make his scheduled court appearance. Instead, he called his pupil and asked her to appear in court on his behalf and ask for a continuance, citing her supervising barrister's indisposition.

Truth be told, Braxton did need a day to rally from what he considered the second major loss in his life. He had texted Judy the night before, but received no reply. This had led him to accept that he would indeed not see her again, and that he should now carry on in the British tradition of stiff upper lip.

He did not send a second text, convinced that sending a second such text without a reply would smack of desperation sure to add to his myriad missteps to date—beginning with his overconfident demeanor that must have given Judy the impression that he truly was a rake, a player, a clone of Hodges, and ending with what to her must have seemed his fatuous declaration when she departed. If he could only take it back, and instead have conveyed a sense of disinterest that might have intrigued her rather than cause her to run away.

He considered squandering the rest of the day watching re-runs of Doc Martin on ITV as a distraction from mindlessly lying around second guessing himself, and rationalizing his failure to win her affection. He told himself that Judy was far too preoccupied with her undertaking to allow herself to become drawn into any new relationship. Should he have been more honest with her about the futility of that undertaking, or would that have only put her off even more? She had recently suffered a loss and was not looking to rebound with any new affair. He decided he wouldn't allow himself to wallow in second guessing, rationalizing, or—god forbid—pity. Instead he would change into his running clothes and shoes, and run a half marathon around

Westminster. When he got back, his mind would be cleared, and he would be ready the next day to take his place as an up and coming barrister practicing his trade in the hallowed halls of the Old Bailey.

Chapter Fifty-Five

Two thousand miles away, Judy sat at the desk on the Gulfstream G-500 and pensively looked down at the snowcapped landscape of Greenland below. Chandler was now dozing on the couch, and her flight attendant was reading a magazine in the jump seat.

She put aside the documents Jake had sent her, and turned her thoughts to the man she was leaving behind in London.

When she had left Braxton in Portsmouth, Judy had been preoccupied with her upcoming interview with Alistair Devon. While she thought Braxton an attractive friend—the kind of friend she might "look up" the next time she visited London—she had given very little thought to his premature, awkward, and Darci-esque declaration. At the time he delivered it, she hardly thought it serious. For one thing, it reminded of her so many similar declarations she had long learned to adeptly field during her life—though not always without causing hurt feelings.

The fact was that she had never liked being "pursued," and preferred to make her own choices. Granted, she had chosen her first husband, and it had not worked out. But she had also chosen Robin, and he had given her the happiest years of her life.

Confident that she had solved the mystery of who had murdered Angela Sterling and poisoned Audrey Sterling, her mind was now sufficiently cleared to allow her to think of what she had to look forward to in life after she returned to Houston, and to her law firm in New York.

Or course, there was still the matter of finding actual proof of what she was now quite certain was the truth. She realized that barring a miracle—though a miracle she was still resolved to create through one additional line of inquiry—she would be unable to provide such proof. The fact that she knew the truth now sufficiently cleared her mind to allow her to entertain thoughts beyond the immediate apprehensions engendered by her undertaking—a venture she had taken on of her own accord. She now turned on her mobile to read for the first time the text Braxton had sent her several days before. It was short:

> Dear Judy,
>   I enjoyed our time together, and apologize for the deficiency of eloquence in my parting words to you in the garage, though I hope you know they came from the heart. In lieu of making yet another feeble attempt, I have attached a rendition of *Hymn a L'amour* by Celine Dion which she sang at the 2015 Music Awards, to express my hope that I may someday see you again. BT

Judy attached her earphones and listened. As her eyes clouded, Chandler woke with a start.

"Everything all right, Judy?"

Judy folded away her mobile and nodded. "Yes, Chandler, I'm fine. Go back to sleep."

Chapter Fifty-Six

As the G-500 landed at Sugarland and taxied to the terminal, Amber and Tyrone were waiting on the tarmac next to the Range Rover.

Chandler unfolded the stairs and then followed the flight attendant down to the tarmac. Judy stood at the door and waved.

Amber ran to Judy and embraced her. "So you've finally come home, little sister! How I've missed you! You must tell me all about your adventures. I was afraid you'd never come back. I have a reservation at Brennan's."

Judy embraced Tyrone and then joined Amber in the Range Rover. At Brennan's, Amber released Tyrone for the night. "We'll get a cab home," she said.

"So," said Amber as the two sat down for drinks, "I can't believe you know who killed Angela. I really need to know, because we have a statute of limitations looming, and I'd like to file the wrongful death complaint for Brenda by next week."

Judy shook her head. "I've got to do one more thing before I tell you. I'm sure, but I want you to be sure as well. Just give me one more day, two at the most, and then I'll tell you everything."

"Okay, but I hope you know what you're doing. So, this confirming evidence you need to check out first—is it here in the U.S., or do you have to rush back to London or Paris? Can't you even give me a hint?"

"I can tell you that the lead I need to follow is here in the U.S. Chandler is taking me there tomorrow morning. If all goes well, I should be back by tomorrow night or the following morning."

"All right, I'll wait. But I have to tell you I can't imagine. But hey, let's talk about this barrister you met in London. Braxton, is it?"

Judy shook her head.

"What, you can't tell me about him either? Come on, baby, I'm your sister, remember? Is it serious? Now you simply must tell me."

"I had a lot of time to think on the flight over. I have to tell you, I've only been apart from him for several days, but...I miss him already."

"That's an important sign, I'd say. Go on."

"I'm afraid I've treated him most shabbily. I've been so focused on this case—your case, and getting to the bottom of Audrey's poisoning—that I really didn't give him the time he deserved. He knew I was going on a wild goose chase, but he still offered to help me. He didn't have to. I think he just wanted to be with me. I think he just wanted to please me."

"And did you let him?"

"Not that way, no. Although I think last Sunday evening it might have come to that when I spent the night at his flat...."

"And so you did...."

"No...I didn't, but I'd been drinking. I think I wanted to see if he would try to take advantage...."

"And did he?"

"Not at all. He was a perfect gentleman. He did carry me to his bedroom, but he slept in the sitting room."

"I'm sure you were driving him crazy, but I guess he passed your little test."

"I wouldn't put it that way...I wasn't really... but I was so tired, and he had had quite a bit to drink that evening and I didn't want him to have to drive me back to the hotel... it was so late...."

"You could have called a cab."

"Well, you've got me there. I didn't want to do that either, by myself, and by that time it was almost the middle of the night...."

"On Tuesday he took me to Portsmouth for the weekend. He reserved a suite at the Queen's Hotel, but it had two bedrooms."

"And you never...."

Judy shook her head. "No, I had too many things on my mind. I went to bed early, and he had to go out alone and get some things for our breakfast the next morning...so no...and then even though I had earlier said I would go back to London with him and watch him in court the next day...I didn't want to stay another night...I was afraid I'd...you know...and I wasn't sure...."

"I get it girl. It's okay. So you sent him back to London alone and you stayed at the hotel yourself the next night before taking that sleeper train the next morning to Scotland. Did you at least part on good terms?"

"They could have been better. He told me that he loved me."

"Really! And how did you respond?"

"I think I just laughed it off. I mean we'd known each other for less than a week...."

"And now you miss him."

"Yes...but I didn't even read his text until I was on the plane home."

"Okay, but back up. How did the trip to Aberdeen go? I take it you would have told me if that had turned up anything....

"Amber, I am very sure I know who poisoned Audrey and killed Angela, but I hope that what I will be telling you—after I get confirmation tomorrow—will not disappoint you."

"Disappoint me? How do you mean?"

"I mean, if I can show you that it wasn't Ronald who killed Angela and poisoned Audrey...."

"What? Of course it was Ronald! Who else could it have been? I know you wanted to eliminate these others who might have had opportunity—I get that...."

"And motive as well...."

"Judy, I want the truth as much as you do. I just hope you know what you're doing."

"Please wait. By tomorrow I think the truth will be clear."

Amber put her hand on Judy's. "I hope so, sister. I hope so. I trust you."

Chapter Fifty-Seven

The next morning at 6 A.M., Judy tapped on Amber's bedroom door. Amber was still sleeping.

"Judy?"

Judy opened the door slightly. "Sorry to wake you up. Just wanted to let you know I'm leaving. If I'm lucky I'll be back by this evening, but if not no later than Wednesday morning."

"Let me get up and make you some breakfast."

"No, Tyrone's waiting. Bye."

As Judy left the house, she took out her mobile and dialed Jake before taking her seat in the Range Rover. "Good morning, Tyrone," she said as she waited for a dial tone.

"Good morning, Judy," said Jake. "Are you on your way?"

'Yes. I'll be leaving Sugarland within the hour, and should arrive by 10 A.M."

"When is your appointment with her?"

"2 P.M. I wanted to meet her at the casino, but early this morning she texted me and said she was going home early today and preferred to meet me at her home in Summerlin instead. She invited me for lunch. I texted you her address."

"Yeah, I got it, but I'm not sure I like that, Judy."

"Actually, it's better. I think she'll feel more comfortable in her own home. Now, will you have someone there to give me the device I asked you to get for me?"

"Yep, and they can insert it as soon as you get off your plane. Shouldn't take more than a few minutes."

"All right, and you'll be on post as well?'

"Everything's taken care of. And you have all the documents?'

"Yep, right here in my brief case."

"You're sure you want to take a cab to her house?"

"Yep, as we planned. I think it's better."

Chapter Fifty-Eight

Madeleine Turner's house in Summerlin was a modest white stucco two bedroom home with a white stucco wall around it.

Judy arrived by cab ten minutes late to see Madeleine standing by the gate to let her in.

Judy paid the cab, which took off. "Sorry I'm late. I think the cab driver missed a turn."

"No problem. Come in, Judy" She led her into her nicely air conditioned living room. "So nice to see you again. Can I offer you some ice tea?"

"That would be nice, thank you."

Madeleine brought out the ice tea, and sandwiches. They made small talk about the Las Vegas heat and the new stadium that had just been completed.

"Last time we met you told me that your associate was bringing a wrongful death suit against my sister Audrey's husband. Have you made any progress there?"

"Yes, actually I have Madeleine, and some of the credit goes to you for endorsing our petition to exhume her body."

"I didn't like the idea of digging up my sister's grave, but I was happy to help in any way."

"Yes, and we sent you a copy of the autopsy report, which showed that she had been poisoned by fentanyl within twenty-four hours of her boarding Concorde."

"Yes, I received that. I was quite surprised that they were able to make that determination."

"We were too, but there have been a number of advancements in toxicity analysis."

"I imagine it must have been quite expensive to get such tests done."

"That's true it was. But in order to narrow the list of suspects in the murder of your sister-in-law, it was necessary to determine who interfaced with your sister in the twenty-four hours prior to death."

"Why, if she died in the Concorde crash?"

"We have no way of knowing if she died after boarding but before the Concorde took off. But we do know that the dose of fentanyl found in her system was sufficient to have killed her even if she had never gotten on that plane."

"But after so many years, how could you possibly know who was with her during those twenty-four hours before her death?"

"Just a couple of days ago, the lab reported that it had conducted more precise tests on the fentanyl in your sister's system. These tests have narrowed the window in which she was poisoned to just one to two hours before she boarded the plane."

"Extraordinary. But still, how could you possibly know who met with her only two hours before she boarded the plane? She could have met with anybody in the lounge that day."

"Actually, we were able to identify and conduct background checks on all the visitors to the lounge on the day of the crash, and none of them had any connection to Audrey—except one person."

For the first time, Judy saw a look of distress on Madeleine's face.

"You wouldn't happen to have taken a trip to Paris about that time to see you sister, would you?"

"Of course not. It was a long time ago, but I shall never get the date of July 25, 2000, out of my mind. I remember it so clearly. I was in my kitchen, listening to the news, when I heard the news about the crash. I wasn't concerned about Audrey, because she had told me she would be returning to the U.S. on the Concorde flight from London, not Paris. You can imagine how horrified I was to later learn that at the last minute she had gone to Paris to take Concorde from there."

Judy pulled out a file from here briefcase, withdrew from the file a photocopy of a plane ticket, and handed it to Madeleine. "It's a copy of a United Airlines ticket to London on July 24, the day before you thought Audrey was going to leave on the Concorde from London. Is that your name on it?"

Madeleine was unable to hide her surprise. "Well, yes. I guess I was mistaken about hearing about the crash for the first time in my kitchen. That proves I was in London on the day of the crash, not in Paris."

Judy next pulled two additional photocopies. The first showed the receipt for Madeleine's stay at the Savoy on July 24, 2000, and the second was a copy of a Eurostar ticket from London to Paris on the morning of July 25—all listing Madeleine Turner as the passenger."

Madeleine's face fell. "Yes, now I remember. So long ago. I did decide to take a trip to London, you know, surprise Audrey, and suggest we do a little sightseeing together."

"So you saw her at the Savoy, then? And then you followed her to Paris the next morning on the Eurostar?"

"You know, I can't remember exactly. I may have surprised Audrey in London, and then gone on with her on the Eurostar."

"And then followed her cab to De Gaulle, and then to the Concorde Lounge?"

"Oh, no. I would never have done that. There would be no reason to do that."

Judy pulled out another document. "This shows that you did enter the Concorde Lounge on the morning of July 25 after paying a First Class Lounge upgrade. Since you never boarded the plane, are you saying you never interfaced with her while you were there?"

"What is this? What if I was there? What are you saying? Anyone could have put those patches in her Nicobans, months before!"

Judy pulled out a final receipt—a De Gaulle gift store receipt showing that Audrey bought a new pack of Nicobans on the morning of July 25."

"So what? Audrey died on that plane, and no one can prove any different. Why are you even doing this? And what motive would I have to poison my own sister?"

Judy pulled out a separate file from her brief case containing Madeleine's medical and psychiatric records. "In fact you hated your sister, didn't you? At age fifteen you stabbed her with a knife. You spent six months in juvenile for that. And then two years later you hit her with your car after an argument and put her in the hospital—but Audrey refused to press charges and they were dropped."

"Yes, I hated her! So what! She was always the pretty one! If I ever got a boyfriend, she was always there to steal him away."

"Did that include Ronald Sterling? Long before he made his millions, you dated him didn't you? We have proof of that. You were going to marry him and live happily ever after. But then your pretty younger sister took him away too. All you had to do was get rid of her, and Ronald would come back to you—or so you convinced yourself."

At this, Madeline stood, her face exploding with rage. "I think you best leave this house right now. You don't know what you're talking about. I should never have taken you into my confidence. But you know you can't prove a thing. The Concorde may have done what I wanted to do, but good riddance as far as I'm concerned."

Judy took the last file from her briefcase.

"But it wasn't enough to get rid of your sister. You weren't going to be satisfied until you punished Ronald too. That's a long time to nurse a grudge, Madeleine. We have the record to show how you made contact with Angela just days before she died. Unfortunately Ronald didn't smoke or use nicotine patches, so you couldn't use your foolproof plan of planting Nicoban patches on him. So you did the next best thing and planted patches in her pack of Nicobans and made it look like he did it. You knew he had a motive to kill her. You didn't' care when Angela came around to applying those patches on herself. No rush, you were happy to bide your time, and your revenge had a flexible timetable."

Madeleine, her face now contorted with rage, turned and walked over to a cabinet and pulled from the drawer a Kel-Tec P32 handgun. Regaining her composure, she said, "Yes, I poisoned my sister, but you'll never prove it. I killed that whore Angela as well. But what will that get you? All that work and research just to get me?"

"Listen, Madeleine, put the gun down. Those murders may be hard to prove, but you'll never get away with killing me. I told people I was coming here."

"Just put down your briefcase—and those files—and put them on the coffee table."

"You can't really believe I don't have copies of these files."

"Just put them down on the table! You came here uninvited, you threatened me. I had no choice but to defend myself."

Just as Madeleine began to pull the trigger, Judy made a leap over the couch. Madeleine wildly fired two more shots as Judy escaped from behind the couch, leaped over a chair and swirled behind the dining room table.

At this moment, Clark County police officers broke down the back door.

"Drop the gun!" one of them cried.

Madeleine swirled to meet them and fired her P32. The fire was returned, and Madeleine fell with a piercing scream.

Chapter Fifty-Nine

Amber brought in a tray of tea and hot muffins fresh from the oven and laid them on the dining room table.

"You know, Judy," said she, "you've really ruined my case against Ronald Sterling."

"Well, big sister, the truth is the truth. What can I say?"

"You're amazing is all I really can say. Without your evidence, at best I would have lost my civil case against Ronald, and at worst I would have obtained a wrongful death judgment against an innocent man."

"Actually, you could probably still bring your case against Madeleine's estate. I'm sure her house is worth maybe half a million, and I'm sure she has other assets as well."

"I guess it's not really about the money, and Brenda understands that. But at least she has closure—though it's not the same as bringing the murderer of her mother to justice in a criminal court of law."

"I think any lawyer worth his salt could have shown Madeleine to be deranged and incompetent to stand trial."

"I suppose, but it's always perplexing to me how anyone can lead a seemingly normal life, but still keep the most evil urges hidden for so long. I'm also sorry we can't take advantage of Rule 404(b). You worked so hard to lay the foundation for its application. It would have been interesting to see how that played out in court. It was your interest in that rule which led you the find the truth in this case. Brides in the Bath. But I have to ask, when did you know that it had to be Madeleine?"

"I'd like to say I knew when I first interviewed her back in early August. There was something about her that didn't ring true. Maybe it was just that her extravagant expression of grief over her sister's death didn't ring true, but I didn't seriously begin to suspect her until I began eliminating the other suspects—one by one."

"And how did you do that? You really had nothing on any of them—I mean beyond the fact that they all had motive and opportunity, especially Ronald.

"I think I just took the role of juror in evaluating the credibility of all of them?"

"What do you mean?"

"Unlike lawyers and judges, jurors have to rely almost exclusively on their ability to judge character. In all the cases I tried at Robin's side, there was not a one in which the stench of perjury did not fill the air. Someone was always lying. It was up to the jurors to decide who that was. In the end, jurors are simply human lie detectors. Sometimes they get it wrong, but most often they get it right."

"And it was your judge of character which finally led you to suspect Madeleine?"

"I can't really say that I judged Madeleine's character very well. She was too good at masquerading as a normal person. And it wasn't until Jake got me all those receipts revealing Madeleine to be the mystery guest at the Concorde lounge, and her long history of psychotic behavior with regard to her sister, that I focused on her—and that was more by process of elimination than anything else. But I do think my judgment of character led me to eliminate the other suspects."

"Even Ronald? I mean his character was, and is most low by all accounts."

"I never had chance to interview him, but from what I learned about the way he treated his wives, I think I know what he was about, and it just wasn't murder. I can't really explain that, nor do I think most jurors can either."

"The same with this Viscount McKenzie and Alistair Devon?"

"The Viscount struck me as essentially harmless—still living, in his own mind, in an age when titles meant not just respect, power, and privilege, but financial security as well—and of the latter he had very little. Devon on the other hand struck me as a typical politician who has deluded himself into thinking that his status also makes him physically attractive to women. But I just didn't see him committing murder. In his case his character was just too weak to pull something like that off. Nor could I see him trudging down incognito to Nogales to barter for black market fentanyl."

"So it all came down to your judge of character?"

"No. I'd like to think so, but no. The case was solved by NXR's incredible investigation and research, and RFL's amazing application of the latest developments in DNA and toxicology."

"If Madeleine had kept her composure and just denied everything, do you think we could have made a case against her in court?"

"Probably not. If she hadn't admitted that she committed the murders, the police could never have gotten a warrant to search her house. As you know, they did search her house and found all kinds of fentanyl compounds tucked away in her attic."

"But would they only have had your word for her confession?"

"Oh no. Jake had me fitted for the very latest in tiny microphones, inserted in my ear and able to transmit to the police in the van outside who duly recorded everything she said for use in getting a warrant. Nothing like the old wires they used to attach to the legs and arms of police informers—which more often than not only succeeded in getting them dispatched by the suspects whose conversations they were trying to record."

"Judy, as I said, you were amazing. But you know, of course that you came very close to getting yourself killed by that madwoman."

"I know. I was very lucky. The police were supposed to come in as soon as they heard her say anything incriminating. But it wasn't until they heard the first shot that they came in."

"So what now, Judy? Are we still on with merging our firms, and carrying on Robin's legacy of keeping the justice system on the straight and narrow?"

"Yes. John is working on getting the documents prepared. How do our partners and associates feel about it?"

"They were appalled when I first pitched the idea to them. All of them were concerned that we wouldn't be able to keep afloat representing impecunious defendants and exonerating those wrongfully convicted. But I guaranteed to all of them a fixed salary commensurate with their past earnings."

"I did the same with my firm."

"You're still not really thinking about becoming a barrister yourself, are you?"

"I don't know if I have the right stuff, but yes, I'd like to try. I know someone who would be willing to help me."

"Braxton?"

"Yes. In fact if you'll excuse me, I'm going to call Chandler and have him get the G-500 ready to take me back to London tomorrow morning."

"Speaking of that, have you… does he know about…you know…our assets?"

"You mean the financial ones."

"Yes," Amber said with a laugh. "Our financial ones."

"No, and I don't plan on telling him. He'll have to figure that out for himself. But first, I need to find out whether he really is my Mr. Darcy."

"Mr. Darcy?"

"First impressions."

"First impressions?"

"Never mind," said Judy. "Never mind."

The End

Author's Notes

After the publication of a novel, readers often ask authors how they arrived at the ideas for their story. In some instances authors may confide that their ideas arose from reading newspaper and media accounts of actual events or from documented historical chronicles. Others are inspired by personal experiences, including those of family and friends, or by visits to historical places around the world. The story which follows arose from a combination of all these sources, but in the first instance from a real life tragedy which horrified the world— the crash of the world's only supersonic passenger airliner which occurred in Paris on Judy 25, 2000, killing everyone on board. After learning that that the Concorde which crashed was the very one on which I had flown with a beloved companion some years before—an adventure which included seeing the curvature of the earth while travelling at the speed of bullet, and which I had been able to experience only through the careful saving of my earnings as a law professor over a period of several years—I began to formulate a fictional tale for the fourth book in my Judy Alexander mystery series that would serve as a fictional bookend for the real life events of the Concorde tragedy.

I was also inspired by a re-reading of Thornton Wilder's second novel which won the Pulitzer Prize in 1928—*The Bridge of San Luis Rey*. That book traces the lives of innocent victims which ended when a rope bridge in Peru broke and knurled them to their deaths, raising the cosmic question of why each of them had to die at that particular time and place. Wilder later confided that he wrote the book to pose the question: "is there a direction and meaning in lives beyond the individual's own will?"

The first in a series of seven historical novels—
Alienation of Affection—provided a format for five historical novels, including the one which follows, the fourth in the Judy Alexander mystery series. (A fifth *Murder in Carcassonne* is forthcoming).

The inspiration for that first book, which motivated me to write historical novels as a means of fleshing out the otherwise boring and uninspiring law books which as a law professor I felt compelled to write—arose from a casual conversation I had with an elderly neighbor walking his dog. He regaled me with a fantastic tale, pointing out to me the spot on the sidewalk where he claimed the nation's most notorious murder had occurred in the year 1911. Intrigued, but skeptical of his amazing tale of intrigue, sex, scandal, and betrayal, I asked my research assistant at the University School of Law to research the 1911 newspaper archives of the Denver Public Library and check the newspaper headlines for that year.

To my astonishment, she returned with copies of six weeks of newspaper headlines detailing the trial of Gertrude Gibson Patterson. Hyped by the Denver newspapers as the "Most Beautiful Woman in America," Gertrude was charged with the murder of her husband, and prosecuted by Denver's most aggressive prosecutor who boasted of having never lost a murder case, and crowed that he had sent no less than sixty-two murder defendants to the gallows. Every day for six weeks, all the Denver newspapers captured the imagination of the nation by characterizing the trial as a titanic struggle between "Beauty and the Beast" and leading with rapturous headlines such a "Frenzied mob struggles to get into court, and women have teeth trampled out and clothing torn from bodies in wild riot." (Really, I asked myself—women having their teeth trampled out to see this trial?).

I then began to read the editorial commentaries which revealed the nature of sex discrimination in the days before women's suffrage: "Not within the memory of police officers and criminologists has there been a period in the United States when so many women killed their husbands as in the concluding months of 1911. Experts in criminal law are struggling to solve the riddle of the cause of this practically wholesale murder of husbands. Criminologists are wondering if it is the altitude of Denver that affects the nerves of women that is the cause of this slaughter."

On November 11, 1911, Columnist Alice Roche of the *Denver Daily News* wrote: "The psychology of beauty is the subject now open for study in the West Side Court. The jury of all men is being selected, and already that subtle thing, feminine charm, is sending its sex waves vibrating across the courtroom. That ineradicable thing—womanly beauty—a beauty that lures and gains its ultimate desire—is on one side of the counsel table and the waves emanate from a pair of women's eyes that look softly, sweetly, appealingly, significantly, invitingly, understandingly into those men in the jury box."

What cemented my determination to write about this trial and its place in American legal history, however, was this story which ran in the *Rocky Mountain News* on November 30, 1911, describing the jurors who, after acquitting Gertrude of shooting her husband four times in the back, visited her in her hotel room to "pour out their personal feelings of admiration at the feet of beauty" and presented her with flowers as their personal tribute.

Surely, I thought this trial must have been documented in books, plays, and films. But no—the trial was soon forgotten, overshadowed within a few months by the *Titanic* tragedy. The only documentation of this trial was what I had found in the archives of the Denver Public Library old newspaper section. (Note: *Alienation of Affection* has been optioned for a film to be presented to Netflix, but as yet no film).

Thus began the second of my series of novels highlighting the evolution of law in the annals of American history in a way which departs from the style of the dry documentary. I sought to do so by means of bookending a real historical event with a fictional story. I followed with *Lily Queen*, a fictional tale told through the eyes of the sole survivor of the Triangle Shirtwaist factory sweatshop fire—which also occurred in 1911. This tale bookended the true story of fire in which some 140 young girls working for pennies a day were burned to death in a tenth story sweatshop factory located in downtown Manhattan. In a subsequent trial, the owners of the factory were charged with negligent homicide for locking all the factory exit doors shut— to prevent the girls from "pilfering"—thus causing the girls' deaths either by being burned alive or impaled on wrought iron stakes on the fence below when they flung themselves out of windows to escape the flames. Nevertheless, the owners were acquitted through the efforts of "America's most successful lawyer," Max Stoyer. This too was a story rarely if ever referenced in books or films, and which I thought deserved retelling as part of my study of the evolution of the law in America. *Lily Queen* does so through the eyes of a beautiful young woman determined to seek justice for those who had died in the fire by using the one weapon she possessed—her beauty.

I followed this novel with the first in the Judy Alexander Mystery series—*The Papyrus*—in which a young woman, Judy, modeled after my heroine in *Lily Queen* seeks justice in an unjust world. In this book, a fictional tale of intrigue in the art world bookends a story set in the halls of a San Francisco Museum of ancient Egyptian history chronicling the life of Egyptian queen Nefertiti.

In the second in the series—*Six Queens Naked*—Judy Alexander seeks to find a kidnapped child in Hong Kong. This story bookends by flashback the long covered up but true story of Japan's second attack on Pearl Harbor on March 2, 1942, by means of Flying Boats operating from French frigate shoals a hundred and twenty miles west of Hawaii.

In the third book in the Judy Mystery series, *Murder at Mont St. Michel*, Judy, now a law student at a small law school in Manhattan, is engaged to solve the mystery of a tycoon's daughter who disappeared from the small island of Mont San Michel without a trace, and to find her killer. This story bookends by flashback the true story of the Nazi occupation of Mont St. Michel during World War II, and was inspired by my trip to that most historic isle with the same companion who had earlier travelled with me on the Concorde.

This brings us to the story that you just read in which Judy inherits a legacy which enables her to pursue justice in the case of a young woman who may have been poisoned prior to her much anticipated trip on the doomed flight of Concorde on July 25, 2000.

In the spirit of the Mary Poppins' song, *A Spoonful Of Sugar Makes The Medicine Go Down,* it is my hope that my incorporation of little known historic events as well as current pressing legal issues—otherwise perhaps boring and academic— may find in the stories of the fictional characters who explore them.

www.ingramcontent.com/pod-product-compliance
Lightning Source LLC
Chambersburg PA
CBHW071054250626
47159CB00002B/468